COUNT TO TEN

KAREN ROSE

headline

First published in Great Britain in 2007
by HEADLINE PUBLISHING GROUP

First published in paperback in Great Britain in 2007
HEADLINE PUBLISHING GROUP

10

Cataloguing in Publication Data is available from the British Library

ISBN 978 0 7553 3697 5

Typeset in Palatino by Avon DataSet Ltd, Bidford-on-Avon

Printed and bound in Great Britain by Clays Ltd, St Ives plc

HEADLINE PUBLISHING GROUP
A division of Hachette Livre UK Ltd
338 Euston Road
London NW1 3BH

www.headline.co.uk
www.hodderheadline.com

*To Martin, for the twenty-five best years of my life.
I love you.*

*To Cristy Carrington, for your beautiful poetry and
seeing emotion in my characters that even I didn't
see. I had a rock. You made it beautiful.*

*To the sisters of my heart who know me and love me
anyway. I love you all right back.*

Prologue

Springdale, Indiana
Thursday, November 23, 11:45 P.M.

He stared at the flames with grim satisfaction. The house was burning.

He thought he heard their screams. *Help me. Oh God, help me.* He hoped he heard their screams, that it wasn't only his imagination. He hoped they were in the most excruciating pain.

They were trapped inside. No neighbors around for miles to call for help. He could take out his cell. Call the police. The fire department. One side of his mouth lifted. But why? They were finally getting what they deserved. Finally. That it should be at his own hand was . . . fair.

He didn't remember setting the fire, but he knew he must have done so. Without taking his eyes from the burning house, he lifted his hands to his nose. Sniffed at the leather gloves he wore. He could smell the gasoline on his hands.

Yes, he had done this thing. And he was fiercely, intensely glad he had.

He didn't remember driving here. But of course he must have. He recognized the house, although he had never lived there. Had he lived there, things would have been different. Had he lived there, Shane would have remained untouched. Shane might still be alive and the deep seething hatred he'd buried for so long might never have existed.

But he hadn't lived there. Shane had been alone, a lamb among wolves. And by the time he'd gotten out and come back, his brother was no longer a happy boy. By the time he'd come back, Shane walked with his head down, shame and fear in his eyes.

Because they'd hurt him. The rage bubbled and popped. In this very house where Shane should have been safe, in the very house that now burned like hell itself, they'd hurt Shane so that he'd never been the same again.

Shane was dead. And now they hurt, just as he had. It was . . . fair.

That his hatred and rage would bubble to the surface from time to time was inevitable, he supposed. It had been a part of him for nearly as long as he could remember. But the reason for his rage . . . that reason he'd hidden from everyone. Including himself. He'd denied it for so long, retold the story so well . . . Even he'd had trouble remembering the truth. There were whole stretches of time that even he forgot. That he made himself forget. Because it had been too painful to remember.

But he remembered now. Every single person who raised their hands to hurt them. Every single person who should have protected them and didn't. Every single person who looked the other way.

It was because of the boy. The boy that reminded him of Shane. The boy who looked up to him for help. For protection. Tonight, the boy had looked up to him in fear and shame. It took him back too many years. It took him back to a time he hated to remember. When he was . . . weak. Pathetic. Useless.

He narrowed his eyes as the flames licked the walls of the wooden house that was burning like dry kindling. He wasn't weak or pathetic or useless any longer. Now, he took what he wanted and damned the consequences.

His good sense started to creep in around the anger as it always did.

Sometimes, unfortunately, the consequences damned him. Especially when the anger took over as it had tonight. Tonight wasn't the first time he'd stood back, looking at something he'd done, barely remembering the deed itself. It was the first fire . . .

He swallowed hard. It was the first fire in a long time. But he'd done other things. Necessary things. Things that would get him sent to prison if he got caught. Real prison this time, not juvenile detention which was bad enough, but manageable if a person had enough brains.

Tonight he'd killed. And he didn't regret it. Not a bit. But he was lucky. This house was far away from any neighbors, any prying eyes. What if it had been a normal neighborhood in the city? What if he'd been seen? He asked himself this same question every time. *What if he got caught?*

One day the rage that bubbled inside him was going to get him into more trouble than he could manage on his own. It ruled him. Made him vulnerable. He gritted his teeth. And being vulnerable was the one thing he would never let happen again.

Suddenly the answer seemed so very clear. The rage had to go.

So the source of the rage had to go. Which meant all the people who'd hurt them, looked the other way, they all needed to go. Standing here, watching the flames, the memory of each one of those people came back. He could see faces. Hear names. Feel hate.

He tilted his head as the roof crashed in, sending sparks flying skyward like a million mini-flares. He'd made one hell of a fireworks show.

It would be hard to top a display like that. But of course he would. He didn't do anything halfway. Whatever he did, he'd need to do well. For Shane. And for himself. Then he could finally close the book on this part of his life and move on.

That last shower of sparks might be enough to summon the local fire department. He'd better get while the getting was good. He got in his car and turned back toward the city, a smile bending his lips. The beginnings of a plan were forming in his mind.

It would be one hell of a show. And when the final curtain fell, Shane could finally rest in peace. *And I'll finally be free.*

Chapter One

Chicago, Saturday, November 25, 11:45 P.M.

A branch slapped the window and Caitlin Burnette's jaw clenched. 'It's just the wind,' she muttered. 'Don't be such a baby.' Still, the howling outside was unsettling, and being alone in the Doughertys' creaky old house wasn't helping. She dropped her eyes back to the statistics book that was responsible for her being alone on a Saturday night. The party at TriEpsilon would have been a hell of a lot more fun than this. Noisier, too. Which was why she was here, studying the most boring subject in the quiet of a boring old house instead of trying to study with a party going on all around her room.

Her stat professor had scheduled an exam for Monday morning. If she failed it, she'd fail for the semester. If she failed one more class, her father would take away her car, sell it, and use the money to take her mother to the Bahamas.

Caitlin ground her teeth. She'd show him. She'd pass

7

that damn test if it killed her. And if she didn't, she had nearly enough money in savings to buy the damn car herself or maybe even a better one. The money the Doughertys were paying her to take care of their cat was chintzy, but enough to put her over the top and—

A different noise had her chin jerking up, her eyes narrowing. *What the hell?* It came from downstairs. It sounded like . . . a chair scraping against the hardwood floor.

Call the police. She had her hand on the phone, but she drew a breath and made herself calm down. *It's probably just the cat.* She'd look pretty stupid calling the police about a twenty-pound, overly pampered Persian. Plus, she really wasn't supposed to be here right now. Mrs Dougherty had been clear about that. She was not to 'stay over.' She was not to 'have parties.' She was not to 'use the phone.' She was to feed the cat and change the litter box, period.

The Doughertys might get mad and refuse to pay her if they found out she was here. Caitlin sighed. Besides, word would get back to her dad and wouldn't he just have a field day with that? All over a stupid fluffy cat named Percy of all things.

Still, it didn't hurt to be careful. Quietly Caitlin moved from the spare bedroom the Doughertys used as an office to the master bedroom where she pulled the small gun from Mrs Dougherty's nightstand drawer and disengaged the safety. She'd found the gun when she was looking for a pen. It was a .22, just like she'd shot dozens of times at the range with her dad. She descended the stairs, the gun pressed against the back of her leg. It was pitch black, but she was afraid to turn on a light. *Stop this, Caitlin. Call the cops.* But her feet kept moving, soundless on the carpet, until two steps from the bottom, a stair creaked. She stopped short, her heart pounding, listening hard.

And heard humming. There was somebody in the house and they were *humming*.

The screech of something heavy being dragged across the floor drowned out the humming. Then she smelled gas.

Get out. Get help. She lurched forward, stumbling when her feet hit the hardwood floor at the base of the stairs. She fell to her knees and the gun flew from her hand, skittering across the floor. Loudly.

The humming stopped. Desperately she made a move for the gun, grasping for it in the dark, her hands frantically patting at the cold hardwood. She found the gun and scrambled to her feet. *Get out. Get out. Get out.*

She'd taken two steps toward the door when she was hit from behind, knocked to her knees. She tried to scream, but she couldn't breathe. Together they slid a few feet before he pushed her to her stomach, lying on top of her. He was heavy. *God, please.* She struggled but he was just too heavy. In a second he twisted the gun from her hand. His breath was beating hot and hard against her ear. Then his breathing slowed and she could feel him grow hard on top of her. *Not that. Please, God.*

She clenched her eyes closed as he thrust his hips hard, his intentions clear. 'Please let me go. I'm not even supposed to be here. I promise I won't tell anyone.'

'You weren't supposed to be here,' he repeated. 'How unlucky for you.' His voice was deep, but fakely so. Like a bad Darth Vader imitation. Caitlin focused, determined to remember every last detail so that when she got away, she could tell the police.

'Please don't hurt me,' she whispered.

He hesitated. She could feel him take a breath and hold it, as time stood still. Finally he let the breath out.

Then he laughed.

Sunday, November 26, 1:10 A.M.

Reed Solliday moved through the gathered crowd, listening. Watching their faces as the house across the street burned. It was an older, middle-class neighborhood and the people standing outside in the cold seemed to know each other. They stood in shock and disbelief, murmuring their fear that the wind would spread the flames to their own homes. Three older women stood to one side, their worried faces illuminated by the remains of the fire that had taken two companies to bring under control. This fire was too hot, too high, too many places within the house to feel like an accidental fire.

Despite their shock, this was the time to interview the onlookers, before they had time to share stories. Even in groups of people with nothing to hide, shared stories became homogenized stories in which relevant details could be lost.

Arsonists could go free. And making sure that didn't happen was Reed's job.

'Ladies?' He approached the three women, his shield in his hand. 'My name is Lieutenant Solliday.'

All three women gave him the once-over. 'You're a policeman?' the middle one asked. She looked to be about seventy and tiny enough that Reed was surprised the wind hadn't blown her away. Her white hair was tightly rolled in curlers and her flannel nightgown hung past the hem of her woolen coat, dragging on the frosty ground.

'Fire marshal,' Reed answered. 'Can I get your names?'

'I'm Emily Richter and this is Janice Kimbrough and Darlene Desmond.'

'You all know this neighborhood well?'

Richter sniffed. 'I've lived here for almost fifty years.'

'Who lives in that house, ma'am?'

'The Doughertys used to live there. Joe and Laura. But Laura passed and Joe retired to Florida. His son and daughter-in-law live there now. Sold it to 'em cheap, Joe did. Brought down all the property values in the neighborhood.'

'But they're not home now,' Janice Kimbrough added.

'They went to Florida to see Joe for Thanksgiving.'

'So nobody was in the house?' It was what the men had been told on arriving.

'Not unless they got home early,' Janice said.

'But they didn't,' Richter said firmly. 'Their truck is too tall for the garage, so they park it in the driveway. It's not there, so they're not home yet.'

'Have you ladies seen anybody hanging around that doesn't belong?'

'I saw a girl going in and out yesterday,' Richter said. 'Joe's son said they'd hired somebody to feed the cat.' She sniffed again. 'In the old days Joe would have given us his key and a bag of cat food, but his son changed all the locks. Hired some kid.'

The hair on Reed's neck stood on end. Call it instinct. Call it whatever. But something felt very bad about all this. 'A kid?'

'A college girl,' Darlene Desmond supplied. 'Joe's daughter-in-law told me she wasn't going to be living in. Just coming in twice a day to feed the cat.'

'What other cars did the Doughertys drive, ladies?' Reed asked.

Janice Kimbrough's brow furrowed. 'Joe Junior's wife drives a regular car. Ford?'

Richter shook her head. 'Buick.'

'And those are the only two vehicles they have? The truck and the Buick?' He'd seen the twisted remains of two cars in the garage. A sick feeling turned in his gut.

All three ladies nodded, exchanging puzzled glances. 'That's all,' Richter said.

'Thanks, ladies, you've been a big help.' He jogged across the street to where Captain Larry Fletcher stood next to the rig, a radio in one hand. 'Larry.'

'Reed.' Larry was frowning at the burning house. 'Somebody made this fire.'

'I think so, too. Larry, somebody might be in there.'

He shook his head. 'The old ladies said the owners are out of town.'

'The owners hired a college kid to watch the cat.'

Larry's head whipped around. 'They said nobody was home.'

'The girl wasn't supposed to stay overnight. There are two cars in the garage, right? The owners only kept one in there. Their other vehicle is a truck that they took with them. We've got to see if she's in there, Larry.'

With a curt nod, Larry lifted his radio to his face. 'Mahoney. Possible victim inside.'

The radio crackled. 'Understood. I'll try to go back in.'

'If it's too dangerous, you come back out,' Larry ordered, then turned to Reed, his eyes hard. 'If she's in there . . .'

Reed nodded grimly. 'She's probably dead. I know. I'll keep canvassing the crowd. Let me go in as soon as you can.'

Sunday, November 26, 2:20 A.M.

His heart still pounded, hard and fast. It had all gone just as he'd planned.

Well, not just as he'd planned. *She'd* been a surprise he hadn't expected. Miss Caitlin Burnette. He pulled her driver's license from the purse he'd taken. A little souvenir of the night. She wasn't supposed to be there, she'd said. Let her go, she'd begged. She wouldn't tell anyone, she'd promised. She was lying, of course. Women were full of lies. This he knew.

Quickly he moved the dirt away from his hiding place and lifted the lid of the plastic tub. Shiny baubles and keys struck his eye. He'd buried this the first day he'd come here and hadn't opened it since. Hadn't had cause to. Hadn't had anything to put inside. Tonight he did. He tossed Caitlin's purse on top of his other trinkets, replaced the lid and carefully arranged the dirt on top. There. It was done. He could sleep now.

He walked away licking his lips. He could still taste her. Sweet perfume, soft curves. She'd practically been dropped in his lap. Like Christmas come early. And she'd fought him. He laughed softly. She'd fought and cried and begged. She'd tried to tell him no. It just made him harder. She'd tried to scratch his face. He'd easily held her down. He shuddered, the memory still so fresh. He'd nearly forgotten how good it could feel when they said no. He was getting excited again, just thinking about it. They always thought they could fight back. They always thought they could say no.

But he was bigger. Stronger. And no one would ever tell him no again.

From a window above the boy watched, his heart pounding. *Tell someone. But who? He'll find out I told.* He'd be so angry and the boy knew what happened when he became angry. Sick with terror the boy went back to bed, pulled the covers over his head and cried.

Sunday, November 26, 2:15 A.M.

It had been a nice house, Reed thought as he walked through what was now a ruined shell. Damage to one side appeared less extensive than the other. It would be daylight soon and he'd be able to get a better view. For now, he flashed a high-powered light on the walls, looking for the burn lines that would lead him to the fire's origin.

He stopped and turned to the firefighter who'd manned the inside line. 'Where was it burning when you got here?'

Brian Mahoney shook his head. 'There were flames in the kitchen, the garage, the upstairs bedroom, and the living room. We got as far as the living room when the ceiling started to crumble and I got my guys out. Just in time, too. Kitchen ceiling caved. We focused on keeping it from spreading to the other houses after that.'

Reed looked straight up through what had been two stories, an attic and a roof, and saw stars in the sky. They could have multiple points of origin. Some bastard wanted to be sure this place burned. 'Nobody hurt?'

Brian shrugged. 'Minor burns on the probie, but he'll be okay. One of the guys got some smoke. Captain sent them both to the ER to get checked out. Listen, Reed, I came back in to look for the girl, but there was still too much smoke. If she was here . . .'

'I know,' Reed said grimly. He started moving again. 'I know.'

'Reed!' It was Larry Fletcher, standing in the kitchen next to the far wall.

Immediately Reed noted the stove pulled away from the wall. 'You guys pull that stove out?' he asked.

'Not us,' Brian answered. 'You're thinking he used the gas to start this thing?'

'It would explain the first big explosion.'

Larry continued to stare down at his feet. 'She's here.'

Reed gritted his teeth and moved to Larry's side. He shone his light down, dreading what he'd see. And drew a breath. 'Goddammit,' he hissed.

The body was charred beyond recognition.

'Dammit,' Brian echoed, tightly furious. 'Do you know who she was?'

Reed moved the light around the body, schooling his mind to be detached, not to think about the way she'd died. 'Not yet. I got the number of the old owner of this place from the ladies across the street. Joe Dougherty, Senior. His son, Joe Junior, lives here now. Joe Senior said Joe Junior and his wife went on a chartered fishing boat twenty miles off the Florida coast for the weekend. He doesn't expect him back until Monday morning. He did tell me his daughter-in-law worked for a legal firm downtown. Supposedly the girl they'd hired was the daughter of one of the wife's officemates. A college kid. I'll see if I can locate her parents.' He sighed when Larry continued to stare at the body on the floor. 'You didn't know she was here, Larry.'

'My daughter's in college,' Larry returned, his voice rough.

And mine will be soon enough, Reed thought, then banished the thought from his mind. Thoughts like that would drive a man crazy. 'I'll get the medical examiner out here,' he said. 'Along with my team. You look like shit, Larry. Both of you do. Let's go outside so I can debrief your crew, then go back to the station and get some rest.'

Larry nodded dully. 'You forgot to say "sir." ' It was an attempt at levity that fell miserably flat. 'You never said "sir," not in all the years you rode with me.'

They'd been good years. Larry was one of the best captains he'd ever had. 'Sir,' Reed corrected himself gently. He pulled Larry's arm, making his old friend move away from the charred obscenity that had once housed a young woman's soul. 'Let's go.'

17

Sunday, November 26, 2:55 A.M.

'I've got the lights set up, Reed.'

Reed looked up from the notes he'd been making sitting in the cab of his SUV. Ben Trammell stood a few feet away, his eyes troubled. Ben was the newest member of his team and, like most of the team members, had been a firefighter for years before joining the fire marshal's office. This was, however, Ben's first death as an investigator and the strain was already visible in his eyes.

'You okay?' Reed asked and Ben jerked a nod. 'Good.' Reed gestured to his photographer who waited in the warmth of his own car. Foster got out, his camera in his hands and a camcorder hanging around his neck.

'Let's go,' Reed said briskly, walking up the driveway, around the debris left by the firefighters. They'd work on processing everything outside when it was daylight. 'For now we touch nothing. We're going to document the scene and I'm going to take some readings. Then we'll see what we have.'

'Did you call for a warrant?' Foster asked.

'Not yet. I want to make sure whatever warrant I request covers the right things.' He had a very bad feeling about the body lying in the Doughertys' kitchen and being a meticulous man, he was mentally preparing for all the legal angles. 'We're good to go in for origin and cause. Any more and I want a court order, especially since the owners aren't here to give us permission to enter.'

Reed led them through the foyer, past the staircase and into the kitchen where the lights shone bright as day. The room was destroyed. The glass had blown from the windows and the ceiling had collapsed in one spot, making it difficult to cross the room without climbing over fallen roof supports. A thick layer of ash covered the tile floor. But most riveting was the victim, who lay where Larry Fletcher had first discovered her.

For a long moment all three men stood motionless, staring down at the victim, forcing their minds to process what was more horrific in the light than it had been in the dark. With a deep breath, Reed finally pushed himself into action, pulling on a pair of latex gloves before pulling his mini-tape-recorder from his pocket. 'Foster, start with the camcorder. We'll get stills once we've done our first walk-through.'

He lifted his own recorder to his mouth as Foster began to shoot tape. 'This is Lieutenant Reed Solliday, accompanied by Marshals Ben Trammell and Foster Richards. This is the Dougherty household, twenty-six November, oh-three-hundred. Outside conditions, twenty-one degrees Fahrenheit with winds from the northeast at fifteen miles per hour.' He drew a breath. 'A single victim has been found in the kitchen. The skin is charred. Facial detail has been destroyed. Gender is not immediately apparent. Small stature indicates a female which is consistent with witness accounts.'

Reed crouched next to the body and with his free hand pulled the sniffer from the bag he wore slung over one shoulder. Carefully he passed the instrument over the body, the sniffer's tone instantly switching to a high-pitched whine. He wasn't surprised. He glanced up at Ben. He could make it a trainable moment at least. 'Ben?'

'High concentrations of hydrocarbons,' Ben said tightly. 'Indicates presence of accelerants.'

'Good. Which suggests?'

'Which suggests the victim was doused in gasoline before being lit.'

'Gasoline, or something.' Reed focused on not allowing the stench to cloud his senses or the image of the dead young girl to tear at his heart. The first was nearly impossible, the second completely so. Still, he had a job to do. 'The ME will be able to tell us exactly what was used on her. Good, Ben.'

Ben cleared his throat. 'Do you want me to call for the dog?'

'I did already. Larramie's on duty tonight. He should have Buddy here in twenty minutes.' Reed straightened. 'Foster, get the victim from the other side, will you?'

'Yep.' Foster videotaped the scene from several more angles. 'What else?'

Reed had moved to the wall. 'Get a shot of this entire wall, then close-ups of all these marks.' He leaned closer with a frown. 'What the hell?'

'Narrow "V,"' Ben noted, steadier now. 'The fire started down at the baseboard then moved up the wall fast.' He looked over at Reed. 'Really fast. Like with a fuse?'

Reed nodded. 'Yeah.' He ran the sniffer across the wall and once again they heard its high-pitched whine. 'Accelerant up the wall. A chemical fuse.' Unsettled, he studied the wall. 'I don't think I've ever seen anything like that before.'

'He used gas from the stove,' Foster commented, turning the camera toward what was left of the appliances. He leaned closer, capturing the area between the stove and the wall. 'The bolt's been removed. Had to have been deliberate.'

'I thought so,' Reed murmured, then brought his recorder back to his mouth. 'The gas was flowing into the room, rising to the ceiling. The fire was ignited low to the floor, then traveled up this line of accelerant. We'll take samples here. But what about this?' He stepped back and took in the pockmarks that mottled the width of the wall.

'Something exploded,' Ben said.

'You're right.' Reed ran the sniffer along the wall. Short screeching bursts emerged, but no long whine as before. 'It's like napalm, the way it sticks to the wall.'

'Look.' Ben was crouching near the door that connected the kitchen to the laundry room. 'Plastic pieces.' He looked up, puzzled. 'They're blue.'

Reed bent down to look. They did look blue. Quickly his eyes took in several more pieces scattered across the floor and a picture formed in his mind. It was a photo in a book. An arson investigation manual, at least fifteen years old. 'Plastic eggs.'

Ben blinked. 'Eggs?'

'I've seen this before. I bet if we can get enough pieces, the lab will be able to put them together like a plastic egg, like kids hunt at Easter. The arsonist fills it with accelerant, either solid or a viscous liquid like polyurethane, runs a fuse through a hole in one end. He lights the fuse and the pressure from the blast blows the egg apart, spewing the accelerant all over.'

Ben looked impressed. 'That explains the burn patterns.'

'It does. It also goes to show if you do this job long enough, you'll see it all. Foster, get all the pieces and their location on tape, then close-up stills of everything in the room. I'm going to call in for a warrant to cover us on the origin and source samples, too. I don't want any lawyer telling us we can use the search samples for the arson, but not for the assault on that poor girl.'

'Cover your ass,' Foster muttered. 'Damn lawyers.'

'We'll get the plastic pieces after Larramie and the dog are finished. Maybe there's a piece big enough for Latent to get a print.'

'You optimist, you,' Foster said, still muttering.

'Just take the pictures. Also get pictures of the doors and first-floor windows, especially the locks. I want to know how he got in here.'

Foster moved his camera away from his face long enough to stare at Reed. 'You know if that girl's a homicide, they're going to yank this case right out from under you.'

He'd already thought of that. 'I don't think so. I'll have to share, but there's plenty enough arson here for us to keep our hands in the pot. For now, we're here. We've got the ball. So move it into field-goal territory, okay?'

Foster rolled his eyes. He wasn't a sports fan. 'Fine.'

'Ben, there are two cars in the garage. The old ladies said the Doughertys had the Buick. Find out who owned the other one. And, Foster, at first light, I want you out there snapping pictures of the ground. With all this mud, he's bound to have left us something.'

'Optimist,' Foster muttered once again.

Sunday, November 26, 2:55 P.M.

His thoughts had cleared after a good night's sleep and now he could consider exactly what he had accomplished. And what he had not. He sat with his hands neatly folded on his desk, staring out the window, analyzing the events of the night. This was the time to determine what went well so that he could do those things again. Conversely, he needed to decide what had not gone well and whether to fix or eliminate those things. Or perhaps even add something new. He'd take it point by point. Keeping it in order. It was the best way.

The first point was the explosion. His mouth curved. That had gone very well, art and science all rolled into one. His little firebomb worked perfectly, the design easy to implement. Not a single moving part. Elegant in its simplicity.

And very successful. He grimaced a little as he tested his sore knee. Maybe a little too successful, he thought, remembering the force of the blast. It had knocked him off his feet, throwing him to his hands and knees as he'd run down the Doughertys' front walk. He guessed he'd cut that fuse a little too close. He'd wanted ten seconds to get out of the house and down to the street. Mentally he counted it out. It had been more like seven seconds. He needed ten. Ten was very important.

The next time, he'd cut the fuse a little longer.

The first egg he'd put in the kitchen worked beautifully, just like his prototype. The second egg, the one he'd put on the Doughertys' bed . . . He'd intended to kill the old man and his wife, then burn them in their own bed. When he'd discovered they weren't there, the second bomb became symbolic, but ultimately not a viable part of his plan.

He'd realized as he stood ready to light its fuse that by the time he ran downstairs and lit the fuse for the kitchen egg the upstairs one would already have blown. That blast might have set off the gas before he was out of the house, trapping him inside. So he'd left it there, hoping it would blow when the fire spread. Judging from the way the fire had burned through the roof of the house, he believed that had happened. But had it not, the police may have found it and learned more than he wanted them to.

So even though the concept of two bombs was sweet, lighting them simultaneously was impractical, the risk too great. From now on, he'd stick with one. Everything else about the explosion itself had been a textbook success. Everything had gone just as he'd planned. Well, not entirely.

Which brought him to the second point. The girl. His smile widened to a grin, wicked and . . . powerful. Just thinking about her made his body tighten.

When she begged, when she tried to fight, something inside him had snapped and he'd used her. Completely. Savagely. Until she lay on the floor quivering, unable to say a word. *That's the way it should be. The way they all should be. Quiet.* If not voluntarily, then by force. His grin faded. But he'd used her without a condom, which was incredibly stupid. He hadn't considered it then, he'd been too wrapped up in the moment. Once again, he'd been lucky. The fire would take care of any evidence. At least he'd had the presence of mind to douse her with gasoline before he ran. She'd be destroyed, along with anything of his own he'd left behind when he'd run.

Which left point three. His escape. He hadn't been seen running to his own car. Lucky, lucky. Next time he couldn't count on that kind of luck. He'd have to come up with a better means of escape. One that, even were he spotted, would do the police no good. He smiled. He knew just what to do there.

He considered his plan. It was good. But, he had to admit, it was the sex that had made the evening complete. He'd killed before. He'd taken sex before. But now, having experienced murder and sex together, he couldn't imagine one without the other.

It should come as no surprise, really. It was, he supposed, his one . . . weakness. And perhaps his greatest strength. Of all the weapons he'd ever wielded, sex was the finest. The most basic.

Of all the ways to put a woman in her place, it was the very best. Young, old . . . it didn't really matter. The enjoyment, the release, was in the taking – and knowing they would never go a day without remembering that they were weak. And he was strong.

His biggest problem was that he'd let them live. It was almost what had gotten him caught before. It was almost what had earned him a punishment far greater than he'd experienced in the laughable juvenile detention system. He'd learned from that, too, as evidenced by Caitlin Burnette. If one planned to rape a woman, make sure she didn't live to tell the tale.

But he had to be completely honest. Technically, the night had gone off much better than he'd dared hope. Realistically, he'd failed. He'd missed his target. In the light of day, the fire, even taking Caitlin, paled. This couldn't be about fire. The fire could only be the tool. This was about payment. Retribution. Old lady Dougherty had escaped her fate. She was out of town. For Thanksgiving. He'd gotten that much from the girl.

But she'd come back and when she did, he'd be waiting.

Until then, he had more to do. Miss Penny Hill was next on his mental list of offenders. She and old lady Dougherty had been thick as thieves. Penny Hill had believed Dougherty's lies. *So did I, in the beginning.* In the beginning, Dougherty had promised them safety. His lips twisted. *Hope.* But in the end she'd turned, accusing them of things they hadn't done. Her promise of safety was mercilessly broken. She kicked them out on the street and Hill had shipped them away, like cattle. *It's for the best,* Hill had said as she'd driven them away, straight into hell on earth. *You'll see.* But it hadn't been for the best.

She'd lied, just like all the others. He and Shane had been helpless, homeless. Vulnerable. Old lady Dougherty was homeless. Soon enough she'd be helpless. And then dead. Now it was Penny Hill's turn to become helpless and homeless. And dead. It was only fair. To use her own words, it was for the best. She'd see.

He checked the clock. He had someplace to be. He didn't want to be late.

Chapter Two

Monday, November 27, 6:45 A.M

'Daddy!'

The shout, accompanied by the banging on his bedroom door, sent the tie tack in Reed's hand skittering to the floor and under his dresser. He sighed. 'Come in, Beth.'

The door exploded, admitting both fourteen-year-old Beth and her three-month-old sheepdog, who took a running leap, landing in the middle of Reed's bed. The dog shook, sending muddy water everywhere.

'Biggles, no.' Beth yanked on his collar, pulling him across the sheets to the floor where he sat, puppy tongue sticking out just far enough to make him too cute to punish.

Hands on his hips, Reed stared in dismay at the muddy streaks the puppy had left behind. 'I just changed my sheets, Beth. I told you to wipe his paws and dry him off before you brought him back in the house. The backyard is a mudbath.'

Beth's lips twitched. 'Well, his paws are clean now. I'll wash the sheets again. But first I need lunch money, Dad. The bus is coming soon.'

Reed pulled his wallet from his back pocket. 'Didn't I just give you lunch money a few days ago?'

Beth shrugged, her hand out. 'You want me to go hungry, or what?'

He shot her an overly patient look. 'I want you to help me find my tie tack. It rolled under the dresser.'

Beth dropped to her knees and felt under the dresser. 'Here it is.' She dropped it in his palm and he handed her a twenty.

'Try to make it last for at least two weeks, okay?'

She wrinkled her nose and in that moment looked so much like her mother that his heart squeezed. Beth folded the bill and slid it down into the pocket of jeans that hadn't seemed that tight before. 'Two weeks? You've gotta be kidding.'

'Do I look like I'm kidding?' He looked her up and down. 'Your jeans are too tight, Bethie,' he said and she got that look on her face. Damn, he hated that look. It seemed to have appeared about the same time as the pimples and the mood swings. Reed's sister Lauren had informed him in a dark whisper that his baby was no longer a baby. God. PMS. He wasn't ready for this. But it didn't seem to matter. His baby was a teenager. She'd be going off to college any day now.

His mind flitted to the victim they'd found in the rubble of the Dougherty house. If she was the college house sitter, she wasn't much older than Beth, and Reed still didn't know her name. He still hadn't heard from Joe Dougherty Junior. He had been able to trace the burned-out Chevy in the garage to a Roger Burnette, but when he and Ben had stopped by the Burnette address, no one had been home. He'd try again this morning after he stopped by the morgue and the lab.

Beth narrowed her eyes, her acidic tone piercing his thoughts. 'Are you saying these jeans make me look fat?'

Reed sucked in his cheek. There was no good answer to this question. 'Not even close. You're not fat. You're healthy. You're perfect. You do not need to lose weight.'

Eyes rolling, her tone became long-suffering. 'I'm not going anorexic, Dad.'

'Good.' He let out the breath he'd been holding. 'I'm just saying we need to go shopping for bigger jeans.' He smiled weakly. 'You're growing too fast, baby. Don't you like the idea of new clothes?' The tie tack rolled in his clumsy fingers, no longer as dexterous as they once had been. 'I thought all girls loved shopping.'

Quickly Beth took over the task, fixing the tie tack and smoothing his tie with a practiced hand. The look he hated disappeared, replaced by a wicked grin that made her dark eyes sparkle. 'I *love* shopping. I bet we could spend six hours in Marshall Field's alone. Sweaters and jeans and skirts. And shoes! Just think of it.'

Reed shuddered, the picture abundantly clear. 'Now you're just being mean.'

She laughed. 'Revenge for the fat comment. So you want to go shopping, Daddy?'

He shuddered again. 'Frankly, a root canal without novocaine seems less painful. Can Aunt Lauren take you?'

'I'll ask her.' Beth leaned up and kissed his cheek. 'Thanks for the lunch money, Daddy. Gotta go.'

Reed watched her dart away, the sloppy pup at her heels. The front door slammed as Beth headed out, the sheets on his bed still muddy from the dog she'd begged him to buy for her birthday. He knew if he wanted to sleep on clean sheets tonight, he'd best change them himself. But the smell of coffee tickled his nose. She'd remembered to flip the switch on the coffee machine, so he'd cut her slack on the puppy prints. Despite her sometimes volatile mood swings, she was a good kid.

Reed would sell his soul to make sure she stayed that way. He glanced over at the picture on his nightstand. Christine serenely stared back as she had for eleven years. Sitting on the edge of his bed, he picked up the picture and dusted the frame with the cuff of his shirt. Christine would have enjoyed Beth's coming of age, the shopping trips, the 'talk.' He doubted even the 'look' would have fazed her. Once he would have damned the world that his wife hadn't had the chance to find out. Today . . . he set the picture back on the nightstand so that it once again covered the dust-free strip of wood. After eleven years, the rage had become sad acceptance.

What was, was. Shrugging into his suit coat, he shook himself. If he didn't hit the road soon, traffic would make him late. *Coffee, Solliday, then get moving.*

He was pulling out of his garage when his cell phone rang. 'Solliday.'

'Lieutenant Solliday?' The voice was frantic. 'This is Joseph Dougherty. I just got back from a charter fishing trip and my dad said you called.'

Joe Junior at last. He put the car in park and pulled out his notepad. 'Mr Dougherty. I'm sorry to have to contact you this way.'

There was a heavy sigh. 'Then it's true? My house is gone?'

'I'm afraid it's true. Mr Dougherty, we found a body in the kitchen.'

There was a beat of silence. *'What?'*

Reed wished he could have spoken to the man in person, but his shock sounded sincere. 'Yes, sir. The neighbors said you had somebody watching your house.'

'Y-yes. Her name is Burnette. Caitlin Burnette. She's supposed to be very responsible.' Panic had taken the man's voice a little higher. 'She's dead?'

Reed thought of the charred body and swallowed his sigh. *Yes, she's very dead.* 'We're assuming the body we found was your house sitter, but we'll have to investigate before we're certain. We'd appreciate you leaving any notification of the family to us.'

'Of . . .' He cleared his throat. 'Of course.'

'When will you be back in town, Mr Dougherty?'

'We weren't supposed to come back until Friday, but we'll try to get home today. When I know our flight times, I'll call you back.'

Reed tossed his phone to the passenger seat, only to have it ring again. Caller ID this time was the morgue. 'Solliday.'

'Reed, it's Sam Barrington.' The new medical examiner. Barrington had taken over when the old ME went out on maternity leave. The old ME had been efficient, astute, and personable. Barrington . . . well, he was efficient and astute.

'Hey, Sam. I'm on my way into the office. What do you have?'

'Victim's a woman, early twenties. Best I can tell she was five-two, five-three.'

Sam wasn't one to call with such basic information. There had to be more. 'And?'

'Well, before I started to cut I did an initial X-ray of the body. I expected to see the skull in fractured fragments.'

Which was the general way of things. Bodies subjected to that kind of heat . . . the skulls sometimes just exploded from the pressure. 'But you didn't.'

'No, because the bullet hole in her skull vented all the pressure.'

Reed wasn't surprised. Still, now he had to share. He got the arson, the cops got the body. Too many damn cooks in the kitchen. He winced. So to speak. 'Any evidence of smoke inhalation?'

'Haven't gotten that far yet,' Sam said briskly. 'I'm going to start the autopsy right away, so you can come by anytime this morning.'

'Thanks. I will.' He pulled onto his quiet tree-lined street, flipping on his wipers against the rain. It had been a while since he'd worked with Homicide, but he thought Marc Spinnelli was still the lieutenant there. Marc was a straight shooter. Reed only hoped the detective Spinnelli assigned wouldn't be a know-it-all hotshot.

Monday, November 27, 8:30 A.M.

Mia Mitchell's feet were cold. Which was really stupid, because they could be warm and toasty, propped up on her desk as she sipped her third cup of coffee. *But they're not, because here I am*, she thought bitterly. Standing on the sidewalk, cold rain dripping from the brim of the battered hat she wore. Staring at her own reflection in the glass doors like an idiot. She'd passed through these doors hundreds of times before but today was different. Today she was alone.

Because I froze like a damn rookie. And her partner had paid the price. Two weeks later, the moment was still enough to make her frozen. She stared at the sidewalk. Two weeks later she could still hear the crack of gunfire, see Abe crumble and fall, the bloodstain on his white shirt spreading as she stood, slack-jawed and helpless.

'Excuse me.'

Mia jerked her chin upward, then up again, her fist clenching against the reflex to draw her weapon, her eyes narrowing beneath the brim of her hat to focus on the reflection behind her. It was a man, at least six feet tall. His black trench coat was the same color as the neatly trimmed goatee that framed his mouth. After a beat she lifted her chin another notch to his eyes. He was staring at her from under an umbrella, dark brows furrowed.

'Are you all right, miss?' he asked, his voice that even, soft tone that she herself used to calm skittish suspects and witnesses. Her lips quirked up mirthlessly as his intent became clear. He thought she was some nutcase off the street. Maybe she looked that way. Either way, he'd gotten the drop on her and that was unacceptable. *Pay attention for God's sake.* She searched her mind for an adequate response.

'I'm fine, thanks. I'm . . . waiting for someone.' It sounded lame, even to her own ears, but he nodded and stepped around her, pulling the door open as he closed his umbrella. Background noise filtered through the open door, and she thought that would be the end of it and him. But he didn't move. He stood, studying her face as if memorizing each detail. She considered identifying herself, but . . . didn't. Instead she met his scrutiny with her own, the cop part of her brain now back on full.

He was a good-looking man, darkly handsome, older

than his reflection had appeared. It was his eyes, she thought. Hard and dark. And his mouth. He looked like he never smiled. His eyes dropped to her bare hands, then lifted, his expression softer. It was compassion, she realized, and the notion had her swallowing hard.

'Well, if you need a place to warm up, there's room at the shelter on Grand. They might be able to get you some gloves. Be careful. It's cold outside.' He hesitated, then held out his umbrella. 'Stay dry.'

Too stunned to speak, she took it. Her mouth opened to set him straight, but he was gone, hurrying across the lobby. He stopped at the desk sergeant's station and pointed at her. The desk sergeant blinked once, then nodded soberly.

Hell, Tommy Polanski was at the desk this morning. He'd known her since she was a snot-nosed kid tagging behind her dad at the firing range, begging for a turn. But Tommy didn't say a word, just let the man walk away thinking she was some street person. Rolling her eyes, she followed the path the man had taken, scowling when a broad grin took over Tommy's face.

'Well, well. Look what the cat dragged in. If it isn't Detective Mia Mitchell, finally come back to do an honest day's work.'

She took off her hat, shook it dry. 'Got tired of the soaps. How's it going, Tommy?'

He shrugged. 'Same old, same old.' But his eyes twinkled.

He was going to make her ask, the old bastard. 'So who was that guy?'

Tommy laughed. 'He's a fire marshal. He was worried you were planning to storm the place. I told him you were a regular' – his grin went wicked – 'and harmless overall.'

Mia rolled her eyes again. 'Gee, thanks, Tommy,' she said dryly.

'Anything for Bobby's girl.' His grin faded, his eyes giving her a head-to-toe once-over. 'How's the shoulder, kid?'

She flexed it inside her leather jacket. 'Just a graze. Doc says I'm good as new.' Actually it hadn't been a graze and the doctor had said she needed another week on disability, but at her growl he'd shrugged and signed her release form.

'And Abe?'

'Getting better.' So the night nurse said, every night when Mia called anonymously at three A.M.

Tommy's jaw stiffened. 'We'll catch the punk that did this, Mia. Don't worry.'

Two weeks later and the little punk bastard that shot her partner was still on the streets, no doubt boasting how he took down a cop twice his size. A wave of rage hit her hard, but she bit it back. 'I know. Thanks.'

'Tell Abe I said hi.'

'I will,' she lied smoothly. 'I need to go. I don't want to be late my first day back.'

'Mia.' Tommy hesitated. 'I'm sorry about your father. He was a good cop.'

A good cop. Mia bit the inside of her cheek. Too bad Bobby Mitchell hadn't been a better man. 'Thanks, Tommy. My mom appreciated the basket.' Fruit baskets filled the kitchen table of her mother's small house, tokens of respect for her father's long, long career. Three weeks after her father stroked out, the fruit in the baskets was going rotten. A fitting end, many would say. No, many wouldn't. Because many didn't know.

But Mia knew. A hard knot filled her throat and she shoved her hat back on her head. 'I gotta go.' She passed the elevator and took the stairs two at a time, which unfortunately brought her all the faster toward the very place she'd been avoiding.

Monday, November 27, 8:40 A.M.

He worked in brisk silence, sliding the razor blade down the straight edge of the rule, trimming the ragged edges from the article he'd pulled from the *Trib*. FIRE DESTROYS HOME, KILLS ONE. It was a small article, with no photograph, but it did mention the home belonged to the Doughertys so it would be a good addition to his scrapbook. He sat back and looked at the account of Saturday night's fire and his mouth curved.

He'd achieved the effect he'd wanted. There was fear in the words of the neighbors the reporter had interviewed. *Why?* they'd asked. *Who could do such a thing?*

Me. That was the answer, all the answer he needed. *I could. I would. I did.*

The reporter had interviewed old lady Richter. She'd been one of the worst of the geezers, always dropping in on old lady Dougherty for tea, gossiping for hours. She was always looking down her nose at them. 'I don't know what you're thinking about, Laura,' she'd say with a sniff. 'Taking in those kind of boys. It's a wonder you haven't been murdered in your sleep by now.' Old lady Dougherty would tell her that she was making a difference in her boys' lives. She'd made a difference, all right. Her difference had sent them straight to hell. Her difference had killed Shane.

Shane had trusted her. And she'd turned on him. She was as guilty of his death as if she'd stabbed him in the back herself. He looked down at his hand. It was fisted, the X-Acto blade clutched like a knife. He carefully put it down, reined in the emotion.

Stick to the facts, the plan. He needed to find old lady Dougherty. He should have waited for her to return. To go ahead without her had been foolish. He'd been too eager to use the means. He'd forgotten about the end.

When would she return? How the hell would he find her now? His eyes settled on the article once more. Old lady Richter had been a gossip then. Some things didn't change. When the Doughertys came back, she'd know. He smiled, a plan starting to form. He was clever enough to get the information without Richter suspecting a thing.

He studied the article, pride bubbling deep within him. The fire investigators had ruled it arson. *Duh.* But they had no leads, no suspects. They didn't even know the identity of the girl yet. They claimed they were withholding her identity pending notification of her family, but they couldn't know who she was. She'd been burned to a crisp. He'd seen to that. No body could have survived that fire.

His hands went still. He'd said those same words the day Shane died. Nobody could have survived. And Shane had not. That the girl had not was . . . fair.

He gave a hard nod to the newspaper clipping he held in his hands. Nice, straight edges. Suitable for framing. Instead, he slid it between the pages of the book on his desk along with the article he'd cut just as carefully from the Springdale, Indiana *Gazette*. THANKS-GIVING NIGHT FIRE LEAVES TWO DEAD. As they should be. Again, it was fair. More than fair. Again, no suspects. No leads. As it should be.

Later, he'd put both articles with the souvenir he'd taken, Caitlin's blue denim purse. Well, it had been blue. Now it was red, splattered with her blood.

He'd been splattered, too. Luckily he'd been able to shower and change before anyone saw the blood on his clothes. Next time, he'd have to take better precautions. Next time he'd need to cover his own clothes before drawing blood.

He stood up. Because he would draw blood again, very soon. He knew exactly where to find Miss Penny Hill. People thought their addresses were secret because their telephone numbers were unlisted. Not so. If a person knew how, they could find out anything about anybody. Of course the person searching had to be smart.

And I am. He was already starting to feel the excitement of the next kill. Penny Hill would not die easily. He would not be so merciful this time. *Time*. Damn. He'd lost track of time. He gathered his things. If he didn't hurry, he'd be late. He needed to make it through the day, then tonight . . . He'd walked through his plan last night, made sure it was foolproof. Tonight . . . he smiled.

She would suffer. And she'd know why. Then she'd count to ten, one for each miserable year of his brother's life. Then he'd send her to hell where she belonged.

Monday, November 27, 8:50 A.M.

Mia rounded the corner to the Homicide bullpen. It looked the same – pairs of desks back-to-back, piled with papers and coffee cups. Except for two. Hers and Abe's. She frowned. Their desks were clean, their folders in neat stacks. Everything else was arranged with an eerie symmetry – coffee cups, telephones, staplers, even their pens were placed in identical mirror-image locations.

'The Stepford wives cleaned my desk,' Mia muttered and heard a chuckle behind her. Todd Murphy leaned against the wall, coffee cup in his hand, a smile bending his mouth. With his rumpled suit and loosened tie, he was a most welcome sight.

'Stacy,' he said quietly, indicating their office clerk. 'She went through what you'd been working on when Spinnelli reassigned your cases. Stacy got a little carried away.'

'He reassigned *all* of them?' Mia hadn't expected their lieutenant to allow their cases to go untouched for two weeks, but hearing that he'd reassigned them all left her a little rocked. It was as if Spinnelli hadn't expected her back for a long while. *Well, I am back.* She had work to do. First and foremost was catching the sorry piece of shit who'd shot Abe. 'Who took Abe's case?'

'Howard and Brooks. They worked it hard the first week, but the trail was ice cold.'

'So Melvin Getts shoots a cop and gets away with it,' she said bitterly.

'They haven't given up,' Murphy said softly. 'Everybody wants to see Getts pay.'

The thought of Getts calmly lifting his gun and shooting her partner twisted her gut and she felt herself freezing up as she had outside. Fighting it, she strode to her desk with a belligerence she had to fake. 'I bet Stacy even washed my cup.'

Murphy followed her and slumped in his chair two desks down. 'It was really gross, Mitchell. Your cup was growing . . . things.' He shuddered. 'Vile, unspeakable things.'

Mia set the umbrella against her desk and shrugged out of her wet jacket, biting her lip against the twinge in her shoulder as she adjusted the holster under her blazer. 'Good old-fashioned mold. Never hurt anybody.' She pulled the worn fedora from her head and winced. No wonder the guy downstairs thought she was a street person. Both the coat and the hat looked like they'd been pulled from a Salvation Army bin. On the other hand, what did she care what he thought? *You have to stop caring what people think.* She sighed quietly. And she'd stop breathing while she was at it.

She turned her frustration to her perfect desk. 'Hell, I can't work like this.' Deliberately she toppled the stack of folders and rearranged the contents of her desk haphazardly. 'There. If Stacy touched the Pop-Tarts in my drawer, she's dead meat.' But her emergency stash was intact. 'She can live.'

'I'm sure she's been quaking in her boots,' Murphy said dryly. He eyed the umbrella. 'Since when did you start carrying one of those?'

'It's not mine. I'm going to have to find the owner and give it back.' Mia eased herself into her chair, her eyes flitting across the unoccupied desk that butted against Murphy's. 'Where's your partner?' she asked. Murphy's partner was Abe's brother Aidan. Mia wasn't looking forward to the censure she knew she'd see in his eyes.

'At the morgue. We pulled a double homicide last night. He won the toss, so I'm calling next of kin.' Murphy's eyes abruptly narrowed. 'You have company.'

Mia turned, a groan catching in her throat when her shoulder burned. Then she forgot all about her shoulder. Striding across the bullpen with a look that would terrify most serial killers was the assistant state's attorney. Abe's wife. Guilt had Mia avoiding Abe's family for two weeks. Now it was time to face the music. Unsteadily she rose and prepared to take what she had coming. 'Kristen.'

Kristen Reagan raised her brows, her lips tightly pursed. 'So you live after all.'

The woman had every right to her anger. Kristen could have been a widow had the bullet hit Abe's gut just an inch lower. Mia braced herself. 'Just say it.'

Kristen said nothing, instead studying her in a way that made Mia want to squirm, bringing back memories of frowning nuns and stinging palms. Finally Kristen sighed. 'You dumb ass,' she murmured. 'What did you think I was going to say?'

Mia's spine straightened at the soft tone. She would have preferred the harsh words she deserved. 'I wasn't paying attention. Abe paid the price.'

'He said you were ambushed. He didn't see them at first, either.'

'My angle was different. I should have seen them. I was . . .' *Preoccupied*. 'I wasn't paying attention,' she repeated stiffly. 'I'm sorry.'

Kristen's eyes flashed. 'You think he *blames* you? That *I* blame you?'

'You should. I would.' She lifted a shoulder. 'I do.'

'Then you're an idiot,' Kristen snapped. 'We were worried, Mia. You disappeared after they sewed you up. We looked everywhere, but we couldn't find you. We thought you'd been hurt, or killed. Abe's been out of his mind worrying about you. And all this time you've been off somewhere sulking, feeling sorry for yourself?'

Mia blinked. 'I'm sorry. I didn't mean . . . .' She shut her eyes. 'Shit.'

'You didn't mean for us to worry.' Kristen's voice was flat. 'Well, we did. Even Spinnelli didn't know where you were until you called last week to say you'd be back this morning. I went by your apartment six times.'

Mia opened her eyes, remembering three of those times. 'I know.'

Kristen's eyes widened. 'You know? You were *there*?'

'Kind of. Yeah.' Sitting in the dark sulking. Feeling sorry for herself.

Kristen's brows furrowed. ' "Kind of"? What the hell is that supposed to mean?'

The room had quieted and everyone watched them. 'Can you keep your voice down?'

'No. I can't. I've sat by Abe's side for two weeks while he waited for you to call. In between morphine drips and surgery, he worried that you'd gone after Getts yourself and were dead in an alley somewhere. So if I'm a little short on patience or sympathy or discretion, then

45

so be it.' She stood, her cheeks flushed. 'You better show up at his hospital room after your shift. Explain to him what "kind of" means. You owe him that much.' She took two steps, then stopped. Slowly she turned, her eyes no longer flashing, but filled with sorrow. 'Dammit, Mia. You hurt him. When he found out you were okay and that you just hadn't come to see him, he was so hurt.'

Mia swallowed hard. 'I'm sorry.'

Kristen cocked her jaw. 'You should be. He cares about you.'

Mia dropped her gaze to her desk. 'I'll be there after my shift.'

'See that you are.' She paused, then cleared her throat. 'Mia, look at me, please.'

Mia raised her eyes. The anger was gone, concern taking its place. 'What?'

Kristen lowered her voice to a mere whisper. 'You've had a hard time the last few weeks, what with your dad and all. Mistakes happen. You're human. And you're still the partner I want watching my husband's back.'

Mia watched until Kristen was gone, then sank down into her chair. They thought she was upset about her father's death. If only it were that easy. 'Shit.'

Murphy's voice was mild. 'You're white as a sheet. You should have taken a few more days.'

'Looks like I should have done a lot of things,' she shot back, then closed her eyes. 'Have you seen him?'

'Yeah. He was a mess for the first week or so. Aidan

says they're letting him out tomorrow or the next day, so unless you want him to hold it over your head that you didn't visit him, you'd better go tonight. What the hell were you thinking, Mia?'

Mia stared into her very clean coffee cup. 'That I fucked up and nearly got my partner killed. Again.' Murphy said nothing and Mia looked up, sardonic. 'You're not going to tell me it wasn't my fault? This time or last time?'

Murphy pulled a carrot stick from a plastic bag on his desk. 'Would it do any good?'

Mia eyed the stack of perfectly cut carrots as Murphy slipped one between his lips. 'You're trying to quit again, aren't you?'

He held her eyes for a long moment, not fooled. 'Two weeks. Not that I'm counting.'

'Good for you.' She stood, her legs steady again. 'I need to tell Spinnelli I'm back.'

'He's in with somebody. But he said he wants to see you right away and you should just come in.'

Mia frowned. 'Why didn't you tell me?'

'I just did.' She'd made it to the door to Spinnelli's office when Murphy called her name. 'Mia. It wasn't your fault. Abe or Ray. Shit happens. You know this.'

Abe, who'd escaped by the skin of his teeth no thanks to her. Ray, the partner before who hadn't been so lucky. The cops sent Ray's wife fruit baskets, too. 'Yeah.' Drawing a breath, she knocked on her lieutenant's door.

'Come,' Spinnelli ordered. He was sitting behind his

desk, a frown bunching his bushy salt-and-pepper mustache, but his eyes softened at the sight of her. 'Mia. Glad you're here. Come in. Sit down. How are you?'

Mia closed the door behind her. 'Cleared for duty.' Her eyes widened as the occupant of Spinnelli's guest chair turned. *Hell*. Then the guy in the trench coat from downstairs was lurching to his feet and he didn't look any happier than she felt.

For a second she could only stare. '*You're* Detective Mitchell?' he said accusingly.

Mia nodded, feeling her cheeks heat. The man had caught her practically asleep on her feet right outside the station house. He'd thought she was a mental case. Any chance at a good first impression was shot straight to hell. Still, she gathered her composure and met his dark eyes squarely. 'I am. And you are?'

Spinnelli stood up behind his desk. 'This is Lieutenant Reed Solliday from OFI.'

Mia nodded. 'Office of Fire Investigation. The arson guys. Okay. And?'

Spinnelli's mouth quirked. 'And he's your new partner.'

Monday, November 27, 9:00 A.M.

Brooke Adler sat on the corner of her desk, aware that half a dozen sets of eyes would be permanently glued to her cleavage for the next fifty minutes. If she was lucky maybe one of the boys in her class would be paying attention to the lesson she'd so carefully prepared. She didn't hold out much hope. Then again, neither did the boys.

The only hope in this place was on the sign on the front door. HOPE CENTER FOR BOYS. Sitting before her were thieves and runaways and juvenile sex offenders. She would have preferred lions and tigers and bears. *Oh my*.

'So how was Thanksgiving?' she asked brightly. Most of the boys had spent Thanksgiving here, in the dorms of the residential school.

'Turkey was dry,' Mike complained from the back row. There really wasn't a back row, Mike just created one every morning. The end chair on the first row was empty.

She searched the faces of her students. 'Where is Thad today?'

Jeff slouched, outwardly cool. But there was always a tension, a coldness in his eyes, that kept Brooke on edge. 'Faggeus stole the leftover pie from the fridge.'

Brooke frowned. 'Jeff,' she said sharply, 'you know that name isn't tolerated. So where is Thad today?' she repeated more soberly.

Jeff's smile made a shiver race down Brooke's spine. Jeff's smiles were mean. Jeff was mean. 'He got a stomach-ache,' Jeff said blandly. 'He's at the clinic.'

Thaddeus Lewin was a quiet kid, rarely spoke. Brooke wasn't sure who'd nicknamed him Faggeus. She was positive she didn't want to know why. She picked up her copy of *Lord of the Flies* with a sigh. 'I asked you to read chapter two. What did you think?'

Linking *Lord of the Flies* to the *Survivor* TV show had produced a flicker of interest the week before. Now their faces were blank. No one had completed the reading. Then to her surprise a hand went up. 'Manny?' Manny Rodriguez never volunteered.

Manny leaned back in his chair. 'The fire was cool,' he said smoothly.

Jeff's brows went up. 'They got fire in this book?'

Manny nodded. 'These kids get stranded on this island, so they start a signal fire to get rescued, but it gets out of control.' His eyes gleamed. 'Burns the whole side of a mountain and takes out one of the kids. Then later they catch the whole island on fire.'

He sounded almost awed and Brooke's skin prickled. 'The signal fire is a symbol—'

'How did they make the fire?' Jeff asked, ignoring her.

'They used the fat ass's glasses like a magnifying glass,' Manny answered. 'The fat kid gets it in the end.' He grinned. 'Boulder smashes his head open. Brains everywhere.' He looked over at Brooke with a leer. 'I read ahead, Teacher.'

'I used a magnifying glass to kill a bug once,' Mike offered. 'I didn't think it would work, but it really does.'

Jeff's smile flashed, wolfish. 'They say that sticking a hamster in the microwave is a myth, but they're wrong.

Cats are even better, but you need a really big microwave.'

'That's enough,' Brooke snapped. 'Manny, Jeff, Mike, stop it.'

Jeff slid back down in his chair, smirking as his eyes slid back to her breasts, slowly so that she would know he stared. 'Teacher likes pussy . . . cats,' he murmured just loud enough for her to hear. Brooke decided it was best to ignore him.

Manny just shrugged. 'You asked,' he said. 'The fire was cool.'

'The fire is a symbol,' she said firmly. 'Of common sense and morality.' She frowned at the class. 'And stay away from the microwave. Now let's talk about the symbolism of the signal fire. You have a quiz on Wednesday.'

Every set of eyes dropped to her breasts and Brooke knew she'd be talking to herself. Three months ago she'd arrived at Hope Center, the ink barely dry on her diploma, fresh-faced and eager to teach. Now she just prayed she'd get through the day. And that somehow, someway she'd get through to these kids. *Please. Just one.*

Chapter Three

Monday, November 27, 9:15 A.M.

Reed Solliday drew a careful breath and let it out. For a split second the woman had looked angrily stunned. Well, that made two of them, because Reed wasn't thrilled about his new 'partner' either. Marc Spinnelli insisted that Mia Mitchell was one of the best, but he'd seen the woman staring at the precinct door like a deer caught in the headlights. He'd stood behind her for a full minute before she'd detected his presence.

Not the highest recommendation for her skills. Plus, with her battered leather jacket, worn-out hat, and scuffed boots she'd looked . . . well, not like a detective he'd want watching his back. Still, he extended his hand. 'Detective Mitchell.'

Her grip was solid. 'Lieutenant Solliday.' She turned to her boss, her face calm, but her spine rigid. 'What's this all about, Marc? Abe's coming back.'

'Of course he is, Mia. OFI discovered a homicide in one of their arson scenes. Abe will be out for a few weeks. Consider yourself on loan. Sit down and let Reed explain.'

They sat and Mitchell gave him her full attention. Her eyes were clear and alert now. And blue, like Christine's china they used only on holidays. The scruffy hat she'd worn kept her short blond hair dry except for the edges that curled around her face. She'd stowed the ratty jacket and fortunately now looked more professional in a black blazer. Unfortunately the thin, clingy shirt she wore under the blazer didn't do a thing to hide her curves. For a small woman, Detective Mia Mitchell had a hell of a lot of curves.

Reed enjoyed staring at a nice set of curves as much as the next guy, but what he needed was a partner, not a pinup and certainly not a distraction. However, he sensed no flirtation in her, no softness, so he wouldn't hold the curves against her.

'On Saturday night there was a fire in Oak Park,' he began. 'We found a body in the kitchen. This morning the ME called. The X-ray showed a bullet hole in her skull.'

'Carbon monoxide in the lungs?' Mitchell asked.

'Barrington was going back to check. He wanted me to know about the bullet since it changes the nature of the investigation.'

'And the jurisdiction,' she murmured. 'You've seen the body?'

'I was going to the morgue after I finished here.'

'You have an ID on the victim?'

'Tentative. The house is owned by Joe and Donna Dougherty. They went out of town for Thanksgiving and hired a house sitter named Caitlin Burnette. She's the right size and age, and the car we found in the garage was registered to Roger Burnette, so for now we've assumed the body we found is Caitlin. The ME will have to make a positive ID based on dental records or DNA.' She flinched at that, though the movement was barely enough to catch.

Spinnelli handed her a sheet of paper. 'We printed a copy of her license from the DMV's files.'

She studied the page. 'She was only nineteen,' she said, her voice gone low and husky. She looked up, her blue eyes now dark. 'You've informed the parents?'

The thought of breaking the news to the girl's parents nauseated him. It always did. He wondered how homicide detectives hardened themselves to the task, doing it every day. 'Not yet. I went by the Burnettes' twice yesterday, but nobody was home.'

Spinnelli sighed. 'There's more, Mia.'

Reed grimaced. 'If the body in the morgue is Caitlin Burnette, her father's a cop.'

'I know him,' Spinnelli said. 'Sergeant Roger Burnette. Vice for the last five years.'

'Oh shit.' Mitchell rested her forehead against her palm before shoving her hand through her short hair, leaving it standing in blond spikes. 'Could it be a grudge kill?'

Reed was wondering the same thing. 'I guess that's what we have to find out. The Doughertys are flying back some time today. I'll interview them when they come home.'

She met his eyes for a brief instant. '*We'll* interview them,' she corrected quietly.

The challenge was implicit. Annoyed, he nodded. 'Of course.'

'We'll need to get a crime scene unit out there.' She frowned. 'You've already been over the house, right? Shit, this rain's gonna make a mess of things.'

'We were out there all day yesterday. I photographed every room and gathered samples for the lab. Luckily we tarped the roof. The rain shouldn't be a problem.'

She nodded evenly. 'Okay. What kind of samples?'

'Carpet, wood. I was looking for evidence of accelerants.'

She tilted her head a fraction. 'And?'

'My instruments say they're there and the accelerant dog picked up two different kinds. Gasoline and something else. The lab said they'd have results later today.'

She shook her head. 'As crime scenes go, this one's going to suck eggs, Marc.'

Reed straightened. 'Our procedure is to gather evidence to support arson as quickly as possible. We got a warrant. We took nothing more than we needed to establish source and cause until we knew how the girl had died. Our search is clean.'

Her eyes softened a fraction. 'I wasn't talking about your search, Lieutenant. I was talking about fire scenes in general.' She glanced at Spinnelli. 'Can you send a uniform to the Dougherty house? Make sure nobody touches anything until we get there.'

'We've got a security guard there at the scene,' Reed said stiffly. 'Although if you're willing to foot the bill for round-the-clock surveillance, I'll send our guy back. Our budget isn't as big as yours.'

'That's fine. Now that it's a homicide I'd rather have a cop on hand anyway. No offense,' she added quickly. 'I'll call Jack and ask him to meet us there with his CSU team.'

'I've got two team members waiting for them at the house. Foster Richards and Ben Trammell. They'll be able to let them in and show them what we did yesterday.' He'd already called the two men and told them to be ready to join the team he knew Homicide would be sending. He'd added a warning to Foster to play nice in the sandbox with CSU. He'd added a warning to Ben to watch Foster.

She rose. 'Good. But first, let's go to the morgue to see what Caitlin can tell us.'

Spinnelli stood as well. 'Call me when you've notified the parents. I'll contact Burnette's captain so his precinct can send flowers or whatever.'

'You'll want to update the warrant,' Reed said. 'Ours was specific to the arson.'

Spinnelli nodded. 'I'll call the state's attorney's office

and have your warrant by the time you get out to the scene.'

Mitchell tilted her head toward Spinnelli. 'Lieutenant Solliday, can you give us a few minutes alone? You can wait at my desk. It's the one next to the clean one.'

'Sure.' He eased the door closed, but instead of going to her desk he leaned against the wall, his head angled toward the door to maximize his eavesdropping.

'Marc, about Abe's case,' she said.

It was the second time she'd mentioned Abe. He glanced over at the clean desk. That would be Abe's, he surmised.

Spinnelli's voice held a warning note. 'Howard and Brooks are on it.'

'Murphy says the trail is cold.'

'That's true. Mia, you—'

'I know, Marc. This is my priority and you know it will be. But if I hear something, if anybody hears anything and I'm available . . . Dammit, Marc, I saw him.' Her voice became fierce. 'If I see the asshole that got Abe, I'll know him.'

'He got you, too, Mia.'

'A damn scratch. Marc, please.' There was a pause. 'I owe it to Abe. Please.'

Another pause, then a sigh. 'If you're available, I'll call you.'

'I appreciate it.' The door opened and Reed made no attempt to move. He wanted her to know he'd heard. Color flooded her cheeks, her eyes narrowing as she saw him standing there. For a few seconds she just stared up at him, annoyance in her eyes.

'Let's go to the morgue,' she said flatly and turned for her desk where she grabbed the ratty jacket and hat. 'Here's your umbrella.'

She tossed it to him, then gingerly she shrugged into the jacket, favoring her right shoulder. Spinnelli said she was fully recovered, but Reed had his doubts. If she wasn't, he was going straight back to Spinnelli for another detective. She took the stairs two at a time, which he suspected was a combination of pent-up anger and the desire to make him jog to keep up. He'd already worked out that morning, so he took the stairs one at a time, letting her wait on the street. He put up his umbrella but she stepped away.

'I don't have my department vehicle back yet and my own car's very small,' she said, not turning around when he caught up. 'You wouldn't fit.'

Her words held obvious double meaning. He chose to ignore the personal dig and focus on the issue of transportation. 'I'll drive.' Reed considered offering her a boost up into his Tahoe, but she swung up into the cab with surprising agility and only a minor grunt of pain. He slid behind the wheel and looked over at her pointedly. 'You're not ready to be back yet, are you?'

She flicked him an angry glance before staring straight ahead. 'I'm cleared for duty.'

He started the engine, then settled back in his seat,

waiting for her to meet his eyes. A minute of silence ticked by before she finally turned her head, frowning.

'Why are we still sitting here?' she demanded.

'Who is Abe?'

Her jaw clenched. 'My partner.'

And you're not, was the silent addendum. 'What happened to him?'

'He got shot.'

'I take it he'll be all right.'

He wouldn't have seen her flinch had he not been looking for it. 'Eventually.'

'You were shot, too.'

Her cheeks hollowed. 'A scratch.'

He sincerely doubted that. 'Why were you staring at the glass this morning?'

Her eyes flashed. 'None of your damn business.'

It was exactly what he expected her to say. Nevertheless, he'd say his own piece. 'I'm afraid I have to disagree. Like it or not, you're my partner for the foreseeable future. Anybody could have gotten the jump on you this morning, gotten your weapon, hurt you or somebody else. I need to know you're not going to be staring off into space when I need you, so I'll repeat the question. Why were you staring at the glass this morning?'

Something in his words struck a chord because her flashing eyes went totally cold. 'If you're worried that I won't be watching your back, worry no more, Lieutenant. What happened this morning was my personal business. I won't allow my personal business to interfere with our work. You have my word on that.'

She'd held his eyes through all her words and now that she was done, she continued to stare in a way that dared him to cross her. 'I don't know you, Detective, so your word means very little to me.' He held up his hand when she opened her mouth to utter what he was sure would be unprintable. 'But I do know Marc Spinnelli and he has confidence in your capability. I'll let this morning pass. But if it happens again, I'll ask Spinnelli for someone else. You have *my* word on that.'

She blinked several times, her teeth clenched so hard it was a wonder they didn't shatter. 'The morgue, Lieutenant. If you please.'

Reed put the car in gear, satisfied that he'd made his point. 'To the morgue.'

Monday, November 27, 10:05 A.M.

Mia was out of Solliday's SUV before he'd come to a complete stop. *Threaten to go to my boss, my ass.* As if he'd never gotten lost in thought in his life. *So blow it off. It's no big deal. Right?* She fought not to grind her teeth as Solliday followed her across the parking garage. *Wrong.* It was a big deal. He was right. Anybody could have surprised her, taken her weapon. She slowed her pace. She hadn't been careful. Again.

He caught up to her at the elevator and she silently

pushed the button. Without a word Solliday followed her in and stood close enough that she could feel the heat from his body. He stood like a granite monolith, arms crossed over his chest, which made her feel about eight years old. It was all she could do not to cower into the corner. Instead, she kept her eyes locked on the display as the numbers went up.

'I hope you accomplished your goal with that little stunt,' he said, surprising her into looking up at him. He stared straight ahead, his mouth turned down in a frown.

'Excuse me?'

'Jumping from the car before it was stopped. I know you were pissed at me, but it's a long way down for you and you could have broken your leg.'

Mia laughed, incredulous. 'You're not my father, Lieutenant Solliday.'

'Be grateful I'm not.' The doors opened and he waited for her to go first. 'I'd have grounded my daughter for a week for a stunt like that. Two, if she gave me any lip.'

Don't give me lip, girl. Mia barely controlled the flinch. When she was a kid, the snarled line was usually followed by a slap to the head that left her seeing stars. When she got older, just her dad saying that line was enough to make her draw back, earning his contemptuous laughter. She'd hated his laugh. She'd hated him. *My own father*.

But it wasn't her father standing next to her. It was Reed Solliday and he was holding the door that led to the morgue. 'Do these things bother you?' he asked. 'The victim's in really bad shape. Charred beyond recognition.'

They did, but she'd die before letting him know about it. 'I'm sure I've seen worse.'

'I suppose you have,' he murmured and stopped at the glass window to the identification room. 'Barrington's busy. We'll have to wait.'

Mia's stomach tightened and it had nothing to do with the body on the metal table covered with a sheet. Aidan Reagan stood next to the ME looking at X-rays. He'd see her, there was no escaping it. Abe's brother would likely be as angry as his wife had been. Aidan turned from the X-rays and immediately frowned, his eyes meeting hers through the glass. He was nodding at something ME Barrington was saying, but he never broke eye contact with her. He came through the door and stopped.

Solliday moved toward the door, but paused when he realized something was brewing. Interested, Solliday looked from Aidan to Mia, those damn dark brows of his lifted. He looked like Satan, for God's sake. Solliday, not Aidan. Aidan just looked upset.

'Can you give us a minute, Solliday?'

He nodded, obviously still curious. 'I'll wait for you inside.'

She turned to Aidan Reagan. 'Kristen already chewed my ass this morning,' she said before he could say a word, 'but I'm going to the hospital to see Abe tonight, so if you want to meet me there and take what's left, be my guest.'

Aidan quietly assessed her face, just as Kristen had done. 'Okay. I will.'

His voice was heavy with disappointment. She hated when people were disappointed. And she hated that she hated it. 'I have to go.'

'Mia, wait.' He held out his hand, then let it drop to his side. 'We were worried.'

'Yeah, I know. Look, Aidan, I fucked up. Somehow I'll make it up to Abe.' She moved toward the door, but Aidan caught her arm and she sucked in a painful breath.

Instantly he released her. 'You still hurt.'

'I'll live,' she said curtly. 'I'm in far better shape than Abe.' Solliday was already talking to the ME. 'I really have to go, Aidan.'

Aidan followed her gaze through the window. 'Who is that guy?'

'Solliday. He's with OFI and my new best pal until Abe comes back or we solve his homicide, whichever comes first. Solliday's fire turned up a body with a bullet.'

Aidan grimaced. 'Yeah, I got a glimpse of it. Better you than me, Mia.'

'Gee, thanks.' She pushed past him into the morgue, trying to ignore the odor that always hovered there. It was much worse today. Chemicals combined with the stench of cooked flesh to make her stomach churn. ME

Barrington was sliding X-rays onto the light board and Mia forced her mind to switch out of self-pity into detective mode.

The X-rays showed a neat round hole at the base of a skull.

'There's no exit wound,' Barrington was saying. 'The bullet's still in there, but I can't guarantee what shape it will be in. Detective Mitchell. Good to see you back.'

'Thanks.' She stared at the X-ray, focusing her thoughts. 'Bullet came from a .22?'

'That would be my guess.' Barrington pulled the X-ray down. 'No carbon monoxide in her lungs. She died before the fire started.'

'He shot her execution style,' Solliday noted and Barrington nodded.

'I found three breaks in one of the leg bones. Two are current. One is healed, the bone set properly, a few years ago at least, so you know she had access to good health care at one time.'

'Her dad's a cop,' Mia said.

He didn't blink. Not a damn flicker of emotion. 'Well, find out who her dentist was. I'll get her records and make a formal ID. Until then, she's a Jane Doe.' The ME walked to a table and carefully pulled back the sheet. Mia took in the sight for a split second. It was all she could manage without losing what little breakfast she'd consumed. It was bad. Worse than she'd expected. Maybe worse than she'd seen before.

Her eyes flashed to Solliday and watched his body

go rigid, his skin just a little paler. He'd seen this body before, probably many others just as bad. But it wasn't revulsion she saw on his face. Just pain. *He has a daughter*, she thought. Young enough to still ground for bad behavior. Thinking that somewhere in the neat suit beat a heart helped her get over her own nausea at the sight of the blackened corpse. She forced herself to look at what remained of a nineteen-year-old girl. She had a job to do.

A macabre blackened face stared up from the gleaming silver of the table. Charred skin stretched tight over her facial bones. A few tufts of hair remained. Blond, like the driver's license photo Solliday had shown her. She'd been such a pretty girl. So young. She'd been smiling for the DMV's camera. Now her nose was gone and her mouth was open grotesquely, as if on a final, eternal scream. *What did he do to you, Caitlin?*

'Was the victim sexually assaulted?' she asked, her voice steady.

'I can't tell. If she was, we may never know, but I think there's a chance she might have been. I found nylon fibers from her clothing melted onto her upper torso, but none below her waist or on her legs. She might have been wearing cotton, but...' He let the thought trail. 'I'll test further, but I'd guess she was only wearing a shirt.'

'Wonderful,' Solliday muttered. 'One more thing to tell her parents.'

On this they could agree. 'We need to see them,' Mia murmured. 'As soon as possible.' She turned away from the charred corpse and closed her eyes for the space of a deep breath. 'First the parents, then the crime scene.'

Monday, November 27, 11:00 A.M.

The Burnettes lived in a tidy little house, the kind you'd expect on a cop's salary. Pretty curtains hung from the windows and a picture of a turkey still covered the door.

Solliday parked his SUV on the street. They'd been silent the better part of the trip as Mia reviewed the notes he'd made of the Dougherty fire scene, but now Solliday's heavy sigh cut through the silence between them. 'You want to lead this?' he asked.

'Sure.' This was the kind of visit she hated most, the kind that made her feel most inept. *I miss Abe.* Her partner always seemed to know what to say to grieving parents. 'This could have been a grudge kill or a random stalking. But Caitlin could have been involved in something. We'll need to explore possibilities no parent wants to consider.'

'I know,' he said grimly. He wasn't looking forward to this any more than she was. Mentally she'd reevaluated Reed Solliday. Having made his point, he hadn't belabored it, instead giving her quiet on the drive over. It allowed her to settle her mind and consider the morning from his point of view. He'd been polite, compassionate. Generous, even. Had circumstances been reversed, she might not have been as nice.

The notes she'd reviewed were concise, his handwriting square and neat. She glanced at his crisply knotted tie and the clean lines of the thin goatee that framed his mouth. His shoes were buffed to a shine. Square and neat. That about summed him up.

But something inside her balked at dismissing him so easily. There was more to this man than met the eye, although what met the eye was really quite nice. He'd given her his umbrella when he thought she was in need. It was . . . sweet. Unsettled, she focused on his notes. 'Three points of origin?'

'Kitchen, bedroom, and living room,' he confirmed. 'He meant that house to burn.'

'And for Caitlin's body to be destroyed.' She slid from the SUV. 'I hate these visits.'

'Me, too.'

Fire marshals had to pay these kinds of visits, too. She'd never given it that much thought before. Then again, who knew which was worse – telling a parent their child had been murdered or that they'd died in a fire so severe that their body was no longer recognizable? Either way, it was the part of the job that sucked the very most.

Mia rapped on the door. The blue curtains parted and a pair of eyes peeked out at them, widening when Mia showed her shield. In a few seconds the door opened and a woman in her late forties stood before them, her face already showing signs of panic.

She was small, like the body on the table. 'Are you Mrs Ellen Burnette?'

'Yes.' She turned. 'Roger! Roger, come here. Please.'

A burly man appeared in his bare feet, his eyes flickering in fear. 'What's wrong?'

'I'm Detective Mitchell and this is Lieutenant Solliday. May we come in?'

Wordlessly Mrs Burnette led them into the living room and lowered herself to the sofa. Her husband stood behind her, his hands on her shoulders.

Mia sat down on the edge of a chair. 'We're here about Caitlin.'

Ellen Burnette flinched as if she'd been slapped. 'Oh God.'

Roger Burnette's hands clenched. 'Was there an accident?'

'When was the last time you talked with her?' Mia asked gently.

Burnette glared at Mia, his throat working viciously. She knew he knew the drill. Avoidance meant the very worst. 'Friday night.'

'We argued,' Mrs Burnette murmured. 'She went back to the sorority, and we left for my mother's for the weekend. I tried calling her yesterday, but she wasn't there.'

Mia steeled her spine. 'We have an unidentified body. We believe it's Caitlin.'

Mrs Burnette slumped forward, covering her face with her hands. 'No.'

Burnette's hands clutched at empty air, then gripped the sofa. 'What happened?'

'Lieutenant Solliday is with the fire marshal's office. The home of Joe and Donna Dougherty burned to the ground this weekend. We believe Caitlin was in the house.'

Mrs Burnette was weeping. 'Roger.' Numbly, Burnette sat next to his wife.

'She was just supposed to get the mail. Feed the cat. Why couldn't she get out?'

Mia glanced at Solliday. His face was hard, but his eyes were pained. And he was silent, letting her lead. 'She didn't die as a result of the fire, sir,' she said and watched Mrs Burnette's head jerk up. 'She was shot. We're ruling her death a homicide.'

Mrs Burnette turned into her husband's arms. 'No.'

Burnette's eyes never left Mia's as he rocked his wife. 'Do you have any leads?'

Mia shook her head. 'None yet. I know this is a difficult time, but I need to ask you some questions. You said Caitlin lived at a sorority. Which one?'

'TriEpsilon,' Burnette said. 'They're good girls.'

That would remain to be seen. 'Can you give us the names of her friends?'

'Judy Walters,' he said through his teeth. 'Her roommate.'

'Did she have any boyfriends?'

'She did, but they broke up. Joel Rebinowitz.' Burnette's jaw was tight.

Mia noted it in her notebook. 'You didn't like him, sir?'

'He played around, partied too much. Caitlin had a future.'

Mia tilted her head forward. 'You argued on Friday. What about?'

'Her grades,' Burnette said flatly. 'She was failing two classes.'

Solliday cleared his throat. 'What classes was she failing?'

Burnette looked furiously bewildered. 'Statistics, maybe? Hell, I don't know.'

Mia steadied herself. 'I'm sorry, but I have to ask. Did your daughter have any issues with drugs or alcohol?'

Burnette's eyes narrowed to slits. 'Caitlin didn't do drugs and she didn't drink.'

It was what she had expected. 'Thank you.' She stood up and beside her Solliday stood as well. She'd saved the worst for last. 'We're going to have to identify the body.'

Burnette lifted his chin. 'I'll go,' he said.

Mia glanced at Solliday, whose face was still stoically expressionless, but his eyes flickered with pity. Mia sighed quietly. 'No, sir. We'll need to use dental records.'

Mrs Burnette lurched to her feet. She ran to the bathroom and Mia winced at the sound of the poor woman retching. Mr Burnette came to his feet unsteadily, his face a deathly gray. 'I'll get the name of our dentist.' He made his way to the kitchen stiffly.

Mia followed him. 'Sergeant. You're limping.'

He looked up from a little black phonebook, his face haggard. 'I pulled a muscle.'

'On the job?' Solliday asked quietly from behind her.

'Yeah. I was chasing . . .' His voice drifted away. 'Oh my God. This was because of me.' He sank onto a barstool at the counter. 'Somebody getting back at me.'

'We don't know that, Sergeant,' Mia murmured. 'We have to ask the questions. You know that. I'll need names of anyone who's threatened you or your family.'

His laugh was harsh. 'You'll need more pages than you've got in your little book, Detective. My God. This is going to kill my wife.'

Mia hesitated, then gave in and laid her hand on his forearm. 'It may have been random. Let us investigate. Now if you'll get me the name of the dentist, we'll go.'

'Dr Bloom. He's local.' Burnette met Mia's eyes directly. 'Tell me,' he said in a low voice. 'Did he . . . ?'

Mia hesitated. 'We don't know.'

He looked away, cocking his jaw. 'I understand,' he bit out.

Mia leaned forward, snagging his attention again. 'No, Sergeant. I mean we really don't know. I wouldn't lie to you.'

'Thank you.' She'd started to move away when he caught her arm hard and it was all she could do not to flinch in pain. But she didn't, shaken when his eyes filled with tears. 'Find the bastard who did this to my baby girl,' he whispered, then let her go.

Mia straightened, her shoulder burning like a live flame. 'We will.' She slid one of her cards across the counter. 'If you need me, my cell phone number is written on the back. I'd appreciate it if you didn't let Caitlin's friends know that anything's happened.'

'I know the drill, Detective,' he said between his teeth. 'Just get her released as fast as you can so we . . .' His voice broke. 'So we can bury our child.'

'I'll do everything I can. We can see ourselves out.' She waited until she was in Solliday's SUV before hissing out a breath of pain. 'Goddammit, that hurt.'

'I have some Advil in the glove compartment,' Solliday said.

Mia moved her arm and winced at the fire that raced up into her shoulder. 'I think I'll accept.' She found the bottle and dry swallowed two pills. 'My stomach's going to hate me later, but my arm thanks you now.'

One side of his mouth lifted. 'You're welcome.'

'I hate these visits. Their kids are never screwed up, never in any trouble.'

'I think it's worse when they're cops,' Solliday observed.

'That's the truth.' It came out more fervently than she'd intended.

He glanced over at her before pulling into traffic. 'Personal experience?'

If she didn't tell him, he'd ask around. 'My father was a cop.'

He lifted a brow, looking like Satan again. 'I see. He's retired?'

'He's dead,' Mia said. 'And before you go asking around, he died three weeks ago.'

He nodded, his eyes glued to the road. 'I see.'

No, you don't. But she wouldn't argue. 'Cops' kids go astray, like everybody else's.'

'Did you?'

'What, go astray? No, I didn't.' And that's all he needed to know. She looked through her notes. 'This could have been random. Somebody could have broken in to rob the Doughertys and found Caitlin there feeding the cat.'

'She wasn't feeding the cat.' He glanced over at her before returning his eyes to the road. 'I didn't want to say anything to Burnette, but I found pages of a statistics book in the Doughertys' spare bedroom. I think she went there to study.'

Mia considered the compassionate restraint he'd shown with the parents. 'The Burnettes don't need to know that,' she agreed. 'That they fought over grades and that she was there to study would be salt in their wound. Let's go to the Doughertys' now. CSU should be there already.'

Chapter Four

A CSU guy met them at the Doughertys' curb as they got out of the SUV, his face breaking into a grin. 'Mia. I'm glad you're back.'

She smiled with true pleasure. 'I'm glad to be back, Jack. This is Lieutenant Reed Solliday.' She looked up at Reed. 'This is Sergeant Jack Unger, CSU. He's the best.'

'I heard you give a lecture last year,' Reed said, shaking the man's hand. 'Use of new analytical methods in detecting accelerants. Good stuff.'

'Glad you got something out of it. Lieutenant, I already have my team inside, working with your guys. They're gridding off the front hall and the living room.'

'Give me a minute to change into my boots.' Mitchell and Unger inspected the front of the house while Reed concentrated on not fumbling the clasps on his boots. His fingers always got clumsier when he was in a hurry. He joined them at the front door and led them into the

74

kitchen. 'We found the body right here.' He pointed to the far wall.

She looked up at the damaged ceiling. 'The master bedroom's up there?'

'Yeah. It's one of the three points of origin. The kitchen here was the main one.'

Her brows furrowed. 'But you think she was in the spare bedroom studying. On the other side of the house. Tell me the time line of the fire from start to finish again.'

'The neighbors reported an explosion about midnight and called 911. That would have been the kitchen. The first company arrived three minutes later and found flames engulfing this whole side of the house, top to bottom. There was a smaller fire in the living room on the other side. They charged a line and hit the blaze just inside the front door. The kitchen ceiling came down shortly after the fire department arrived and the chief pulled the firefighters out of the house. I got here at 12:52. They'd knocked it back by then. They shut off the gas line to the house when they arrived, so there wasn't any more fuel for the fire in the kitchen.'

'Heat, fuel, oxygen,' Mitchell murmured. 'Good old fire triangle.'

'Eliminate one and you can knock down the fire,' Reed agreed.

Unger looked at the wall with a frown. 'The "V" pattern's narrow. Like it ran straight up fast until it hit about five feet high. Then everything's black the rest of the way up.'

'The valve to the gas line was removed. He started a leak, waited for gas to build up, then left a device to get the fire started. The room exploded when the flame reached the gas, which rises. He ran a line of accelerant up the wall to make sure it did.'

'What did he use to start it?' she asked.

'The lab's doing an analysis for the exact structure, but it was a solid accelerant, probably in the nitrate family. Mode of delivery was a plastic egg.'

Mitchell's blond brows went up. 'Like an Easter egg?'

'No, bigger. Like the eggs panty hose used to come in. He probably mixed the nitrate with guar gum so it would cling to the wall. When the solid ignited, it would have burned straight up. That's why you see the narrow "V." But it also exploded out, which took care of everything below the gas line. Most likely he drilled a hole in the egg, filled it with the mixture, and ran the fuse. He wouldn't have had much time to get away. Probably no more than ten or fifteen seconds.'

'He likes life on the edge, then,' she said. 'How did he get in the house?'

'Through the back door,' Reed answered. 'We took pictures of the lock, but we didn't touch it to get prints.'

She looked up with a frown. 'Why not?'

'I was afraid it was a homicide yesterday. I didn't want some judge throwing out our evidence because it was collected under an arson warrant.'

She looked reluctantly impressed. 'Did you get prints, Jack?'

'Yeah, but I'm betting they don't belong to our guy. If he was smart enough to pull all this together, he was smart enough to wear gloves. Although we could get lucky.'

'Can you check for shoe prints?' she asked Unger. 'Although the rain's probably destroyed any chance of that. Dammit.'

'We got a number of shoe prints,' Reed said, 'most of them from firefighters' boots, but there were a few that weren't. We made plaster casts of those yesterday.'

Again she looked reluctantly impressed. 'They're at the lab?'

'Along with the egg fragments. They're checking for prints on those, too.'

She crouched next to where they'd found the body. 'Jack, let's get samples here.'

Reed crouched next to her, so close he picked up a lighter, much more pleasant scent than the smell of charred wood that hung over the room. She smelled like lemons. 'I took samples around this area. We found traces of gasoline.'

She frowned, troubled. 'He doused her with gasoline. That's why her body burned so hot the fibers of her shirt melted onto her skin.'

'Yes. I picked up traces of hydrocarbons in the air space above the body. You can also see the checkerboard pattern here on the subfloor. It's what happens when gasoline seeps between the tiles. The adhesive is softened and the floor beneath it gets scorched. He probably poured gasoline over her and splashed some on the floor.'

'I can't imagine him taking a chance on lighting a match with all that gas in the room,' Unger said thoughtfully.

'I think when the plastic egg exploded, bits of the burning accelerant would have landed on her. Either way, gasoline burns off pretty quickly unless you have a constant supply. That's why there was enough bone left for Barrington to X-ray.'

Mitchell stood up, her jaw clenched. 'So where did the little fucker shoot you, Caitlin?' She walked around the fallen rafters and into the hall where one of Jack Unger's men worked with Ben, gridding off the room with string and stakes. 'Hello.'

'Ben, this is Detective Mitchell from Homicide and Sergeant Unger from CSU.'

Ben nodded. 'Nice to meet you. Reed, we found something just a few minutes before you got here.' He carefully stepped across the gridded area, a small glass jar in his hand. 'Looks like it came from a necklace.'

Reed held it up to the field lights. 'The letter "C." ' He handed it to Mitchell.

'Where did you find it?' she asked, studying it with a frown.

Ben pointed to the grid. 'Two up, three over. I was just looking for the chain.'

She turned her eyes to the staircase. 'You said you found pages from her statistics book upstairs. That means she was studying upstairs, so she had to come down the stairs at some point. Either alive or dead.'

Unger nodded. 'If he shot her upstairs and then dragged her down the carpet, there will be traces of blood in the fibers. We'll take the whole carpet and check it out.'

'He may have shot her in the kitchen,' Reed pointed out.

'Then we take the whole damn floor,' Mitchell said grimly. 'Shit. I hate fire scenes. There's just nothing left.'

Reed shook his head. 'There's lots left. You just have to know where to look.'

'Yeah,' she grunted, holding the glass jar up to the light. Her eyes went fierce. 'They fought here,' she said, one hand fisted at her throat as if she clenched a necklace. 'Caitlin must have heard something, come down the stairs.'

'He discovered her, overpowered her,' Reed continued.

'Grabbed the necklace. The chain broke and the charm flew. Then he shot her.'

'Then I'll find spatter on the carpet.' Unger looked around. 'We'll bring some bright lights in here and go over the place with a fine-tooth comb. You said three points of origin. We've seen the kitchen. What about the other two?'

'The one in the master bedroom was the same accelerant – another egg.'

'What about the living room?' Unger asked.

Ben had done most of the living-room analysis. 'Go ahead, Ben,' Reed said.

Ben cleared his throat. 'That fire was started in a trash can with newspaper and a cigarette, probably filterless. It would have smoldered for a few minutes before escaping the can. It caught the drapes on fire, but the truck put that one out pretty fast.'

'Can we see the master bedroom?'

'Carefully.' Reed led them up the stairs, then stopped in the doorway. 'Don't go in. The floor isn't stable.'

'The hole in the floor was caused by the fire?' Mitchell asked.

'Yes, it was. The hole in the ceiling was cut by the firefighters to vent the heat.'

Mitchell drew a breath and grimaced. 'I need to get some air.'

'You okay, Mia?' Unger asked, concern in his voice.

'I took some Advil on an empty stomach,' she said. 'My stomach is now protesting.'

Reed frowned. 'You should have asked me to stop. I could have gotten you lunch.'

'That would mean she was actually taking care of herself.' Unger took her elbow. 'Go get lunch. We'll be here a while. I'll call you if I find anything earth-shattering.'

She glanced over at Reed. 'Lunch, then the sorority?'

'That sounds like a plan.'

COUNT TO TEN

Monday, November 27, 12:05 P.M.

Brooke Adler rapped on the door to the school counselor's office and felt it give. She poked her head in to find Dr Julian Thompson sitting behind his desk and one of the other teachers sitting in one of the guest chairs. 'I'm sorry. I'll come back later.'

Julian waved her in. 'It's okay, Brooke. We're not talking about anything important.'

Devin White shook his head with a smile that made her heart flutter. She'd noticed him many times since she'd come to Hope Center. But this was the first time they'd actually exchanged words. 'I have to disagree, Julian. It was of universal importance.' He lifted a brow. 'Bears or Lions on Sunday?'

Brooke knew little about sports, but Chicago was home. 'Bears?'

Devin scowled playfully. 'I guess we can't argue with hometown loyalty.'

Julian gestured toward the chair next to Devin. 'Devin's betting on the Lions.'

'It's a personal weakness,' he said. 'Do I need to leave? Is this a private matter?'

Brooke shook her head. 'No. I could actually use another teacher's perspective. I have some concerns about some of my students. One in particular.'

Julian leaned back in his chair. 'Let me guess. Jeffrey DeMartino.'

'No, not Jeff. Although he as much as admitted

81

sending Thad Lewin to the clinic.'

Julian just sighed. 'Thad's not talking. He's too scared to give Jeff up and we don't have any proof. So if not Jeff, who?'

'Manny Rodriguez.'

Both men were surprised. 'Manny?' Devin asked. 'He's never given me a problem.'

'Me, either. But this morning he was unusually interested in the lesson. We're reading *Lord of the Flies*.'

Julian's brows shot up. 'Are stories about teen anarchy wise around here?'

Brooke shrugged. 'Dr Bixby thought it would make a good study.' The school's director had recommended it, in fact. 'Anyway, today we talked about the signal fire.'

Julian tilted his head. 'Manny's eyes glazed over, didn't they?'

'He was practically salivating.'

'And you want to know if Manny started fires before he came here.'

'Yeah, I do. I mean, I'm happy he's interested, but . . . It was creepy.'

Julian rested his chin on steepled fingers. 'He set fires, yes. Lots of little fires, from the time he was five years old. Then he set a very bad one that destroyed his foster home. It was then he was brought here. We've been working on impulse control.'

Brooke sat back in her chair. 'I wish I'd known. Should I do a different book?'

Devin scratched his chin. 'What would you read

instead? Anything that's worth discussing will have some controversial theme affecting at least one kid in your class.'

'I thought that,' she confessed.

'This may not be a bad thing,' Julian said. 'Now that I know what Manny has been reading, we can use it in our therapy. This is a place he can't start a fire, so presenting him with tempting images here is about as safe as you can make it. We can work on constructive ways to manage his impulses while they're fresh in his mind.'

Brooke stood up and both men followed suit. 'Thanks, Julian. I'll send you a report every few days. Let me know if it gets to the point that changing books is the right thing to do.'

Devin held the door open. 'I hear it's mac and cheese and Tater Tots day in the cafeteria.'

Her lips curved. 'Then we'd better get in line. Tater Tots always go fast.'

Devin grinned. 'And they don't hurt when they throw them at you. Bye, Julian.'

'I haven't been in a food fight yet,' she said as they walked down the hall together.

'I was last summer. Unfortunately it was apples day. That really hurt. I wouldn't worry too much about *Lord of the Flies*, Brooke. So many of these kids have seen far, far worse.' His smile faded. 'It's enough to break your heart.'

'You care about them,' she said quietly.

'It's hard not to. They tend to grow on you.'

'Mr White!' A trio of boys caught up to them, looking panicked.

Devin gave the boys a smile. 'What's up, guys?'

'We need help before the quiz today,' one said and Brooke's heart deflated a little.

So much for Tater Tots, she thought. *I'll be eating at my desk again.*

Devin gave Brooke an apologetic smile. 'I'm sorry. I'll get with you later.'

With a silent sigh she watched him go. Tater Tots with Devin White was about as close as she'd come to a real date in a long time, which was pathetic. She turned toward her classroom. Then stopped short just as she rounded the corner.

Manny Rodriguez was looking both ways as he shoved something into the trash can just outside the lunchroom. A newspaper? That Manny had a newspaper for any constructive reason was unbelievable. She waited until he was gone then lifted the lid of the trash can and, wrinkling her nose, fished the newspaper out. She'd expected to feel something heavy wrapped inside, but as she gingerly shook it, there was nothing.

It was today's *Trib*. Frowning, she pulled the paper apart until she found a hole with jagged edges. He'd ripped something out of the paper. An article? A picture? Whatever it was, it had been on page A-12. Briefly she considered keeping the paper, but ended up tossing it back into the trash can. Half of it was covered in cheese sauce. If it was something wrong, it would be information Julian could use in therapy.

She'd go to the school library, check the *Trib*. Perhaps it was nothing more than an ad for a video game. But remembering the look in Manny's eyes, she doubted it.

Monday, November 27, 1:15 P.M.

'So how old is your daughter?'

Reed looked up in surprise. They were the first words Mitchell had spoken since they'd sat down with their trays in the burger joint she'd chosen. He'd thought she was still angry about this morning. Nobody liked hearing the truth when it hurt and Reed had simply told the truth. If she wasn't capable, he'd ask for somebody else.

If she wasn't capable, it was understandable. A few quick questions to the ME had cleared the puzzle and Mitchell herself had added the final piece. A hurt partner and a dead father. Add the shoulder and she'd hit the trifecta. No wonder she'd been zoned out this morning. But he hadn't seen a single lapse in focus since. She'd been strong and sure with the girl's parents, saying the right things to ease the father's pain as best she could. And at the Doughertys' she'd pulled together the same scenario he had.

Maybe her silence was her way of processing

information and not due to residual anger. Either way her question was an olive branch of sorts.

'Beth is fourteen.' He grimaced. 'Going on twenty-five.'

'That's a tough age,' she said sympathetically. Her eyes flicked to a point behind him. 'I wouldn't go back to that age for all the tea in China.'

'On that we agree. What's back there?'

'Barracuda.' Eyes narrowed, she followed the approach of a woman with a long blond braid. 'Carmichael. To what do I owe the pleasure?'

The woman pulled up a chair and sat down. 'Is that any way to greet me after two whole weeks?' She eyed Reed with interest. 'I thought Reagan was coming back.'

'He is, in a few weeks.'

The woman put out her hand. 'I'm Joanna Carmichael.'

He wasn't sure if he should shake it. 'Lieutenant Solliday—'

'OFI, I know. I ran the plates on your SUV before I came in.'

Reed frowned. 'I don't think I like having my privacy invaded like that.'

Carmichael shrugged. 'Goes with the territory. I'm with the *Bulletin*.'

He looked at Mitchell, who looked excessively annoyed. 'You have groupies?'

Carmichael laughed. 'She makes good copy. You're back sooner than I thought.'

'I'm a fast healer. I don't have anything for you, Carmichael. All my cases were reassigned while I was on disability.'

'This time I have something for you. I've kept my ear to the ground for you. One of my sources tells me that your partner hit one of the guys who shot at you before he was hit. Ripped a nice neat hole in the guy's arm.' She lifted a brow. 'Kind of like yours.'

Mia shook her head. 'Nobody matching their description's visited any of the hospitals for a GSW any time in the last two weeks. I've checked. Every damn day.'

'Your punk's mommy is a nurse's aide. Word is she did a do-it-yourself job. Not too shabby either. Apparently he's a fast healer, too.'

Mitchell's eyes had narrowed dangerously. 'What's your punk's name?'

'Oscar DuPree. Is he your punk, too?' Carmichael asked with deceptive laziness.

Mitchell nodded curtly. 'That's one of them. Where is he?'

'Hangs at a bar called Looney's. But he didn't shoot your partner. His pal, however, has been talking it up. Big bad cop took one in the gut. Fell like a rock. Bitch cop took one in the shoulder while she stared like a deer in the headlights.'

Color was rising in Mitchell's cheeks. 'Fucking little bastard. I owe you, Carmichael.'

'No, you don't.' Carmichael stood up. 'You were nice

to me once. I pay my debts. Now we're square.' She checked her watch. 'I've got to be going. Nice to meet you, Lieutenant. If you get a good lead on your fire/ homicide, I'd appreciate the heads-up.'

Reed kept his face poker straight. 'Excuse me?'

'Oh, cut the bullshit, Lieutenant. You're arson, she's homicide. It doesn't take a rocket scientist to put the pieces together. So, what about it? What's the story here?'

Mitchell was methodically folding her burger wrapper into a paper football. The look she spared Carmichael was fierce. 'You'll be the first to know. I pay my debts, too.'

Carmichael chuckled as she walked away. 'Last one to Looney's is a rotten egg.'

'I take it we're taking a detour on our way to the sorority,' Reed said dryly and Mitchell looked up, surprise in her round blue eyes.

'This is mine to do. If you drop me off at the precinct, I'll drive myself.'

'Show me full rotation. Wind it up like you're going to pitch from the mound.'

She tried to throw the paper football into the garbage and grimaced. 'Shit. That hurts.'

'You need to be back on disability, but you're not going to do that, are you?'

She met his gaze directly. 'My partner was shot down like a dog in the street, Solliday. He's a good man and he was nearly worm food. The punk ass that did it is bragging. If it were you, would you go home and climb under the covers like a little girl?'

She had a way of articulating her thoughts so very clearly. 'No. I wouldn't. Look, I'll drive you, but you call Spinnelli first. You get backup or I'll call this in myself.'

She stood up, her expression determined. 'It's my collar.'

'That's fine. You get your collar, then we get back to Caitlin Burnette.'

'Let's rock and roll, Solliday. With any luck, the vermin will be gathering at their local watering hole. We could be at the university by two-thirty. Three at the latest.'

Reed picked up their trays and slid the garbage into the can. 'Three. Right.'

Monday, November 27, 4:00 P.M.

'Hello, may I speak to Emily Richter, please?'

'If you're selling something—'

'I'm not, ma'am,' he cut in quickly. 'My name is Harry Porter. I'm with the *Trib*.'

'I talked with you guys already.'

'I know,' he said soothingly. 'But I'm looking for a comment from the homeowners, the Doughertys. Do you know where I can find them?'

She sniffed. 'They're not home. They're on vacation.'

'Oh. Well, thank you for your time, ma'am.'

'You people at the paper should really talk to each other instead of bothering me,' she snapped and he wanted to snap her neck. But for now, he needed her.

He'd try again tomorrow. He pocketed his cell with a scowl and pushed Laura Dougherty from his mind. Tonight was Penny Hill's turn to dance. He couldn't wait.

Monday, November 27, 4:00 P.M.

Mrs Schuster looked up from her computer when Brooke came into the library. 'Hello, Brooke. What can I do for you today?'

Brooke pointed to the periodical rack. 'I just wanted to look at today's paper.'

'The sports section is gone,' she said, with a resigned little sigh. 'Devin took it. He's working the stats so he can win the football pool next week. I think a math teacher doing the pool is an unfair advantage. Like insider trading.'

Brooke chuckled. 'I take it you lost this week.'

Mrs Schuster grinned. 'Big-time. Take your time with the paper, Brooke.'

'Thanks.' Brooke flipped to page A-12. And sighed. The article Manny had ripped out was about a home fire. The house had burned to the ground. One fatality.

She made two copies of the article, wondering how many others Manny had clipped. Although the boy couldn't set fires at Hope Center, Manny was at least feeding his addiction passively. It would be one more thing they could discuss in therapy.

She stopped in the mailroom and slid one of the copies into an envelope for Julian Thompson. She'd just put it in his box when the door opened and Devin White came in with two other teachers. It was the end of the day when everyone stopped in to check their boxes, so his coming in wasn't any real surprise. Still her heart gave a little jolt.

'Brooke.' Jackie Kersey gave Brooke an encouraging smile. 'We're all going out for a drink. Come with us.'

Brooke made a quick glance in Devin's direction, but his face was averted, looking in his box which was on the very bottom row. From this vantage point, she had a very nice view of his rear end. 'I really shouldn't,' she murmured.

Jackie's lips twitched, noting the direction Brooke's gaze had taken. 'It's happy hour at Flannagan's, two for one. I'll order a beer and you can have my second.'

Devin looked up from his mail and smiled. 'Come on, Brooke. It'll do you good.'

She laughed, a little too breathlessly. 'I was just going home to grade papers anyway. I'll meet you all there.'

Chapter Five

Mia opened her eyes when Solliday stopped the SUV. They sat in front of a convenience store. 'Why are we here?' Mia asked stiffly. Every square inch of her body ached like she'd been put through a meat grinder. But worse yet would be having to tell Abe that the bastard who'd shot him was still on the streets.

He lifted a brow. 'I had three cups of coffee waiting for your pal.'

Mia winced. 'I'm sorry. I didn't think it would take that long.' They'd sat for two hours when DuPree finally showed up with his arm in a sling. Still they'd waited for Getts, the shooter, until she'd spotted DuPree sneaking out the back door. He'd taken off at a run and she'd had no choice but to take him down. Even with his arm in a sling, he'd been a fighter. 'You should have interviewed the girls at the sorority house.'

'What, and miss the fun?' he said dryly. 'Watching

you take down a drugged-out SOB twice your size was worth the price of admission, even if you didn't catch Getts.'

'Slimy little sonofabitch,' she snarled softly. 'He must have made us.'

'You'll get Getts. And you can sleep tonight knowing his pal's in a six-by-eight.'

He looked positive and sincere. In fact, he looked damn impressed. Maybe she'd been given a second chance to make a first impression. 'Thanks for driving through that back alley and cutting DuPree off. At least I can give my partner that tonight. Let's get to the sorority so you can get home.'

He got out of the SUV. 'Later. The second reason we're here is that I'm starving and you need something in your gut so you can take some more medicine for that pain. It's a wonder you didn't dislocate your shoulder. What do you take on your hot dog?'

'Anything except ketchup. Thanks, Solliday.'

All day she'd walked beside Reed Solliday, feeling small. Now she could watch him as he walked through the store. He moved with a fluid grace unusual for a man his size. And watching Solliday move, she thought of Guy. The comparison had been inevitable, she supposed. It had been a while since she'd thought of Guy LeCroix, which was telling in itself, but now she remembered with stunning clarity.

Guy had moved just like that. It's what had attracted her from the beginning, that panther grace in a big man.

He'd thought he loved her, but ultimately wanted far more than she could give. She didn't really miss him, which was also telling. But she hadn't wanted to hurt him either. She hoped he'd found what he was looking for with his new wife, that he was happy. Since Guy the well had been relatively dry. She'd seen a few men here and there. Mostly there. Nobody serious.

Thinking objectively in the quiet of her mind, she could admit none were better looking than Reed Solliday, even though he did look like Satan when he did the eyebrow thing. Although that little goatee of his did frame a nice mouth. Mia imagined a mouth that nice would prove an asset in certain areas. As would that panther grace.

Mrs Solliday must be a very content woman. For a split second, Mia felt a twinge of wistful envy for Mrs Solliday, whoever she was. But quickly she squelched it. She didn't do cops. It was her life's mantra. *But he's not a cop.* 'He's close enough,' she murmured aloud. Still, a girl could watch. Reed Solliday was a very watchable man.

He was at the counter now, paying for their food. The clerk frowned, then dumped a handful of change into the sack Solliday held open. Shaking his head Solliday opened his door, and corralling her wayward thoughts, Mia took the food from his hands.

'My biggest fear is that Beth will bring home a guy like that and I'll have to pretend to like him,' he grumbled, settling into his seat. From the sack he pulled a handful of packets. 'The condiment pumps were empty. You'll have to make do with these.'

'I'm sure I've had worse. Come to think of it, I have worse every time Abe picks the place we eat. He's into that vegetarian crap. Thank you.' Mia ripped open one of the mustard packets while Solliday opened the center console between the seats. Nestled among a half dozen cassette tapes was a mason jar half-filled with change. Solliday poured the change from the sack into the jar and closed the console lid.

Mia blinked at him. 'Wow. You've got to have ten bucks in change in that thing.'

'Probably.' He took one of the hot dogs and proceeded to eat it plain.

Appalled, she gaped. 'No toppings? Not even mustard?'

He looked at the hot dog with distaste, hesitating. Then he shrugged. 'I have trouble manipulating small items.'

The jar of change now made sense. 'Like pennies and nickels?'

He took a bite and made a resigned face. 'Yep.'

'And mustard packets?'

'Unfortunately, yes.'

Mia rolled her eyes. 'Give me your damn hot dog, Solliday. I'll put on the mustard.'

He handed it over. 'Relish, too?'

She shook her head. 'Relish, too. Why didn't you just ask?'

He shrugged again. 'Pride, I guess.'

'Given your assessment of me this morning, I should think it would be shame,' she shot back and he laughed. He had a nice laugh, deep and rich, and his smile changed his face from Satan to . . . well, wow. For a moment she stared. Wow. Then with a hard blink she dropped her eyes to the carton in her lap. Mrs Solliday was a very lucky lady.

'Touché, Mitchell. Although for the record, as of this afternoon I'm duly impressed with your capability. I haven't seen a move like that since high school.'

She handed him his food. 'Let me guess. Linebacker?'

'Tight end. But that was a long time ago.'

They ate in silence, then Mia folded her wrapper. 'So what happened?'

He eyed her over the last bite of his hot dog. 'None of your business.'

She laughed. 'Touché, Solliday. Give me your trash, I'll throw it away.' When she climbed back into the cab, he was pocketing his cell phone. 'Emergency?'

'No. I just needed to call home.'

Mia sighed. 'I'm sorry again. You have a family to get home to.'

'My hours are as flexible as yours. I have somebody to take care of Beth when I have to work at night. Take something for your shoulder.'

So there was no Mrs Solliday. The sudden thump of her heart was merely interest, Mia told herself, not relief. She popped a few pain relievers, wondering what had happened to his wife, but stopped herself from asking. 'So where are we going now?'

'Greek Row.'

It would be a while before they got there. 'Can I look at your notes again?'

He handed her his notebook. 'So what nice thing did you do for Carmichael?'

'Somebody close to her was murdered last year. Abe and I were primary. She was pretty hysterical and I stayed with her until she'd gotten through the worst of it. It was no more than I'd do for any victim's family.'

'Obviously more than she expected.'

'I guess. Anyway, I've become her personal news source. Every time I turn around that girl is there. But she gave me DuPree. If I get Getts, she'll be on my Christmas list forever.' She scanned his notes. 'Was the bed made in the spare bedroom?'

He looked surprised. 'Yes, why?'

'When I was in school, I studied at the kitchen table. I don't think I would have used somebody else's bedroom, for sure. What was Caitlin doing studying up there?'

'Maybe she got sleepy.'

'That's why I asked about the bed. But she could have slept on the couch. Sleeping in somebody else's bed, especially when you've expressly been told not to live in . . . That's just . . .' She searched for the word. 'Cheeky.'

His lips twitched. 'Cheeky?'

She shook her head with a smile. 'Don't laugh at my adjectives. It's like she was playing Goldilocks, studying and sleeping where she wasn't invited.'

'There was a desk in the bedroom. With a computer.'

'Ah. We should have it taken in. Check for e-mails and Web surfing.'

'I talked to Ben when you were processing DuPree. He said Unger took the computer this afternoon. They'll try to check for e-mails, et cetera, before morning.'

'Okay. So walk with me. Caitlin's studying or surfing the Web or something. She hears something, comes downstairs and he's there. They struggle in the foyer. Maybe he rapes her. At some point he shoots her. But he doesn't burn her to utterly destroy her. Unless he thought she'd be burned to ash and he's just a novice. Are we dealing with a novice?'

'I don't know. He had the solid-accelerant device down just right. But I've been thinking about the sheer spectacle of the explosion . . . He went to a lot of trouble to be noticed. That seems immature, almost childish. But his method was sophisticated. I'd be surprised if he hasn't done it before.' He hesitated. 'Or if he doesn't do it again.'

'Are we talking serial arsonist?'

'It's crossed my mind,' he admitted. 'His MO was so well planned. So grandiose. I can see him thinking it would be a shame to only use it once.'

'Shit. So all we really have is a dead girl and some pieces of a plastic egg.'

COUNT TO TEN

Monday, November 27, 6:40 P.M.

Joel Rebinowitz's roommate was pre-law and proud. Zach Thornton stood between Mia and Solliday and the bathroom door, through which came the sounds of Joel's sobbing. 'He's not going to say another word to you without a lawyer,' Zach snarled.

Mia sighed. 'God save us from baby attorneys. Look, kid, move yourself out of the way, or I'll haul your ass in for obstruction.'

'You can't do that,' he said belligerently.

'Wanna bet?' Zach's belligerence faltered. 'I didn't think so.' She rapped on the door. 'Joel, come out. We need to talk to you and we're not leaving until we do.'

'Go away, dammit.' Joel's voice was ragged. 'Leave me alone.'

Mia looked at Solliday. 'You want to go in after him?'

Solliday grimaced. 'Not really. But I will.'

Thornton changed tactics, his expression gone drastically sincere. 'You just told him his girlfriend is dead. Burned beyond recognition. What do you want from him?'

'The truth,' Mia responded. 'Joel, five seconds or my partner comes in after you.'

Joel staggered out of the bathroom, his face pale and his eyes swollen from crying. 'I'm not talking to you and I'm not going downtown with you.'

Zach nodded, back to smug. 'You want him, get a warrant.'

'Joel, help us clear you so we can focus on the real bad guys.'

'The real killer,' Zach jeered. 'Right.'

Mia lifted on her toes, putting herself inches from Thornton's face. 'Shut. Up. Or I swear to God you will spend the night in a cell. I am not bluffing. I have had enough of you. Sit down and shut up or you'll find yourself surrounded by bullies named Bubba who want to be your best buddy, if you know what I mean.'

Solliday whistled softly. 'It isn't often they get pretty boys tossed into their cage.'

Mia swallowed a smirk as Zach sat down on his bed without another word. She turned soberly to Joel. 'Joel, help me find who did this. When did you last see her?'

'Saturday night. Seven o'clock or so. She said there was a party at TriEpsilon that night but she needed to study. I told her to stay here, but she said if she did we'd . . . well, she wouldn't study. She didn't want to give her father the pleasure of seeing her fail.' He closed his eyes. 'This is all my fault.'

'Why do you say that, Joel?' Solliday asked.

'She partied with me too much. I should have backed off like her father said.'

Either this kid was innocent or he was a damn fine actor. Mia was pretty sure it was the first one. 'Did you hear from her at any time that night?'

'She IM'd me at eleven. She said she loved me,' he ended in a ragged whisper.

Mia glanced over at Solliday, saw they were in agreement over this kid. 'Where were you all evening, Joel?'

'Here until eleven. I IM'd her back, then met some friends at the arcade.' He rattled off six names and she had little doubt they'd corroborate his story.

Mia hated to press him at this point, but it was necessary. 'Did anybody else want to hurt her? Anybody following her? Anybody making her uncomfortable?'

He sagged against the wall, dropping his chin to his chest. 'No. No. No.'

'One more question, Joel,' Solliday said. 'When you didn't hear from Caitlin all day yesterday or today, weren't you worried?'

His head snapped up, fury in his eyes. 'Of course I was. But I thought she'd gone home. I couldn't call her at her parents' house. She'd told them we were through. I figured she'd call when she could. When I didn't see her in class this morning I asked around. Nobody had seen her. I called her parents, frantic. Left two messages on their answering machine. But they'd rather see me in jail than tell me that she was dead,' he finished bitterly. 'God *damn* them.'

Under the circumstances, Mia could see his point of view.

Back at Solliday's SUV she shook her head. 'If I ever have kids, I'm not going to interfere.'

Solliday opened her door for her, as he'd been doing all day. 'Never say never. I can understand both sides.

103

Father wants the best for his daughter. Daughter wants to run her own life. I don't think Joel's involved.'

'Neither do I. I think our guy chose the Doughertys' house. Either he stalked her there, or he happened on her and took advantage of the opportunity.'

'And Burnette could still be the real target.' He closed her door, then came around to his side. The engine was roaring to life when she heard his deep chuckle. ' "Bully named Bubba who wants to be your best buddy." It's poetic. Can I use it?'

She smiled at him, oddly at peace for the moment. 'Be my guest.'

It was quiet during the drive back to the precinct, both using the time to check their voice mail. He stopped the SUV next to her car. 'Wow,' he said. 'Nice.'

Mia looked at her little rebuilt Alfa Romeo fondly. 'It's my one splurge.' Then she slid down to the ground, turning to look at him. 'Barrington made Caitlin's ID official.'

'And the lab found an instant message in the cache of the Doughertys' computer. Time corresponds with Joel's story.'

'Then we make some progress. How about meeting at eight tomorrow in Spinnelli's office? He has this thing for eight o'clock meetings when we catch a big case.'

'I'll see if I can get the lab report on the samples I took before then,' he said, 'and I'll meet you at your desk. The Doughertys left me a voice mail saying they were getting into O'Hare at midnight. We can talk to them after we're done updating Spinnelli.'

'I'll ask Jack to come to the meeting tomorrow, too. He can tell us what he found when he analyzed the carpet. At least we'll be able to better picture where things occurred.' She was quiet for a minute, then sighed. 'I was seeing my partner go down.'

It took him a second. 'You mean this morning when you were staring in the window? What happened that night?'

'We wanted these guys for a homicide in South Side. Getts and DuPree. It was a drug thing that got out of hand and they killed two women caught in the cross-fire.' She sighed. 'Anyway, we got a tip they were hiding out in an apartment, but they weren't.'

'It was a setup.'

'Looks that way. But I saw them. And they shot Abe.'

'And you, too,' he said and her lips curved sadly.

'Just a scratch. While I was gone Spinnelli reassigned the case.'

'To the two guys he sent this afternoon. They stood back while you took DuPree.'

She smiled at the disbelief she heard in his voice. 'It was . . . a gift, actually. They let me have the collar. They knew how much it meant to me.'

'I guess I understand that. Look, I'm sorry about this morning. It's just that the jacket and the hat made you look . . . unsavory.'

'Unsavory?' she asked with a grin.

'Don't laugh at my adjectives,' he said, his voice light.

'Okay.' She sobered. 'My good jacket had a rip where the bullet hit my arm and it was nasty with blood.' Mostly Abe's blood. 'I have to get another paycheck before I can afford a new coat.' Her smile was self-mocking. 'Spent all my cash on the car.'

One brow lifted. 'What about the hat?'

'Sorry, the hat stays 'cause it's comfy. Just hope it doesn't rain. See you.'

She'd started to swing the door closed when he stopped its path. His eyes held sympathy, but they also held respect. 'I'm sorry about your partner, Mitchell. And your father.' He leaned back, settling himself behind the wheel once again. 'Eight o'clock.'

She closed his door and got into her own car, feeling calm and keyed up all at the same time. She started the engine, cursing the cold air the heater spit out at full blast. She still had to see Abe. What she'd say when she got there was anybody's guess.

Monday, November 27, 6:40 P.M.

'This was fun.' Brooke had nursed that one beer for an hour and a half.

'Told you it would do you good,' Devin said smugly.

Brooke's heart fluttered, but she was determined the beer would not make her lose her good sense. Devin had laughed and joked, but no more with her than with the other teachers they'd met at the bar. Brooke was surprised just how many teachers gathered for happy hour. Evidently she wasn't the only one stressed over the job.

'When do they all go home?'

He looked surprised. 'It's Monday night. We stay and watch the game.'

'The game.'

'*Monday Night Football*. The game. Please tell me you're joking.'

'Nope. My family didn't do sports.'

Devin slid down in his chair, getting comfortable. 'So what did you do for fun?'

'Scrabble. Risk. Trivial Pursuit.'

His lips twitched. 'And I thought I was a nerd.'

I don't think so. The thought left her light-headed and she mentally scrambled for words to untie her tongue. 'The librarian says you're using your math powers for evil.'

He threw back his head and laughed. 'She's just mad because I keep winning the pool.' He lifted a brow. 'You should join the pool. I could make you a fortune.'

His laugh made her warm all over. 'A fortune, huh?'

He shrugged. 'Well, at least you'd only lose five bucks.'

She sighed. 'Five bucks *is* a fortune.'

He looked philosophical. 'Nobody gets rich being a teacher. You knew this, right?'

'*That* I knew.'

'But other stuff you didn't?'

'I had dreams of helping kids learn to love books. It's not working out that way.'

'Manny and the fire really has you worried, doesn't it?'

'I hate the thought that I could be pushing him to do something terrible.'

Devin sighed. 'Brooke. You can't make anybody do what they don't want to do. All of these boys have issues. For Manny, it's fire. For Mike, it's stealing.'

'What about Jeff?' she asked glumly and he rolled his eyes.

'Nobody understands Jeff. I've been trying to get through to that kid for months. There's something cruel in him. Unfortunately, he's one of the brightest kids I've met.'

Brooke blinked. 'Jeff?'

'Yeah. Kid's a math whiz. If he weren't in juvie, he'd be getting scholarships.'

Something inside Brooke rallied. 'His record will be sealed when he's eighteen. None of this should affect his chances for getting into a good school.'

'Doesn't matter. That kid'll be arrested within a month of getting out of Hope.'

Brooke felt her temper flare. 'How can you say that? How can you give up on him?'

Devin signaled the waitress for another beer, then looked back at her, regret in his eyes. 'I didn't give up on him. He's the one giving up on himself. I'd give my eyeteeth to change it, but I've seen it too many times. So will you.'

'I don't want to become jaded like . . .' She brought her temper to heel.

'Like me? Good. But be careful, Brooke. These boys are dangerous.' He lifted his eyes to the television mounted over the bar. 'Looks like they're calling for snow.'

It was an abrupt topic change, but effective. Brooke gathered her purse and coat. 'I'm sorry, Devin. I was out of line.'

He looked sad. 'No, you're right. I am jaded. Unfortunately you have to be or they get to you. I find myself torn between wanting to save them and wanting to lock them all up forever. Sometimes they scare the hell out of me.' He eyed her coat. 'You're not staying for the game?'

She was starving, but Christmas shopping had taken a big bite out of her budget. No eating out until January. 'Nope. Gotta get home and prepare tomorrow's lesson.'

To her surprise he came to his feet and helped her with her coat. 'It's dark outside and the neighborhood's not the best. I'll walk you to your car.'

Monday, November 27, 7:45 P.M.

Reed grunted at the sudden sharp elbow in his gut. He glared down at his sister, who glared up with equal fervor. He dropped the plate back in the sink. 'That hurt.'

'It was meant to. Sit down before I really get mean.' Lauren gave him a mock glare. 'We have an agreement. You don't keep up your end very well. Sit down, Reed.'

Reed sat. 'You pay the rent on time and take care of Beth. That's enough.'

'The deal was cheap rent for babysitting and cleaning. Shut up, Reed.'

The cheap rent on the other side of Reed's duplex allowed Lauren to work part-time while she took classes at the university. Her flexible schedule meant Reed never had to worry about who was watching Beth when he had to work. In his mind, it was more than a win-win. Still, Lauren had her pride. 'Did Beth ask you to take her shopping?'

Lauren laughed. 'She did. Big man like you afraid of a few racks of clothes?'

'You see racks of clothes. I see monsters with price tags for fangs. So will you?'

'Of course. If you want, I'll even pick up a few things you can put under the tree.'

Christmas. 'I've never waited so long to do my shopping before. I just don't know what she likes anymore.' And the knowledge left him . . . bereft somehow.

'She's not a little girl anymore, Reed.'

'So you keep telling me.' He cast a wistful look up at the ceiling. Just a few months before, nothing could have pried Beth from the Monday night game. But now she always excused herself after dinner, saying she had studying to do. 'I never thought growing up meant she'd start disliking all the things we used to like.'

Lauren shot him a sympathetic look. 'You've had it easy. A girl who could tackle, jump, and check as well as any boy. But tomboys grow up and start liking frilly stuff.'

'Tomboy' made him think of Mia Mitchell and her 'comfy' hat. 'Not all tomboys. You should meet my new partner.'

Lauren's eyes widened with surprise. 'You hired a woman down at OFI?'

'No, she's a homicide detective.'

She grimaced. 'Ooh. Nasty.'

Reed thought about Caitlin Burnette, lying in the morgue. 'You have no idea.'

'So tell me more. What's the new chick like?'

Reed gave her a censorious look. 'If I called her a chick, you'd hit me.'

Lauren grinned. 'That's what I love about you. You're such a smart man. So dish.'

'She's an athletic kind of woman.' Who'd been able to respond to every challenge thrown her way that day, whether it was a grieving father, a two-hundred-pound crackhead, or an arrogant baby lawyer. She'd dealt. Very capably, in fact. 'That's all.'

Lauren rolled her eyes. 'That's all. So what's her name?'

'Mitchell.'

Again her eyes rolled. 'Her *first* name.'

'Mia.' And he found he liked the sound of it. It suited her. 'She's a real pistol.'

'And? Is she a blonde, brunette, redhead? Short, tall?'

It was his turn to roll his eyes. 'A blonde. And small.' The top of her head barely reached his shoulder. His shoulder twitched as the image flashed into his mind of her blond head resting there. *Like that would ever happen.* Somehow he couldn't see Mia Mitchell leaning on anyone. That the thought had even crossed his mind was disturbing in and of itself. *Don't even consider going there, Solliday. She's not for you.*

Lauren had sobered. 'Too small to watch your back?'

In his mind he saw her taking down DuPree. 'She'll be fine.'

Lauren was watching him carefully. 'She obviously made an impression on you.'

'She's my partner, Lauren. That's all.'

'That's all,' she mimicked. 'I'm never going to have any more nieces and nephews.'

Now his mouth dropped open. 'What? Whatever made you think you would?' He shook his head. 'Have your own babies. Not me. Not again. I'm too old.'

'You are not old. You just act like it. When was the last time you were out on a real date? And not a meeting with one of Beth's teachers or a visit to the dental hygienist.'

'Thanks for reminding me. I need to schedule a teeth cleaning.'

Her fist shot out of the suds to sock his arm. 'I'm serious.'

He rubbed his arm. 'Ow. You keep hurting me tonight.'

'Well, you keep pissing me off. When, Reed? When was your last date?'

That he'd entered into willingly? Sixteen years ago when he'd taken Christine out for coffee after the classical poetry class he'd dreaded until the night he'd met her. Afterward she'd read her own poetry, just to him, and he'd lost his heart right then and there. 'Lauren, I'm tired. I've had a long day. Leave me alone.'

She was undeterred. 'You haven't had a date since . . . Christmas three years ago.'

He shuddered. 'Don't remind me. Beth hated her.' So did I.

'Beth's support is important. But you're a young man. One of these days Beth will be grown and you'll be alone.' Her mouth drooped. 'I don't want you to be alone.'

Her words hit him hard, the picture of Beth grown and gone too real in his mind. But Lauren cared. So Reed swallowed back a curt command for her to mind her own business and kissed the top of her head. 'I like my life, Lauren. Get Beth some jeans that don't make her look twenty-five, okay?' He retreated, her glare boring into his back.

Upstairs, the loud pounding of Beth's music assaulted his ears through her bedroom door. This, he supposed, along with everything else, was part of her growing up. Still, he wished it weren't happening so fast. He knocked on the door, hard. 'Beth?'

The music abruptly stopped and the puppy yapped. 'Yeah?'

'I just wanted to talk to you, honey.'

The door opened and her dark head poked out high, the puppy's low. 'Yeah?'

Reed blinked and suddenly had no idea of what to say. Her brows went up, then back down, bunching in a frown. 'You okay, Dad?'

'I was just thinking that we hadn't done anything together in a while. Maybe this weekend we can go . . . to the movies or something.'

Her eyes narrowed suspiciously. 'Why?'

He laughed. 'Because I miss you?'

Her eyes flickered. 'One of my friends invited me to a sleepover this weekend.'

He tried to swallow his disappointment. 'Which friend?'

'Jenny Q. You met her mom at open house at the school last September.'

Reed frowned. 'I don't remember. I'll have to meet her again before you can go.'

She rolled her eyes. '*Fine.* She and I are also doing a science project together for school. You can take me there tomorrow night and meet her mom then.'

'I can take you? How about "Please, Dad"? And *don't* roll your eyes at me,' he snapped when she did just that.

He sighed. He hadn't come to fight with her, but it seemed to be happening a lot more lately. 'I'll meet her tomorrow.'

Beth's frown softened. 'Thanks, Dad.' She closed the door with a soft click and he stood staring for a long moment before going on to his own room.

Where he stopped and sighed. Muddy paw prints still ran across his sheets. He remade the bed, then sat on the mattress and picked up Christine's picture. Christine had been . . . the one. He missed her. *But I like my life just the way it is.* The way he'd made it. Although, sometimes he did wish there was someone to talk to in the quiet hours. And there were, he admitted, the physical aspects as well. It had been a long time since he'd been with a woman. Lauren hadn't needed to remind him of that.

He'd never sought anyone to replace Christine. What woman could? She'd brought beauty to his world, nourished his soul. But his body had needs. He'd thought, in the early years after Christine's death, that he could . . . vent his need discreetly with women who weren't interested in long-term relationships. He'd quickly found there were no such creatures on the planet. Every woman who'd promised no strings had ended up needing them. And each one had been hurt because Reed was a man of his word.

Unfortunately no strings plus no hurt equaled no sex. So he'd gone without. Not pleasant, but not the end of the world everyone made it out to be. There was discipline after all. The lessons he'd learned in the military had stood him in good stead. He liked his life. His quiet life. But tonight the quiet seemed more intense than it usually did.

He set Christine's picture down and pulled open the nightstand drawer where he'd kept the book hidden for eleven years, nestled under the stack of birthday and Father's Day cards. Carefully he pulled it from its place of safekeeping and caressed the cover with the pad of his thumb. It was no bigger than the palm of his hand. But so full of her. He let the book fall open to the page that was most worn. She'd called it simply 'Us.'

Pale shoot of golden green,
supple stem and tentative leaves
too new to be certain.
Held tight in a fist of craggy rock
that shadows shelters,
holds the angel hair roots firm,
beating back the wind,
softening the drops of rain
to a kiss.
Huddled against the rock's stubbly face,
she unfurls her fronds,
drinking in morning light.
Nourished by his mineral core,
she grows lush in the life he offers her
until it is unclear who saved whom.
Her canopy, now the roof above his head.
His stony crevice, her very foundation.

A light knock on his door had his pulse rocketing. He put the book away under the cards, feeling foolish. It was just a book. No cause to hide it like a guilty secret.

No. It wasn't just a book. It was a memory. *Mine*. 'Come in.'

Lauren stuck her head in, looking unhappy. 'I'm sorry, Reed. I pushed too far.'

'It's okay. Let's just leave it alone.'

'Well . . . Good night.' She closed the door and Reed sighed.

Then chuckled, because from out of nowhere came the mental picture of Mia Mitchell on her toes in the face of that arrogant little lawyer-boy. 'Bully named Bubba who wants to be your best buddy,' he murmured. Somehow he suspected a poetry reading wouldn't be her ideal first date. Mia Mitchell would want to go somewhere physical. Football, hockey. *If I asked her out, we'd go to a game*, he thought, then shook his head at his own meandering. He would never ask her out.

There would be no first date with Mia Mitchell. She was definitely not his type. He took a long look at Christine's picture. *She* was his type. His wife had been grace and elegance with a sparkle in her eye when she felt mischievous or fun. Mitchell was brash and bold, every movement packed with pent-up energy, every word laid bare of nuance.

His gaze rested on the drawer where the book lay hiding. The words there had been Christine's heart. And his own. He couldn't see a woman like Mia Mitchell appreciating the delicate balance of words and emotions. Not that it made Mia a bad person. Not at all. Just not his kind of woman.

Not that it mattered. Theirs was a temporary business relationship. When he found Caitlin Burnette's murderer he would be back to normal. Which was just the way he liked things. He gathered the dirty sheets. He had time to do a load of laundry during halftime. Football, leftover pizza from the weekend, and a beer. It was a good life.

Monday, November 27, 8:00 P.M.

Beth Solliday took off the bathrobe she'd hastily donned at her father's knock and stepped in front of her full-length mirror. Her eyes critically analyzed the balance of color and style in the outfit she'd chosen for the weekend. Jenny Q had ordered it for her online. There was no way her father could know she'd bought it. She'd skipped lunch for two months to pay for this outfit, but it would be worth it.

She dialed Jenny. 'It's Beth.' She grinned. 'I mean Liz.'

'Are we on?'

'Laid the foundation. I told him he'd met your mother already last fall.'

'Fine. I'll tell my mother that she met him. She never remembers anything.'

'Good. See you tomorrow night.'

'Bring the goods.'

'Oh, I will.' Beth hung up, did one last twirl. Then she changed into her pajamas and hid the outfit. Soon she'd step out. Experience life. She wasn't a little girl anymore.

Chapter Six

Monday, November 27, 8:00 P.M.

Mia flashed her badge at the nurse. 'I'm here to see Abe Reagan.'

'Visiting hours are over, ma'am.'

'I'm here to discuss Detective Reagan's gunshot wound. We have a lead.'

The nurse sucked in one cheek. 'Uh-huh. What's in the bag, Detective?'

Mia looked down at the brown paper sack that contained baklava, one of Abe's favorites. She looked back up and with a straight face said, 'Mug shots.'

The nurse nodded, playing along. 'He's the third door from the end. Tell him if his blood pressure goes up from eating those mug shots, my needle is extra large tonight.'

'Man, you guys are evil,' Mia muttered, hearing the nurse chuckle behind her. Slowly she approached Abe's room, her stomach in a knot. She stopped outside the door and nearly turned around. But she'd given her word. Lightly she knocked.

'Go away. I don't want any more Jell-O or applesauce or whatever you have,' came the cranky reply and despite her trepidation Mia had to grin.

'What about this?' she asked, holding the bag out as she walked in.

Abe was sitting up in bed, the game on the TV. He muted the sound and turned to her with a guarded look that wiped the smile from her face. 'Depends. What is it?'

He peeked in the bag, then looked up, his expression inscrutable. 'You can stay.'

Awkward, Mia stuck her hands in her pockets while she searched his face. He was thinner. Gaunt. Her heart skipped a beat as new guilt piled high. He said nothing, just sat looking at her, waiting. She puffed her cheeks and blew out a breath. 'I'm sorry.'

'For what?' he asked evenly.

She looked away. 'Everything. Letting you get shot. Not coming to visit you.' She shrugged. 'Getting you poked with a really big needle if you eat what's in the bag.'

He grunted. 'Nurses' trash talk. They don't scare me. Sit down.'

She sat, but couldn't meet his eyes. She took the silence as long as she could before blurting, 'So . . . Where's Kristen?'

'Home with Kara.' Their daughter that Abe treated

121

like the precious treasure she was. 'Mia, look at me. Please.'

No anger blazed in his blue eyes. Instead there was sorrow there that she didn't know if she could take. She lurched to her feet, only to have him grab her arm.

'Sit down, Mia.' He waited until she had, then muttered a soft curse. 'Did you think for a moment, one single moment, that I blamed you for this?'

She met his eyes squarely. 'I thought you should. I knew you wouldn't.'

'I didn't know if you were all right. Mia . . .' He swallowed hard. 'I thought you'd gone after them,' he said harshly. 'And I wasn't there to watch your back.'

She laughed sadly. 'I did. But I couldn't find them.'

'Don't do that to me again. Please.'

'What, let you get shot up?'

'That, too,' he said dryly. 'Kristen said she tore you a new one this morning.'

'I hope I never have to face her across a courtroom. I felt about an inch tall.'

'You would have been a layer of slime on the floor if she hadn't felt sorry for you. You told her you weren't paying attention that night. Why?' He stopped her mid-denial. 'Don't. We've been partners too long. I knew something was bothering you.'

She drew a breath. 'I guess my dad and the funeral . . . It just caught up to me.'

His eyes narrowed. He hadn't bought it. Somehow

she hadn't thought he would. 'Is it so bad that you can't tell me?'

She closed her eyes, saw the headstone that lay next to her father's. The stranger's eyes meeting her over it. 'If I say yeah, will you be hurt?'

He hesitated for a heartbeat then asked in a quiet voice, 'Are you in trouble, Mia?'

Her eyes flew open, saw the concern on his face. 'No. It's nothing like that.'

'Sick?' He winced. 'Pregnant?'

'No. And way no.'

He sighed his relief. 'And it's not a guy because there haven't been any in a while.'

'Thanks,' she said sarcastically and he smiled. 'I'd nearly forgotten.'

'Just trying to help.' The smile faded. 'If you need to talk, you'll come to me, right?'

'Yeah.' She was glad that was over. 'I have news. Remember Getts and DuPree?'

'I have a vague recollection,' he said, his voice gone dry again.

'Well, it seems you got DuPree before Getts got you.'

His eyes narrowed, focused. 'Good. Hope the sonofabitch hurts a lot.'

'DuPree hurts worse now.' Her smile was a mere baring of teeth. 'I got *him* today. Joanna Carmichael told me where he was.' His eyes widened in surprise and she nodded grimly. 'Shocked the hell out of me, too. I guess all that skulking around she does is finally paying a dividend. But . . . Getts got away.'

'Damn,' he said softly.

'I'm sorry.'

'Mia. You idiot. He shot you, too. Now he knows you know where he hangs. You got his buddy in custody. He's either going to go under or come out fighting.'

'I'm betting he'll hide.'

'Until he catches you unaware. I didn't see either of their faces, but you did. You're the only one who can identify Getts. We wanted them for murder before. Now we're tacking on attempted murder of a cop. You think he's gonna want you around?'

She'd already considered it. 'I'll be careful.'

'You tell Spinnelli you want a partner to watch your back. Until I come back.'

'I got one already. Temporarily,' she added hastily when his dark brows went up.

'Really? Who?'

'I've been loaned to OFI. Arson/homicide case. Guy's name is Reed Solliday.'

Abe leaned forward. 'And? Is he old, young? Rookie, experienced?'

'Experienced enough. A little older than you. Old enough to have a fourteen-year-old.' Her shudder was exaggerated. 'Keeps his shoes too shiny.'

'He should be flogged.'

She chuckled. 'He seemed obnoxious early on, but it looks like he might be okay.'

Abe opened the bag and she knew all was forgiven. 'You don't want any, do you?'

'I ate mine on the way. And if the nurse asks, the bag's got mug shots in it.'

He cast a furtive glance at the door. 'Do you hear her?'

Her lips twitched. 'I thought you weren't afraid of the nurses and their trash talk.'

'I lied. The night nurse is the antichrist.' He snagged a piece of the dessert and settled back against his pillow. 'Tell me about the arson case. Don't leave out anything.'

Monday, November 27, 11:15 P.M.

Penny Hill wasn't home. *Why wasn't she home?* He glanced at his watch, then fixed his gaze back on the house he'd scoped so carefully the night before. She'd been here last night, tucked into bed by eleven. He'd returned tonight, ready to roll and she wasn't here. He peered in her front window, hidden from the street by thick evergreens. There was only a great big dog sleeping on the living-room floor. He clenched his teeth.

He had three choices. One, come back tomorrow night. Two, torch the place without her in it. Three, be patient and wait. He considered the options. The risks of waiting here, of perhaps being seen. The rewards of the hunt. Last time he surrendered the kill, anxious for the fire. Tonight he wanted more. He remembered little Caitlin with a shiver of restless pleasure. He could remember the energy pulsing through his body. That incredible rush.

He wanted that rush again. The complete and total power of life and death.

And pain. He wanted the bitch to feel such pain. To plead for mercy.

He wanted Penny Hill to pay. His lips curved, wolfish. He'd wait. He had time. All the time in the world. She didn't. She'd count to ten and go to hell.

Monday, November 27, 11:25 P.M.

Mia climbed the stairs to her apartment. She'd hoped an hour run would get rid of all her nervous energy, but all it had done was soak her in sweat and make her taped shoulder throb. The second she pushed her door open she felt the difference. The air was warm and it smelled like . . . peanut butter?

'Don't shoot. It's just me.'

A breath rushed from her lungs. 'Dammit, Dana, I could have shot you.'

Her best friend sat at her dinette table, hands up. 'I'll replace the peanut butter.'

Mia closed her apartment door and flipped the dead bolts. 'Ha-ha. Nobody loves a dead comedian. When did you get home?' Dana and her husband had taken their foster kids to Maryland's Eastern Shore to spend Thanksgiving with Ethan's old friends.

'About midnight last night. Getting the kids up for school this morning was *such* a joy. Ethan and I put them on the school bus and went back to bed.'

Mia pulled two beers from the fridge. 'Going to bed with Ethan is *such* a hardship.'

Dana grinned. 'I'll survive.' She shook her head at the offered beer with a grimace. 'No thanks. Doesn't go with the peanut butter.' She waited until Mia was slouched in a chair. 'You didn't return any of my phone calls. I was worried.'

'Join the chorus.' Then she sighed when irritation flashed in Dana's brown eyes. 'I'm sorry. God, I feel like a fucking broken record today. Sorry, sorry, sorry.'

Dana lifted a brow. 'You done?'

'Yeah.' It came out surly and childish. Which was about right at this point.

'Okay. Look, I just wanted to check on you. Make sure you weren't dead or something. Nobody loves a dead sulker. So what have you been doing with yourself the last two weeks, Mia, besides avoiding me, and apparently everybody else?'

Mia took a long drag from the bottle, then went to her kitchen cabinet and pulled out . . . the box. It was a simple wooden box, no decoration or labels. It was incredible that such a little box could hold so much hurt. She put it down in front of Dana. 'Ta-da.'

'Why do I feel like Pandora?' Dana murmured and

lifted the lid. 'Oh, Mia.' She lifted her eyes, under-standing now. 'At least now you know. About the boy, anyway.'

'I found the box in Bobby's closet when I was pulling together clothes to bury him in. I didn't open it until I got home from the cemetery. I was going to put his shield in it.'

With great ceremony the shield had been presented to her mother at Bobby Mitchell's graveside, lying atop the flag that had draped his coffin. Her face haggard and worn, Annabelle Mitchell had turned and placed them in Mia's hands. Too stunned to react, Mia had accepted them. The trifolded flag was now propped up against her toaster. The flag probably had Pop-Tart crumbs in its folds, but apart from a reluctance to dirty an American flag, it was hard to care.

She pointed at the box with her bottle. 'Instead, I found that.'

Dana pulled the photo from the box. 'Damn, Mia. He looks just like your baby pictures.'

Mia's laugh was hollow. 'Bobby had some powerful genes.' She walked around to look over Dana's shoulder at the chubby-faced boy sitting in a little wooden rocking chair, a red truck clutched in his fist. The boy she'd never seen, although she now knew his name. His birthday. And his death day. 'That should look like my baby picture. That's our rocking chair, mine and Kelsey's. Bobby had our pictures taken in it, too.'

'How tacky.' Dana's words were bland, but her

mouth was set in a firm line. 'But then we knew that about him.'

Only Dana knew. Dana and Kelsey. And perhaps Mia's mother. Mia wasn't entirely sure what her mother knew. She stared at the little boy's face. 'He has Bobby's blond hair and blue eyes, just like me. And like *her*, whoever the hell she is.'

'You've spent the last two weeks trying to find her. I thought you would.'

She was the stranger Mia had seen at her father's burial. A young woman with blond hair and round blue eyes . . . *just like mine*. For one brief instant it had been like looking in a mirror. Then the woman had dropped her eyes and disappeared into the crowd of cops paying their final respects. After the burial service Dana had searched the crowd, leaving Mia to accept the respects of each and every cop there.

That had been the hardest part of the whole sham. Nodding soberly to each uniform as they grasped her hand, told her in hushed tones that her father had been a good cop. A good man. How could everyone on God's earth have been so damn snowed?

When the last uniform was gone and Mia stood alone with her mother she'd lifted her eyes to Dana, who'd shaken her head. The woman was gone. One look at her mother's face had told her all she'd needed to know. Annabelle Mitchell had seen her, too. But unlike Mia, her mother hadn't seemed the least bit surprised. And like so many times in her life, her mother's eyes had shuttered. She was unwilling to discuss the woman, the little boy. The damn headstone. LIAM CHARLES MITCHELL, BELOVED SON.

'I'm glad you saw her, too. Otherwise I might be on the shrink's couch right now.'

'You didn't imagine her, Mia. She was there.'

Mia finished off the beer. 'Yep. I know. Then and later.'

Dana's eyes widened. 'She came back?'

'A few times. She never speaks, just looks at me. I'm never close enough to grab her. I swear this is driving me crazy, Dana. And I know my mother knows who she is.'

'But she won't tell you.'

'Nope. Good old Annabelle. I did get her to tell me about the boy.' She set the beer down, its taste suddenly bitter. 'I've got to tell Kelsey. She needs to know.'

The last time she'd spoken with her sister had been the day their father died, through the Plexiglas as she always did. Mia never asked for any special visitation with her sister. Having the other inmates know Kelsey Mitchell's sister was a cop would not be in Kelsey's best interest.

Kelsey needed to know what she'd found. Maybe she could finally find peace.

'I can go tell her,' Dana offered.

'No. It's my responsibility. But thanks. I'll have to fit it in. I got a new case today.'

'With who?'

Mia studied her bottle carefully. 'With Reed Solliday. Arson.'

Dana's brows lifted, knowing her moods well. 'And?'

'Seems like a nice guy. Not married. Fourteen-year-old kid. Moves like a dancer.'

'I never understood how that was such a turn-on for you.'

Mia chuckled ruefully. 'Me, either. Good thing he's off-limits.'

'You said he wasn't married.'

She sobered. 'I also said he was a nice guy.'

Dana made a frustrated sound. 'Mia, you piss me off.'

'I don't mean to.'

Dana sighed. 'I know. So . . . What will you do with the box?'

'I don't know.' Her mouth twisted. 'I put my dog tags in it.'

Dana's eyes dropped to her chest. 'Then why are you wearing them now?'

Mia fingered the chain around her neck. 'Because once I put them in the box, I couldn't sleep. I don't know, it was like a panic attack or something. So I got up and put them back on.' She lifted a brow. 'That was the night before Abe was shot.'

'You were shot, too, Mia.'

'And look at me.' She spread her arms wide, sardonic. 'Good as new.'

'I can't understand how a smart woman like you is so superstitious.'

Mia shrugged. 'I'd rather be superstitious and alive than logical and dead.'

'And if it were a rabbit's foot, I'd say no harm, no foul. But they're Bobby's, Mia, and until you take them off, you're still connected to him.' With a frustrated sigh, Dana stood and put on her coat. 'Ethan will be worried about me so I have to go. Come out to the house tomorrow. I'll fix you a special treat for dinner. The kids brought you something.'

'Please say it's not another goldfish,' she begged and Dana smiled.

'No, not a goldfish.' She gave Mia a hard hug. 'Get some sleep.'

Monday, November 27, 11:35 P.M.

Penny Hill breathed a sigh of relief. Her garage door was several inches closer than it usually was. *I never should have had any of that punch. But it was my retirement party, after all. Should have called a cab.* She'd been lucky not to have hit another car or been stopped by a cop for DUI. *Wouldn't that look just dandy in my file?*

But her file was now officially closed. After twenty-five years with Social Services, she was calling it quits. A lot of families had come her way. A lot of successes. A lot of regrets. One moment of shame. But that water had flowed under the bridge years before. She couldn't change it now.

She was free. She tugged at her briefcase, teetering on her feet. It was unusually heavy. She'd cleaned out her desk and stuffed the briefcase full. Too much punch made her too unsteady to haul it in tonight. *I'll get it tomorrow.* Now, all she wanted was a strong antacid and a soft pillow. Wearily she opened her front door.

And flew forward, violently. Her head smacked the newel post as the door closed and she was jerked to her feet by a pair of strong hands. Pulled against a hard body. She started to scream but a cold gloved hand covered her mouth and she felt the bite of a blade against her throat. She stopped fighting, feeling a spear of hope when her daughter's dog bounded into the room. *Please, Milo. Don't be friendly for once.*

But the dog just stood there wagging his tail and the man behind her relaxed. He forced her forward, into her kitchen. 'Open the door,' he said. 'Let the dog out.'

She did as he said. Happily Milo bounded away across her fenceless backyard. 'Now lock the door, just like it was before,' he said and she obeyed. He let go of her mouth just before he forced her to her knees. Then flat on her face. She cried out as he grabbed her hair and smashed her head into the linoleum. Hard.

'If you scream, I'll cut out your tongue.'

She drew a deep breath into her lungs to scream anyway. Laughing softly he pressed her face into the floor again, his knee hard against the back of her neck. He shoved something into her mouth. Cloth. She tried to spit it out and gagged. Don't throw up. *You'll die if you throw up. You'll die anyway. Dear God. I'm going to die.*

A whimper of terror escaped her throat and he laughed.

He tossed the Ziplock bag holding the used condom into his backpack. He'd been lucky with Caitlin. He wouldn't rely on luck this time. If by any chance he failed to completely incinerate Penny Hill, he'd made sure there would be none of his DNA left behind. She lay on the floor, curled in a fetal position. She was in pain. But not enough. She would be, though. A few more things to do and he could be on his way.

In the backseat of her car, which he'd left running in her driveway, he'd found her briefcase. The briefcase was an unexpected find. Who knew what information he'd find inside?

But first things first. He spread the same nitrate gel over her torso that he'd used in the egg and ran a fuse out of the room, alongside the fuse that led to the egg. He'd come prepared this time. Caitlin Burnette had been unplanned and he hadn't been thinking. He'd used gasoline on her when he should have used the gel from the second egg. Gasoline burned off too quickly. He wanted Miss Hill to burn very thoroughly. But in the event she did not, he didn't want her surviving to tell tales. That would be bad.

Once more he returned to his backpack, pulling out the two garbage bags he'd packed. He pulled one of the bags over his head and poked his arms through the sides. With the wrench he removed the valve on the gas line behind the stove. In a few minutes the top half of the room would be filled with gas.

He'd crouched down next to Penny Hill, the knife in his hand, before realizing he'd nearly forgotten the most important thing. Quickly he ran to the far corner of her house, crumpled some newspaper and threw it in the trash can. Then he pulled the filterless cigarette from his pocket and carefully lit it, set it on one end so that the burning tip rested away from the paper. In a few minutes, the cigarette would burn to its end.

Back to Miss Hill. He ran back to the kitchen and grabbed her arm. Hard. Her eyes slowly opened. 'For Shane,' he said. 'You remember Shane. You placed him and his brother in some godforsaken foster home in the middle of fucking nowhere.' Her eyes flickered in startled recognition. 'You never came to check on them. For a whole year. They were sodomized there. So now you understand why I had to do that to you.'

Quickly he sliced her arm, just above her elbow, and blood spurted all over the plastic bag he wore, warm and wet. 'You'll die,' he promised. 'But first, you'll burn.' He crouched closer, until he was in her face.

'Count to ten, bitch. Then go to hell.'

He pulled off the plastic bag, rolled it up and put it in the clean bag, threw his tools in his backpack, shouldered it, then lit the fuses from the relative safety of the laundry room. *Ten . . . nine . . .* he ran to the front door, pulled it firmly closed . . . *eight . . .* Then he was in her car, peeling out of the driveway, counting down all the while.

Three, two . . . and . . . Right on cue the air shook with the explosion, broken glass flying from the windows of Hill's house. He'd done a much better job of estimating the length of his fuses this time. He was at the end of the street before the first neighbor ran from their house. Carefully he drove, making sure to arouse no suspicion. Driving on, he pulled far off the deserted side road where he'd left the car he'd stolen that evening. He covered Hill's car with evergreen branches. Nobody would find it there.

He changed cars, making sure to take his backpack. Settling behind the wheel, he pulled off the ski mask and drove away. Penny Hill would be in a lot of pain right about now. He'd savor the satisfaction later.

Tuesday, November 28, 12:35 A.M.

'You were right. He's done it again.'

Reed turned. Mia Mitchell stood behind him, her gaze fixed on the inferno that used to be the residence of Penny Hill. She'd gotten here fast. 'It appears so.'

'What happened?'

'Residents reported an initial explosion at about five

minutes after midnight. Companies 156 and 172 responded at 12:09 and 12:15 respectively. They arrived at the site and the battalion chief immediately saw the similarity to Saturday's fire. Larry Fletcher called me at 12:15.' He'd immediately called Mitchell, expecting a cranky middle-of-the-night reception. Instead she'd been instantly alert, professional. He glanced at the crowd, dropped his voice so only she could hear. 'They think the homeowner was home. Her name is Penny Hill. Two guys went in to look for her.'

Horror and pity and sad resignation flickered in her eyes. 'Aw, shit.'

'I know. The pair checked the right side of the house, but she wasn't there.'

'They check the kitchen?'

'Can't get close enough yet. They've turned off the gas and run a line into the house. They're working it. There was a smaller fire in the living room.'

'Trash can?' she asked and he lifted a brow.

'Yeah.'

'I've been mulling it over. The trash can was the odd thing at the Doughertys'.'

'Agreed. The solid accelerant was sophisticated. The gasoline was like an afterthought, but the trash can was almost . . .'

'Childish,' she supplied. 'I bounced it off Abe tonight. He thought the same thing.'

Abe, her partner who was laid up in a hospital bed. 'How is he?'

She nodded once, briskly. 'He's good.'

So then, he suspected, was she. Which made him glad. 'Good.'

'You talk to the crowd?'

'Yeah. Nobody saw anybody before, but everybody was inside, asleep or watching TV. Then all of a sudden, the big boom. One of the neighbors heard the squeal of tires just before the explosion, but he's pretty shaken up.' Reed pointed to a man standing at the front of the crowd, his expression one of shocked horror. 'Daniel Wright. There are skid marks on the driveway and Miss Hill's car is gone.'

'I'll put out an all points for her vehicle.'

'I already did.' His brow lifted when hers went up. 'Hope you don't mind.'

Her eyes had blinked with surprise, then settled. 'Of course not. Just so it gets done.' She turned her gaze back to the fire. 'They've got it under control.'

'Knocked this one down faster. It hadn't caught hold in the top floor yet.'

'He wanted that bed to burn in the Doughertys' house,' she noted. 'Why not here?'

He wondered the same thing. Two firefighters emerged from the house. 'Come on,' he said and started toward the truck where Larry stood with his radio. 'Well?'

Larry's expression was grim. 'She's in there. Mahoney says she looks like the last one. We couldn't get close enough to get her out in time.' He eyed Mitchell. 'You are?'

'Mia Mitchell, Homicide. You must be Larry Fletcher.'

Larry's expression went from grim to wary. 'I am. Why Homicide?'

She looked up at Reed, her blue eyes accusing. 'You didn't tell him?'

Reed scowled. 'I left him a message to call me.'

'Tell me what?' Larry demanded and Mitchell sighed.

'The victim in the last fire was dead before it started. This one may have been, too.'

Larry's frown was troubled. 'I shouldn't feel relieved, but I do.'

'Human nature,' she said. 'There wasn't anything you could have done.'

'Thanks. Maybe we'll sleep tonight. You'll want to talk to the guys who went in. Mahoney and the probie. Hey!' he shouted at the men. 'Mahoney. Hunter. Over here!'

Mahoney and the newest probationary member of their company trudged toward them, still in full gear with the exception of their breathing apparatus which hung around their necks. Both wore looks of exhausted devastation. 'We were too late,' Brian Mahoney said, his voice rough from the smoke. 'She's charred, just like the last one.'

The probie just shook his head. 'My God.' His voice was thick, horrified.

Mitchell stepped forward, peering up under the brim of the probie's hat. 'David?'

The probie pushed his hat back. 'Mia? What are you doing here?'

'I should say the same thing to you. I knew you took the exam, but I thought you were still waiting for an assignment.'

'Been with the 172 for three months. I guess since you're here we should assume these were homicides. That the fire was just to cover them up.'

'That's a good assumption. Do you know Solliday?'

The probie shoved his hat under his arm. Sober gray eyes met Reed's and annoyance prickled as Reed studied his face. Even dirty, this guy was a calendar boy. 'No. I'm David Hunter, the new guy.'

'Reed Solliday, OFI. I take it you know each other.'

One side of Mitchell's mouth lifted wryly. 'Yeah, we've had our fun in the past.'

The thought of Mitchell having fun with the pretty probie sent a wave of irritation through Reed, so hard and fast it shocked him. *Whoa.* If Mitchell and Hunter were a number, it was none of his damn business. This fire was. 'Tell me what you saw.'

'Nothing at first,' Hunter admitted. 'The smoke was too thick. Black. The spray went to vapor right away. Showered back down on us. We kept moving, checked the bedrooms and didn't find anybody in the beds. We finally got close to the kitchen.' He closed his eyes and swallowed convulsively. 'I almost stepped on her, Mia. She was . . .'

'It's okay. Not an easy sight even if you've seen it before. How was she laid out?'

Hunter took a breath. 'Fetal.'

Mahoney took off his hat, wiped at the sweat on his brow. 'The fire was high up, Reed. Char lines at eye level. Just like the last one. And the stove was pulled away.'

'What about the trash can in the living room?' he asked.

'Just a metal wastebasket filled with newspaper,' Mahoney said.

'The girl we found Saturday was dead before the fire,' Larry said. 'This one probably was, too.'

Mahoney blew out a breath. 'Thanks. It helps a little. You done with us?'

Reed looked down at Mitchell. 'You done?'

'Yeah. David . . . Tell your mom hi,' she said in what was an obvious substitution.

Hunter's mouth lifted. 'I will. Don't be a stranger.'

Mahoney and Hunter walked away and Reed unclenched his jaw. 'You can't go in yet,' he said, annoyed with himself for his curt tone. 'Your boots won't protect your feet from the heat.' He turned for his SUV, Mitchell following behind him.

'When can Jack and his team go in?'

'An hour. Ben and Foster and I will go in first, but go ahead and call Unger.' He sat on his tailgate to change into his boots. Her call completed, she dropped her phone in her pocket and watched him, fists on her hips.

Her watching him, combined with the cold air and his own ire, made his fingers even clumsier on the clamps of his boots. Finally, Mitchell lightly smacked his hands away and took over the task.

'Are you always so stubborn about asking for help?' she snapped.

'Are you always so sensitive to other people's feelings?' he shot back and her chin immediately lifted, her eyes narrowed. Cold.

'No. That's why people like dealing with Abe better. But Abe's not here, so you're stuck dealing with me.' She dropped her hands and stepped back. 'Now you're ready, Sluggo. Check on our victim if you don't mind, since I don't have appropriate footwear.'

Her sarcasm took the starch from his shorts. 'Look, I . . .' *What? You what, Solliday?* 'Thanks.' He grabbed his kit and headed for the house. 'Can you get somebody to keep the crowd back while I go in? Also, call the ME.'

'Will do.'

Mia watched him enter Hill's house, flashlight in one hand, his bag of gizmos in the other. *Nice going.* Once again, she'd stepped on toes without meaning to. Or fingers, in this case. *Just get to work, Mia.*

She drew Mr Wright off to the side. 'I'm Detective Mitchell. You knew Mrs Hill?'

His shoulders sagged. 'She's dead, then? Penny's dead?'

'I'm afraid so. I'm sorry. Can you tell me exactly what you saw?'

He nodded. 'I was asleep, but this squealing woke me up. I ran to the window and saw Penny's car take off down the street. A second later . . . Her house exploded.'

'Did you see anybody behind the wheel, Mr Wright?'

He shook his head miserably. 'It was dark and it happened so fast . . . I'm sorry.'

So was Mia. 'Did she normally park her car in the driveway?'

'Just recently. Her daughter had to move out of her house into an apartment, so Penny was storing her stuff in the garage.'

'Did you know Mrs Hill's daughter?'

'I talked to Margaret once or twice, a month ago. She used to live in Milwaukee. I don't know where she's living now. Penny has a son in Cincinnati. His name is Mark.'

'Do you know where Mrs Hill worked?'

'She was a social worker.'

Alarm bells went off. Social workers made great grudge targets. 'Thank you.' She pressed one of her cards in his cold hand. 'If you remember anything, please call me.'

She canvassed the crowd, but it seemed only Mr Wright had seen anything of value. She walked to the back of the fire engine as they were rolling up the hose. David Hunter leaned with his back against the engine, his eyes closed, his face drawn.

'How are you, David?' she murmured and wearily he turned to look at her.

'How do you stand it?' he asked instead.

'Like you will. One day at a time. Most of yours won't be this way. Thankfully, most of mine won't, either.' She rested her good shoulder against the side of the truck and looked up at him. He was taller than Solliday by several inches, but not nearly as broad. And David was clean-shaven, so there was none of that devil-look Solliday had down so well. 'You sell your garage when you joined up?'

'No. I hired someone to run it for me. I go out there on my off days and yank engines. Whatever I need to do.' He lifted a brow. 'Your Alfa need a tune-up?'

'No, it's still good from the last one you gave it. So you're keeping busy.'

He met her gaze squarely. 'It seemed like the wisest thing to do.'

David Hunter had a bad case of a wounded heart. Long ago he'd fallen for Dana, but Mia's friend had never seen it. Then Dana had fallen in love with someone else, and nobody who'd seen Dana and Ethan Buchanan together thought they were anything less than perfect for each other. Mia was happier for her best friend than anyone else, but seeing the stark pain in David Hunter's eyes had always been like a kick in the gut. 'Nobody knows, David. If it's up to me, nobody ever will.'

His smile was sardonic. 'I guess there's comfort in

that somewhere.' He pushed himself away from the truck. 'So what's going on here, Mia. Really?'

'We don't know yet. Listen, have you seen any other fires that looked like this?'

'No, but I've only been here three months. You should ask Mahoney.'

'I will. How about trash-can fires? How many of them have you seen?'

'I'd have to think. A few, at least, but most of them are set by little kids, elementary school age.' He looked back at the house. 'This wasn't done by a kid.'

She frowned. 'Most arsonists are under the age of twenty, right?'

'Yeah. But your friend Solliday would be better for that kind of information.'

He's not my friend. The sharp edge of the thought was unexpected. *He's just temporary.* 'I'll ask him. Now I need to talk to Mahoney before you guys head out.'

Tuesday, November 28, 1:35 A.M.

Now that, he thought, *had gone a great deal better*. He tossed a shovelful of mud to one side. *Practice makes perfect, after all.*

Quickly he covered the hole he'd dug, burying what he'd taken from the scene. The condom and bloody plastic bags would keep until he could come back and dispose of them properly. He should have stopped to dispose of them on his way back, but he'd been paranoid, constantly watching his rearview mirror.

His caution had been unnecessary. Nobody had followed him. Nobody had seen him. Penny Hill's car was now abandoned, its license plates and VIN tags removed. He'd moved it far enough off the deserted road to keep it from being found for a while. He knew he'd left nothing behind, but one could never be too careful. One hair could convict him.

Of course, they'd have to catch him first. And that, they'd never do.

He'd been careful. He'd been skillful. He'd been ruthless.

He smiled as he gave the earth a good stamp with his foot. She'd suffered. He could still hear Penny Hill's moans. Unfortunately they'd been muffled by the gag in her mouth, but that had been a necessary evil. But the gag hadn't hidden the hollowed, glazed look in her eyes when he'd finished with her. And she'd known exactly why. That made it all the sweeter.

He stopped abruptly, one hand gripping the shovel handle. Shit. He'd forgotten the briefcase. Penny Hill's briefcase was still in the backseat of her car. He made himself calm down. It was okay. He'd go back and get the briefcase when he could. He'd hidden the car well enough that nobody would bother it before then.

He looked up at the night sky. There were still hours before dawn. He could get a little sleep before his day officially began.

*

The boy watched at the window, his heart in his throat. He was there, again. Burying something, again. He should tell. He should. But he was so afraid. He could only watch as he finished, covering his hiding place once more. His imagination conjured all kinds of hideous pictures of what he'd just buried. But the reality of what he'd do if he told was every bit as bad. This the boy knew for sure.

Chapter Seven

Tuesday, November 28, 7:55 A.M.

She looked tired. It was Reed's first thought as he stopped in the doorway of the Homicide bullpen, one hand clutching a pair of firefighters' boots, the other carrying a carton with two cups of coffee. Mitchell sat back in her chair, her scuffed boots propped up on her desk, her attention focused on a thick file in her lap.

Her eyes flew up when he let the heavy boots drop to her desk. She eyed them, then looked up with a half-smile. 'It's not even Christmas. yet. I'm touched, Solliday.'

He extended his hand and saw true appreciation light her face. 'Now you're talking.' She set the file on her desk and took one of the Styrofoam cups from his carton.

'It's real coffee,' he said. 'Not like that sludge over there in your pot.'

'Yeah, but the caffeine concentration in the sludge is enough to keep us going for days.' Warily she looked up at him, a plastic cream packet in her hand. 'You want me to put the cream in yours, or are we going to insult each other again?'

He chuckled. 'I take mine black.' He looked down at the folder on her desk. 'Roger Burnette's case files?'

'Not his files from Records. I requested those yesterday, but our clerk hasn't brought them up yet. These are Burnette's own notes. He was waiting when I got here this morning. Names, addresses, dates of anybody whose Wheaties he's pissed in the last few years. I think it helped him to feel like he was doing something.'

'And?'

She grimaced. 'Everybody in here had a grudge.'

'So you're back to Caitlin being the tool to her father's payback.'

She added cream to her coffee and snapped the lid back into place. 'I don't know. I do know that Penny Hill was a social worker. She's probably taken a lot of kids from a lot of homes over the years. Disrupted a lot of lives, from a certain point of view. I think it will be interesting to cross-reference Roger Burnette's cases with Penny Hill's. See if anybody hated them both.'

'Did Roger Burnette know Penny Hill?'

'No. I was so hoping he did, but he'd never heard her name.' She swung her feet to the floor. 'Now it's time for morning meeting. I asked Jack and the ME to come.' She grabbed the file and her coffee. 'I also asked our psychologist to stop by. His name is Miles Westphalen. I filled him in. I've worked with Miles before. He's good.'

Before Reed could say a word she was off down a side hallway, motioning him to follow. A *shrink*, was all he could think. *Oh joy.*

A large table dominated the center of Spinnelli's conference room. Spinnelli himself sat at one end, flanked on either side by Jack Unger from CSU and Sam Barrington from the ME's office. An older man sat next to Jack. He would be the shrink.

Spinnelli searched their faces, and winced. 'You two get any sleep at all?'

'Not much,' Mitchell said. She smiled warmly at the shrink. 'Hey, Miles. Thanks for coming. This is Lieutenant Reed Solliday from OFI. Reed, Dr Miles Westphalen.'

Reed shook the old man's hand, keeping his face blank. He hated most shrinks. Hated the way they tried to read your mind. The way they turned everything into a question. He especially hated the way they blamed propensity for evil on upbringing. He laid odds that Westphalen would have this arsonist reduced to a poor soul with no father and an abusive mother before the meeting was over.

Westphalen sat back, mildly amused. 'Lieutenant Solliday, it's nice to meet you. But don't worry, I won't read your mind. Not before my first cup of coffee, anyway.'

Reed's jaw tightened as Mitchell took the chair next

to Westphalen. 'Leave him alone, Miles,' she chided wearily. 'He's had a long night. We both have. Sit, Solliday. Please.' She looked over at Barrington. 'Have you had a chance to check her out?'

'Only a cursory look,' Barrington answered as Reed sat next to Mitchell. 'But I'm willing to bet I find something else on the body other than gasoline. The burns are far deeper. This fire burned longer, at least on the victim.'

'So about the victim,' Spinnelli interjected. 'Who is she?'

'Penelope Hill, age forty-seven,' Mitchell said. 'She was an employee of Social Services for twenty-five years.' She blew a breath up through her bangs, sending them flying. 'Last night was her retirement party. I talked to one of my old friends in Social Services this morning. Hill was well respected and well loved. She'd been written up in the paper several times for her community service.'

'"Well loved" is relative,' Westphalen noted. 'By her coworkers, maybe.'

'But by parents whose kids she's taken away?' Mitchell continued Westphalen's thought. '"Well loved" probably isn't a description they'd use. I thought of that, Miles.'

'A cop's daughter and a social worker,' Spinnelli mused. 'Any connection?'

She shook her head. 'Burnette didn't know her. We'll need a court order for Hill's files so we can cross-check their case-loads. But the fires themselves were the same in a lot of ways.'

Spinnelli raised his brows. 'Reed?'

All eyes turned to him. 'Both were started in the kitchen. Both used natural gas as the primary fuel. Both used a strip of solid accelerant up the wall as a chemical extension of the fuse. The lab came back with the analysis of the solid accelerant used in the Doughertys' house. Ammonium nitrate mixed with kerosene and guar gum. Highly flammable. I should have the lab's analysis on the mix used in Hill's house by the end of the day, but I expect it to be the same.'

Spinnelli stroked his mustache. 'Are we dealing with a professional arsonist?'

'Not in the traditional sense. Arson for profit is normally committed by property owners for the insurance or by torches who are providing . . . a service. This doesn't feel like it's about money. It's personal. I mean, he didn't just set a fire. He blew up their houses. How he knew the victims we still haven't figured out, but the use of an explosion just screams *Look at me. Look at what I can do.*'

'And *Look at them. Look how they died,*' Mitchell murmured. 'It's like a flashing neon arrow.' She looked over at Westphalen. 'A cry for help?'

Westphalen lifted shaggy gray brows. 'More like a cry of rage.'

Reed was surprised. He'd expected the shrink to run with the 'cry for help' mantra. It was another thing he hated about shrinks. Nothing was anybody's fault. If a criminal committed a crime they were crying for help. That was bullshit. Criminals committed crimes because they got something out of it. Period. If they wanted help, they'd ask nicely, not by nearly blowing up a damn neighborhood.

Spinnelli pushed away from the table and walked to the whiteboard. 'So we have what?' He started writing, creating two columns he headed Dougherty/Burnette and Hill. 'Time of the crime?'

'Both about midnight,' Reed said. 'Both were residential structures in middle-class neighborhoods. Both used incendiary devices with a fuse.'

'Don't forget about the trash can,' Mitchell murmured.

'And both had a separate fire,' Reed added. 'Set in a wastebasket with newspaper and a filterless cigarette. Without the filter, the cigarette burns down to the end, setting the newspaper on fire. It's a very simple but effective time-delay device.'

Spinnelli noted it, then turned around. 'Now that sounds more like a novice.'

'It means something,' Mitchell said quietly. 'It's ... symbolic.'

'You're probably right. What else?' Spinnelli asked. 'Sam?'

'Both bodies were charred beyond visual recognition,' Barrington offered. 'As I said, the degree of the damage appears much greater in the second victim.'

'Mrs Hill,' Mitchell murmured. 'Her name was Penny Hill.'

Something in her face squeezed at Reed's heart but Barrington just lifted his blond brows. 'The killer used something different on the second victim. Something that didn't burn off as fast.'

'Check for the nitrate mixture,' Reed said. 'I'll have the lab fax you the formula.'

'I'll be waiting for it. Get me the second victim's dental records, Detective. I'll make a positive ID as quickly as I can.'

'Yeah,' Mitchell said flatly. 'I'll be on that today.'

Barrington stood. 'If there's nothing more, I have a great deal to do today.'

'Call us when you have something,' Spinnelli said and Barrington left.

For a moment Mitchell glared at the door the ME had closed, then slowly flattened her fist on her thigh. When she spoke, it was quietly. 'Marc, Caitlin Burnette's body was incinerated with gasoline. Penny Hill's with something . . . hotter.'

'Probably not hotter,' Reed inserted. 'Just something that didn't burn off as fast.'

She shrugged, annoyed. 'Whatever. My point is, it was a difference. He changed. Improving on his MO, maybe.'

Spinnelli's mustache bent down as he considered it. 'Sounds like a reasonable assumption. What are the differences?'

'In the first house he left two devices,' Reed said. 'One in the kitchen and one in the master bedroom. In the second, he didn't leave one in the bedroom.'

Spinnelli seemed intrigued by this. 'Why?'

'A specific rage for the Doughertys maybe,' Westphalen said. 'It was their bed.'

'Or he may have decided he got plenty of bang with one device, so why risk a second,' Reed countered. 'A common mistake of novice arsonists is leaving too many incendiary devices. They think one is good, so five is better. But if one of the five doesn't go off, it's evidence. Simplifying could be part of his learning curve. But we'll ask the Doughertys if they have any enemies.' He glanced at Mitchell. 'They called me this morning. I told them we'd meet them at their house sometime after nine.'

'That's fine.' She frowned though. 'Miles, if the Doughertys were the target, I'd agree. But if Caitlin was the victim, why the master bed? I mean, Caitlin was studying in the spare bedroom. What good did burning a bed she'd never touched do him?'

'It's a good question,' Westphalen admitted. 'Go talk to the Doughertys.'

'Other differences?' Spinnelli asked.

'He left Caitlin's car in the garage and used Penny Hill's to get away,' Reed said.

'It does seem like he's organizing his method,' Westphalen commented.

Spinnelli scribbled on the board. 'Jack?'

'We found blood spatter on the carpet we took from the Doughertys' house. Ben Trammell also found what could have been the metal button from her jeans. It was in the hall, in a crevice against the staircase. We didn't find any trace of her jeans in the hall, but they could have burned. If they did, we should find some remnants in the ash.'

'What about the gasoline?' Mitchell asked.

'None on the carpet. Only in the kitchen around where the body was found.'

'So he raped and shot her in the hall, then dragged her into the kitchen and doused her with gasoline.' Mitchell clenched her jaw. 'Sonofabitch.'

'Next of kin,' Spinnelli said. 'Have Penny Hill's been informed?'

'Not yet,' she said. 'I've called all the Mark Hills in Cincinnati, but none of them are related to Penny. Human Resources at Social Services will be at their desks in another half hour or so. I'll get contact information from them.'

Spinnelli sat down. 'Miles, can you give us a profile, or at least a place to start?'

Westphalen cast a cautious glance in Reed's direction. 'Lieutenant Solliday probably has a better understanding of arsonists.'

Reed gestured for him to continue, interested in what he had to say. 'Go ahead.'

Westphalen took off his glasses and polished the lenses with his handkerchief. 'Well, about twenty-five percent of arsonists are under fourteen and light fires for excitement or due to compulsion. I don't think that's the case here. Another twenty-five percent are fifteen to eighteen.' He shrugged. 'I don't want to believe a teenager could do this, but we all know they're capable. Rarely are arsonists over thirty years old. If they are, they're the torches the lieutenant mentioned – purely for profit. Adult arsonists who aren't for profit are almost always seeking revenge. The majority are white. Almost all are male. I'd almost guarantee this perpetrator has a record.'

'We couldn't find any prints,' Unger said. 'He didn't leave anything behind that we've found so far, so we have nothing to lead us to him or his record.'

Westphalen frowned. 'Well, when he leaves something behind, I'm betting you'll be able to link it to someone, somewhere in the system. The fact that he was seen driving away from Mrs Hill's house seconds before the explosion indicates he either planned the timing of his escape poorly or that he planned it well and has a high need for risk.'

'A high sensation seeker,' Mitchell said and Westphalen nodded.

'Perhaps. Arsonists in general have had an unstable childhood. Absent fathers, emotional abuse from the mother.'

Reed's jaw tightened. There it was. He'd known it was impossible for any psychologist not to blame upbringing. Westphalen's eyes met his and Reed could see the shrink had picked up on his irritation, but the older man just mildly continued. 'Many times arson is a stepping-stone for sex crimes,' Westphalen added. 'I've treated a number of sexual predators who have used arson as a means of sexual gratification early on. Then the fires aren't good enough anymore. They graduate to rape.'

'So you're not surprised that this guy would rape and burn,' Mitchell said.

Westphalen put his glasses back on. 'No, it doesn't surprise me at all. What does surprise me is that he didn't stick around to watch his fire burn. He plans such a giant blast and then doesn't stay for the performance.'

'I thought the same thing,' Reed agreed, stowing his irritation. 'I checked the crowd last night. I didn't see anybody in either crowd that didn't live in the neighborhood and I didn't see anybody last night that was at the Doughertys' fire.'

'What's next?' Spinnelli asked.

'I'll analyze the samples we took from Hill's house last night,' Unger said. 'I don't anticipate finding much in the kitchen, but we did sweep the front part of the house where there was less damage. I'm going to take a team back again this morning, to check things out in the daylight. If he left a hair and it didn't burn, we'll find it. Can I count on Ben Trammell, Reed? He was a huge asset yesterday.'

'Of course.'

'We'll talk to the Doughertys,' Mitchell said. She

looked up at Reed. 'Then I'd like to go back to Penny Hill's house, too.'

'We should also go back to the university. We need to know who else knew where Caitlin would be or if anyone was seen around campus that didn't belong.'

'And then to the arcade to check out Joel Rebinowitz's alibi. I drove by after I left Penny Hill's last night, but they were closed. They open again at noon.' Mitchell looked over at Spinnelli. 'We need a court order for Penny's files and I still need Burnette's case files. Can you send Stacy to get them?'

Spinnelli scratched a note on his notepad. 'I'll take care of the court order. How far back do you want Stacy to go?'

She looked over at Westphalen. 'What do you think, Miles? A year?'

The old man shrugged. 'It's a place to start. I don't know, Mia.'

'Me, either,' she said grimly. 'We can stop by Social Services and get access to Hill's records on the way back then we cross-check until something common pops.'

'Reed, have you run a database check for similar fires?' Spinnelli asked.

'Yep. I ran queries through the BATS database, Sunday morning and again this morning before I came. BATS is the Bomb Arson Tracking System that's maintained by the ATF,' he added in response to Mitchell's puzzled look. 'I got a lot of hits on solid accelerants, but mostly in commercial properties. I didn't get any hits when I added in the murders. I got thousands when I queried trash-can fires. I set up a query to run automatically a few times a day in case our guy does something like this somewhere else. We'll see.'

Spinnelli frowned. 'So basically our best bet is finding a link between our own cases at this point. Update me before you leave for the day, Mia. Good luck.' He and Unger left the room, but Westphalen hung back, aimlessly fiddling with his tie.

'You don't believe in the impact of home life on criminals,' Westphalen said, his voice still mild. Reed hated shrinks' 'mild' voice. It was like fingernails on a chalkboard.

'I think it's society's panacea,' he said, not nearly as mildly. 'Everybody's got issues, Doctor. Some people get dealt a harder deck than others. Too bad. Good people deal with it and become productive citizens. Bad people don't. It's that simple.'

Mitchell looked at him, her blue eyes curious, but said nothing. Westphalen pulled on his overcoat. 'Such conviction.'

'Yes,' Reed answered, knowing his answer was curt and not giving a damn. Shrinks used ploys like that to learn things most sane people would rather keep private.

'We'll have to talk more someday,' Westphalen said, mild amusement in his voice, then he turned to Mitchell with a warm smile. 'I'm glad to see you back, Mia. It wasn't the same around here without you. Don't go getting shot again, okay?'

Her mouth curved, her affection for the old man obvious. 'I'll do my damnedest, Miles. Say hi to the missus.' When Westphalen was gone, she looked up. He thought she'd press him on why he'd been so curt with the shrink. But she didn't, simply gathered her notes. 'You ready to roll, Solliday? The faster we talk to the Doughertys and check out Penny Hill's house, the faster we can get to the files, which is my absolute favorite part of the job.' Her sarcasm said it was anything but.

'I thought threatening belligerent boys with bullies named Bubba was.'

She grinned unexpectedly and his heart lifted a little, the sour mood brought on by the shrink fading away. 'Not bad, Solliday. Added a few more poetic words there. Not bad at all. Let's stop by a drive-through on the way to the Doughertys'. I'm starving.'

Tuesday, November 28, 8:45 A.M.

He blinked down at the front page of the newspaper. Wow, the reporter moved fast. He hadn't expected to see the story until tomorrow. But there it was on the front page of the *Bulletin* – SERIAL ARSONIST/MURDERER AT LARGE.

I'm not all that large, he thought and smiled at his own joke.

They'd named Penny Hill as the victim right off the bat. None of the 'withholding name of the victim pending family notification' crap. He read on and frowned. Somebody had seen him driving away. Well, they couldn't identify him even if they did since he'd been wearing the ski mask. It wouldn't matter if they'd seen the license plates of the car – they belonged to Penny Hill herself.

'The victim was Penny Hill, forty-seven years old.' Hmm. She looked pretty good for an old lady. At least she had. Once again he chuckled. Now she looked like a marshmallow left in the fire too long.

At least he imagined she did. What he really wanted was to see the body. To see the house. To see the destruction he'd caused. But that wasn't prudent as long as the law was on the case. So who was chasing him? He scanned the article. Lieutenant Reed Solliday, OFI. A lieutenant. They'd sent a higher-up looking for him. None of this junior G-man shit. Good. This Solliday was decorated. Experienced. He'd prove a worthy adversary. That just meant he'd have to work hard to keep his work area clean. Leave nothing for the good lieutenant and his partner to find. So who was his partner?

His lips curled into a sneer. Detective Mia Mitchell. A woman? They'd actually picked a woman to try to find him?

They'll never catch me in a million years. But overconfidence would not be his downfall. He'd plan and act as if two qualified men chased him. But he'd sleep easy.

He tore the article from the paper and scanned it a last time. They mentioned Caitlin. He'd missed it the first time, so anxious had he been to see Penny Hill's name in print. 'The victim of the first fire is nineteen-year-old Caitlin Burnette, daughter of Sergeant Roger Burnette—' His heart nearly stopped. 'A twenty-year veteran of CPD.'

Shit. He'd killed the kid of a *cop*. What was the daughter of a cop doing there anyway? *Shit*. Furious, he shoved the article into his book, along with the one on the Dougherty fire from yesterday's *Trib* and the other one from Friday's Springdale *Gazette* on the Thanksgiving fire. *Shit*. The police would hunt him now, like he was a dog. He swept all his things into his bag with one angry swoop. Dammit. This totally *sucked*.

He headed for the door, his heart racing as fear set in. *I have to stop.*

Then he stopped in his tracks. *No*. He couldn't stop. He wouldn't stop. He was doing this for his own future. *The anger has to go, remember? You can't stop until you're done. Or it would be like . . . like not finishing a bottle of antibiotics. It'll just be worse, stronger, more powerful the next time*. The next time he could lose his head and get caught. But right now, he was in full control. He hadn't lost his head last night, nor would he. He was conscious of every action. He was thinking smarter. Working smarter.

He wouldn't stop. Not till he was done. He'd have to

be fast not to get caught. He'd have to be perfect. But right now, he had someplace to be. He had to be on time.

Tuesday, November 28, 9:05 A.M.

Mia was folding her breakfast sandwich wrapper when they pulled in front of what had once been the Doughertys' home. A middle-aged couple stood on the curb staring up at the blackened structure in shock. 'I think that's the Doughertys,' Mia said quietly.

'I'd say you were right.' Solliday blew out a sigh. 'Let's get this done.'

Mr Dougherty turned as they approached. 'You're Lieutenant Solliday?'

'I am.' He shook hands with the man, then his wife. 'This is Detective Mitchell.'

The couple exchanged a worried glance. 'I don't understand,' Dougherty said.

'I'm with the Homicide division,' Mia said. 'Caitlin Burnette was murdered before the fire was started in your house.'

Mrs Dougherty gave a strangled cry, her hand covering her mouth. 'Oh God.'

His face horrified, her husband put his arm around her. 'Do her parents know?'

Mia nodded. 'Yes. We informed them yesterday.'

'We know this is a bad time,' Solliday said. 'But we have to ask some questions.'

'Wait.' Dougherty shook his head, as if to clear his thoughts. 'You said the fire was *started*, Detective. This was arson?'

Solliday nodded. 'We found incendiary devices in the kitchen and your bedroom.'

Mr Dougherty cleared his throat. 'I know this sounds insensitive and please be sure we'll do everything in our power to help you . . . But what do we do now? Can we contact our insurance company? We don't have a place to live.'

Beside him, Mrs Dougherty swallowed convulsively. 'Was anything left?'

'Not much,' Solliday answered. 'Contact your insurance company. Just to prepare you, they'll be conducting an investigation.'

Now Mr Dougherty swallowed. 'Are we suspects?'

'We'll rule you out as quickly as possible,' Mia interjected calmly.

Mr Dougherty nodded. 'When can we go in to see what we can salvage?'

'Our wedding photos . . .' Mrs Dougherty's voice broke and her eyes again filled with tears. 'I'm sorry. I know Caitlin's . . . But, Joe . . . Everything's gone.'

Dougherty rested his cheek on the top of his wife's head. 'It'll be all right, Donna. We'll get through this, just like we got through everything else.' He met Solliday's gaze. 'I assume either you or the insurance company will be checking our financial records.'

'That's standard practice,' Solliday confirmed. 'If

you've got something to tell us, this is a good time, sir.'

'We were sued five years ago. A customer fell in our hardware store.' Dougherty's mouth twisted. 'The jury found in favor of the plaintiff. We lost everything.'

'It's taken us five years to dig our way out,' Mrs Dougherty said wearily.

'When my dad retired two years ago, he sold us his house, cheap.' Bitterly he looked up at the ruins. 'We were starting all over again. Took our first vacation in years. And now this. We had the minimum insurance on this place. Just enough to get a policy. There's no financial incentive for us to destroy our own home.'

'Where do you work now, Mr Dougherty?' Solliday asked.

'At a home improvement superstore.' Again his mouth twisted. 'I'm in charge of nuts and bolts. My boss is a kid half my age. My wife is a secretary. She takes in sewing to make ends meet. We're not rich people, but we did not do this.'

'Mr Dougherty,' Mia said quietly and the man met her eyes without flinching. 'Can you think of anyone who'd have a grudge against you and your wife, specifically?'

'Besides the kook that sued us?' He shook his head. 'No. We kept to ourselves.'

'The neighbors said you changed all the locks on the doors,' Solliday commented and Mia glanced up at him. His expression was calmly unreadable.

'Emily Richter,' Mr Dougherty bit out. 'The biggest

busybody. My parents always asked her to watch the house when they went away. I didn't want her in my house.'

'She would have gone through our things,' Mrs Dougherty said. 'And then told everyone about our finances. She was angry when we got the house at such a bargain.'

Mia took out her notebook. 'Who was the kook who sued you?'

Mr Dougherty peered over the top of her notebook. 'Reggie Fagin. Why?'

She smiled at him. 'Just asking the questions. May save me some time later.'

'You never told us when we can go into our house,' Mr Dougherty said.

'We'll get you back in as quickly as possible,' Mia assured them without giving a real answer. They seemed like nice people, but she'd check them out, just the same. 'Do you have any valuables you'd like us to hold in the meantime?'

'My wedding album,' Mrs Dougherty said. 'Other than that, I can't think right now.'

Mr Dougherty's face changed, abruptly. 'Um . . . We have a gun, upstairs in our nightstand drawer. It's registered,' he added defensively.

Solliday looked surprised. 'I didn't find any guns registered in your name.'

Mia looked up at him, surprised herself that he'd checked.

'It's registered in my maiden name,' Mrs Dougherty said. 'Lawrence. I bought it before we got married. It's just a .22, but I'd hate for it to fall into the wrong hands.'

'Excuse us a minute,' Mia said and motioned Solliday with her head.

He followed her, his jaw tight. 'No, I didn't find a gun,' he muttered before she could ask. 'And I looked in that nightstand drawer.'

'Shit. He could have brought his own gun and then found theirs.'

'Or Caitlin could have found it when she was up there studying and he took it during the struggle. He may have come unarmed. We could be back to Caitlin as an accident. Wrong place, wrong time.'

'This muddies everything,' she grumbled. As one they turned back to the waiting couple. 'We didn't find your gun,' Mia said. 'We'll report it stolen for you.'

The couple looked at each other, then back, dread in their eyes. 'Was Caitlin killed with our gun?' Mr Dougherty asked heavily.

'We don't know,' Solliday said. 'Was it loaded?'

Numbly Mrs Dougherty nodded. 'I kept it loaded with the safety on. I never fired it except at the firing range, and that's been . . . years.'

'Did you know a woman named Penny Hill?' Mia asked and both shook their heads.

'I'm sorry, that name doesn't ring any bells,' Mr Dougherty said. 'Why?'

'Just asking the questions.' Mia smiled again to calm them. 'Might help me later.'

'I'll see if I can find your wedding album. Anything else?' Solliday asked.

'I know this sounds horrible, what with Caitlin . . .' Mrs Dougherty's eyes were filled with a combination of anxiety and guilt. 'My cat, Percy, was in the house. He's a white Persian. Did . . .' She drew a breath. 'Did you find him?'

Sympathy flickered in Solliday's dark eyes. 'No, ma'am, we didn't. If we do, we'll let you know. I'll be right back, Detective.'

Mia turned back to the couple. 'Where will you be staying?'

'For now, we're at the Beacon Inn.' Mr Dougherty's brief smile was entirely without mirth. 'I guess we're not supposed to leave town.'

'For now, it would be easier if I or the lieutenant could contact you when we need you,' Mia agreed neutrally. 'Here's my card. Call me if you think of anything else.'

'Detective.' Mrs Dougherty was tentative. 'The Burnettes . . . Ellen is a friend of mine. How are they?'

'As well as you can expect under the circumstances.'

'I can't even imagine,' she murmured.

They were silent then, waiting for Solliday's return. Minutes passed and Mia frowned. He should have been back by now. He'd stressed how dangerous the compromised structure was, but she'd heard nothing to indicate the roof had fallen in on his head. Still . . . 'Excuse me,' she said. Halfway up the driveway she stopped, her eyes widening as Solliday appeared from around the back. 'What the hell is that?'

Solliday grimaced at the filthy bundle he held at arm's length. 'Somewhere under all this dirt is a white Persian. He was curled up against the back door in the mud.'

Mia grinned up at him. He seemed so disgusted. 'That's so nice of you.'

'No. I'm mean. Hateful. Take it. He stinks.'

'No way.' She laughed. 'I'm allergic to dirty cats.'

'My shoes are dirty,' he complained and she laughed again.

She turned to Mrs Dougherty. 'It appears the prodigal cat has been found. Whoa,' she said as Mrs Dougherty ran up, hope in her eyes. 'For now, this cat is evidence.'

'Excuse me?' the Doughertys said together.

Solliday just scowled and kept the cat as far away from his trench coat as he could.

Mia sobered. 'Whoever did this must have let him out or Percy slipped out when he was breaking in or leaving. We'll take him in, give him a bath and check him out. We might be lucky and get some physical evidence. If not, we'll return him to you quickly.'

'He's probably hungry,' Mrs Dougherty said, biting her lip.

'We'll feed him.' Mia's lips twitched. 'Won't we, Lieutenant?'

Solliday's eyes narrowed in a way that promised retribution. 'Sure.' He held out a padded album that had also once been white. 'Your wedding pictures have a good bit of water damage, but a restorer might be able to salvage some of them.'

Mrs Dougherty let out a shuddering breath. 'Thank you, Lieutenant.'

Solliday's scowl softened. 'It's okay. See if you can find a box for Percy. I don't want him making a mess in my truck.'

Tuesday, November 28, 9:25 A.M.

Thad Lewin was back. Brooke leaned against her desk as she watched the students take their places. Mike pulled his chair to the back, Jeff lounged and Manny said nothing at all. But it was Thad she watched. The boy was normally shy, but today was different. Today his head was down, his steps shuffling. He lowered himself to his chair, tenderly. Brooke blinked, not liking the picture that was beginning to form in her mind. She glanced at Jeff, who lifted one side of his mouth in a cruel amusement that made her blood go cold.

'Mornin', Teacher,' he drawled. 'Looks like the gang's all here.'

She didn't drop her gaze, challenging him silently until his eyes slid down to her breasts. *God help us when he gets out.* It was a common phrase uttered by every teacher, male and female. She thought about what Devin said last night, that Jeff would reoffend and be back in jail within a month of leaving this place.

She didn't want to be on the receiving end of that offense. 'Open your books,' she said. 'Today we're going to talk about chapter three.'

Chapter Eight

Tuesday, November 28, 9:45 A.M.

Reed was just happy to get his hands clean. He came out of the men's room at the convenience store still scowling at his shoes. He should have changed them before going into that house. That's why he kept several pairs in the back of his truck.

Nasty cat. Covered in mud and a number of other things best left unidentified, it was currently being restrained in the box on Mitchell's lap. From where he stood, Reed could see her in the truck, her elbows propped on the box, face intent as she talked on her cell phone. She'd been on hold with Social Services when he'd come in to wash up, waiting for information on Penny Hill's next of kin. Now her expression changed, grew softer. Pained. She was informing Hill's son, some three hundred miles away. But her face had looked like that when she'd informed the Burnettes in person.

Hill's family wasn't just an entry in Mia Mitchell's notebook. She'd insisted on using Penny Hill's name, rather than *the victim*. She cared. He liked that.

A yawn cracked his jaw. It had been a sleepless night and an afternoon of reading the fine print of case files loomed. He carried two cups of coffee to the cash register, then froze as his eyes dropped to the stack of newspapers at his feet.

'Will that be all?' the cashier asked.

Reed glanced up, then back down to the paper. 'The coffee and a paper. Thanks.'

When he got outside, she'd finished her call and was staring straight ahead. But when he knocked on her window she was quick to respond, rolling it down so she could take the coffee from his hands. 'What's that?' she asked, looking at the paper.

'Your friend Carmichael. She was following you last night.'

'Dammit,' she said, scanning the page. 'It's not the first time she's followed me to a crime scene. It's like she has radar or something. I wonder when the woman sleeps.'

'*I* wonder where she was hiding. I checked the crowd. I should have seen her.'

'She seems able to disappear. If she saw us, she would have hidden.'

Reed started the engine. 'How'd she get the story in this morning's edition?'

One side of her mouth lifted wryly. 'The *Bulletin* goes to press at one A.M.'

'You know this from experience.'

She shrugged. 'Like I said, it's not the first time. Looks like she's got a couple of big stories on the front page. The fire is above the fold and me tackling DuPree yesterday afternoon is below.' She made a hissing sound. 'She named Penny Hill. Dammit.'

He'd seen that. 'You were able to inform the family before they found out?'

She looked glum as she read on. 'The son, yes. Not the daughter.'

'It says the authorities were unavailable for comment.'

'Which means she called me on my office line while I was at the scene. She's a real piece of work.' She sighed. 'The neighbors talked, after I asked them not to.'

'Some people like to see their name in print.'

'Hopefully you do, because you're in the article, too.' She busied herself adding cream to her coffee, using the box on her lap as a tray. 'Stay still, cat,' she muttered when the box shifted. 'Says here that you're decorated. So dish, Solliday.'

'A few citations, like yours. Next stop is the lab so we can get rid of that cat.'

Mitchell patted the box. 'Poor kitty.'

'Dirty kitty.' Reed pulled out into traffic. 'That cat reeks.'

She laughed. 'He does have a certain . . . bouquet. What, don't you like animals?'

'Clean ones, yes. My daughter has a puppy. Big muddy paws all over everything.'

'I always wanted a pet.' She said it almost wistfully.

'So get one.'

'Too much guilt. I tried goldfish once. Kind of a test. I failed. I pulled a thirty-six-hour shift and when I got home I was so tired I forgot to feed it. Fluffy ended up floating.'

He had to smile. 'Fluffy? You named a goldfish Fluffy?'

'I didn't. My friend Dana's foster kids did. It was kind of a group effort. Anyway, all my friends have pets so I just play with theirs. That way I can't hurt anything.' She sipped her coffee, quiet for so long that he turned to look at her. Immediately she straightened her back, as if she'd realized her thoughts had drifted. 'Penny Hill's son said he'd drive up to claim his mother's body. He'll be here tomorrow morning.'

'What about Hill's daughter? The neighbor thought she lived in Milwaukee.'

'The son said his sister got divorced recently and moved back to Chicago.'

'Do you have her address?'

'Yeah. She's about a half hour from here.'

'Then let's drop off Percy and pay her a visit.'

Mitchell sighed. 'I just hope she doesn't read the *Bulletin*.'

Tuesday, November 28, 12:10 P.M.

Manny Rodriguez looked both ways before throwing the newspaper into the garbage outside the cafeteria. Behind Brooke, Julian swore softly. 'You were right,' he said.

'I saw him with the newspaper at the end of first period. You want to fish it out?'

Julian lifted the lid. 'This is the *Bulletin*. Yesterday was the *Trib*.'

'Both are available at the front desk,' she said.

'Well, whatever he cut out was front-page news. You go eat your lunch. I'll check to see what Mr Rodriguez was reading. It could just be an article about sports.'

'Do you really think so?'

He shook his head. 'No. Did you have any issues with him today during class?'

'No. He was actually very quiet. He didn't say a word, even when we started talking about the signal fire in the book. It was like he was bothered by something.'

'I'll talk to him. Thank you, Brooke. I really appreciate your help in this.'

With a frown Brooke watched Julian walk away. He didn't seem very worried by any of this. *Maybe I'm just green,* she thought. *Maybe I'm just making a big deal out of nothing.* But she didn't think so. She wondered what other items Manny collected. She wondered if Julian would have Manny's room searched. If he didn't, he should. *I would.*

'Brooke? Is something wrong?' Devin was coming out of the cafeteria.

'I'm just worried about Manny. He's clipping newspaper articles about arson.'

Devin frowned. 'That doesn't sound good. Did you tell Julian?'

'Yes, but he doesn't seem very concerned. What does it take to have a student's room searched?'

'A valid concern. I'd say yours qualifies, Brooke. Talk to the security dean. He'd want to know something like this.'

Brooke considered Bart Secrest, the dour-faced head of security. He made her nervous. 'Julian might think I'm going around him.'

'He'll understand. Let me know if you want me to go with you to talk to Bart later. Bart looks mean, but he's really a cream puff.'

'A cream puff.' She shook her head. 'Sour cream maybe.'

Devin just grinned. 'Talk to Bart. His bark is far worse than his bite.'

Tuesday, November 28, 12:30 P.M.

Jack's team was at Penny Hill's house when she and Solliday got there. Instead of Jack's normal smile, she was met with a scowl. 'Thanks a lot, Mia.'

She blinked at him. 'What?'

'What were you thinking, dropping a damn cat off at the lab?'

Mia's lips twitched. 'He's evidence, Jack.'

Jack's scowl deepened. 'You ever try to bathe a cat?'

'Nope,' she said cheerfully. 'I'm bad with pets.'

Behind her Solliday chuckled. 'Just ask Fluffy the goldfish.'

Jack rolled his eyes. 'Next time you drop off a live animal, call first, okay?' He motioned them to follow him. 'Cover your feet. We think we found something.'

CSU had gridded off the kitchen and Ben was sifting through debris near the stove. Ben looked up, sweat running lines through the grime on his face. 'Hey, Reed. Detective.'

'Ben.' Solliday looked around with a frown. 'You find anything?'

'More egg fragments, just like the other house. I sent them to the lab to see if there were any pieces big enough for prints. And then there's the floor. Show 'em, Jack.'

Jack stopped near where they'd found Hill's body. He ran a gloved finger along the floor and showed them a finely ground dust, dark brown.

Mia immediately sensed a change in Solliday as he grabbed Jack's hand and held it up to the light. 'Blood,' he said, then looked back at Mia. 'Or it was. At temperatures of this fire, the proteins begin to degrade. It was too dark to see this last night.'

'There was a lot of blood,' Jack said. 'It soaked through the seams in the linoleum.'

Mia stared at the floor, in her mind seeing Hill's body as they'd found it, curled up in a fetal ball, her wrists still bound together. 'So he shot her, too?'

Jack shrugged. 'Barrington could tell you for sure.'

'You find any prints in that blood?' she asked.

'No.' Jack stood up. 'We haven't found any prints anywhere. He probably wore gloves. But . . .' He led them to the front door. 'Look here.'

The doorknob had a brown smear. 'He came out this way with bloody hands,' Solliday said. 'It's consistent with the neighbor's story. He heard tires squeal, then saw Hill's car tearing down the street.'

Jack tapped the air above the newel post. 'Now look here.'

Mia got close to the wood, then looked up at Solliday. 'Brown hair caught in the wood grain. They fought here.'

'Just like Caitlin,' Solliday murmured.

'We'll bag that and take it in,' Jack said. 'The brown hair has gray roots, so I'm thinking it's your victim's and not the killer's. Sorry.'

'I wouldn't think she'd be strong enough to knock his head into the newel post,' Mia agreed as she pushed at the front door, checking out the tree-lined front porch. The evergreens had been badly burned but neighbors had told her that the trees had been full and thick. 'You didn't find any evidence of forced entry on the back door, did you?'

'None,' Jack confirmed.

'Char patterns indicate the back door was closed through the fire,' Solliday added.

'Then he probably came in through the front. He could have easily concealed himself behind those trees and waited for her to come home. It's late. She's tired. I talked to her supervisor this morning when I called to get her next-of-kin info. He said she'd had a little too much of the punch at her retirement party. When I first called he thought I was calling to say she'd been hauled in for DUI.'

'So she's unsteady on her feet,' Jack said. 'He waits for her to open the front door, then pushes in behind her and knocks her into the post.'

'He surprised Caitlin inside the house. He was waiting for Penny outside in the cold. Why didn't he just break in?' Mia scanned the wall. 'I don't see an alarm panel.'

'There isn't one,' Solliday said. 'Here or on the back door.'

'That doesn't make sense,' she said with a frown. 'He waits for her *outside* in twenty-degree weather, pushes his way in, overpowers her, then forces her to the kitchen where he shoots her, sets the place on fire, then steals her car.'

'We found her car yet?' Jack asked.

'Not yet.' Mia looked around the foyer. 'Did you sweep this area?'

'Twice,' Jack said dryly. 'Debris's on its way to the lab.'

She ignored his tone. 'Did you find a shopping bag of presents? Or a briefcase?'

'No, neither.'

'Her supervisor said she left the party at 11:15 last night with a bag full of gifts and her briefcase. He thought we'd find her Day Planner in the briefcase.'

'It was late,' Solliday said. 'Maybe she left the bags in her car.'

'Maybe.' Mia drew in a breath. 'I'd sure as hell like to have her Day Planner.'

Jack made a sympathetic grimace. 'No chance she had GPS in her car?'

'No. Her car was ten years old and her son said she didn't have any fancy electronics.' She blew out a breath. 'I'm still stuck on why he waited for her here. Why didn't he break in the back door like he did at the Doughertys' house? It's not like she had a big . . . Hell. Wait.' Quickly she walked back to the kitchen, and carefully stepped her way across the grid to the cabinet. It had collapsed along with the counter. Glass and ceramic pieces littered the floor. 'Did you check through this stuff yet, Ben?'

'Not yet,' Ben said.

Mia crouched down and started picking through the pottery.

Jack crouched down next to her. 'What are you looking for?'

'Something like . . . this.' She pulled a thick fragment out of the pile, between her thumb and forefinger. She wiped the fragment clean and held it up. 'Paw print.'

Solliday sucked in one cheek. 'A dog dish. She had a dog.'

'Who is AWOL,' Mia said flatly. 'I don't get this guy. He lies in wait for this woman, shoots her and leaves her to burn, but he spares the dog just like he spared Percy.'

'He doesn't fit the profile,' Solliday said. 'Most arsonists would have killed the pets.'

'None of the neighbors mentioned a dog,' Mia said. 'Why not?'

Solliday's brows rose. 'Let's ask them.'

'I have Mr Wright's number.' She dialed her cell. 'Mr Wright? This is Detective Mitchell. I talked to you last night. I have a question. Did Mrs Hill have a dog?'

'No, but her daughter did. I didn't even think . . . Oh, God, that poor animal. He was a nice dog, too. Her daughter's apartment didn't allow dogs, so Penny kept the dog.'

'Daughter's dog,' Mia mouthed. 'What kind of dog is it, Mr Wright?'

'Golden retriever, Great Dane mix. He was huge, but friendly. Penny would joke . . .'

Mia could hear him take a shuddering breath. 'She would joke what?' she asked.

'That the dog was so friendly it would lead a burglar to the silver for a Milk-Bone.'

'Mr Wright, if you see him wandering the neighborhood, can you call me? Thank you.' She hung up with a sigh. 'Big dog. Dane-golden mix. That's why he waited. The dog was big. He thought he was vicious.'

'But he didn't shoot him when he had the chance,' Solliday commented.

'Have you talked to the daughter?' Jack asked.

'No. I called a half dozen times and we stopped by her apartment, but the landlord said she hadn't been home since Saturday morning. Her car's gone.'

'You checked the inside of her place?'

'Under the circumstances we thought it was prudent,' Solliday said. 'But she wasn't there. Her answering machine was flashing with a number of calls. Mia called for a warrant, so if we don't hear from her in a few hours, we'll go back.'

Mia blinked, a little startled at hearing him use her first name. He'd started calling Jack by his first name, too. Apparently the lieutenant was feeling more at home. Unfortunately Mia wasn't ready to let him settle in. She was still Abe's partner.

But before she could reply, Solliday's cell phone rang. 'It's Barrington,' he told them. 'What do you have, Sam?' He listened for a moment. 'We'll be right down.' He flipped his phone closed, his mouth gone flat. 'He's got something.'

Tuesday, November 28, 1:35 P.M.

'He's autopsying somebody else's case right now,' Sam's tech told them, motioning to the door. 'You can go in and talk to him through the glass.'

'Can't he come out here?' Mitchell asked, then squared her jaw. 'I just ate, okay?'

The tech chuckled. 'I'll tell him you're here.'

'Hill's body is going to be worse than an autopsy,' Reed cautioned quietly.

'I know. I remember.' She closed her eyes for a second, just long enough for a shudder to shake her. 'I hate to watch them cutting. I know it makes me a wuss, but—'

'It's all right, Mia,' he interrupted.

'So we're on a first-name basis now,' she said. 'I thought you'd slipped before. You must have decided to keep me after all,' she added, her voice hard with sarcasm.

'The first time was a slip,' he admitted. 'But why stand on formality now?'

'Why indeed?' she murmured, then turned as Sam emerged, pulling at the surgical mask he wore. 'What do you have?' she asked.

Sam walked to a sheet-covered body. 'Your vic had carbon monoxide in her lungs.'

'Whoa,' she said.

'Wait,' Reed said at the same time. 'CSU found blood at the scene. We thought he'd shot her like he shot Caitlin Burnette.'

'No. X-rays show skull shattering, consistent with the pressure caused by the high temperature. No vent holes this time. She was alive when the fire started.'

Mitchell's brows had snapped together. 'How long was she alive?'

'Carbon monoxide levels indicate maybe two to five minutes. Not much more.'

Reed was almost afraid to ask. 'Was she conscious?'

'I didn't find any evidence of pre-mortem head trauma.'

Mitchell's face had gone a bit pale. Reed drew a breath, unable to imagine the pain the woman must have experienced if she had been conscious. Grasping at straws, he asked, 'Is it possible she was drugged, Sam?'

'I've sent out for a tox screen to look for drugs in her system. Her bladder was essentially destroyed, so I couldn't do a urine tox. The blood samples I took indicated a blood alcohol level of .08. That's a lot of alcohol for a woman of her size.'

'She'd been to a party,' Mitchell murmured, then straightened her spine and strengthened her voice. 'If he didn't shoot her, then where did the blood come from?'

Carefully Barrington pulled back the sheet and Reed felt Mitchell tense beside him. 'I have to be careful,' Barrington said. 'The body's very fragile. But come here.' He moved to one side, motioning them closer. 'Look at her arms.'

Hill's torso was black, but her arms and legs were blistered, the skin loose and . . . Reed's stomach took a roll and beside him, Mitchell's swallow was audible.

'God,' she murmured, then again straightened. 'Her arms looked blacker before.'

'Soot. We had to swab the skin. Her torso took the greatest brunt of the fire. It's really difficult to totally destroy an adult body in a house fire,' Barrington said, as if lecturing med school students. 'The body is composed of so much water.'

'He coated her torso with the solid accelerant, but not her limbs,' Reed said quietly.

'I found ammonium nitrate on her torso. It was helpful knowing what to look for.'

'The blood, Barrington?' Mitchell bit out. 'Where did the blood come from?'

Unperturbed, Sam pointed to his own inner arm, just above his elbow. 'He cut her brachial artery, here. If you look closely, you can see the skin curls in around the slice.'

'He sliced her?' Mitchell shot a puzzled look up at Reed, then back at Sam, her eyes narrowed. 'How long would it have taken her to bleed out?'

'Two to five minutes,' Sam said.

Mitchell's face hardened. 'Sonofabitch. He wanted her to bleed out slowly. Shooting would have been too merciful.'

Reed exhaled slowly. 'He wanted her to feel the pain. He burned her alive.'

'How long would she have been conscious?' she asked between her teeth.

'Without drugs? A few minutes. It's hard to say.'

'Her hands are intact,' Reed said. 'Did you check them?'

'Yes, but I didn't find anything. If she scratched at him, she didn't get skin.'

'Did you check her teeth?' Mitchell asked and Sam shook his head.

'Not yet, but I will.'

Mitchell blew out a breath. 'What kind of knife are we looking for?'

'Probably not serrated, but very sharp. There's no evidence of sawing, just a slice.'

Mitchell stepped back from the body. 'We'll need to see if any knives are missing from Penny Hill's house. Hopefully her daughter will know what she had in her kitchen.'

Reed checked his watch. 'Your clerk should have pulled Burnette's case records by now. Let's go by Social Services and get Hill's records, then we can start cross-checking.'

She took one long last look at Hill's body, her jaw tight. 'Yeah. Let's go see who hated Penny Hill enough to do this.'

Tuesday, November 28, 3:15 P.M.

Mia's arm was throbbing, but she gritted her teeth as she held on to the box of Social Services files. Solliday carried the heavier box, his expression grimly stark as hers must also be. It was as if their moods had combined into one dark cloud. After leaving the morgue, she'd felt angrier than hell. But now, she felt completely drained.

Penny Hill had been well loved. The grief at Social Services had been palpable. Phones rang and social workers moved through their daily business, but there had been a hush over the place. Like in a church before a funeral. Or at a graveside after.

The elevator slid open and Mia walked into the bullpen, counting the seconds until she could drop the heavy box, but she stopped short at the sight of her desk, piled high with more boxes. Abe's desk, conversely, was still well-ordered and immaculately clean, with not a folder to be seen.

'God save me from pissy clerks,' she muttered. Stacy had been miffed that Mia hadn't been more appreciative of her desk-cleaning efforts. Now Mia couldn't see her desk at all. Without a word she marched to her desk and dropped the box on the floor. Solliday more sedately slid his box onto Abe's desk and sank into Abe's chair. Before she could quell the reflex, Mia's hand stretched out, a protest rising in her throat. 'No.'

Solliday's head lifted and his eyes met hers as her cheeks heated.

'I'm sorry,' she said. 'That was stupid.'

His lips curved inside his goatee. 'I promise I won't put my dirty shoes on his desk,' he said, and the wry humor in his voice made her smile as she dropped into her chair.

'I am sorry. Abe would want you comfortable. It's just that I haven't been so tired in a long time.'

'I know. We were up most of the night. And then . . . that kind of grief.' He pulled a stack of files from his box. 'It drains the very life out of your soul.'

Mia blinked. 'That sounded remarkably poetic, Solliday. I mean . . . like a real poem. Not like my "bully named Bubba."'

His eyes dropped to the files. 'How do you want to handle these?' he asked and struck with curiosity, she leaned forward. His cheeks were decidedly red.

'Solliday. You're blushing.'

He cocked his jaw to one side, stubbornly refusing to meet her eyes and Mia found herself thoroughly charmed. 'Let's go through the files Hill's boss cherry-picked first,' he said.

'Ah, yes. The many arsonists Penny Hill tried to place in foster care. We need a system or we're never going to find a connection. How about you write down all the names you come across in Hill's files, I'll do Burnette's. In an hour we break and compare.' She frowned at the boxes. 'If I can figure out where to start.'

He reached into his pocket and pulled out a bottle of pain reliever. 'Start with this. You make me hurt just looking at you. You carried in that damn box like you didn't have a hole in your shoulder.' He tossed the bottle across their desks and Mia caught it.

'Are you always such a mother?' she asked.

He looked surprised. 'No, I'm a father. Why can only mothers make you take medicine?'

'Because—' She bit her tongue. *Because fathers are the reason you have to take medicine in the first place. Mothers just give you a pill and tell you not to provoke him anymore.* She grabbed the top file and started reading. 'Let's just get to work, okay?'

She could feel his eyes on her, watching, but in the end he said nothing, just settled himself into Abe's chair and began to read.

Tuesday, November 28, 4:00 P.M.

Bart Secrest was a scary-looking man. Kind of like Mr Clean, but mean. His office was dark and stark, without one picture or personal memento to soften his image.

Brooke took the chair he offered with a silent gesture.

'You did the right thing, Miss Adler,' he said without preamble.

'I didn't want to cross Julian.' Who'd been livid over the search of Manny's room.

'Julian will live,' Bart said in a tone that made Brooke think there was no love lost between them. 'You were right to worry about Manny Rodriguez, Miss Adler.'

'So you found something?'

He nodded. 'Lots of stories about fires.'

'Local fires, like the two articles I saw him clip?'

'No, those were the only local articles. The others were more how-to.'

'Oh Lord. He was collecting articles on how to set fires?'

'He was.' Secrest leaned back in his chair. 'And we found a pack of matches hidden in one of his shoes. Obviously smuggled in from somewhere.'

She frowned. 'But we're in lockdown. How could something get smuggled in?'

'Every castle has a bolt-hole, Miss Adler.'

She blinked at him. 'Excuse me?'

His smile was brief and somehow still made him look mean. 'Every institution has a supply pipeline for contraband. Even this one. But I'll find it. That I guarantee.'

He stood and she guessed the interview was over. 'Well . . . good night.'

His answer was a curt nod as she backed out of his door. She'd turned the corner toward the main entrance when she heard her name. Julian was standing outside his office, looking furious. 'Brooke, what the hell have you done?'

Brooke straightened her spine. She'd done the right thing. Bart Secrest said so. 'I reported suspicious behavior, Julian. The way you were supposed to.'

Julian came closer until he was practically standing on her toes. He leaned over her, invading her space and tickling her nose with the aroma of pipe tobacco that lingered in his jacket. 'You insolent little . . .' He hissed a breath between his clenched teeth. 'Don't you dare tell me what I should have done. You have ruined months of progress with that boy. Months. Thanks to you, any trust I'd built with him is gone.'

Brooke's heart was hammering so hard she thought he could hear it. He was big and way too close and breathing her air. Still she lifted her chin and stared up at him defiantly. 'You said he wouldn't start any fires here at the school.'

'And he wouldn't have.'

She shook her head. 'Secrest found matches in his room.'

Julian narrowed his eyes. 'Not possible.'

'Talk to Secrest. He'll tell you. Manny could have started a fire that put every teacher and student in danger. I did the right thing, even if you don't agree.'

Shaking from head to toe but proud she hadn't caved and apologized, she made it to her car and drew a deep breath as she buckled herself in. Hands trembling, she pulled the two articles she'd copied in the last two days. One from Monday's *Trib*, the other from today's *Bulletin*. Two fires, local. Two fatalities. Manny had been withdrawn that morning in class. Preoccupied. Disturbed. And they'd found matches in his room.

That Manny could have been involved in these fires was impossible. He couldn't leave the property. But someone had managed to smuggle matches in. These two fires were the only local articles he'd clipped. What made these fires so special? Or had she reignited Manny's compulsion and any articles on fire would have sufficed?

She winced. *Ignited*. Poor choice of words. Two people were dead because of these fires. She wouldn't be able to sleep as long as she worried she herself was somehow . . . *To blame* was also a poor choice of words. *Connected* was better. She needed to find out if Manny was somehow connected, and through him . . . *me*.

She could call the police. That would be the sensible thing to do. But it was more than likely she was being compulsively ridiculous and there was no connection at all. It would be a wild-goose chase for the police and that wouldn't be good.

But if there was a connection, the police should be told. There was one way to find out. The second fire was in a neighborhood close to the school. She'd see for herself.

Tuesday, November 28, 4:15 P.M.

'Mia. *Mia*.'

She looked up from Burnette's files with a jolt, blinking furiously to bring Solliday into focus. *Shit*. She'd dropped off, right here at her desk. 'You ready to trade names?'

He shook his head. 'We have company,' he said quietly. A woman was crossing the bullpen, her eyes red and swollen. 'She matches the description of Hill's daughter.'

Mia came to her feet, alert now. In the woman's hand was a copy of the *Bulletin*.

'I'm Margaret Hill. I'm looking for Detective Mitchell. She left me a message.'

'That's me. You're here about your mother.'

'Is it true?' she whispered, holding the paper. 'What this says about my mother?'

'I'm sorry, Miss Hill. Let's go somewhere we can talk more privately.' She led her into a small room next to Spinnelli's office. Still clutching the newspaper, Margaret Hill sank into the chair and closed her eyes. Sollliday closed the door behind them.

'Miss Hill, I'm so sorry for your loss. This is Lieutenant Solliday with the fire marshal's office. We're investigating your mother's death together.'

Margaret nodded and swiped her cheeks with her fingertips. Solliday put a box of tissues in her lap and leaned against the edge of the table so that Margaret was between them. 'Miss Hill.' His voice was so very gentle it made Mia's throat thicken. 'You know from the newspaper that your mother's house burned down last night.'

Margaret looked up, her cheeks streaked. Her gaze locked onto Solliday's face. 'It says . . . It says the police think she was murdered.'

'She was, ma'am,' Solliday said and Margaret began to cry again.

'I'm sorry,' she whispered. 'I just can't . . . My God. Oh, Mom.'

Mia touched her hand. 'Did she mention anyone or anything that worried her?'

Margaret visibly controlled herself. 'Mom was a social worker. She took children from crackhead mothers and abusive fathers every week for twenty-five years.'

'Did she worry about all those mothers and fathers?' Solliday asked.

'Not really. She worried sometimes about going into their houses. Once she was shot and she almost died. I was so happy she was retiring. I thought for once she could finally sleep at night.'

'She wasn't sleeping? You said she didn't worry about the parents,' Mia said.

'She didn't.' Margaret's smile was hard and bitter. 'She was so terrified she'd miss something. Miss a detail, and a child would get hurt. She used to wake up screaming. It got worse after she got shot. We thought we'd lost her then. I was only fifteen.'

'What happened to the shooter?'

'He got jail time. He only shot Mom. He killed his wife.'

'Is he still in jail?'

'I think so. They were supposed to tell us if he got out.'

Mia noted it. 'Miss Hill, did anyone else have a personal issue with your mother?'

Margaret nodded. Slowly. 'My ex-husband wanted to kill her.'

Solliday's brows lifted. 'Why?'

'Because my mother finally convinced me to leave

him. Two months ago I filed for divorce. Mom should have said "I told you so." But she never did.'

'Why did you leave him?' Mia asked and Margaret rolled up her sleeves. Solliday didn't quite manage to control his flinch. Small round scars were scattered up and down her arms. Cigarette burns. Mia pursed her lips briefly. 'Okay. That answers that.'

'Where is your ex-husband now, Miss Hill?' Solliday asked tightly. He was very angry, Mia could tell. But still in control. That was good.

'In Milwaukee.'

Mia pulled Margaret's sleeves back down. 'Your mother knew about the abuse?'

'I managed to hide it from her for a while. But she found out.'

'So what did your ex-husband do when he found out you were gone?'

'Doug tried to push his way into Mom's house, but she threatened to call the cops and he left, cursing her. I was hiding in the back room the whole time. Looks like I ended up running from Doug just like I ran from Mom.'

Solliday's brows crunched. 'How do you mean?'

'Mom and I had a hard relationship. I think I married Doug just to punish her. High-and-mighty social worker, can't control her own kid. You can't possibly understand.'

Mia thought about her own sister. *I need to tell Kelsey what happened at Bobby's grave.* 'Yes, I can. We'll need your husband's full name and address.'

Her jaw tight, Margaret wrote. 'His last name is Davis. I hate that SOB.'

'I can understand that, too,' Mia said. She could feel Solliday's eyes watching her, looking deeper than she wanted him to see. It sent a prickling shiver down her spine. Steadfastly she focused on Margaret. 'Miss Hill, does your ex-husband like animals?'

'No. He hates dogs. When I left, I took Milo to Mom's and . . . Oh, no. Is Milo alive?'

'He didn't appear to be in the house at the time of the fire,' Solliday said.

Relief and confusion battled in her eyes. 'Mom never let him out without his leash.'

'We'll call you if we find him,' she said. 'Your brother is coming up tomorrow.'

Margaret closed her eyes. 'Oh, wonderful.'

'You don't get along with your brother?' Solliday asked.

'My brother is a good man, but no, we don't get along. He warned me that one day I'd cause more trouble for Mom than she'd be able to clean up. I guess he was right. He usually is.' She stood up unsteadily. 'When can I see my mother?'

'You can't,' Mia said gently. 'I'm sorry.'

Tortured emotion twisted the woman's face before she nodded and walked away.

'Well,' Mia said. 'Doug may be a spouse-abusing prick, but I don't think he did this.'

'Me, either. But the sooner we rule him out, the sooner

Margaret Hill can let go of some of her guilt.' He checked his watch. 'You can call Milwaukee PD while I drive.'

Mia frowned. 'Where are we going?'

'Back to the university. We still have to talk to Caitlin's friends. I called the housemother at the sorority house. She's going to have all the girls there at five thirty.'

'When did you do that?'

'When you were asleep.' He waved her quiet when she opened her mouth. 'Don't say you're sorry. You were up all night. You tackled that guy yesterday and you should still be on disability. I think even you need to sleep, Mia.'

There'd been a wry admiration under his criticism. 'Thanks. I think.'

Tuesday, November 28, 4:30 P.M.

'Hello,' he drawled. 'May I speak with Emily Richter, please?'

Her sigh was long-suffering. 'This is she. With whom am I speaking?'

'My name is Tom Johnson. I'm calling from the Chicago *Bulletin*.'

'How do you reporters keep getting my phone number?' she demanded.

'You're listed in the phone book, ma'am,' he said politely. *Damn idiot woman.*

'Well.' She sniffed. 'I talked to one of your reporters already. A woman. Her name was . . . Carmichael. You should talk to her if you want details about the fire.'

'Well, ma'am, I'm not covering the fire itself. I'm with a different department. I'd like to feature your neighbors in a small piece. Let the community know they have a need. Give folks a way to help out, this being the holiday season and all. My deadline's in just a few hours. If you could help me out, I'd sure appreciate it.'

'Well, what do you want from me?' she snapped.

I'd love to shut you up, you old bag, he thought, then injected a lazy smile into his voice. 'I've been trying to reach the Doughertys, but nobody knows where they are. I'd like to talk to them, find out what they need the most, things like that.'

'They just got back this morning.' She sniffed. 'From Florida. They were here, talking to the police. I went out after the police were gone, to offer my help, of course.'

Of course. 'Did they mention where they were staying by any chance?'

'I didn't ask. But they had a parking permit from the Beacon Inn.'

Thank God for gossiping old busybodies, he thought with a grin. 'Thank you, ma'am. Happy holidays.' He hung up, satisfied.

Mrs Dougherty, you and I have a date. A hot one. He chuckled. A hot date. *Sometimes I slay myself.* He dragged the mammoth phone book from below the phone and found the hotel's number, dug in his pocket for more change and dialed.

A perky voice answered. 'Beacon Inn, this is Tania. How can I help you?'

He deepened his voice. 'Yes. I'd like the room number for Joe Dougherty, please.'

'I'm sorry, sir. We don't give out the room numbers of guests. I can connect you.'

The back of his neck heated in anger. 'Actually, I'm having flowers delivered to him and his wife. I just need the room number to tell the florist.'

'Just tell the florist our hotel name and location. We'll deliver them for you.'

Her smug tone clawed at him. *We'll deliver them for you.* She wasn't going to tell him, the high-and-mighty bitch. He gritted his teeth against the impotent rage. 'Thank you, Tania. You've been so helpful.' He hung up and narrowed his eyes at the phone.

Flowers it would have to be. And Tania would wish she really had been helpful.

Chapter Nine

Tuesday, November 28, 6:45 P.M.

Reed yawned as he pulled into the parking space beside Mitchell's little Alfa.

'Don't do that,' she protested. 'I still have tons of reading to do tonight.'

'You're not going back to your desk. I know I need some sleep. So do you, Mia.'

'I won't go back right away. I have something I need to do first. But I've got to get through some of those files. We've got nothing so far.'

'The info we got from the sorority was disappointing,' he agreed glumly.

'They can't tell us what they didn't see. If this guy stalked Caitlin, he was damn careful about it. At least we can rule out Doug Davis and Joel Rebinowitz.'

'Lucky for Doug he has a temper. Being held without bail for aggravated assault in a Milwaukee jail gives him a tight alibi. We can tell Margaret Hill he's not to blame.'

'And luckily the arcade has a security camera.' It had

clearly shown Joel playing pinball during the hours in question. She scrubbed her cheeks with her palms and shot him a weak smile. 'Go home and see your daughter, Solliday. Fluffy is dead so he just isn't the conversationalist he used to be. I won't be missing anything at home.'

He didn't smile back. Fatigued frustration flared and with it his temper. 'No way. Tired people have accidents. People die. Go the hell home.'

She blinked at him, surprised. 'I'm not that tired.'

'That's what the guy said who ran a red light and broadsided my wife.' Immediately he wished the words back, but it was too late.

Her blue eyes flickered sympathy. 'And she died?'

'Yes.' The one word vibrated with an anger that surprised him. But at the moment he wasn't sure whom he was most angry with.

She sighed. 'I'm so sorry.'

So was he. 'It was a long time ago.' He gentled his voice. 'Go home, Mia. Please.'

She nodded. 'Okay. I will.'

That had been too easy. It didn't take a detective to realize she wasn't going home.

Something perverse nagged at him. She was going to get herself killed, and dammit, she was starting to grow on him. He now understood why Spinnelli spoke so highly of her. He also had to admit she'd piqued his own curiosity.

Reed waited until she'd driven away, and then

followed. At the first traffic light she hadn't detected his presence. *She really must be tired*, he thought. He pulled out his phone and said, 'Home,' and waited for voice recognition to do its thing.

'Hey, Dad,' Beth said, startling him. Caller ID still caught him unaware sometimes.

'Hi, sweetie. How was school today?' The light changed and Mitchell continued onward, not trying to lose him. So far, so good.

'Okay. When are you coming home?'

'I'll be a little while. Something's come up on this case.'

'*What?* You promised you'd take me to Jenny Q's tonight. Meet her mother. So I can go to her party this weekend, remember?'

The vehemence in her voice took him aback. 'Well, I can go over there tomorrow.'

'I have to study with her *tonight*.'

It sounded as if every word was being spat from her mouth. 'Beth, what's wrong?'

'You're not keeping your promise is what's wrong. Oh!'

It sounded like she stifled a sob and alarmed, he sat up straighter. Hormones again. He could never keep track of which week to be careful. 'Honey? This will be all right. I'll ask Aunt Lauren to go meet her mother if it's that important to you.'

'Okay.' She shuddered a breath. 'Sorry, Dad.'

Reed blinked. 'It's okay, honey. I think. Put Aunt Lauren on the phone.'

'What was that about?' Lauren asked a minute later.

'She wants to go to a party at her friend's house this weekend and I was going to meet the girl's mother tonight, but I'm working late.' It was a small lie. Little and white. Still he winced. But made no move to turn around. 'Can you take her over there to study and give the mom the third degree?'

'Do I get to use the bright lights and rubber hoses?'

He chuckled. 'Knock yourself out. I'm not sure when I'll be home.'

'Reed, are you working that fire that killed the social worker?'

Reed grimaced. 'How do you know about that?'

'It's all over the news. My God. That poor woman.'

'Which news?'

'Local. It was one of their lead stories. You want me to tape it for you at ten?'

'That'd be great. Remember, Beth's got to be home by nine.'

'I've been doing this a long time, Reed,' Lauren said patiently. 'You shouldn't worry about my taking care of Beth. You should be more worried I'll get married.'

'Are you planning a big wedding any time soon?' he teased.

'I'm serious. One of these days I'll leave. You need to consider my replacement.'

'Oh. This is about me dating.' Lauren was good at back-alley arguing.

'Finding a good wife is a lot easier than hiring a good

nanny. And my biological clock is ticking. I've got to find a husband before they're all taken. Talk to you later.'

Reed hung up, a scowl furrowing his forehead. What *would* he do with Beth when Lauren flew the nest? He did know he wasn't going to get married just to get a live-in nanny-slash-maid. He'd had a good marriage once. There was no way in hell he'd make do with anything less. He let his mind drift as he tailed Mia Mitchell's car, remembering Christine. She'd been the perfect wife. Beautiful, smart, sexy. He sighed. Yes, sexy. He had to stop letting his mind drift, because it kept drifting to sex.

But it was hard to control his mind when he was this tired, much less his body. He could remember everything so vividly. Just how she'd looked, how it had felt to make love to her in the quiet of the night. Touching her skin, her hair. The way she whispered his name when she was so close, begging him to take her to the sun. And how it had felt when she came, taking him with her. But most of all, he remembered the amazing peace he'd felt afterward, holding her spooned against him.

Stop. Something was wrong with that fantasy. Different. Reed blinked hard, bringing all the taillights in his path back into focus. Whoa. Troubled, he blinked again, but the picture in his mind was unchanged. The woman in his mental wanderings wasn't tall and dark with the lithe body of a dancer. The woman in his mind was blond. Her body strong and compact. Her breasts . . . her legs . . . different. Her eyes weren't dark and mysterious. They were wide and blue like the summer sky.

Hell. The woman he'd been making love to in his mind hadn't been Christine. It had been Mia Mitchell. Restlessly he shifted, the picture of Mitchell still stubbornly filling his mind. Naked and waiting for him. And now that he'd seen her like that, even if it was only in his mind, it was going to be damn difficult to see her any other way.

'Well, that's just perfect,' he muttered. Making love to a memory was safe. Dreaming about a real live woman was way too dangerous. So he'd push the very thought from his mind. This he could do. This he'd done before. This was discipline.

Four cars ahead, Mia was signaling her merge onto the interstate, going south. If he had a brain in his head he'd drive right on past the merge ramp, turn around at the next intersection and go home. But he didn't. For some reason he didn't try to fathom, he followed, wondering where she would take them.

Tuesday, November 28, 7:00 P.M.

He slid the vase full of flowers onto the hotel's counter. 'Delivery, ma'am.'

A small woman stood behind the counter, typing. Her name tag said TANIA and below it in smaller letters,

ASSISTANT MANAGER. Around her neck she wore a photo ID and clipped behind it, a key card. He'd bet it was a master key. And he needed one of those.

She looked up with a tired smile. 'I'll be with you in just a minute.'

He yawned, then pushed the dark-rimmed glasses up on his nose. They were just ten-dollar reading glasses, but they altered his looks. Combined with the long wig he'd picked up cheap, the difference would be enough to fool the security camera. 'Take your time.'

'You're working late,' she said sympathetically.

His yawn had been no fake. He'd had a couple of very late nights recently. 'Got a few last-minute orders. But this is my last delivery tonight. I get to go home.'

Her smile was rueful. 'Lucky you.'

He let her type another thirty seconds. 'The roads are really slick, so be careful when you drive home. They're calling for more snow tonight.'

'Thanks, but I'm not going home any time soon. I'm here all night.'

He grimaced. 'All night? Jeez.' *All night? Damn.* He wanted her key.

She shrugged as she typed efficiently. 'I have two people out with the flu, so I'm pulling a double. Don't get off till seven tomorrow morning.' She finished typing and turned, giving him her full attention. 'Oh, what pretty flowers.'

They should be. They cost him fifty bucks. 'They go to . . .' He pulled a sheet of paper from his pocket.

'Dougherty. Can you confirm I've got the right place?'

'You do,' she said. 'The Doughertys are guests.'

'They'll get delivered tonight?'

'I'll deliver them myself as soon as I can step away.'

Tuesday, November 28, 8:15 P.M.

After twelve years Mia should have been used to watching her little sister walk across the visitation area in a prison uniform. Kelsey dropped into the chair, waiting.

Mia picked up the phone on her side of the Plexiglas and after a moment's hesitation, Kelsey did the same. 'He's buried,' Mia said and Kelsey's lips quirked up.

'I should hope so. He'd be pretty ripe by now.'

Mia's own mouth curved sadly. 'I wish you'd been there.'

'Dana was there for you.'

'Yeah. She was and I'm grateful for it. But I needed you.'

Kelsey's eyes flickered. 'I would have been there for you. Not for him.'

It was understandable. 'I know.'

'Why are you here, M?' It was always 'M.' Never 'Mia.' Kelsey took pains to keep herself removed in case somebody inside recognized Mia for the cop she was. Fortunately there was no family resemblance to link them. Kelsey looked like their mother, while Mia was the image of Bobby Mitchell. He'd been a blond charmer in his younger days, blinking those blue eyes to look sincere when the occasion called for it. Mia had always suspected he'd been a ladies' man. Now she knew for sure.

'Something happened you need to know about. When I got to the cemetery the day of Bobby's funeral . . .' She could see the small headstone in her mind. It had been a cold shock. One more betrayal to add to all those that had come before. 'The plot next to him had already been taken.'

Kelsey tilted her head back, her eyes narrowing. 'By good old Liam.'

Mia's mouth dropped open. Finally she found her voice. 'You *knew*?'

Kelsey's brows lifted, her eyes cool. 'You didn't? Interesting.'

'*How* did you know?'

'Found a picture in a box in his closet when I was looking for money once. Cute kid, sitting in our chair. The "true heir" to the kingdom.'

Mia was floored. 'I found the box when I was going through his suits for the funeral home. I didn't open it until I got home from the cemetery. I saw Liam's name on the gravestone on the plot next to Bobby's when I got to the cemetery for the burial. Until that moment, I had no idea Liam even existed.' *Liam Charles Mitchell, Beloved Son.*

A shadow passed over Kelsey's face. 'I'm sorry. I

wouldn't have wanted you to find out that way. I really thought you knew. So what did she do?'

'*She*' was their mother. 'At the cemetery? She zoned out.' Later, she'd talked. Mia hadn't been patient with her mother. It would be a long time before the two of them spoke cordially again. *That should bother me more than it does.* 'He was born when I was ten months old. He died a year later. I checked Liam's birth certificate. It said his mother was a Bridget Condon.'

'I know.'

Mia blinked. 'Bobby told you?'

Kelsey lifted a shoulder. 'I waited till he was drunk one day and asked him.'

Mia closed her eyes. 'Which time was that?'

'Just before Christmas when I was thirteen.'

Mia remembered. 'You had to get six stitches in your lip.'

'And *she* told the hospital I'd fallen off my skateboard.'

It was their mother's way. Juggle emergency rooms, juggle the lies. Anything to keep the secret. 'Hell, Kelsey.'

'It's done, M. He's in his own private hell now.'

'He gave the baby his name.' It had been bothering Mia for three weeks.

'He'd moved in with Bridget. He was going to marry the mother of his son.'

'He was going to leave us because Bridget had a son. And Annabelle didn't.'

'And he came back after the baby died.'

'Yeah. I know. Annabelle told me that much.' After Mia had confronted her after the funeral, in the privacy of her mother's house. 'And Annabelle took him back.'

'And nine months later, out popped me. Another girl.'

'He rejected two children because neither of them had a dick.' She clenched her teeth on a wave of fury. 'All those years I tried to please him. Appease him.' Mia sighed. 'So what do you know about the other daughter?'

Kelsey blinked. 'Excuse me?'

Mia blinked back. 'At the cemetery . . . I saw a woman. She looked like me, just a little younger. She had my eyes.' Bobby's eyes. 'It was uncanny.'

Kelsey was clearly at a loss. 'That I didn't know. Can't help you there, M.'

'Well, thanks for believing me at least. I know it sounds crazy.'

'You've never lied to me.' Kelsey sat back, considering. 'So there are three of us misbegotten non-male spawn.'

'That we know of. Maybe more. God knows how many times he tried for a boy.'

Kelsey's lips quirked in amusement. 'Well, it looks like Bobby shot mostly X's. No little Y's to make little Bobbys.'

Mia smiled, despite the weight on her shoulders. 'God, I miss you.'

Kelsey swallowed, hard. 'Stop. Don't make me . . .'

She drew a breath, took a surreptitious glance side to side. 'It's like blood in the water, M.'

'You come up for parole again in three months.'

'Like I don't know the exact time to the minute? It won't do any good.'

'I'll be there. I promise.'

'You've always been there, every hearing. And I'm grateful. But Shayla Kaufmann is always there, too, and her grief carries more weight than your good words.'

Mia clenched her fist. 'It's been twelve years, Kelsey.'

'But her husband and son are still dead.'

'*You* didn't shoot them. The store video showed it clearly.' Kelsey had stood there, her hand shaking so bad she'd nearly dropped the gun. Her boyfriend Stone had done the shooting and was serving life without parole. Kelsey had cooperated, earning her a deal. Eight to twenty-five. At the time, Mia had been relieved Kelsey's sentence hadn't been stiffer. Twelve years later, Mia knew exactly how slowly time could pass.

Kelsey's face was immobile, but her eyes had darkened with a torment she rarely let Mia see. 'I didn't shoot, but I stood there while Stone did. I didn't do anything to save that man and his son. That father's last action was to shield his son with his own body.' She held herself rigid and focused on a point over Mia's shoulder and Mia knew they were both thinking that was something their own father never would have done.

'Dammit, Kelsey, you were young. Scared. You were high.'

'I was *guilty*.' Her lips trembled and she pursed them. 'And I still am.'

Mia bit the inside of her cheek, hard. 'I'll still be there at the parole hearing.'

Kelsey's eyes closed for a long moment and when she opened them, they were again cool and detached. 'I hear you took a bullet, kid.'

The subject of parole was now closed. 'Yeah. Two weeks ago.'

'How's your pal?'

'Abe? He's in the hospital, but he'll be okay.'

'Don't drop your guard.' One side of her mouth lifted. 'You're the only one who ever comes to visit me in here. I'd hate for anything to happen to you.'

Mia cleared her throat. 'Okay.'

'Oh, yeah. And tell Dana I said thanks, but no thanks.'

'For what?'

'I got a postcard from her vacation to the beach. Big ugly crab on the front. She said she wished I could have been there to help her eat them. They look like bugs.'

'I'll tell her. I've got to get back now. I have another few hours of reading to do after I smack a man silly.'

Kelsey's brows lifted in lazy interest, but her eyes were sharp. 'Police brutality?'

'Nope. This is my temporary partner. He followed me all the way from town and now he's waiting out in the parking lot.' She huffed. 'Thinks I didn't see him tailing me.'

Amusement now lit Kelsey's eyes. 'Now why would he do a thing like that?'

'Because he . . .' Mia thought about all the kind things Reed Solliday had done for her over the last two days. Coffee, medicine, opening doors like she was . . . a lady. It would appear that Reed Solliday was an old-fashioned gentleman and a nice guy. Who'd played football. And liked poetry. And seemed to feel the pain of the victims as keenly as she did. She sighed. 'He was worried about me. Apparently somebody wrecked his wife's car when they were too tired to drive.'

'So he's married?' Kelsey shook her head reproachfully. 'M.'

'He's a widower with a kid. And don't get that look in your eyes,' she added, when Kelsey did just that. 'He's temporary, just until Abe gets back.'

'What does he look like?'

The man was big. And built. 'A little like Satan.' She ran her thumb and forefinger around her mouth. 'He's got this goatee thing going on.' That framed a very nice mouth.

'Interesting.' One brow went up. 'So is this Satan a fallen angel or a gargoyle?'

Mia shifted in her chair uneasily. 'He's . . . easy enough on the eyes.'

Kelsey nodded, her mouth bent in speculation. 'And?'

And he's decent. And I like him. She drew a breath. *Hell.* 'That's all.'

Kelsey stood up. 'Okay, if that's how you're going to play it, I'll wait for Dana's next letter. She'll give me the straight scoop.' And without saying good-bye, Kelsey hung up the phone and walked away. She never said good-bye, she always just walked away.

For a minute Mia just sat there, her heart aching. Then she carefully hung up the phone and went to give Solliday his just deserts.

Tuesday, November 28, 8:30 P.M.

It took her long enough, he thought sourly, as Tania exited the hotel lobby carrying the flowers. The inside of the car he'd taken was nice and warm and he'd nearly fallen asleep waiting for her. All the doors were on the outside of this motel, so he knew she'd need to pass this way sooner or later.

Slowly he drove through the parking lot, keeping her in his sight all the time. Finally she stopped and knocked. The door opened, not wide enough for him to see inside. But that was okay. He lifted his binoculars and focused. Room 129. *Go, me.*

He yawned again. He was so tired. He wanted old lady Dougherty, but he didn't want to be so tired he didn't enjoy it, or worse, that he made a mistake. It was a foolish man who took chances when he was fatigued. Besides, he needed a key card and Tania didn't get off till seven tomorrow morning. He could take it now, but somebody would notice when she didn't come back to the desk. Because after he took her key card little Tania and her smart mouth wouldn't be going anywhere.

He had time. It wasn't like the Doughertys had a place to go. So he'd go home, get some sleep and be back tomorrow morning to make sure Miss Tania got home safely.

Tuesday, November 28, 8:45 P.M.

Reed was dreaming. He knew inside the dream that he was dreaming, but that made it a little more okay. Because he knew even as he dreamed that it would not come true. He would not pull Mia Mitchell into his bed. He would not tear the clothes from her body. He would not kiss every inch of her creamy skin. And he certainly would not come inside her with enough force to make her blue eyes glaze over.

So because none of those things would ever happen, he knew he'd better enjoy the dream as long as it lasted. And he was enjoying it. As was she. Her tight body was arched up, her internal muscles gripping him as he moved. 'God, Reed,' she was moaning, not the delicate little whispers of Christine, but loud, loud enough to penetrate his own pleasured stupor. '*Reed.*'

Reed woke with a start, his eyes flying to his car window where Mitchell stood pounding her fists on the glass. She rolled her eyes when she saw him jolt to awareness. 'Dammit, Solliday, I thought you were passed out from carbon monoxide.'

He rolled the window down, still reeling from the dream that had been way too real for his comfort. He nearly reached for her, knowing now how her face would feel between his palms. But he didn't really know. Nor would he. 'I guess I fell asleep.'

She looked mad. Why was she mad? 'What the hell are you doing here?'

Here? He looked around, saw the fence, the security post. Prison. *Oh, yeah.* The drive out from the city came back with clarity. So much for a surreptitious tail. *Damn.* He'd been made. 'Um . . .' His mind was utterly blank. His body utterly hard.

Her eyes still snapping, she stared at him. 'Did you really think I didn't see you?'

Some of the blood was returning to his brain, making things more comfortable on both counts. 'Maybe. Okay, yeah, I didn't think you saw me. I blew it, didn't I?'

Her frown softened. 'Yeah, but your intentions were good. You have a nice nap?'

He felt his cheeks burn, as if his dream were a scarlet letter branded on his forehead. 'Yeah. I did.' He looked up at the prison building, its lights glaringly bright against the night sky, then back at her. 'If I ask what brought you here, will you tell me it's none of my business?'

Her eyes narrowed slightly. 'You are the nosiest of men.'

'Sorry.'

'You also seem to be nice and relatively harmless.'

His dream flashed back, vivid and clear and in full Technicolor. What she didn't know wouldn't hurt either of them. 'Most of the time, yes.'

'And you did bring me coffee twice today and a hot dog yesterday.'

That sounded promising. 'And I let you pick where we ate lunch, both days.'

Her lips curved. 'Yes, you did.' The small smile faded. 'I was visiting my sister.'

It was not what he'd expected. 'What?'

'You heard me. My younger sister's in for armed robbery. Shocked?'

'Yeah. I have to say I am. How long has she been in?'

'Twelve years. I come during visiting hours like everybody else. I don't want anybody inside to know her sister's a cop.'

Stunned, he had no idea what to say. One side of her mouth lifted, likely in sympathy for his inability to speak. 'Like you said yesterday, sometimes it's worse with cops' kids. My sister is paying for some really bad decisions. If she doesn't make parole, she'll go on paying another thirteen years.'

'So you really do understand how Margaret Hill felt about her mother.'

She just stood there, watching him. Saying nothing.

'Well.' He scratched his face where new stubble was starting to itch. 'What now?'

'Now I go back and read files.'

There were dark shadows under her eyes. 'Or we could grab some dinner.'

She studied him carefully. 'Why?'

'Because my stomach's growling so loud I'm surprised you can't hear it.'

Again her mouth quirked. 'I can hear it, actually. I meant why did you follow me?'

'You were tired and you feel guilty because you haven't processed information in those files in one night that will probably take both of us days to get through.' She hadn't bought his explanation, so he gave the only answer that would satisfy them both. 'For some reason I like you. I didn't want anything to happen to you. That's all.'

She flinched, her eyes taking on a suspicious glint that rocked him as she took a giant step back from his window. She turned her head to look up at the prison building. When she looked back, her eyes were clear, her smile slightly mocking. 'Then let's get something to eat. But not around here, okay?'

He nodded. 'Okay. This time you follow me.'

Tuesday, November 28, 10:15 P.M.

Reed stepped out of his garage and waited as Mitchell's little Alfa turned into his driveway. He was a little surprised she'd stuck with him when it became clear they were headed to his house, but here she was, ratty jacket and all. He'd had partners over for dinner before after all. Foster, a bachelor with a hot plate, was a regular.

But Foster sure as hell didn't look like Mia Mitchell. Reed's heart thudded heavily in his chest as she got out of her car. From where he stood, he could see her every curve. *You're crazy*, he thought. *This is a bad idea. B-A-D.* But there had been something in her eyes, a soft vulnerability. He'd thought she had no softness in her yesterday morning. He could see now that he'd been very wrong.

She stopped three feet from him, blond brows lifted. 'Café du Solliday?'

'I don't know about you, but I can't stand the thought of another burger in a sack.'

Her lips curved, amused. 'You gonna cook for me?'

'That depends on your definition of cook. Come.' He led her through the garage into the kitchen where Beth stood at the microwave as popcorn popped. 'Hi, honey.'

Beth turned only her head to glare at him. Rolling her eyes, she looked away.

Conscious of Mitchell behind him he took a step toward his daughter. 'Beth?'

'*What?*'

'What's wrong now?'

Beth set her jaw. 'Nothing.'

'I think I'll go,' Mitchell murmured and he held up his hand.

'No, it's okay. Beth, this is Detective Mitchell, my temporary partner. This is my daughter, Beth. My *polite* daughter, Beth.'

Beth shook her head with a disgusted huff. 'It's nice to meet you, Detective.'

'It's nice to meet you, Beth. Look, Solliday, I can—'

His smile was strained. 'You can sit. Please. Beth, if you won't tell me what's wrong in a reasonable way, then you can go to your room.'

'What's *wrong* is that everybody continues to treat me like I'm four years old. All I wanted was to stay over at Jenny's tonight. I even brought my *toothbrush*, for God's sake. But Lauren . . .' She gritted her teeth. 'Lauren embarrassed me in front of *everyone*.'

'Who was everyone?'

'Never mind.' The corn continued to pop, each sound like another punch of tension.

'Lauren followed my instructions. You know no sleepovers on school nights.'

The microwave beeped and Beth grabbed the bag. 'Fine.' She slammed the microwave door and a minute later slammed her bedroom door. Reed turned to Mitchell with a wince.

'I swear I had a nice daughter once.'

She smiled ruefully. 'Aliens. Pods. Body snatchers. It's the only explanation.'

With a tired chuckle, he took off his overcoat and suit coat and laid them across a chair. 'I'll give her a chance to cool off before we discuss which privileges that little tantrum cost her. Take off your coat, Mia. Stay awhile.'

Coming to his house was a really bad idea. But as Mia watched Solliday move around his kitchen, it was damn hard to mind. He'd shed his coat and set his dirty shoes outside. They still bore the remnants of mud from that morning, although Mia was quite certain they'd be shiny enough to see her face in by eight o'clock tomorrow.

Meeting his daughter had been interesting. But Beth was fourteen and Mia supposed that said it all. What had been more revealing was his response. Patient, firm, and bewildered. Bobby would have backhanded her to the floor. Even Kelsey had never defied him in front of company. But Mia pushed Bobby from her mind and focused on the different but equally unsettling thought of Reed Solliday.

He was tugging at his tie and Mia found the sight a lot more intimate than she would have liked. The play of his muscles beneath the fabric of his shirt as he pulled the tie free of his collar sent a flutter through her gut and a sharp zing straight down.

Reed Solliday was a very watchable man, and in the quiet of his kitchen she could admit to herself that she was interested. *Watch yourself*, she told herself firmly. *You don't do cops. But he's not a cop*, her mind reasoned as she fought to keep from staring at the dark coarse hair that now peeked from his open collar. *Fucking technicality. Get a grip.* She dragged her eyes up to find him staring at her, eyes nearly black.

'What's wrong?' he asked, his voice low and gravelly, as if he read her thoughts.

What was wrong was that Reed Solliday looked way too good standing there with his tie off and that it had been a very long time since she'd had a man and that desire had suddenly, *unwantedly* come knocking. Pounding. Crashing at the damn door. But as none of those were appropriate responses, she shrugged. 'I'm not sure why I'm here.'

His brows lifted in challenge, his gaze still fixed on hers. 'Dinner?'

She swallowed. 'I thought we were going to stop someplace close to the precinct.'

He looked away, severing the invisible thread that had connected them. He pulled a glass casserole dish from the refrigerator. 'I like to eat real food when I can.'

Real food Mia could appreciate. 'So what is it?'

He peeled back the foil. 'Looks like lasagne.'

'You didn't make it?'

'Nope.' He slid the dish into the oven. 'My sister Lauren did. She's a good cook.'

So his sister was the one who watched Beth when he had to work late. Mia had wondered. Now she was relieved. And annoyed that it mattered at all. Casting her eyes aside, she watched him rummage in the fridge for lettuce. 'Do you want help?'

'No, thanks. I'm not the cook my mom was, but I can manage a salad.'

Was. 'So she's dead? Your mother.'

'Five years ago. She had cancer.'

'I'm sorry.' And she was. From the wistful tone of his voice, he'd loved his mother and obviously missed her. She thought about Bobby and wished for just a fraction of Solliday's grief. But there was none and would never be. 'What about your dad?'

'He remarried and retired to Hilton Head. Plays golf every day.' The words were tempered with affection and she felt a pang of jealousy that made her ashamed.

He set the salad bowl aside and pulled a pitcher of tea from the fridge. 'I called for my messages while I was waiting for you back there at . . . Well, back there. Ben left me the analysis on the accelerant from Hill's house. It's ammonium nitrate, the same as the Doughertys'. It's commercial grade, could have been bought in any feed store. I hate to send Ben off chasing wild geese until we have something more to go on.'

'Once we've gotten some leads from the files we can show some photos around. See if any of the local fertilizer distributors remember anything. What about the plastic eggs? I've been trying to remember the last time I saw a panty hose egg in the store.' She made a face. 'Not that I go looking for such devices of torture myself.'

He smiled as he sat down with two glasses of iced tea. 'I Googled them Sunday. The company changed from plastic eggs to cardboard boxes in ninety-one.'

'But our boy had at least three of the eggs.'

'The sites I checked said that they're used for arts and crafts, but again, without a suspect, we're looking for a needle in a haystack. I did have Ben call all the arts-and-crafts stores in the area, but he came up empty. The eggs do come up occasionally on eBay so his source might not even be local. All we really have is some blood and hair, both belonging to the victim, and shoe prints that could have belonged to anybody.'

She could hear the frustration in his voice. 'Give Jack some time. If our guy dropped anything, he'll find it.' She checked her watch, concern nagging at the back of her mind. 'It'll be midnight soon. You think he'll strike again?'

'If not tonight, then soon. He likes the fire too much to stay away.'

Mia bit at her lip. 'Why fire? Why does he like fire?'

'Fire can be fascinating, hypnotic. It can destroy with seemingly effortless ease.'

'It's powerful,' she said and he nodded.

'And wielding that power makes the arsonist invincible, for just a little while. He can create chaos, bring trucks full of firefighters speeding to the scene. The arsonist commands the actions of others. He sees it like making puppets dance on a string.'

'It's a compulsion,' she murmured and watched his eyes flash.

'No. That makes it sound like they can't help it. They can. They just choose not to.'

Mia remembered his words to Miles. 'You don't believe in compulsions?'

'People say that they have compulsions when they really mean gratification means more to them than the people they'll hurt. When they don't want to be held accountable.'

She frowned. 'You don't believe in mental illness?'

He frowned back. 'Don't put words in my mouth, Mia. I do believe some people are mentally ill. That they truly hear voices or think they're being pursued. I've never met an arsonist that wasn't declared mentally competent. It's not compulsion. It's choice.'

There was something there. Something very deep. Right now, she was too tired to see it clearly so she let it go. 'You've done this a long time,' she noted quietly instead.

He visibly forced himself to relax. 'About thirteen years.'

She traced a pattern in the moisture on her glass. 'You were a firefighter before you joined OFI. If I asked why you changed, would you say it was none of my business?'

'I'd say I owe you one secret revealed, Detective. Christine asked me to change. She was afraid I'd get hurt. I'd always been interested in the investigation side and I'd just finished my degree. The time seemed right and it made her happy.'

Christine must have been his wife. Again jealousy

227

pricked, which was irrational. 'I assumed it had something to do with your hands.'

'That would be two secrets. But okay. It's not something I'm particularly proud of. I lost it for a little while after Christine died. Drank too much. One night I was working on my car. I shouldn't have been drinking but I was, and I dropped the battery. It cracked and acid leaked on my hands, damaged the nerves in my fingertips. Stupid, really.'

Stupid she could understand. 'We all do stupid things when we're distracted.'

He met her eyes, held them for a long quiet moment. 'What's distracting you, Mia?'

She opened her mouth, unsure. Disturbed because she suddenly wanted to tell him everything. All her secrets. But she was saved an answer by a sleepy voice.

'Reed?'

A woman stood in the doorway, rubbing her eyes and clutching a videotape. Mia looked at the woman, then rapidly back at Solliday. To say there was no family resemblance would have been the understatement of the year.

The woman walked across the kitchen, her hand extended, her smile bright white against her ebony skin. 'You must be Detective Mitchell. I'm Lauren Solliday.'

Mia shook off her surprise and shook the woman's hand. 'It's nice to meet you. I hope I'm not imposing, coming in so late.'

'Not at all.' She sniffed. 'You found the lasagne?'

Solliday nodded. 'And I made a salad.'

Lauren's lips twitched. 'Domesticity in a male. Can you beat it?'

'His domesticity trumps mine,' Mia admitted.

'We grew up in a big family. Everybody had to cook. Even Reed.' She handed him the tape. 'I set it to copy the whole show in case I fell asleep. Which of course, I did.'

'What did you tape?' Mia asked.

'Lauren told me the fire at Hill's house made the news. Let's take a look.'

He led them into the living room, popping the video in the machine while Mia scanned the room. It was elegance without intimidation, a delicate balance, Mia suspected. She wondered if Lauren or Christine had done the decorating. The mantel over the fireplace was packed with photos and a half dozen framed cross-stitched works of art. The one on the end was of wild roses with 'CS' stitched in the corner. So this room was Christine's. Solliday caught her looking, mistakenly thinking her attention focused on one of the pictures that looked like a UN photo.

'That was the last reunion before Mom died,' he said. 'My parents . . . and all of us.'

Mia blinked as she took a quick count. 'Holy shit,' she breathed.

He chuckled. 'We were an intimidating bunch.'

'So I take it that your parents did a lot of adoptions.'

Lauren's smile flashed. 'They adopted six of us formally. Reed was the first.'

Mia pushed the wistful feeling away. 'My best friend is a foster mother.'

'The friend whose kids named your goldfish Fluffy,' Solliday said dryly.

'She's the one. This is what Dana wants to build. You had a happy family.'

Lauren took the picture and put it back on the mantel with fond precision. 'We did.' She smiled over at Solliday. 'We still do.' She gave Mia an assessing sweep, head to toe and back again. Then her lips twitched. 'It's very good to meet you, Mia Mitchell.'

'Lauren.' It sounded like a warning but Lauren just grinned at him. 'Let's watch the news.' He sat at one end of the sofa and Lauren quickly took the other end, leaving Mia with the middle, uncomfortably close to Solliday. She was certain she'd been manipulated, but her attention was diverted when Hill's charred house came into view.

A pert reporter stood on the curb, Hill's house in the background, and Mia's pulse spiked. 'Holly Wheaton,' Mia said in disgust. She truly hated that woman.

'She drove me nuts last year when I was working an apartment fire. She doesn't like me very much.'

'That makes two of us. Was this live at six, Lauren?' Mia asked. 'Or at ten?'

'I know it was live at six. This looks like that same segment, rebroadcast.'

Holly Wheaton aimed an earnest face toward the camera. 'Behind me is what's left of the home that belonged to Penny Hill, a social worker. Last night this house was ablaze, the work of an arsonist. But not only did this arsonist steal Ms Hill's home, witnesses say police believe he also stole Ms Hill's life.'

The picture sliced to a home video of the fire. 'This is what the scene looked like last night when flames consumed this house,' Wheaton voiced-over. 'A quick-thinking neighbor shot this video, all the while terrified the fire would spread to his own home.'

One of Penny Hill's oh-so-caring neighbors had taken video and sold it to the press. Mia gritted her teeth. 'Sonofabitch.'

Beside her on the sofa, Solliday blew out a breath. 'On that we agree.'

'This is the second suspicious blaze in less than a week,' the reporter went on as the home video ended and the picture cut back to the ruins. 'Both fires resulted in fatalities. We're told the police are treating both deaths as homicides.'

The camera panned back as the reporter continued, showing Hill's house draped with yellow crime scene tape, then farther back to show the houses on either side and the neighbors who'd turned out to observe the cameras. Mia jerked forward. A woman stood at the edge of the picture next to her car, looking up at the house. There was something in the way she held her body as she stared up at the blackened house. The camera had picked up on a fine tension that went beyond simple curiosity.

'Look,' Mia said.

'I see her,' Solliday returned tightly.

'Police Lieutenant Marc Spinnelli issued a "no comment" statement earlier this afternoon, but has since scheduled a press conference for tomorrow morning. We'll keep you informed as news breaks. This is Holly Wheaton, Action News.'

Mia was staring at the screen. 'Rewind.'

Solliday already was. He slowed the tape, then took it frame by frame. 'We can't see the license number on her car. It's a blue . . . Hyundai. Four or five years old.'

'She could just be a bystander or a sensation seeker,' Lauren said doubtfully.

Mia's skin was tingling, her fatigue chased away. 'I don't think so. You want to pay Holly Wheaton a visit tomorrow? Maybe they caught more on tape.'

Solliday smiled, a sharp feral smile that told her his instincts had been awakened as well. 'She might still be at the station. Let's call her now.'

Mia shook her head. 'It's almost eleven. Nobody's going to be answering the phones.'

His expression shifted. 'I have her direct line and cell,' he admitted. 'And home.'

A twinge of annoyance had her brows crunching. 'I thought she didn't like you.'

'I thought she drove you crazy last year,' Lauren added more glibly and he glared at her. Lauren just grinned. 'I'll wrap up your dinner so you can take it with you.'

When Lauren had left the room he turned his glare on Mia. 'Five people *died* in that apartment fire last year.' Pain flashed in his dark eyes. 'Three of them were kids. One baby still in a crib. Wheaton didn't care about that, about any of them. She just tried to cuddle up for an exclusive. I wasn't interested. Even if I had been, I sure as hell wouldn't have been after that. I'm not that kind of man, Mia.' He stopped abruptly, his eyes locked on hers. 'I only kept her card because I never throw anything away.'

It was one of those moments, Mia thought, when the depth of a person was truly revealed. He wouldn't be interested in a woman whose only care was camera angle and her number of minutes on air. That wasn't the kind of man he was. The annoyance vanished, replaced with a deep respect and with it a resurgence of desire, deeper than before. Dangerous ground. Mentally she edged back. 'Then let's call her now.'

He nodded once, hard. 'Okay.'

Chapter Ten

Tuesday, November 28, 11:15 P.M.

Wheaton was waiting for him at the front door of the
studio smiling – until Mitchell walked in. Wheaton's
mouth pursed hard, and lines marred her famous face.

Wheaton's face was classically beautiful. And
her body . . . Well, Reed wasn't dead. She disgusted
him personally, but his hormones apparently had
no ethics. They hadn't when she'd sidled up to him
while he investigated that apartment fire last year,
either. Her blouse had been unbuttoned so that he
could see the lace of her bra and the swell of her breast.
Then she'd opened her mouth and that had been the
end of that.

'We saw your piece on the fire at Penny Hill's house,'
he said.

She preened. 'It was good, wasn't it?'

'Yes, very. We want the tape. All the tape you took
while you were there tonight.'

Wheaton studied his face. 'What's in it for me?'

'You won't be broadcasting from a jail cell,' Mia said acidly.

Wheaton's eyes narrowed. 'I don't respond to threats, Detective.'

Mia smiled then, and it wasn't nice. 'I haven't yet begun, Miss Wheaton. We're specifically interested in the video the neighbor took. Which neighbor was it?'

'You know I won't tell you that. I protect my sources.'

'This is a homicide investigation, Miss Wheaton,' Mia snapped. 'Two innocent people are dead. Cooperate or I'll have a court order tomorrow morning banning any more showing of that tape. I want the tape you shot and the neighbor's tape. Now.'

'Holly, it's been a very long day,' Reed said, making his voice soothing. 'We've been on this case nonstop for twenty-four hours. We could get a court order, but nobody here wants to do that.'

'I do,' Mia muttered and Holly's chin went up and her mouth opened.

'We don't,' Reed said before either woman could speak. 'Truly. We're trying to put a killer behind bars, Holly. You can help us do that.'

She jutted her jaw to one side. 'In return for?'

Reed glanced at Mia from the corner of his eye. 'An interview when it's all over.'

Wheaton's eyes went sly. 'It could be weeks. How about a chat every morning?'

'How about once a week?' Reed countered. He wanted a killer off the street. He wanted that tape.

'Two times a week, days and locations to be determined by me.'

Reed swallowed his sigh. 'Fine,' he said wearily. 'Can we have the tape now?'

Her smile was feline. 'I'll send it tomorrow if I have time. Thursday at the latest.'

Beside him, Mia opened her mouth. 'Fu—'

Reed cleared his throat, cutting off the rest of Mia's curse. 'Tonight. Now. Or the deal's off and Detective Mitchell gets her court order.' He lifted his hand when Wheaton started to talk. 'And I'll personally see that every engine company in town bars you from any and all fire scenes and,' he added softly, 'your boss will know why.'

Wheaton's mouth went grim and Reed knew they had a deal. 'Wait here.'

When she was gone he turned to Mia. 'I'm sorry,' he murmured.

Her blue eyes were cold. 'I'll wait for you outside,' she answered.

With a sigh he watched her go. Thirty minutes passed and finally Wheaton reappeared, a videotape in her hand. 'It has the neighbor's video?' Reed asked.

When she didn't see Mia, Wheaton smiled. 'I would never welsh, Lieutenant.'

'Of course you would if it benefited you. If this is missing anything, the deal is off.'

Her smile went flat. 'And how would you know if it were missing anything?'

'Detective Mitchell will tell me after she seizes all tapes made since last Saturday. I expect she'll have her court order by ten tomorrow at the latest.'

She cocked her jaw, fury in her eyes. 'I could erase them all.'

He smiled and pulled his micro-recorder from his pocket, hit rewind and let it replay her last words as her eyes narrowed to angry slits. 'I wouldn't. Mitchell would love to see your ass in jail. I don't think you'd find the accommodation to your liking.'

'You sonofabitch,' she hissed.

He pocketed his recorder and stuck the tape under his arm. Her assessment was very true in a basic kind of way. 'Good night,' he said. 'I'll see myself out.'

Mia was leaning on the hood of her little car, eating lasagne out of Lauren's plastic bowl. When she saw him coming she tossed the container on the front passenger seat, her face a stony mask. He handed her the tape but she shook her head. 'We'll watch it tomorrow,' she said. 'Eight o'clock.' She was walking away when he rolled his eyes and caught up to her.

'Mia, you're being childish,' he said and she whirled, fury snapping in her eyes.

'You undermined me,' she hissed. 'The next time I go to get evidence, I'll have to work twice as hard. Dammit, I could have had a court order by tomorrow morning.'

'But you have the tape *now*.' When she just looked at him, he sighed in frustration. 'You weren't going to get what you wanted that way, Mia. Sometimes it pays to be—' He cut himself off, but she'd already taken a step back as if he'd slapped her.

'Nice,' she finished, her voice brittle. 'I'll make a note of it.' She walked around her car, shoulders hunched against the wind. She looked small. And hurt.

Let her go, the voice in his head cautioned as she fired up her engine. *By tomorrow she'll be fine.* But he'd seen the look in her eyes. *She'll bounce back. She'll get over it by morning.* Trouble was, he didn't think he would. *That's not the kind of man I am.*

He got in his SUV, considering all he'd learned about Mia Mitchell. She cared, too much, but she coated her feelings with a sarcastic veneer so that nobody would know. He thought about that moment in his kitchen, when he'd caught her looking at him . . . She'd been interested. He was sure of it. Then when he'd denied interest in a woman like Holly Wheaton – *That's not the kind of man I am*, he'd said – in Mia's eyes he'd seen respect. So what kind of man was he? Perhaps it was time to find out.

Wednesday, November 29, 12:30 A.M.

Mia lived on a quiet street lined with identical apartments. They weren't fancy, but they appeared clean. Flower boxes hung from most of the windows. He didn't think Mia had one. He couldn't see her taking the time for flowers any more than she'd taken the time for

Fluffy the goldfish. Christine had been quite a gardener. She'd loved her roses.

Mia had left so little space behind her car that maneuvering his SUV had been a challenge, his front bumper nearly kissing her rear. Too many double entendres there, he thought. *Leave it alone.* He watched her get out of her car wearily. *Leave her alone.*

He knew he should. But for some reason he seemed unable to. She was watching him with steady eyes. Then she approached, waiting as he rolled down his window.

'Tell me something, Solliday. Do you always follow your partners around?'

It was a fair question, he thought. 'No.'

'Then why me? Am I that pathetically inept that you have to watch over me?'

'No.' The trouble was, he wasn't really sure why he was here. No, that wasn't true either. He knew. He just didn't like it. *Go home, Reed. Do not get out of this vehicle.* He got out of the SUV. 'I didn't want to leave it like that.'

Her jaw tightened. 'It was nothing. We went to get the tape. We got the tape.'

Technically, he'd gotten the tape. And she had not. Holly Wheaton had made sure the distinction was crystal clear. Now, looking in Mia's eyes, he could see that she still smarted from the confrontation. 'Mia, she's just a vindictive woman.'

Color rose in her cheeks. 'I'm all right. I promise I won't cry myself to sleep.'

'Will you sleep?'

'If you ever go home, I might,' she said irritably. 'I've dealt with bitches far bitchier than Wheaton, trust me. Hell, I'm far bitchier than Wheaton. Look, I appreciate your concern. But go home. We'll study that damn tape backward and forward tomorrow. I promise.' She turned and squeezed through the space between their vehicles.

He followed her, all the while telling himself to just do as she asked. *Go home.* But his feet didn't obey and placing one hand on the SUV's hood for support, he nimbly sprang over their bumpers, landing on his feet. 'Mia.'

'Dammit, Solliday.' She yanked open the passenger door. 'For the last time, I am okay. For the last time, go home.' She bent over, her hand searching under the seat.

For a second he damned the ratty jacket that effectively covered her past her hips. Then he thanked it. 'What are you doing?'

'Getting your sister's plastic bowl.'

'You don't have to give it back now. She has plenty of bowls.'

'I wasn't going to give it back. I only ate half of mine. I'll eat the rest for breakfast.'

He winced. 'Lasagne for breakfast.'

'It's got all the major food groups, so don't knock it.' She straightened, lifting the plastic bowl in the air like a trophy. 'Lasagne, breakfast of champions.'

His eyes followed hers to the container she held, then shifted to the left when he caught a movement from the corner of his eye. A car approached, too fast for the speed limit on her street. The window was rolling down and a face peered out. Reed had a split second for recognition to dawn before he saw a flash of light as the streetlamp reflected against the steel barrel of a gun.

'Reed! Get—'

Mia's words barely registered as his reflexes took over. He leaped, and in the next moment they were both on the sidewalk, his body covering hers.

A heartbeat later a shot cracked the air and her driver's-side window shattered. He pressed her flat to the ground as a second shot took out her windshield and a third pinged off the hood inches from the top of his head as the car sped away, tires screeching and the odor of burning rubber filling the air. They were gone. At least the car was. It would be stupid for the gunman to leave the safety of his vehicle. But the guy had shot at a cop in front of her own apartment, so how smart could he be?

Reed lay there, straining to hear footsteps over the pounding of his heart in his ears, waiting for a fourth shot that never came. His body fully covered hers, one arm hooked around her waist, his face buried in her hair. His shoulder had taken the brunt of the fall where he'd landed and rolled. Her right arm extended straight out from beneath him, her weapon looking huge in her small hand. She'd drawn as he'd taken her down. He'd done the same. Gripping his nine-mil, he lifted his head.

'Are you hit?'

'Only . . . by you.' Her elbow jabbed his ribs. 'Dammit, Solliday, I can't breathe.'

You're welcome, he thought sourly and lifted himself a fraction of an inch so she could breathe. 'God.' She shuddered out the breath, greedily took in another. 'You hit?'

'No.' He sucked in a deep breath of his own. Now that it was over, his muscles didn't seem capable of any movement at all. 'I got a glimpse of his face. Looked like your Getts.'

'I know. I saw him, fucking little bastard. Same MO that got him in this mess to start with. Drive-by shootings, killing innocent bystanders. You'd think the fucker would learn his lesson, but no. He's still shooting up the damn neighborhood with no care for bystanders caught in the crossfire.' She was muttering as her breath hitched. 'He's already ditched the car by now. He always does.' Her body sagged beneath him and she rested her cheek against his forearm. 'Dammit.' The last was a weary murmur, as if she hadn't the energy for more.

His own body slumped. Any of those bullets could have hit them. If he'd been a second later, she could have been dead. If her car had been any smaller, he could have been dead, too. That last shot had come way too close for comfort. He dropped his head and took another breath, this time smelling the lemon of her hair instead of burning rubber or gunpowder. Awareness was returning in degrees as the adrenaline began to ebb.

Glass was everywhere around them. The sidewalk was hard against his elbows and his left knee would have a hell of a bruise by morning. But she was small beneath him, soft and round. And for the moment, leaning on him. It was a vulnerability he suspected she let few people see.

That she let him see was . . . sweet. Thrilling. And combined with the feel of the soft curve of her rear end against him . . . undeniably arousing. *Get up, Solliday, before you*— But it was too late. He grimaced as his body stirred and with an effort he pushed himself to his hands and knees, hoping he'd been fast enough, hoping she hadn't noticed. Carefully he straightened, wincing as the discomfort in his knee took his mind off the ache elsewhere. He shook his shoulders free of pebbled glass, then bent his head and brushed more glass from his hair.

She pulled herself up to sit against her car, every movement slow and tentative. It was the second time in as many days she'd taken a blow to her injured shoulder. He'd tried to take most of the brunt of the fall himself, but he'd obviously hurt her just the same.

'I'm sorry,' he murmured. 'I didn't mean to hurt you.'

She drew a breath and took her radio from her belt. 'I'm okay. Just knocked the wind out of me.' But she didn't meet his eyes as she called for Dispatch and he wasn't sure if she had noticed his physical response or if she was just embarrassed that he'd seen her as anything less than a superwoman.

'This is Detective Mitchell, Homicide. We've had

shots fired at 1342 Sedgewick Place from a moving car. Shooter and driver have escaped in a late-model Ford, brown.' She rattled off the license plate and he was amazed she'd had the presence of mind to notice. 'You'll probably find the car abandoned within a block radius. Send a CSU team. Tell responding units there are plainclothes officers on the scene.' She clipped her radio back on her belt.

'What do you want to do?' he asked.

Sirens were faint in the distance. 'He's gone,' she said.

Reed pushed himself to his feet and bent his knee. 'If he's on foot, we can search,' he said, but she shook her head.

'Let the uniforms search the area and I'll call Spinnelli.'

She looked up at him then, understanding in her eyes. 'You couldn't have done anything. You definitely shouldn't chase him. You're not a cop.'

You're welcome, he thought again, twice as irritated as before. He wasn't a cop, but he was law enforcement. He carried a gun. Her attitude was so typical of cops, it made him pissed. But it wasn't worth fighting that one tonight.

She stood up, gingerly. 'You're angry,' she said and he gritted his teeth.

'Getting shot at kind of makes me pissed,' he said sourly. He waited for her to say something else . . . like *thank you*, but when she didn't, he frowned and moved past her.

She stopped him, grabbing his arm. 'Thank you, Reed. You saved my neck.'

He looked down into her face, let himself shudder over the thought of how close they'd both come to being shot. Even though she was safe, her cheek was a mess, scraped and raw. Gently he cupped her chin, ran his thumb along her jaw, felt her flinch. He now understood she was more likely to flinch at tenderness than at real pain. 'I'm sorry. I didn't mean to hurt you. Just now or back at the newsroom.'

Just as gently, she pulled away. 'I know.' The sirens now screeched down her street. 'The cavalry's here.'

Apartment windows had started to open and residents were cautiously poking their heads out now that it appeared to be safe. Two cruisers with flashing lights rolled to a stop in front of her car.

'Goddammit,' she snarled and Reed's head whipped as he checked the area. All he saw was broken glass and the beginning of a small crowd.

'What?'

She pointed at one of the cruisers. Just behind the right front tire was the remnants of Lauren's plastic bowl, smashed to smithereens. 'Now I'll have to eat Pop-Tarts.'

He couldn't help it. He had to laugh.

Wednesday, November 29, 6:00 A.M.

He'd had a good night's sleep and now his mind was working efficiently once more. He'd looked all over for Young, the next name on his mental list. There were four Youngs. One had known, but was merely a coward. His death would be less painful. Two knew and looked the other way. They would suffer. But one . . . he'd caused great pain. He'd killed Shane. *He'll wish he was dead a thousand times before I'm done.* He'd been unsuccessful in locating any of the Youngs. Until now.

How could he have missed it? The one he sought sold real estate. Realtors plastered their names everywhere – including on the high school alumni website. Tyler Young now lived in Indianapolis. Finding him would be easy. He would finish off the Doughertys tonight, then head south.

But he still needed to find the other Youngs. If he had to, he'd go back. He didn't want to. But he had to find the other Youngs. He'd faced down a lot of ghosts already. What was one more? But it wasn't just any ghost. It was Shane's. And his own.

Wednesday, November 29, 7:25 A.M.

Mia was waiting on the curb when Solliday pulled up in his SUV, her plastic garment bag slung over her shoulder. He leaned over to open her door. 'You look like hell.'

Folding the hanging bag, she tossed it in the back and swung up into the passenger seat with a wince. Her head ached, her shoulder burned and the whole right side of her body was sore, despite the way he'd tried to cushion their fall with his own body the night before. 'Good morning to you, too, sunshine,' she muttered as she buckled up.

'Did you get any sleep?'

'Some.' Maybe an hour total, spread over four. She kept waking up, normal after an adrenaline rush like she'd experienced. But when she woke it wasn't to the sound of shots and shattering glass, but to the memory of his body stretched over hers, hard and aroused. And when she woke, she reached for him. That was the worst part. 'You?'

'Some. Do you think we can be a little late for Spinnelli's eight o'clock meeting?'

She studied him warily. 'Why?'

He looked away, but not before she saw his cheeks redden and suddenly the cab was too warm. He was remembering last night, too. Which was why it was against regulations for partners to have any extracurricular involvement. Which was why it wouldn't happen.

'I watched the tape when I got home last night. In the home video the guy with the camera was shouting at somebody to get behind him, to stay away from the fire.'

'Probably didn't want whoever it was to block his shot,' she said sardonically. 'So?'

'So he called the person Jared. Maybe it was another neighbor. Or his kid.'

'Very cool,' she said slowly. 'So we find out who Jared is, hopefully before the neighborhood's left for work. I'll call Marc, but he won't be able to move the meeting too far. He called last night after you left. Wanted to be sure we were both still alive. He said there's a press conference at ten. We're expected to put in an appearance.'

He made a disgusted face. 'Why?'

'Because we're primary on the case. Spinnelli will field all the questions, but we'll be there as the poster children of cross-agency cooperation. Relax. Your shoes are already shiny. I've got to change into my dress uniform and my shoes pinch.'

He grimaced. 'So we're window dressing.'

'More like bait.'

His brows shot up. 'Who will they let into the press conference?'

Mia's smile was sharp. 'Spinnelli told them not to be too picky about credentials.'

'He's hoping the arsonist shows up.'

'He's certainly not doing it for the exposure. Spinnelli hates wearing his dress blues even more than I do.'

'Suddenly I feel a smile coming on.'

She chuckled. 'Drive, Solliday. I've got calls to make.'

Wednesday, November 29, 7:25 A.M.

Tania Sladerman staggered down the stairs to her apartment, exhausted from the double shift. She knew the manager at the Beacon Inn wouldn't even thank her for covering, but at least the overtime pay would help cover next semester's tuition.

She missed twice before shoving the key into her dead bolt. Then jerked upright when a hand grabbed her hair and yanked back her head. *A knife. To my throat.*

A scream broke free, but his other hand clamped her mouth, muffling it. 'Don't say a word,' he breathed. 'Or I'll slit your fucking throat.'

Wednesday, November 29, 7:55 A.M.

'This was easier than I thought,' Reed said as they walked up to Jared's father's house. The kids at the bus stop had given up their comrade without blinking an eye.

'It's always easier to ask kids. They don't worry about selling their video to the highest bidder.' Mia rapped on the door and waited, her head tilted in apparent repose, but Reed knew better. She'd been livid when she found out who Jared's father was. The door opened and Mr Wright's eyes widened.

Mia's smile was not pleasant. 'I hope you remember me, Mr Wright. Or perhaps Oliver Stone would be more appropriate? I hear you're in the filmmaking business.'

Wright's eyes hardened. 'I didn't do anything wrong.'

'Illegal, no. Immoral, plenty. She was your neighbor and you profited from her death. You stood there with tears in your eyes. Were those for the camera, too?'

'I told you what you wanted to know. Besides, it was my son that took the video. Duane. He's in high school. It was . . . homework.'

Mitchell's mouth twisted. 'You can call it what you like while you're handing it over.'

Wright's mouth dropped open. 'You can't do that. It's private property.'

'It's evidence. There are a few ways to do this. You can wait here while I call in for a warrant. Or' – she held up a finger when Wright would have protested – 'you can go to your office and then I can show up with a warrant in an hour or two once everyone is at their desk. I've got to go to a press conference this morning, so I'll still be in full uniform, escorting you to the door. Or, you can give me the video now and go on with your day.'

Wright's jaw tightened. 'Are you threatening me, Detective?'

Reed vividly remembered the scene with Wheaton the night before. This was the same song, second verse. And the more he'd thought about Wheaton, the more he realized Mia had been right. He had usurped her authority. It wasn't the way partners behaved.

'Yeah, she is. Which is it going to be, Mr Wright? Door

number one, two, or three? And I wouldn't think of trying to destroy the videos because then I think she'd make sure she hauled you downtown and the charge would have more teeth. Like obstruction.'

Mia nodded. 'Sounds good, Lieutenant. Obstruction it would be.'

'Wait here.' He slammed the door in their faces.

Mia looked up, her eyes once again full of respect. 'Well, done, Monty Hall.'

The door opened and she turned her attention back to Wright, who slapped a videocassette into Reed's hand, barely waiting for Mitchell to write him out a receipt before slamming the door so hard the house shook.

'Thank you for doing your civic duty with such a cheerful spirit,' she murmured. 'Let's get this back to the office and see if we can figure out who our mystery lady is.'

Reed followed her back to his SUV. She frowned at him. 'Are you okay, Solliday?'

Reed nodded, grateful he'd regained some of the moisture in his mouth. Because the moment she'd looked up, so serious, his mouth had gone completely, utterly, bone dry. He clenched his jaw as they headed back to the city. This was damn inconvenient and a totally bad idea. *She* was a totally bad idea. But the images that had taunted him during the night returned and with them a yearning that left him breathless.

It was Lauren's fault, he decided. She'd put the idea in his mind that he needed someone. That he'd be alone. Of how long it had been since he'd had a relationship. It was just bad luck that fate had paired him with a woman detective at the same time. He damned Lauren and damned fate. And wondered how Mia felt about strings.

'Solliday, your face is . . . pasty. If you need to throw up, let me drive.'

Grimly he laughed. Mia Mitchell did have a way of articulating the obvious. 'I'm fine. Besides, your feet won't reach the pedals.'

She made a sarcastic face. 'Smart-ass. Just drive, Solliday.'

Wednesday, November 29, 10:10 A.M.

Mia scanned the crowd who sat impatiently waiting for Spinnelli to appear. It was cold outside but Spinnelli had wanted to maximize access. There were reporters in the crowd, but also a half dozen cops in plain clothes. Spinnelli had set up surveillance in advance and there were several cameras recording the event from several angles. Holly Wheaton sat in the front row, her eyes shooting daggers, although they seemed to be aimed at Solliday. Mia glanced up at him, standing beside her, his feet spread, his arms folded over his chest. He looked like a bodyguard.

'Wheaton looks like she wants to do you some serious harm,' she murmured.

'She said some things after you left. I suggested she might . . . reconsider.'

Something in her warmed. 'You took up for me?'

His mouth curved inside his goatee. 'Something like that.'

'Okay. Thanks, I guess.'

'You're welcome.'

Mia rocked slightly on her sore feet as she studied faces. 'See anybody you know?'

'No known firebugs, if that's what you mean. But check out the back. Ten o'clock.'

Mia had to bite back a scowl. 'One blond bitch with a braid,' she muttered. 'I'm still pissed that she printed Penny Hill's name before we could inform the family.'

'But she did give you DuPree. You said she was on your Christmas list forever.'

'I lied,' she muttered and heard his deep chuckle. The warmth inside her spread, soothed, even though she wanted no part of it.

Spinnelli walked up to the podium. The crowd sat up straighter. 'We've had reports in the press of a string of fires and homicides. We're here today to set the record straight. We've had two fires in the last week, presumably set by the same arsonist. At each fire site, one body was discovered. We're treating each death as a homicide. At this time we are pursuing a number of leads. Leading the investigation are Detective Mitchell, Homicide, and Lieutenant Solliday from the OFI. Both are decorated, seasoned professionals with many years' experience between them. They have the full support and resources of both departments at their disposal. I'll take a few questions now.'

A *Trib* reporter stood. 'Can you confirm the first victim was the child of a cop?'

'This is true. The deceased is Caitlin Burnette, a nineteen-year-old college student. We ask that you respect her family in this time of mourning. Next?'

Holly Wheaton rose gracefully and Mia gritted her teeth. 'The second victim was a social worker. It's hard not to make a connection between the two. A cop's daughter and a social worker. Are we talking about someone with a mission of revenge?'

'At this time, the motive behind these homicides is not known. Next?'

'Smooth,' Solliday murmured.

'That's why he wears the stripes.' Mia kept her eyes trained on the crowd as the reporters asked the same questions a dozen different ways. Spinnelli stayed calm and unruffled. He was extending the exposure, she knew. Giving them time to study the crowd, to look for any suspicious behavior. But nothing jumped out. Nothing looked—

She went completely still. Beside her, Solliday tensed.

'What?' he demanded in a low whisper.

Mia swallowed hard, unable to break eye contact with the blonde across the crowd just as she'd been unable to look away when their eyes had met over her half-brother's gravestone. The woman just looked at her, her expression unreadable.

'Who do you see?' he asked. 'Is it the woman from the video?'

Mia managed to shake her head. 'No.'

He pushed out a frustrated breath. 'Then who?' he hissed between his teeth.

The woman touched her fingertips to her temple in a small salute and slipped away. 'I don't know,' Mia said. 'Cover me.' She stepped behind Solliday's body, grateful for his size as she slipped to the sidelines, her radio in her hand. 'This is Mitchell. There's a woman walking west. Five-six, shoulder-length blond hair, dark suit. Stop her.'

Mia made it to the back of the crowd and looked around. The uniforms stationed at this area looked puzzled. 'Nobody matching that description came through here, Detective.'

Mia swore softly and set off at a jog when she saw her. She was walking fast, a scarf covering her head. And now . . . She was getting into a white Chevy Cavalier. Mia started running, but the car pulled away from the curb, made a quick turn, and was gone before Mia could get more than the first three letters of the license plate. 'DDA—' *Shit*.

Mia stopped abruptly in the middle of the street. Dammit. The woman was like a damn ghost. Disgusted, she headed back. Spinnelli was still on the platform.

Solliday pushed his way around the crowd and met

her along the side. 'The woman on the tape had brown hair. Why did you chase a blonde?' he demanded.

'I honestly don't know. But getting mad at me won't help, that I can guarantee.'

'Look, we're in this investigation together, Detective,' he said, his voice tense and too controlled. 'Don't ever tell me to "cover you" then slip away again. What if it had been someone we needed to follow? I had no way of knowing if you needed backup.'

'It was personal, all right? I don't think it had anything to do with this case.'

Solliday's eyes flickered. 'You walked away from a press conference we threw to draw out a killer because of something *personal*?'

Put that way, she could see his point. 'Yeah.'

Spinnelli came up to them, his eyes narrowed. 'What was that all about, Mia?'

Mia pursed her lips. 'I . . . I'll explain.'

'Damn straight you will,' Spinnelli snapped. 'Debrief in my conference room in ten minutes. Don't be late.'

Mia watched him walk away, managing to control her wince. Solliday still stood staring at her, dark eyes flashing. 'I'm sorry,' she said. 'It won't happen again.'

'To paraphrase your leader, damn straight it won't.' Then he walked away.

'Goddammit.' But Mia wasn't sure who she was swearing at. After a minute, she went inside the precinct, deciding she was swearing at herself.

Chapter Eleven

Wednesday, November 29, 10:45 A.M.

All eyes were on her when she walked into the conference room. Spinnelli, Jack, Miles. And Solliday. She sat next to Jack, her stomach churning.

'Did the woman from the news video show?' Spinnelli barked without preamble.

Solliday cleared his throat. 'No. Mia thought she saw somebody she recognized, but it turned out not to be the video woman. We got some more amateur video taken yesterday evening. We're hoping to find a lead there.'

He was covering for her. Mia bit down on the inside of her cheek. As angry as he'd been, he was covering for her. He was acting like a partner. *But I didn't.*

Spinnelli pushed. 'You must have seen somebody you knew to disappear like that.' He frowned. 'Without communicating your intentions. Who did you see?'

Mia met Spinnelli's hard gaze. 'I didn't see the woman from the video. Sir.'

Spinnelli drummed his fingers once. 'Then who was she?'

Mia laced her fingers together, hard. 'It was a personal matter.'

Spinnelli's eyes narrowed. 'Well, it just became public knowledge. Who was she?'

Her churning stomach turned upside down. *Now everyone would know*. 'I don't know her name. I saw her for the first time three weeks ago. She's popped up a few more times in the last few weeks. Then again today.'

Spinnelli's eyes widened. 'She's been following you?'

'Yeah.' Mia swallowed hard, but the bile still burned the back of her throat.

'What does she say, Mia?' Solliday asked, very quietly.

'Nothing. She just looks at me. Then runs before I can find out what she wants.'

'She saluted you today,' Solliday said.

She saw it in her mind. That little salute with that small reluctant smile. 'I know.'

Miles leaned back, his eyes sharp. 'You do know who she is.'

'I know who I think she is. But she has nothing to do with this case. Sir.'

Spinnelli cocked his jaw. 'She's following you. Last night you were shot at.'

Mia frowned quickly. 'That was different. That was Getts.'

Spinnelli leaned forward. 'You don't know that for sure. So tell me, Mia.'

It was not a request. 'All right. I found out the day of my father's burial that he'd had a son with . . . with a woman not my mother. The boy is buried in the plot right next to his. The woman who's been following me was there, at the burial. She looks just like my father.' She lifted her chin. 'I assume she's his daughter, too.'

There was a long moment of uncomfortable silence. Then Jack reached over and covered her hands with one of his. She hadn't realized how cold she was until she felt his warmth. 'You're going to pull your fingers out of their sockets,' he murmured, loosening the death grip she had on her hands.

Spinnelli cleared his throat. 'I take it you never knew about these . . . siblings.'

'No, sir. But that's not really important. The fact remains that I diverted my attention from a stakeout for personal reasons. I'll accept the consequences.'

Spinnelli looked at her, hard. Then blew out a breath. 'Everybody out. Except you, Mia. You stay.' Chairs scraped as Miles, Solliday and Jack rose to their feet.

When the door was shut, she closed her eyes. 'Just get it over with, Marc.'

She could hear his footsteps as he paced the length of the room. Then he stopped. 'Look at me, Mia.' Bracing herself, she did. He stood on the other side of the table, his fists on his hips, his mustache bunched in a frown. 'Hell, Mia. Why didn't you tell me?'

'I . . .' She shook her head. 'I don't know.'

'Abe said you told him you were distracted that night. Now I guess it all makes sense.' He sighed. 'I'm not sure I'd have done anything differently.'

Her heart thumped hard in her chest. 'Sir?'

'Mia, we've known each other too long for this shit. You have a personal problem, you take personal time, okay? But under the circumstances, I would have followed her, too. You think she's a danger?'

Mia drew her first easy breath in an hour. 'I don't think so. Like Solliday said, today she saluted me. It was almost . . . respect. All I could think was that we were watching for suspicious faces and there she was. But she showed up before the arson started.'

'She just gives you the creeps.'

'Yeah. Makes me wonder how many more there are out there.'

'Well, figure it out on your own time,' he said, but gently. 'Now, get back to work. I want to know who that woman in the news video is, ASAP. You're dismissed.'

Mia made it to the door, then paused, her hand on the doorknob. 'Thanks, Marc.'

He just grunted. 'Get out of those monkey shoes, Mitchell.'

Mia got back to the bullpen and stopped. Dana stood next to her desk, a small cardboard box clutched in her hand. 'What's up?' she asked, dropping to her chair.

Dana lifted her brows. 'I've come to report a

homicide.' She set the box on Mia's desk and pulled out a crab, its claws wrapped with rubber bands. It wasn't moving.

Mia wrinkled her nose. 'Jeez, Dana, what the hell is that?'

'It *was* a Maryland crab. I caught it with my own hands. It was alive and would have *been* alive if you'd come last night. Now it's dead and you're to blame. I want justice.'

'I can't believe people eat those. They look like giant bugs from a bad fifties flick.'

Dana dropped the dead crab back in the box. 'They're pretty tasty, which you would have found out if we could have cooked this one for you. I heard there was a press conference, so I figured you'd be here. I've been worried. How's your shoulder?'

'Good as new.'

'And now you've got a new owie. What did you do to yourself now?'

'Dodged a bullet,' she said carelessly and Dana's eyes narrowed.

'This new case?'

'No.'

'You'll tell me later. For now, I need to know what's happening on this arson case.'

'You know I can't tell you specifics, Dana.'

Pain flashed in Dana's brown eyes. 'I knew Penny Hill.' And she was mourning her, Mia could see. 'She was a good person. You'll catch who did this?'

'Yes.' Now if they had a lead or two, she'd feel better about that promise.

'Good.' Dana tilted her head. 'And everything else? How's all that?'

'I had to tell Spinnelli. She was at the press conference.'

Dana blinked in surprise. 'Damn.'

'She got away again, but I got half her license plate this time.'

'You want Ethan to track her down?'

Dana's husband was a PI with a way around computers. 'Not yet. I'll try first.' Mia's gaze swerved to the edge of the bullpen, where Solliday had entered, a small television under one arm and a VCR under the other. He'd covered for her when he didn't have to. Dana twisted around to see what she was looking at and whistled softly.

She looked back, her appreciation evident. 'So who is he?'

'Who?' But it was a bad plan to play dumb. 'Oh. Him.'

'Yeah, him.' Dana's lips twitched. 'Want me to run a background check on him?'

Mia felt her cheeks heat, knowing exactly what Dana meant. She'd run Ethan through the system herself when Dana got all floppy-eyed over him and they'd been married just a few months later. It didn't take a detective to connect the dots. 'Not necessary. That's my new partner.'

Dana's eyes now flashed amusement. 'You were a little sparse on the details, girl.' She stood up as Solliday put the video equipment on Abe's desk. 'Hello, there. I'm Dana Buchanan, Mia's friend. And you are?'

Solliday shook the hand Dana extended. 'Reed Solliday, her temporary partner.' His mouth curved, his eyes warming. 'You're the foster mother.'

Dana's smile broadened. 'I am. Right now I have five, but I'll get another soon.'

'I was a foster kid. My parents were active in the system for years. Good for you.'

Dana still held his hand, studying his face in a way that made Mia's cheeks hotter. 'Thank you.' She let go of his hand and turned back to Mia. 'Call me later, or I'll come find you. That's a promise.' She gave a backward wave as she walked away.

Mia grabbed Wright's video. 'Thanks for getting the TV.'

'No problem.' Watching her friend from the corner of his eye, Reed tossed Mia the cord. 'Plug it in and I'll set it up.' When the redhead got to the edge of the bullpen, she stopped and looked back. Her brows lifted in silent challenge, then she disappeared into the hall. There had been a comforting quality to her voice and in the way she'd held his hand, as if they'd been old friends. 'She forgot her box,' he said.

Mia glanced up and laughed. 'She would. It's got a dead crab in it.'

'Your friend brought you a dead crab?'

'It was supposed to be a culinary delight.' She ducked under her desk to plug the cord in, then stood, briskly tugging at her dress uniform. 'Let's look at Mr Wright's opus.'

Reed popped in the video. 'This is the footage of the fire we saw last night.' In silence they watched the fire scene, watched themselves. Reed swallowed the wince when the camera caught him fumbling with his boots and Mia taking over the task.

'I'm sorry about that,' she murmured and he remembered the look in her eyes when he'd rebuked her. Remote, as if she'd pulled back from a slap. *But you're stuck with me.* The words were telling in light of what she'd just divulged. What a shock it must have been to find her father had a second family. He searched for something to say.

'Mia, about what happened in Spinnelli's office . . .'

Her eyes never left the small screen, her jaw going taut. 'Thanks for trying to cover for me. You won't have to do it again.'

'I didn't mean that. That woman. Your . . .' He faltered. 'It must have been a shock.'

Her eyes narrowed at the video as a young woman with a braid came into the picture, briefly. 'There's Carmichael, skulking around.'

She'd shut the door on the subject. 'She kept to the background,' he said.

'I should have seen her.'

'Maybe. You'll be looking for her next time.'

She shot him a guarded glance. 'Carmichael, yes.'

He held her eyes for a moment before she looked away, back to the screen where the scene had changed. Wheaton stood at the curb, fluffing out her hair and checking her makeup. 'Jared's brother Duane was standing pretty far back,' he said.

'It's going to make it hard to get anything unless he ventures closer.'

'It's still quarter to six according to the time stamp. The woman's not here yet.' He pulled Mitchell's chair around their desks. 'Sit down. This could take a while.' The picture focused on Wheaton, before finally zooming out. Reed sat up straight, suddenly alert. 'She's there.' The blue Hyundai was parked off to the side and the woman was standing at her car door, staring up at the house, just as she had on *Action News*'s video.

Mitchell had leaned forward, squinting. 'Can we get a make on the plate?'

'Maybe your computer enhancement guys can,' Reed said doubtfully. 'Duane's still too far away for me to see anything and the angle's bad.'

Then as if heeding their wish, the camera crept a little closer, taking a trip along the outer boundary of cars and onlookers. Reed held his breath. 'Just a little farther.'

'Holly's on,' Mitchell said. 'Her people are paying attention to her. Duane's getting a little braver. Come on, boy. Move your ass closer.' Duane did, the video inching closer to the car. Finally it stopped, the plate still too small to read, but in full view.

'Closer, boy,' she murmured, but the camera hovered in place for a few seconds, then abruptly moved back to Wheaton's camera crew who were dismantling equipment. Then there was static as the video stopped.

'I think that's the best we're going to get,' Reed said. 'Let's take this to the computer guys. Maybe we'll get lucky.'

Mitchell pushed her chair back. 'The computer guys are on the fifth floor. You take them the video. I'll change and meet you. Don't have any fun until I get there.'

He watched as she jogged from the bullpen. She'd closed herself off, just as she had when he'd touched her face. He should let it go. But he wasn't sure he could.

Wednesday, November 29, 1:05 P.M.

Mia stared out the window of the SUV as Solliday slowly drove past the teachers' parking lot. 'There it is. One blue Hyundai, registered to Brooke Adler, English teacher.'

'Your computer guys did a good job blowing up that video frame.'

'Technology is a beautiful thing,' she agreed as he pulled into a visitor's space. 'Adler's got a clean sheet. She doesn't seem like a likely arson suspect.'

'Agreed. But she knows something. Or thinks she does.'

'Agreed. If she'd set the fire, I think she'd look satisfied, but she just looked guilty.'

'The fact that she works with delinquent kids is as good a tie as any so far.'

'Our arsonist isn't a novice. You said so yourself. Could he really be a kid?'

'I said his fire-setting methods were sophisticated. I don't think he's a little kid. A teenager would certainly fit the profile.' He angled his head. 'What's wrong, Mia?'

She met his eyes, troubled. 'Penny Hill was burned alive. On purpose.'

'And part of you doesn't want to believe a kid is capable of that,' he said quietly. 'While the other part knows better.'

She nodded, the truth of it a bitter taste in her mouth. 'That about sums it up.'

He lifted a shoulder, sympathetic. 'We could be wrong.'

'I hope not. It's the first real lead we've gotten.' She slid to the ground. 'Let's go.'

She walked through the school door he held open, thinking she could get used to somebody like Reed Solliday. Doors, chairs, coffee. She was getting spoiled.

A woman sat behind the glass. Her badge said she was Marcy. 'Can I help you?'

'I'm Detective Mitchell and this is Lieutenant Solliday. We've already provided ID to your security guard at the gate. We'd like to speak with Miss Adler, please.'

'I'm afraid she's in class right now. May I take a message?'

Mia smiled obligingly. 'You may not. You may tell her to come talk to us right now.'

A man appeared to their left. 'I'm Dr Bixby, director of Hope Center. Can I help?'

Mia distrusted him at first sight. 'Only to assist us in speaking to Miss Adler. Now.'

'Marcy, arrange for coverage in Miss Adler's room. Come with me.' He led them to a small room, spartanly furnished. 'You can wait here. It will be more private than the lobby. As her employer, I have to ask. Is Miss Adler in some kind of trouble?'

Mia kept smiling. 'We just want to talk to her.'

Uncertainly the man closed the door, leaving them alone with an old desk and two worn chairs. The single window was covered with black bars. It was what it appeared to be – a prison for bad kids. 'I always wonder if they've got places like this bugged.'

'Then let's ask her to step outside,' Solliday said simply and Mia looked up at him.

'No "Don't be so paranoid, Mitchell"?' she asked.

'Does Abe say that?'

'No, never. He just flips a coin to choose lunch. Heads is good. Tails is vegetarian.'

He paced the length of the small room and once again she was taken with the fluid grace with which he moved. A man his size should look cramped and out of place in a room this small. Instead, he moved like a cat, balancing on the balls of his feet. Graceful, but . . . restless. 'I take it you're not taken with vegetarian fare,' he murmured.

'No. We were a meat and potatoes family.'

He'd stopped at the window and now stood looking between the bars, his expression pensive. 'So were we, after.'

His mood had altered dramatically in the minutes they'd been here. 'After what?'

He threw a look over his shoulder. 'After I went to live with the Sollidays.'

The look was a guarded one that warned her to proceed cautiously. 'They adopted you out of the foster-care system?'

He nodded, turning back to the window. 'I'd been in four homes before they took me in. I'd run away from the last two. I was too close to being sent to a place like this.'

'Then we owe the Sollidays a great deal,' she said softly and watched him swallow.

'Yes, we do.' He turned and sat on the arm of one of the chairs. 'I do.'

'Sometimes there's a fine line between going good and going bad. One good experience, one kind soul can make all the difference in the world.'

One side of his mouth lifted. 'I still think good people deal and bad people don't.'

'Way too simple. But we'll save that debate for another day. Somebody's coming.'

The door opened and Mia found herself looking at the woman from the video. She was very young. 'Miss Adler?' she asked and the woman nodded, eyes wide. Scared.

Adler stepped into the room, Bixby behind her. 'Yes. What can I do for you?'

'I'm Detective Mitchell and this is my partner, Lieutenant Solliday. We'd like to talk to you,' Mia said evenly. 'Would you step outside with us?'

Bixby cleared his throat. 'It's cold, Detectives. We'd be more comfortable in here.'

'I'm not a detective,' Solliday inserted smoothly. 'I'm a fire marshal.'

The color drained from Adler's face and Bixby looked down at her with a frown. 'Miss Adler, what's happened?'

She clenched her hands together. 'Did Bart Secrest talk to you yesterday?'

Bixby's mouth tightened almost imperceptibly. 'What have you done, Miss Adler?'

It was a not-so-subtle move to distance himself from his employee. Flinching, Adler moistened her lips. 'I just went to see one of the houses in the articles. That's all.'

Mia took a step forward. 'Um, hello? We'd like to know what's going on here, now.'

Dr Bixby leveled Mia a stern look that she imagined would have reduced the trembling Miss Adler to tears before briskly moving to the telephone on the wooden desk. 'Marcy, can you call Bart and Julian? Have them meet us in my office right away.'

'Miss Adler, we'd like to talk to you alone, first,' Mia insisted. 'We won't be long. Although we'd be happy to wait while you get a coat.' She held the door open, ignoring the director, who'd opened his mouth but closed it without saying a word.

Adler shook her head. 'No, I'll be all right.'

Wednesday, November 29, 1:25 P.M.

He could see the parking lot from the window. He stood there now, watching as three people left the building to stand in the sun. Two had gone in. A woman and a man. The woman was Detective Mia Mitchell. He recognized her from her picture in the paper. The man then could only be Lieutenant Solliday. His heart would continue to beat normally. He would not lose his head.

They were talking to Brooke Adler, because she'd gone to the fire scene, the idiot. Not because they knew anything. They had nothing. No evidence. No suspects. So there was no reason to fear. They could search the whole school and find nothing, because there wasn't anything here. He smiled. *Except me.*

Mitchell and Solliday would have their little talk with Adler, learn what everyone else already knew – the new English teacher was an insignificant, airheaded little mouse. With, he had to admit, exceptional breasts. He'd often had thoughts about her body – enjoying it, even allowing her to enjoy it. But now, all that would have to change. At least the part about her enjoying it. For bringing them here, she'd have to pay.

But the fun would need to wait. Right now there were cops on the property. But they wouldn't stay long. When they were satisfied there was nothing here, Mitchell and Solliday would leave. *And I'll go on.* Tonight he'd finish Mrs Dougherty. He was already getting excited thinking about the new challenge.

But again, the fun would need to wait. Right now, he had someplace to be.

Wednesday, November 29, 1:25 P.M.

Brooke willed her teeth not to chatter as the cop looked her up and down scathingly.

'You were at our crime scene yesterday evening,' she began sharply. 'Why?'

'I . . .' She wet her lips and felt them burn dry from the cold air. 'I was curious.'

'Are you nervous, Miss Adler?' the fire marshal asked gently. Brooke didn't watch much television, but she'd seen enough to know the man was the good cop. The small, blond woman played the bad cop very well.

'I haven't done anything wrong,' she said, but she sounded guilty, even to her own ears. 'If you'd go inside, we can explain everything to you.'

'We will soon,' the fire marshal said. His name was Lieutenant Solliday. She needed to remember that. She needed to remember she hadn't done anything wrong and stop acting like an idiot. 'But first, tell us why you went to the burned-out house last night.' His smile was kind. 'We caught you on the ten o'clock news.'

She'd had a bad feeling when she'd seen herself on the news. Her biggest fear had been that Bixby or Julian would see her. This was worse. 'I told you, I was curious. I'd read about the fires and I wanted to see them for myself.'

'So who is Bart Secrest and what did he tell Bixby?' the woman asked.

'Please ask Dr Bixby.' She looked over her shoulder. Dr Bixby was standing just inside the front door with a scowl. 'You're going to get me fired,' she murmured.

Solliday smiled, still kindly. 'We'll haul you downtown if you keep wasting our time.'

She blinked at the clash between his kind tone and harsh words. Her heart was beating hard and she was sweating despite the cold. 'You can't. I didn't do anything.'

'Watch us,' he said softly. 'Two women are dead, Miss Adler. Maybe you know something useful and maybe you don't. If you do, you'll tell us. If you don't, you'll stop whatever game you're playing because every minute we stand here is a minute he has to plan another attack. I'll ask you again. Why did you go to the burned-out house?'

Her mouth went dry. Two women, dead. 'One of our students was clipping the articles from the paper about

273

the two fires. I reported him to Bart Secrest, our security dean. The rest you'll have to get from him.'

The woman's eyes narrowed. 'Him, who? Him, Secrest or him, the student?'

Brooke closed her eyes, visualizing the cold expression on Manny's face that morning. She doubted anyone would be able to pry anything out of Manny now. 'Secrest,' she said and shivered hard. 'I've honestly told you everything I can.' The two detectives shared a glance and Lieutenant Solliday nodded.

'All right, Miss Adler,' the detective said. 'Let's go talk to Dr Bixby.'

Wednesday, November 29, 1:30 P.M.

Bixby was waiting for them in the lobby. The look he shot Adler was cold and Mia couldn't help but feel a little sorry for the woman.

He led them to an office as rich as the waiting room had been sparse. He gestured to leather chairs around a mahogany conference table. Two men were already seated. One was in his mid-forties with a kindly face. The other looked like he bashed in walls with his bald head for fun. 'Dr Julian Thompson and Mr Bart Secrest,' Bixby said.

The nice-faced one rose, a smile creasing his face. Immediately Mia distrusted him as much as Bixby. 'I'm Dr Thompson, the school's counselor.'

Secrest just scowled and said nothing.

'Sit,' Bixby said. He drummed his fingers while he waited for them to do so. Mia took a few extra seconds, just to watch Bixby frown. Finally she sat next to him.

Mia looked at each of the men. 'Who is the student and where are the articles?'

The counselor hid his flinch, but not well. Secrest continued to scowl.

'We investigated the student and saw no need to pursue the matter. Miss Adler felt some . . . personal need to view the scene herself, likely due to her sense of compassion for the victims. Isn't that right, Miss Adler?' Bixby asked.

Adler nodded unsteadily. 'Yes, sir.'

Mia smiled. 'Uh-huh. You're contracted by the state, aren't you, Dr Bixby? Subject to state audits and surprise visits by the licensing board?'

Bixby's jaw tightened. 'Please don't threaten me, Detective.'

Mia looked at Solliday, amused. 'I'm starting to hear an echo. So many people telling me not to threaten them.'

'Maybe because everyone we've talked to has known something we needed to know, but didn't want to tell us,' he said, very quietly. Almost ominously. His tone was perfect.

'That must be it.' She leaned forward, sliding her palm flat on the table until she could look up into

Bixby's face. It was a power-shifting move that she normally found very effective. Judging by the annoyed flicker in Bixby's eyes, it was effective once more. 'I wonder what you know, Dr Bixby. You said you investigated. I assume this means you didn't think this student was clipping articles for a school book report.'

'As I told Miss Adler,' Solliday said in the same ominous tone, 'we have two women in the morgue. Our patience is thin. If your student is not involved, we'll be on our way. If he is, he's a danger to the rest of your students. You don't want that kind of publicity.'

A muscle in Bixby's jaw twitched and Mia knew Solliday had hit the right chord. 'The student does not leave this facility. There is no way he could be involved.'

'All right,' Mia said, relaxing. 'Tell us about the facility. Do all students live here?'

'Twenty percent are day students,' Dr Thompson said. 'The rest are residential.'

Mia smiled. 'Residential. That means they're locked up?'

Thompson's returned smile was strained. 'It means they can't leave. They are not locked in cells as they would be in a jail, no.'

Mia widened her eyes. 'You never let them outside?' She blinked. 'Ever?'

Bixby's eyes flashed. 'Residential students are given supervised time outdoors.'

'The exercise yard,' Mia said and Bixby's cheeks

burned. Mia held up her hand. 'I know, this isn't a jail. But your neighbors wouldn't be happy to know that a possible murderer was right here, less than a mile from their homes. From their children.'

'Because there isn't,' Bixby said tightly. 'I've told you already.'

'And we heard you the first time,' Solliday said mildly. He looked over at Mia, one dark brow lifted. 'You know you did promise Carmichael she'd be the first to know.'

She beamed at him, in perfect accord. 'Yes, I did.'

Secrest leaned forward, eyes narrowed. 'That's extortion.'

'Who is Carmichael?' Bixby asked.

'The reporter who wrote the article in yesterday's *Bulletin*,' Secrest said.

Thompson's mouth fell open. 'You can't give false information.'

Mia shrugged. 'She asks me where I've been. I'll tell her I've been here. No lie. Sometimes she even follows me around, looking for news. She might be outside your gates as we speak. I guess as publicity goes, that would suck. The whole not-in-my-backyard thing and all.' She stared Bixby down. 'And your total lack of cooperation will affect your standing with the state. I'll see that it does.'

Bixby looked ready to explode. He hit a button on the intercom. 'Marcy, pull Manuel Rodriguez's file.' He jabbed the button. 'I hope you're satisfied.'

'I hope I am, too,' Mia said with all sincerity. 'So do the families of my two victims.'

Thompson's face had gone florid. 'Manny's an innocent young man.'

Mia lifted her brows. 'He's *here*, Dr Thompson. He's obviously not *that* innocent.'

'He didn't set these fires,' Thompson insisted.

'You searched Manny's room, Mr Secrest?' Solliday asked, ignoring the counselor.

'I did.' Secrest's eyes were like stone.

Mia lifted her brows. 'And?'

'And I found a book of matches.'

'Were any missing?' Solliday pressed. 'And to save us time, if yes, how many?'

'Several. But the matchbook had been used by someone else.'

She noticed a twitch in Thompson's cheek. 'Do you know where he got them?' she asked. From the corner of her eye she saw Secrest roll his eyes.

'He took them from Dr Thompson's office,' Secrest said. 'He smokes a pipe.'

Mia leaned back in her chair. 'Bring Mr Rodriguez to us, please.' Everyone stood. 'Miss Adler, please remain.' She looked at Bixby. 'Alone.'

When the doors were closed, Mia turned to Adler, who was pale. 'Now tell us *why* you went to Penny Hill's house.'

She licked her lips. 'I told you. I was curious. Because of the articles.'

Solliday shook his head. 'No. We saw you, Miss Adler, on the video. You didn't look curious. You looked like you felt guilty.'

'It was the book.' In her eyes Mia saw pure, unadulterated misery. 'I assigned *Lord of the Flies* right before Thanksgiving. Right before the first fire.' She pursed her lips hard. 'Right before the first woman was killed.'

'Interesting timing,' Solliday murmured. 'Still, why go to the victim's house?'

'I needed to know what the police knew. To know if I'd done . . . caused . . .'

Mia frowned at Solliday. 'I'm missing the connection to the book,' she murmured.

'*Lord of the Flies,*' he murmured back. 'Teens stranded on an island without adults descend into anarchy. They have a signal fire. Later they burn most of the island down.'

'Oh. Dots connected.' Mia turned her attention back to Adler, who sat quietly, tears running down her face. 'Was that really a good choice of a book here?'

'Dr Bixby approved it, encouraged it even. He wanted to observe the students' reactions. I offered to assign a different one, but Julian said it would be useful in Manny's therapy.' She struggled for control. 'All I could think was "What if I caused him to do this? What if my book gave him the idea?" And then there was another fire and another woman died. What if those women are dead because I got him started?'

Solliday sighed. 'If Manny did this, you are not responsible, Miss Adler.'

'I'll believe you when you find out who really did it. Can I go now?'

'Sure,' Mia said, more inclined to be gentle now. 'Don't leave town, okay?'

Adler's smile was thin and bitter. 'Somehow I thought you'd say that.' She shut the door hard, leaving Mia and Solliday sitting side by side. Solliday looked around the ceiling and the walls, then abruptly bent close to Mia's ear.

'This could be a wild-goose chase,' he murmured. 'A waste of time.'

A shiver raced down her back, unexpected and hard as his heat warmed her and the scent of him filled her head. Unbidden, her body tightened, as the memory of him lying on top of her shoved at her logical thought. She made herself focus and leaned up to whisper in his ear. 'Maybe. But we're here. Other than boxes of files, this is all we have. Cops, social workers, angry kids . . . And these guys are hiding something. I've got a feeling about all this.' And that, she told herself, would be cop instinct and not the fact that her cheek still tingled from where his beard had brushed against her skin.

The door opened and Bixby appeared. 'Manny is being brought up front. I will stay with him through your questioning as he is a minor. Is there anything else you require?'

Solliday stood up. 'We'd like to search the boy's room ourselves.'

Bixby nodded stiffly. 'As you wish.'

Mia's lips curved. 'Your . . . cooperation is noted, Dr Bixby. Keep Manny here while we do our search. We'll come back to talk to him when we're ready.'

Wednesday, November 29, 2:45 P.M.

Reed stifled a sigh as Bixby led Manny Rodriguez from the room. A search of his room had turned up nothing and Manny was as closed as any youth he'd ever met. 'If he did it, he's not giving anything up. But I don't think he did. I think we just wasted an afternoon chasing an English teacher with an overdeveloped sense of guilt.'

'Win some, lose some.' Mia shrugged into that god-awful coat. It looked worse from the slide on the pavement she'd taken last night. 'Let's go back and hit the files.'

Reed held the door, then followed her to the front desk where a grim-faced Marcy was ready to sign them out. He walked by the front display cases, then stopped when something shiny caught his eye. He backed up a few steps and stared, his pulse picking up a few beats. 'Mia, look at this.'

She stared at the students' displayed art. 'Interesting painting,' she said, her eyes taking in the row at her eye level. It was dark with a hint of insanity.

'Look up,' Reed said and she did. 'Higher,' he said and she blinked.

'Well, well.' She rocked herself on her toes to get a better view of one budding artist's rendition of a Fabergé egg tucked away on the top row. It sparkled with intricate beads and crystals set in geometric patterns. 'Pretty. I wish I could get closer to see.'

'You want a boost?' he asked and she shot him a glare, but her eyes were amused.

'Smart-ass,' she muttered. 'It took one hell of a chicken to lay that egg.'

'I think the chicken had some help.' He bent close to her ear. 'It's the right size.'

'And the right color,' she murmured. 'I think we need a warrant. I'll take care of it.'

His smile was satisfied. 'And I'll tell Dr Bixby that we'll be staying a little longer.'

She walked away, flipping open her cell phone. 'Damn, you get to have all the fun.'

Wednesday, November 29, 3:15 P.M.

The art teacher was built like Reed Solliday, Mia thought as she looked around the room. His muscles bulged beneath the paint-spattered T-shirt he wore. His bald head gleamed like polished onyx. His fingers were bigger than hot dogs, the really expensive kind. His name was Atticus Lucas and he did not look happy to see them.

'Which student did the egg?' Solliday asked.

'I don't have to—'

'Uh-uh-uh,' Mia interrupted. 'Yes, you do have to tell us. Tell him, Mr Secrest.'

'Tell them,' Secrest muttered.

Lucas looked slightly embarrassed. 'None of them did.'

'So it's a real Fabergé?' Solliday asked, tongue in cheek.

Lucas glared. 'No need for the sarcasm, Lieutenant,' he said. 'I did it.'

Mia turned to face him, blinking. 'You?'

He stood as if at military attention, nodding. 'Me.'

She looked at his thick fingers. 'All that dainty work? Really?'

He scowled at her. 'Really.'

'Did you do all the art in the display case?' she asked.

'Of course not. I was trying to show the kids that art could take different forms. I wanted them to think another student did it so that—'

'They wouldn't think it was gay,' Mia finished with a sigh.

'Something like that,' Lucas said tightly.

'Well, now that your art's been outed,' she said, 'where are the rest of the eggs?'

'In the supply cabinet.' He walked to a metal cabinet and pulled the doors open. He took a tub and pulled at the lid. And blinked. 'They were in here. They're gone.'

Solliday glanced at Mia. 'We'll want to get fingerprints on the tub and the cabinet.'

'I'll call Jack. But first, Mr Lucas, when was the last time you touched the tub?'

'I made that egg in August. I haven't touched the tub since then. Why?'

'How many eggs were there?' Mia pressed.

Lucas looked perplexed. 'They're just plastic eggs. I don't get the big deal.'

'Just answer her question,' Solliday snapped and Lucas glared at him.

'A dozen, maybe. They were there when I got here two years ago. Nobody ever touched them except for me and only when I did that one egg.'

'A dozen,' Solliday murmured. 'He's used three. He's got nine more to play with.'

Mia pulled out her cell phone to call Jack. 'Shit.'

Solliday motioned to Secrest. 'Take me to the lab. I want to check your chemicals.'

Mia held up her hand as they started to walk away. 'And we'll be taking Manny downtown. Arrange for a guardian or advocate.'

His jaw taut, Secrest nodded.

Wednesday, November 29, 3:45 P.M.

Solliday stood sideways in the small chemical storeroom because his shoulders wouldn't fit. On any other man, the goggles on his face would look geeky, but they didn't hurt Solliday's looks one bit. Because it wasn't the time to think so, she focused.

'You know your way around a lab,' she observed.

'A lot of fire inspectors major in chemistry,' he said.

'Did you?'

'Kind of.' He was checking bottles against the inventory he'd found on a clipboard hanging on the door. 'My dad was a chemical engineer and I guess I had something to prove, so I majored in that, too.'

That he spoke of his adoptive father was understood. 'I thought you were a firefighter before OFI.'

He crouched down to check out the bottom shelf. 'I was. Being a firefighter was all I'd ever wanted to do. I applied for the academy the day after I got out of the army.'

Well, the army explained his obsession with shiny shoes. 'But?'

'But my dad encouraged me to get a degree while I was still young, before I had a family to take care of. So I went to school on my GI money full-time until I was accepted into the academy and part-time after that until I finished. Took me a bunch of years, but it was worth it.' He looked up. 'How about you?'

'Law Enforcement on a soccer scholarship. What are you looking for?'

'There are a couple of different ways to get ammonium nitrate. One is in a bottle.' He picked one up. 'But this has its original seal and the inventory says they only had one.'

'When was it delivered?'

'August, three years ago.' He squinted at the label. 'I'm really surprised a school this size has an inventory this extensive.'

'The previous teacher left it behind. I haven't had to buy anything since I got here.'

Mia turned to find the science teacher observing from a few feet away. 'How long have you been teaching here?'

'About a year. I'm Mr Celebrese.'

'Dectective Mitchell and my partner, Lieutenant Solliday.'

'You'll find the nitric acid in the locked cabinet, Lieutenant. Here's the key.'

Mia passed it to Solliday, who checked it off. 'I take it a second way to get ammonium nitrate uses nitric acid.'

'Yeah, it does.' Solliday checked the cabinet and locked it back. 'Still sealed.'

'We don't use a lot of the stronger chemicals here,' Celebrese said.

'Afraid the kids will splash each other with acid?' Mia asked.

Celebrese's jaw went taut. 'Did you find what you were looking for?'

Solliday emerged from the closet, the goggles still on his face. 'Not yet.' Ignoring Celebrese's scowl, Solliday walked to the far wall, to a booth with a glass front.

'Looks like a salad bar with an overactive sneeze guard,' she said and he laughed.

'It's a hood. People use volatiles here because it's ventilated.' He pulled out the sniffer he'd used to measure hydrocarbons at Penny Hill's house, pulled the glass window up a crack and slid the sniffer underneath. Immediately it began to squeal and Solliday smiled, a dark edgy smile that said he'd found what he was looking for.

'Jackpot,' he murmured. 'Celebrese, when was the last time you used the hood?'

'I – I've never used it. Like I said, I don't use strong chemicals.'

Solliday pulled the window back down. 'Detective, can you ask Sergeant Unger to come down here as quickly as possible? He'll want to take samples here.'

Her smile was one of admiration and respect. 'My pleasure, Lieutenant.'

Behind the goggles his dark eyes flickered. 'Thanks.'

Chapter Twelve

Reed came out of Interview to find Spinnelli, Westphalen, and state's attorney Patrick Hurst waiting on the other side of the glass. 'You rang,' Reed said.

In Interview, Manny sat slumped in a chair, his arms crossed over his chest. Mia sat on the boy's end of the table, crowding him, trying to bully Manny into offering details, hoping he would correct her mistakes. So far all she'd gotten was a bored look.

'That's him?' Spinnelli asked.

Reed nodded. 'Manuel Rodriguez, fifteen.'

'Who's the woman?' Patrick asked, referring to the wispy-looking woman who sat at Manny's other side looking at turns angry and uncomfortable.

'His court-appointed advocate. We were shocked she let us go on this long.'

'Our gain,' Patrick said. 'His history?'

'Manny's been at Hope for six months. Before that he burned down his foster house. He used gasoline and a

288

match, nothing sophisticated. His foster mother was seriously burned. He seems to have remorse for hurting her, but not for setting the fire.'

'They searched his room last night?' Hurst asked. 'And found matches?'

'Yeah. At first the matches was all they'd admit they'd found, but after we found the eggs, they admitted that they'd found his stash of reading material. How-to articles on arson, but all on liquid accelerants, like the right mix of gasoline and oil. None mentioned the plastic egg as a delivery device. None mentioned ammonium nitrate.'

'Did they also find pornography?' Westphalen asked quietly, his eyes on the boy.

'Yes, but that wasn't a big surprise. It's common with arsonists,' Reed told Hurst when the man's brows lifted. 'Many arsonists start fires, then . . . gratify themselves.'

'I get the picture,' Hurst said dryly. 'So did he do it?'

'I didn't think so the first time I talked to him, at the school.' Reed shrugged uneasily. 'I still don't. This boy loves the fire. Practically salivates when you show him pictures of burning buildings. If he started a fire, he would have stayed to watch it burn. I don't think he could have forced himself to run away. Also, I don't get the sense of fury in this kid. Manny hurting his foster mother seems to have been an accident.'

'But our guy used gasoline on Caitlin Burnette,' Spinnelli pointed out.

'But pouring it on a person is different than on a

floor,' Reed countered. 'Manny has no history of direct violence against people, just structures.'

Spinnelli turned to Westphalen. 'Miles, what do you think?'

'I'm inclined to agree. But first, do you have photos of the bodies, Lieutenant? I want to see his response to the results of his handiwork, if it is indeed his.'

'Mia has them in her briefcase.' It was in the chair next to her. 'We didn't want to show him actual photos of the scene or the bodies without Patrick's okay.'

Patrick considered for a moment. 'Do it. I want to see his response, too.'

Spinnelli tapped on the glass. Mia leaned closer, delivering a few more parting verbal shots. The boy continued to look bored, never breaking his disaffected pose.

'The killer's fury has been pointed at women so far,' Reed murmured. 'We wanted to see if she could get a rise out of him. Intimidate him.'

'But he's not taking that bait,' Westphalen commented. 'Another reason I'm inclined to agree with you.'

Mia shut the door. 'He's not budging, but I have his advocate shaking in her boots.'

'What do you think, Mia?' Spinnelli asked.

'He's hiding something, I think. He's got motive and means – his history of arson, possession of matches, and all those how-to articles – but I still get stuck on opportunity. I mean, the kid's been in lockup.

How the hell did he get out to kill Caitlin and Penny and if he could get out, why the hell did he bother to go back?'

She'd voiced this concern on the way back from the school and it was valid. Reed had given it a lot of thought. 'If found a way out, he might come back just because it's more convenient to do so. It's cold outside and Hope Center is warm and gives him three squares a day. He'd have his cake and eat it, too.'

Mia's brows bunched as she considered it. 'It's possible. I'll be more inclined to believe he's involved if we can tie him to Caitlin or Penny. So what now?'

'The doctor wants you to show Manny the photos of the bodies,' Reed said.

'Okay, but you should go in. He talks to you. He just stares at my chest.'

And for that, Reed thought, no man on the planet could blame the boy. 'Anything special, Doc?'

Westphalen thought a second. 'See if you can get him off his guard before you show the pictures. I don't want that bored look. He hides too much behind it.'

'I'll try.' Reed walked back into the interview room and closed the door at his back.

The advocate lifted her chin. 'Manny is tired. He's told you what you want to know. When are you going to stop this nonsense and let him go back to Hope Center?'

'I'm not sure he's going back. He might stay here tonight, as our guest.'

Manny's chin jerked up. 'You can't do that. I'm a kid.'

'We have a special area for men under eighteen accused of capital crimes.' He took his time finding the photos, watching Manny from the corner of his eye.

Manny's face was panicked. 'What's a capital crime?'

Reed glanced up. 'Death penalty.'

Manny jumped up. 'I didn't kill anybody.' He turned to the advocate. 'I didn't.'

'Lieutenant.' The advocate drew herself up straighter, although her voice shook. 'You're just scaring him. He's done nothing.' She pointed to a chair. 'Sit down, Manny.' He sat and she folded her hands on the table. 'He wants a lawyer. Now.'

'He hasn't been arrested,' Reed said carelessly. 'Should he be?'

'No!' Manny exploded.

Reed walked behind him, leaned over him and put the photos of the charred bodies on the table. 'Should you be?'

Beside him the advocate covered her mouth and gagged.

Manny pushed his chair back, but Reed kept him from going anywhere. 'Look at them,' Reed said harshly. 'This is what your fire did, Manny. This is what you did. This is what you'll look like when they pull your sorry ass off the electric chair.'

Manny grabbed the table and pushed away with all his strength. *'Let me go.'*

Hearing the boy's panicked tone, Reed stepped back and the chair flew to the floor, but it was too late as Manny retched.

It was a good thing they had more copies of the photos. It was a better thing that Reed had an extra pair of shoes in his SUV. The boy sank to his hands and knees, heaving, sobbing. Grimacing, Reed went into the anteroom to talk to the others.

Mia shot him a wince. 'Sorry. If I'd known he'd do that . . .'

He narrowed his eyes at her. 'You still would have asked me to go in.'

She nodded philosophically. 'Probably. I gotta say though, not bad, Solliday. Especially the part about the electric chair. I'll have to remember that.'

'I didn't know if he'd know we hadn't used the chair in years,' Reed said absently as he watched. The advocate was trying to help him. Manny just jerked away and hung there, shuddering. Reed shook his head. 'He didn't do this. I think if he did he'd have been intrigued by the pictures. Fascinated, even.' Manny crawled to the wall, arms around his knees, rocking. His eyes were closed and his lips moved. 'He's not.'

'No,' Mia murmured. 'He's scared. Listen to him.' She turned up the volume.

'Can't tell.' Manny muttered it to himself over and over. 'Can't tell. Won't tell.'

Everyone turned to Patrick. 'Well?' Spinnelli asked. 'Can we hold him?'

Patrick huffed in frustration. 'What do you have, exactly?'

'We've got missing eggs and lots of fingerprints,' Mia said. 'Jack found more than twenty different prints in the art and science rooms. He's cross-checking all the prints against the teachers and inmates.' She lifted her brows. 'I mean children.'

Patrick looked unhappy. 'That's all?'

Mia smiled at Reed. 'You found it,' she said. 'You get to share the best part.'

It was the plum. 'We also found remnants of chemicals used in the devices.'

This caught Patrick's interest. 'Explain.'

That Mia's eyes held respect and admiration shouldn't make him feel as good as it did. But it did. 'We checked out the science class lab. Under the hood I found evidence of hydrocarbon vapors and on the countertop remnants of gunpowder and sugar.'

'Used for?' Spinnelli asked.

'What's a hood?' Patrick asked at the same time.

'A hood's a contained area with a ventilation shaft. I'm betting the samples Jack took today will show traces of kerosene – our analysis of the solid showed our guy mixed it with the ammonium nitrate. Mixed with liquid fuel, fertilizer becomes explosive.'

Patrick looked appropriately impressed. 'And the gunpowder and sugar?'

'Homemade fuses. He would have used the gunpowder and sugar to coat regular shoelaces.' Reed shrugged. 'I've seen it done before. Terrifyingly simple to find on the Internet. One of the pages Manny had hidden away gave the instructions.'

Spinnelli's eyes were intense. 'But you still don't think he did this?'

'Not alone,' Mia said. 'Just listen to him. Unless he's a really good actor . . .'

Behind the glass, Manny still rocked himself, still muttered the same words.

'Patrick, is this enough to hold him?' Spinnelli asked.

'Hell, yeah. I'll petition a new trial with family court based on what you found. That'll give you a few days to figure out what he knows and who else is involved.'

'One night in holding will be all Manny needs to convince him to talk,' Mia said.

'We'll see,' Westphalen said quietly, still watching the boy. 'I hope you're right.'

'And next?' Spinnelli asked.

'Jack's got Latent analyzing prints and the lab analyzing the powder Solliday found in the lab. And we're back to the files, to see if we can find a connection between Roger Burnette, Penny, and anybody in that screwy school.' Mia pointed at Patrick. 'When this is done you guys need to check that school *out*. They're just plain *off*.'

'I'll add it to my list,' Patrick said dryly. 'Call me tomorrow with an update.'

'I'll set up time tomorrow for a formal exam for Manny,' Westphalen offered.

Spinnelli followed them out. 'We appreciate it, Miles.'

Behind the glass an officer escorted Manny back to holding and the advocate gave them a hard look through the glass before leaving through the same door Manny used.

And then, they were alone in the dim anteroom. Mia sighed. 'Now we hit the files.'

'First I change my shoes.'

Her lips twitched. 'I'm really sorry about that.'

Reed had to chuckle. 'No, you're not.'

She grinned up at him. 'You're right.'

He met her eyes, intending to raise her one better, but he stopped. And really looked. The laughter faded from her eyes, uncertainty taking its place. And as he watched, her uncertainty mixed with awareness and his throat grew thick. Once again they were connected on a different level, just as they'd been the night before in the quiet of his kitchen. Gently he grasped her chin and tugged her face toward the light. The bruise on her cheekbone was beginning to yellow, the scrape on its way to healing.

She wasn't a classically beautiful woman, but there was something about her face that drew him. He knew it wasn't wise. He told himself to let her go, but he didn't seem able. No, that wasn't true. He just didn't want to. And that was something that hadn't happened in too many years to remember. His thumb grazed her jaw and he watched the awareness in her eyes treble.

'You should have gone to a doctor. You might have a scar.'

'I don't scar easily,' she murmured, so low he almost didn't hear it. 'I guess I'm lucky that way.' She pulled away, took a step back, both physically and emotionally. 'I've got to get to those files.' And she was gone before he could open the door for her.

Wednesday, November 29, 5:00 P.M.

Brooke paused, trembling as she stood before Dr Bixby's office door. She'd been summoned. It didn't sound good. Drawing a breath, she made a fist and knocked hard.

'Come.' Dr Bixby looked up from his desk, his expression forbidding. 'Sit.'

She did, as quickly as her knocking knees would carry her. She opened her mouth to speak, but Bixby waved his hand. 'Let's cut to the chase, Miss Adler. You did a stupid thing. Now the police are crawling all over my school and this will not sit well with the advisory board. You have jeopardized my work. I should fire you right now.'

Her mouth slightly agape, Brooke could only stare. Bixby's lips curled in a sneer.

'But I won't,' he continued. 'Because my lawyers have advised against it. Seems like your Detective Mitchell spoke to the attorney while she was searching the premises this afternoon. Said you were worried about getting fired. Said any move to terminate you would look bad in the event of a lawsuit. Are you planning to sue me, Miss Adler?'

Brooke somehow found her voice. 'No, sir. I had no idea Detective Mitchell had spoken to anyone about me.'

'We're compiling your file, Miss Adler. We'll be able to terminate you with just cause very soon. It would be better for all concerned if you resigned. Immediately.'

Brooke fought back a wave of hysterical nausea. Thoughts of rent and bills and student loans charged through her mind. 'I – I can't do that, sir. I have responsibilities.'

'You should have thought about that before you went on an unauthorized jaunt. I'll give you two weeks. At the end of that time I'll have enough in your file to let you go.' He leaned back in his chair, looking powerful, and something in Brooke snapped.

She surged to her feet, her face hot. 'I did nothing wrong, and anything you manage to gather against me will be lies.' She opened the door, then paused, her hand clenching the knob. 'If you try to fire me, I'll go to the press so fast your head will swim.'

His lips thinned. 'Spin,' he said dryly. Mockingly. 'My head will *spin*.'

She nearly faltered, then saw his knuckles whiten as he clenched a pen. Her chin came up. 'Whatever. Don't try it, Dr Bixby, or you'll be the one who's sorry.'

Slamming the door, she marched out of his office and into Devin White, who stood waiting in the hall. His lips were twitching. 'Make his head *swim*?' he asked.

Now that it was over, tears burned her eyes. 'He's going to fire me, Devin.'

His amusement fled. 'On what grounds?'

'He's making them up.' A panicked sob welled in her throat.

Devin kneaded her shoulders restlessly. 'He's just threatening you, Brooke. I know a good lawyer or two. Let's get a beer, calm you down, then we'll decide what to do.'

Wednesday, November 29, 6:05 P.M.

Reed thought a half hour was enough time. It allowed Mia to reestablish her composure and allowed him to change his shoes and get them both a decent cup of coffee. He should have gone straight home, it was past six and he needed to set things straight with Beth. He thought about the way he'd dealt with his daughter the night before and the way he'd dealt with Mia Mitchell a half hour before and wondered if females ever hit an age where the men in their lives knew the right thing to do or say.

But he had done the right thing with Mia. It sounded cheesy, but it felt too right to have been wrong. Of course she'd be wary, uncertain. But he wasn't so out of practice that he didn't recognize good chemistry when he stumbled across it. A relationship with a cop would be difficult. Priorities would at times interfere. But the more he thought, the surer he became that if there was a woman who wouldn't want strings, it would be Mia.

And if she does? The question slyly insinuated itself, rattling him. If under that rough and sarcastic exterior beat the heart of a woman who wanted a home, husband, and children? Then he'd regretfully, but respectfully, walk away. No harm, no foul.

Reed started across the bullpen, his steps slowing as he approached her empty desk. The files she'd been reading were gone and so was Mia.

'She went home,' said a cop in a rumpled suit who held something skinny and orange between his lips. A carrot, Reed decided. Another, younger, man sat across from him, typing with hurried strokes, a dozen red roses in tissue paper on top of a foil-wrapped gift box at his elbow. 'You must be Solliday. I'm Murphy,' the rumpled one said, his tone easy although his eyes were watchful. 'And this is Aidan Reagan.'

Reed recognized the younger man. 'We met, kind of.'

Murphy looked surprised. 'When?'

Reagan glanced up at his partner. 'In the morgue on Monday. I told you I'd seen him there.' Then he dropped his eyes back to his keyboard and Murphy's lips twitched.

'Don't be hurt by my partner's bad manners. He's a newlywed and today's his one-month anniversary.'

Aidan looked up, his eyes narrowed. 'Actually it was yesterday, but I had to work and missed it. If I miss it tonight . . .' He shook his head. 'I will *not* miss it tonight.'

Murphy's chuckle was just a tad evil. 'I hope not. I hate to even think about the mood you'll be in tomorrow if Tess doesn't try what's in the box tonight.'

Reagan didn't even look up. 'You're trying to break my concentration, but it won't work.' He tapped a few more keys and hit the button on his mouse with fanfare. 'There. My report's done and submitted. I'm off to have dinner with my wife.'

'And dessert,' Murphy said.

Reagan's eyes rolled heavenward as he pulled on his coat. 'God, yes. Don't work too late, Murphy. Nice to see you, Solliday.' He dashed off, the roses under one arm and the wrapped box under the other.

Murphy's sigh was lusty. 'I was with him when he bought what's in the box. Almost made me want to get married again.' He looked over at Reed. 'You married, Solliday?'

'No.' But his imagination was working overtime, envisioning what had been in the box. Envisioning it on a certain curvy little blonde. 'I take it that you're not, either.'

'Nope.' Murphy absently crunched on his carrot stick, but his eyes had gone from watchful to sharp and Reed got the feeling that the man was annoyed with him.

'How did Mia get home?'

'Spinnelli got her a department car.'

'Oh. Well, was she all right when she left?'

'Sure. She packed her files and said she'd read them at home. Said to tell you to meet her in Spinnelli's at eight tomorrow morning. Oh, and she took a message for you.' Murphy pushed a piece of paper to the edge of his desk and sat, waiting.

Reed sighed when he read the words.

Holly Wheaton called. She'll meet you for dinner at seven tonight at Leonardo's on Michigan. Wear a tie. She says their pasta is divine and it's her treat.

'Dammit. She had my cell number. Why did she call Mia?'

'I expect she wanted to rub it in Mia's face. Having her take a message like she's your secretary just sweetened it. You and Wheaton have something going?'

Reed flinched. 'God, no. The woman's a viper. I made a deal with her so that she'd give us some video she'd made of one of our fire scenes. I've done it before – traded an interview for information. I just had no idea Mia would get so angry about it.'

'Most of the time Mia's just like one of the guys, fairly predictable. But when Wheaton crosses her path . . . Stand back because the claws come out.'

He'd seen a little of that last night. 'Why?'

'You'll have to ask her that. It was personal. Was that coffee for her?'

'Yeah.' Reed handed Murphy one of the cups. 'You've known her a long time?'

'Ten years. Back before Ray Rawlston was her partner.'

'What happened to him?'

'He died.' Murphy looked away. 'Line of duty. Mia took out the guy that did it. Took a bullet herself.' He looked back, his face pained. 'We almost lost her.'

Reed sat on the edge of Aidan's desk, stunned. 'My God.' He couldn't think about her that way, almost being gone. 'And then she and Abe get shot? What are the odds?'

'I don't know. I do know she's very . . . vulnerable right now.'

It was a warning and Reed had the good sense to take it as one. 'She had a shock this morning, seeing that woman in the crowd. But I think having to admit it to us might have been even harder for her.'

Murphy nodded. Slowly. 'She's strong, mostly. But she's got heart, and that sometimes yanks her under. Don't yank her under, Solliday.'

'I won't.'

'Good. Now, throw me that box of Pop-Tarts in her drawer. I'm tired of these damn carrot sticks. Kicking the habit's a bitch.'

Reed tossed him the box, brows lifted. 'She won't like you eating her stash.'

Murphy shrugged. 'I'll just blame it on you.'

Wednesday, November 29, 7:15 P.M.

'That was delicious,' Reed said. 'You'll have to make this recipe again.'

Beth beamed. 'We made it in Consumer Tech.'

'Home Ec,' Lauren supplied. 'He's right, Beth. This is terrific.' She lifted a teasing brow. 'I might just be replaced as cook of the household.'

Beth laughed. 'I don't think so. Besides, this was homework. I get points when you fill out the questionnaire.' She pulled two pens from her pocket. 'If you gush too much, Mrs Bennett'll think you're lying, but be nice enough so that I get an A. Nines will be good, but give me a ten for cleanliness. Bennett's a neat freak.'

'And here I thought you were trying to weasel something out of me,' Reed murmured, scanning the questionnaire. 'Or perhaps to apologize.'

Beth scrunched her mouth in a frown. 'Da-ad.'

He'd leveled the worst punishment he could think of. No weekend party. 'What?'

'I thought you might let me out this weekend. Just to go to Jenny Q's house.'

Reed reached over and tapped her nose. 'You don't have to bribe me, Bethie. Just say the words. I'm . . . sorry.' He drew them out and she rolled her eyes.

'I'm sorry.' She snapped it out, fast and far less sincerely than he'd wanted.

'For what?'

'Dad!' She bristled, looking so much like Christine in

a snit. A dramatic sigh rustled the papers on the table. 'I'm sorry I was difficult last night.'

'You weren't difficult, Beth. You were downright rude. And in front of a guest.'

Her eyes went sly. 'New lady partner. Does this mean Foster won't be coming for dinner anymore? That would be a real shame.'

'Sure he will. Detective Mitchell is a temporary partner. Why worry about Foster?'

'I dunno. He's kind of hot in a . . . artsy kind of way. Cameras. Film. Maybe he can take some shots of me. For my modeling career.' Then she laughed as his jaw dropped. 'Just kidding.' She propped her chin on her fist. 'So how about the dame?'

Lauren was laughing by now. 'Yeah, Reed, how about the dame?'

Reed drew a breath, still reeling from the 'Foster hot' comment. 'Just to be straight, were you kidding about Foster being hot or you having a modeling career?'

She peered over at his paper. 'Ten on cleanliness and nine on taste?'

His eyes narrowed. Women and their deals. Thoughts of facing Holly Wheaton across a table left him nearly as cold as the thought of Foster being hot. 'Deal.'

Beth smiled. 'Both.' She looked down at her plate, then back up. 'I'm sorry, Dad. I was rude. I was just so mad you wouldn't let me stay over at Jenny's house that I . . .' She trailed off when he lifted his brows. 'I'm sorry. That's all.'

'Accepted.' He filled out the questionnaire and handed it back to her. 'And done.'

She brightened. 'So I can go to Jenny's for a sleepover this weekend.'

Lauren put a cup of coffee next to his plate, her expression saying she was ready to take cover over what was coming next. 'No,' he said. 'The punishment stands.'

Beth's mouth dropped open. 'Dad!' She lurched to her feet. 'I can't believe this.'

'*Sit down*,' he said and was shocked when she obeyed. 'You were insufferably rude. You raised your voice to me and slammed the door so hard you knocked a picture off the wall upstairs. I'm usually so proud of you, but last night I was ashamed.'

Her eyes dropped to the table. 'I understand.' When she lifted her eyes, they were calm. 'That science project that Jenny and I have been working on is due tomorrow. Can I at least go to her house to finish it? It's not fair that her grade suffers, too.'

Reed looked over at Lauren, who shrugged. 'All right,' he said. 'Get your things. I have a meeting to go to, so I'll pick you up when I'm done.'

Her jaw clenched, Beth nodded and walked away.

Reed sighed. 'I'm a sucker, aren't I?'

'Yep. But you love her. I'm so glad she has this life, but sometimes I wish she could understand how much harder it is to say no. My birth mother didn't care enough to.'

'Mine, either.' Reed brooded into his coffee. 'She was never sober enough.'

Lauren's face scrunched with worry. 'I'm sorry. I didn't mean to make you remember.'

'It's okay.' He looked up. 'It's just that Mia and I had to visit juvie today.'

'So now she's Mia. So, Reed, to quote Beth, what's the deal with the dame?'

'She's my partner, Lauren.'

Lauren's mouth curved. 'But no "that's all." I call that progress.'

'I'm ready,' Beth said from the door.

Reed stood up. 'Then let's rock and roll, kid.'

Wednesday, November 29, 7:45 P.M.

Dana eyed Mia's clean plate, then nodded. 'You're done. Finally.' They were the last two sitting, Dana's foster kids having cleaned their plates long before.

Mia rolled her eyes. 'You're a bully. I hate vegetables.'

'You come here because you want me to bully you. I'm always glad to oblige.'

Much of her temper over Holly Wheaton's call had dissipated over dinner. Being around Dana's kids made it hard for her to stay mad. But she still had enough mad left for a final jab. 'You'd make a good dominatrix,' Mia grumbled and Dana laughed.

'Dana the Dominatrix. I like the sound of that.'

'So do I.' Dana's husband, Ethan, wandered into the kitchen and kissed the back of her neck. 'We could have some fun with that. Gives me ideas.'

Dana smacked him playfully. 'You don't need any new ideas.' She pulled his head down for a kiss and Mia felt the pang she always felt when she saw them together. Except tonight, it wasn't the same. It was sharper, somehow. Darker. Normally the pang was happiness for Dana and sometimes wistful longing for herself.

But tonight it was jealousy and . . . resentment. Troubled at herself, she cleared her throat. 'Guys? For God's sake, do you mind already?'

Ethan was the first to pull away, looking puzzled at her harsh tone. 'Sorry, Mia. I'll take care of overseeing homework tonight, honey. You two can talk.' Tenderly he ran the back of his fingertips over Dana's face before he left the room, and Mia couldn't block out the sensation of Reed Solliday's thumb brushing against her jaw.

She'd run tonight. She'd gotten scared and run like a little girl. Wheaton's phone call was just an excuse to be angry with him. It was easier than dealing with what she'd felt when he touched her face. He'd done it last night as well. She'd pulled away then, too.

'I'm ready whenever you are,' Dana said quietly.

Mia slid a nickel across the table and Dana smiled. 'It's a quarter now,' Dana said. 'Inflation. But I'll just put it on your tab. Go ahead. Talk to me.'

'I'm a stupid idiot.'

'Okay.'

Mia scowled. 'You're not earning your quarter.'

Dana's laugh soothed. 'Point me in the right direction, Mia. I'm not psychic.' She sobered. 'I'll make it easier for you. A, it's the woman you think is your half-sister. B, you're ripped up because two people are dead and you can't bring them back to life because you're not God. C, you were almost killed last night, which you haven't mentioned once by the way, or D, Reed Solliday.'

'How about E, all of the above?'

'Mia.'

Mia sighed. 'E, all of the above, but at this moment mostly D?'

'Is he being mean to you?' Dana asked, as if she were comforting a five-year-old.

She opened her mouth to say something snide, but her repository of comebacks was suddenly empty. 'No, he's been a perfect gentleman. He opens doors, pulls out chairs, holds umbrellas over my head.'

'He should be shot,' Dana drawled in a deadpan voice.

'I'm serious, Dana.'

'I know, honey. So besides making you feel awkward by treating you with the respect you deserve, what else does he do?'

'Ooh, you're good.'

'Thousands agree. Stop stalling.'

'Last night he followed me to the prison. I went to tell Kelsey about Liam and *her*.'

'That's interesting. So how is Kelsey?'

'Stubborn as ever about the parole board. And she knew about Liam and his mother, but not the woman. Oh, and she said you could keep your crabs.'

Dana's lips twitched. 'I'm not touchin' that with a ten-foot pole. Okay, time-out's over. He's handsome, kind, and I'm betting he's interested and you're scared.'

All those years as a social worker had honed Dana's observation skills. All the years as Mia's best friend had sharpened them to a razor edge. 'Essentially, yes.'

Dana leaned forward conspiratorially. 'So, has he kissed you yet?'

A laugh bubbled up. 'No.' She sighed. 'But it's headed that way.'

'And?'

'And . . . I'm not looking for a relationship.'

'Neither was I.'

'That's different.'

Dana lifted a brow. 'How?'

'You love Ethan. You *married* him.' And for Dana, that had been a huge step.

'At first I only planned to use him for sex and cut him loose when I was done.'

Mia blinked. That one she hadn't heard before. 'Oh?'

'But I didn't get done with him. I'm still not done. Don't think I'll ever be done. He's just too good in bed.

All those muscles and all that energy . . .' She fanned her face.

Mia found herself tightening her thighs against the throbbing between her legs. 'Not fair. You know how long it's been since I've had any and you're just rubbing it in.'

Dana laughed. 'I'm sorry. I couldn't resist. Oh, Mia.' Her smile became sad. 'Look at yourself. You're thirty-four years old and all you have is work. You go home to a dark, cold apartment and an empty bed. You wake up the same way. Your life is passing and you're just watching the days go by.'

Mia swallowed hard, but the lump still closed her throat. 'Not fair,' she whispered.

'I'm tired of being fair,' Dana whispered back. 'I'm tired of watching you throw your life away because you don't think you deserve any better. Dammit, your father's dead, Mia. Kelsey's in jail and your mother . . . God only knows about her. But you, you I know. You I care about. And if you think it's not fair to live like you do, you should be the one to watch you do it. It breaks my heart, Mia.' Dana's voice broke. 'And *that's* not fair.'

Because her own heart ached, Mia lifted her chin and dropped her eyes. 'I'm sorry.'

Dana slapped the table. 'Goddammit, Mia, yank that stick out of your ass and listen to me. You deserve a life. Don't tell me you don't want that.' She spread her arms wide. 'That you don't want this. Look me in the eye and tell me you don't want this.'

Mia looked around the kitchen, at the cheerful colors, the sink filled with dishes, the refrigerator covered with the artwork done by small hands. And she wanted it, so fiercely it stole her breath. 'Yes,' she hissed. 'I want it.'

'Then take it.' Dana leaned forward, her eyes turbulent. 'Find someone and take it.'

'I can't.'

'You mean you won't.'

'Fine. I won't.'

Dana leaned back in her chair, her shoulders sagging. 'Why not?'

'Because I'd ruin it.' She jerked her eyes away from Dana's devastated face and finished it. 'And I'll be damned if I'll ruin two kids like he ruined us.'

There was silence, then Mia heard the sound of the nickel sliding back across the table. 'I can't help you, Mia,' Dana whispered. 'I'm sorry.' For minutes they sat not speaking, then Dana sighed. 'Can I give you some free advice?'

'Can I stop you?'

'No. Human contact is a need, just like food. No food, you starve. If you deprive yourself of human contact it can do the same to your soul. You're attracted to Reed?'

Mia drew a breath. 'Yeah.'

'Then don't run away from him. See where this takes you. You don't have to have a house with kids and a husband to have a relationship. And despite the Valentine's Day cards, not every relationship is meant to last forever.'

'Would you accept less than forever?'

'No, because I've tasted it and now I can't imagine being satisfied with anything less. But if you're bound and determined not to have filet mignon, then don't push away the hamburger. If you're honest with the man, hamburger might be enough sustenance to get you through. And who knows? Maybe he only likes hamburger, too.'

'See, that's where you're wrong. Only the sleazebags only like hamburger.'

'And Reed Solliday is no sleazebag,' Dana said heavily.

No, he wasn't. 'Dana, I don't want to hurt anyone like I hurt Guy. Reed's a nice man. So it's hands off. I've gotta go. Thanks for dinner.'

From her kitchen window, Dana watched Mia drive away. Ethan came up behind her, slid his hands around her waist. She leaned into him, needing him more than ever.

'Did you tell her?' he murmured and she shook her head.

'No, the time wasn't right.'

Ethan splayed his hand against her abdomen. 'You have to tell her sometime, Dana. She's a big girl and she loves you. She'll be happy for us.'

That, of course, was the issue. 'I know she'll *want* to be happy for us, Ethan. I guess I'm selfish enough to want to wait until I know she will be.'

'Well, don't wait too much longer. I want to tell

people. I want to shop for cribs and booties and stuff.' He turned her in his arms and kissed her soundly. 'But first, let's talk a little about that whole dominatrix thing.'

Dana laughed as he'd meant for her to. 'I do love you.'

He pulled her close, held her tight. 'I know.'

Wednesday, November 29, 7:55 P.M.

Holly Wheaton watched Reed approach like an angry cat watches a recalcitrant mouse. Of course, Reed wasn't a mouse. But that didn't make Holly Wheaton any less a cat. A cat in a low-cut sheer blouse, suede miniskirt, and killer pumps.

It was abundantly clear what the woman had had in mind. Reed found himself curiously affected and repelled and . . . making comparisons. He wished Mia could be here to put this woman in her place. But also because he just wanted her here. Mia didn't have Wheaton's features, that face that made men's fingers pause on the remote as they channel surfed. But Mia had something more . . . natural. More appealing. Just . . . more. He let his eyes dip briefly below Wheaton's chin. Mia had her there, too. Hands down. Or hands on. *Focus, Solliday. The shark is circling*. He seated himself across from Wheaton and shook his head when the waiter appeared to fill his glass.

'No thank you.' He handed the waiter the menu. 'I won't be staying.'

Wheaton's cheeks flushed. 'I recall a deal. And speaking of such, you're late.'

'I had another dinner engagement.'

'You could have broken it.'

'No, I couldn't have. Nor would I have. I don't have much time, Miss Wheaton. I promised you an interview. Please commence.'

'Very well.' She put her recorder on the table. 'Tell me about the investigation.'

'I can't comment on any ongoing investigation.'

Her eyes narrowed. 'You're welshing?'

'No. You asked for an interview. I didn't promise to answer your questions. Now I will, of course, provided you ask me something I'm at liberty to divulge.'

She sat for a moment, then smiled and the hair on the back of his neck stood straight up. 'So who was the woman that Detective Mitchell pursued today?'

Reed just looked at her, perplexed on the outside, but raging-bull mad on the inside. 'Oh, you mean at the press conference. She thought she saw someone we wanted to talk to, but she was mistaken.' He shrugged. 'No mystery.'

Wheaton huffed a chuckle before pulling a personal DVD player from the leather bag at her feet. She handed it to him. 'Just hit play. The resemblance is uncanny.'

He did and the rage inside him grew as he watched the camera pan the crowd and focus on the woman who was most likely Mia's half-sister. This was none of Wheaton's business. It was Mia's pain and he'd be damned if Wheaton would cash in on it. She took the player from his hand. 'Tell me what I want to know or I'll go public with this.'

'With . . .' he asked mildly. 'She's not a person of interest. Just a face in the crowd.'

She lifted a shoulder. 'Fine. I'll find out on my own.'

'You do that. When you find out, let me know. I might like to go to dinner with *her*.'

Wednesday, November 29, 8:00 P.M.

He sat at his desk, damning Atticus Lucas when he should be running through the evening's logistics one last time. One egg in the corner of the display case and the cops were all over the school. What the hell was a grown man doing playing with beads?

He'd been in that art room. The cops would find his prints somewhere. Sometime. And if they were the least bit good at their jobs, they'd realize something wasn't quite right. But it would take them . . . oh, days, at least to get to that point.

Unfortunately, they'd found evidence of his work in the lab as well. It was impossible. He'd cleaned so thoroughly and run the fan the entire time he worked in the hood. But they'd found something. He wouldn't panic. He needed time to finish. Time to do it right. But now, because of Adler and her idiocy, he'd have to hurry the job.

But all that was a distraction. He had work to do. Soon it would be time to move. He knew exactly where to go, what to do. There was an energy in the air. It would be something new. He was growing bored with houses anyway. He was ready to move on.

He'd timed it all well, but he'd need to be quick before the sprinklers and smoke detectors alerted the motel staff. Which at the chosen time of night would be one lone person at the front desk drinking coffee and trying to stay awake.

He'd already scoped it the night before. He was ready. Mr Dougherty wouldn't suffer. It wasn't his fault that he'd married a bitchy woman. Mrs Dougherty, though . . . she had a lot to answer for. Very soon, she'd begin.

By answering to me.

The ringing of the phone jarred him back to reality. His first reaction was fear, but rage followed quickly. Rage at Adler for bringing the police to his doorstep. *Which brought the fear to me.* Was it the police? What did they now know? He answered the phone on the fourth ring. 'Yes.'

'I need to talk to you.'

He blinked, more at the fierce tone than the words. 'Okay. Why?'

'I've talked with Manny. He told me everything.'

His fist clenched the phone, then he forced himself to

relax. He injected a note of amused incredulity into his voice. 'You believed him? Come on.'

'I don't know. I need to talk to you.'

'Okay. Meet me and we'll discuss it rationally.'

There was a long pause. 'Okay. Flannagan's Bar in half an hour.'

He looked at his list. He'd checked nearly everything off, but there were still a few ends to tie off before he visited the Doughertys in their hotel. 'Make it forty-five.'

He stood, carefully loading his eggs into the backpack. Then he drew his blade from its sheath and turned it this way and that, catching the light, admiring its gleam. He'd sharpened it after Penny Hill. A responsible weapon owner cared for his tools.

The boy watched, a terrible fear clutching his heart. He knew firsthand what that blade could do. He also knew what the blade would do if he was ever discovered. So he pulled himself into a tighter ball and hid from the monster who haunted his dreams.

Chapter Thirteen

Wednesday, November 29, 8:40 P.M.

Reed could see her coming in his rearview. He shouldn't be here. He should have just waited until the morning to tell her. There wouldn't be anything she could do tonight anyway. But he knew she'd want to know. He knew she wasn't the type to ... how had she phrased it? To hide under the covers like a little girl.

She slowed the borrowed department car, rolling to a stop next to his SUV. For a moment she sat there, looking at him, then parked her car along the curb. Feeling like he dragged an anchor, he got out and walked up to her car, his hands in his pockets.

She popped her trunk and looked up at him from the corner of her eye. 'Something break on the case?' she asked. Inside her trunk were a half dozen grocery bags.

He shook his head. 'No.'

'Need somebody to tie your shoes or tear your mustard packets?'

'No.' He nudged her aside and grabbed the bags in both hands. 'Is this all?'

She slammed the trunk shut. 'I don't eat much.'

Without another word she led him up three flights of stairs and into her apartment. It was sparsely decorated as he'd known it would be. No pictures hung from the walls. Furniture was minimal. The TV was tiny and rested atop an old Styrofoam cooler. This wasn't a home. This was merely the place she slept when she wasn't working.

His eyes settled on the small wooden box on her dinette table just before she whisked it and a trifolded flag into her coat closet that was equally bare. That the flag had belonged to her father was not a huge leap. He'd been a cop. He'd get a cop's funeral. His widow would get the flag.

That the box had also been his was logical. That the daughter had the flag and not the widow was telling. But given what she'd shared this morning, completely understandable. How hard it must have been to learn of her father's infidelities while standing at his grave. How much harder for the widow. He thought of how he himself might have felt, learning that Christine had betrayed him. He simply couldn't imagine it.

That Mia Mitchell managed to stay focused at all was testament to the kind of cop she was. 'You can put the groceries on the table,' she said and he did, all the while wondering how he would tell her that her privacy was on the verge of being threatened.

He unpacked a bag, stacking frozen dinners. 'I just got finished meeting with Holly.'

Her eyes flashed. 'I trust you left Miss Wheaton well and happy.'

His temper rose. 'I don't like her, either, Mia. And I don't like your insinuation.'

She shrugged fitfully. 'You're right. I'm sorry,' she muttered. 'Doesn't matter anyway.' She reached for the stack of frozen dinners and he grabbed her arm.

'Dammit, Mia. What's wrong with you?'

For a split second, the anger in her eyes changed to fear. Then just that fast, it was gone, defiance taking its place. She jerked her arm and shaken, he immediately let her go. 'Go away, Reed. I'm not good company right now.'

She grabbed the cartons and disappeared into the kitchen. He heard the freezer door open, then slam shut. She reappeared, fists on her hips. 'You're still here.'

'So it would seem.' She stood there scowling, blue eyes flashing, somehow sexier in khaki pants and scuffed boots than Wheaton had been in a suede miniskirt and killer pumps. And he wanted her, scowl and all.

'Look. You seem like a nice man. You deserve better than I've treated you. I'm not warm and fuzzy, but I'm not usually this rude.' The smile that curved her lips was obviously forced. 'I'll try to be nicer. Let's get this case solved and you can walk away, hopefully none the worse for the wear.' She started for the front door, dismissing him.

Not just yet. 'Mia, I need to talk to you about Holly Wheaton. It's important.'

She stopped five feet away, her back to him. 'I really don't care.'

He sighed. 'About this you will.'

She turned to face him, wary. 'What's she done?'

'Your absence from the press conference this morning didn't go unnoticed.'

She closed her eyes. 'Oh shit.'

'She knows about the woman you followed, that she's important to you. She has video of her in the crowd. I thought you'd want to know, so you could be on your guard.'

Her eyes opened, narrowed. 'Goddamn, I hate that bitch.'

'I'd have to say the feeling is mutual. Why does she hate you so much?'

'We had a child rape/homicide and she tried to cuddle up to Abe for an exclusive, just like she tried with you at that apartment fire. Didn't matter that Abe is married. Abe and I agreed the best way to get Wheaton off his back was to give an exclusive to somebody else. We talked to Lynn Pope of *Chicago on the Town*.'

'I've seen her show, but I've never met her.'

'Lynn's a classy lady. I trust her. When Holly found out she filed a formal complaint with Spinnelli. He supported us, of course, and the next time *he* had a story, he gave the exclusive to Lynn. So Holly blames me for trying to ruin her career.'

'Why you?'

'Because the men couldn't possibly have resisted her on their own. I had to have turned them against her. She's a menace.' She sighed bitterly. 'She's also good at finding what she wants to know. Most men aren't capable of resisting a pretty face like hers. Most are even less capable of resisting a short skirt or the twitching ass inside it.'

There was a compliment buried in there somewhere, Reed knew, because he had resisted. But there was also something else, an acceptance that she, Mia Mitchell, didn't have those same attributes and was somehow less desirable. Which pissed him off, because he was living, breathing, aching proof of just how desirable she was. 'Nobody knows about your relationship to the blonde except the men in the room this morning. I won't say a word. Spinnelli, Jack, and the shrink won't say anything, either.'

She pressed her fingertips to her eyes. 'I know. I appreciate you coming by to tell me. Now I'm really sorry I snapped at you.'

Reed wanted to go to her. To take her in his arms and hold her. But she'd pulled away twice and he was afraid she'd make it three times. And he'd be out. So he stood where he was, hands in his pockets. 'It's okay.' He injected a note of humor in his voice. 'If I'd known how much you hated her, I would have let you get your court order.'

One side of her mouth turned up sadly. 'I knew you were a gentleman.'

You've said your piece. Now go. But his feet stayed planted where they were. He couldn't leave her looking so defeated. 'Mia, I've watched you for three days now. You care about the victims. If they suffered. Finding them justice. You care about the families. Giving them support and dignity. That's important to me. More important than warm fuzzies and especially more important than a twitching ass in a short skirt.'

Her eyes were serious as she studied him from five feet away. 'Thank you. That's the nicest thing anybody's ever said to me.'

Now you can go. Dammit, just go. But still he stood. 'Although you'd look every bit as good in a short skirt.'

Her eyes heated and his heart turned over. 'Second nicest.'

He took a step forward, testing. She held her ground, but he could see her pulse flutter at the hollow of her throat. At her sides her hands flexed and clenched and he came to a stunning realization. He made her nervous. It was an ego-boosting, courage-building discovery. 'About last night,' he said. 'I knocked you down.'

She lifted her chin. 'I know. I was there.'

'I haven't been shot at since I was in the army. My reflexes were a little rusty.'

She sucked in one cheek. 'Not all of them.'

It was the opening he'd been waiting for. 'So you did notice.'

'It would have been difficult not to,' she said dryly. 'So was it reflex or interest?'

She'd regained her stride, her cocky balance. And somehow that made what came next more . . . fair. If he'd pressed his advantage when she was sad and defeated it wouldn't have been. 'And if I said both?'

'You'd be honest at least.' She regarded him levelly for a moment. 'You could have waited until tomorrow to tell me about Wheaton. Why did you come tonight?'

The moment stretched as he considered his answer, then snapped as with two steps he eliminated the remaining distance that separated them. He slipped his hand around her neck, his fingers up into her hair and did what he'd wanted to do for days. When his mouth covered hers he felt her stiffen, then her arms were around his neck as she lifted on her toes and kissed him back.

He shuddered, as much from relief as release. It had been a long time since he'd held any woman this way. A long time since he'd tasted a woman's lips, felt the surge and surrender in her response. It was sweet, he realized. And familiar, as if he'd been here, done this before. Mindful of her bruised cheek he kept it much lighter than he wanted, much briefer than he wished. Stoically ignoring the coiled want in his gut, he ended the kiss, but held her tight against him.

'I wasn't sure you wanted this,' he admitted. 'You pulled away from me.'

She rested her forehead against his chest. 'I know.'

It was said so wearily that he pulled back to see her face. 'Why did you pull away?'

'Because I didn't want to want this. But I do.' Her lashes lifted and it was as if he'd been sucker punched. Her blue eyes were darkly aroused. His pounding heart climbed into his throat and with difficulty he forced it back down so he could breathe.

'Why? Why don't you want to want this?'

She hesitated. 'How much time do you have?'

Time. Shit. 'What time is it?'

'A little past nine. Why?'

'I promised Beth I'd pick her up at nine and that's clear on the other side of town.'

She nodded. 'I understand. We can talk more later.'

He grabbed his coat from the old sofa and took two steps toward the door, then stopped and turned back around to face her. 'She'll be fine for another few minutes. In fact, she's probably happy I'm late.'

Her lips curved. 'So how do you propose using another few minutes?'

'Doing what you don't want to want.' He caught her chin and tilted her face up and this time she met him more than halfway, instantly taking the kiss to the next level. Hot and wet and full of motion, it set his body throbbing and left him wanting much, much more. Conscious of the time, he abruptly pulled away, and was gratified to see she was breathing just as hard as he was. 'Warn me when you start wanting to want it,' he said. 'I'll make sure I bring along a defibrillator.'

She laughed. 'Go home, Solliday. We'll take this up

again tomorrow.' Her smile sobered a shade. 'But not around the office, okay?'

'Okay.' He leaned forward for one more kiss, then turned on his heel with an oath. 'I have to go. Lock the door behind me.'

'I always do.'

He paused on the landing outside her door. 'I'll see you at eight tomorrow.' With a little physical distance, his mind began to clear. 'Don't go out alone tonight, okay?'

She looked amused. 'Solliday, I'm a cop. I'm supposed to tell other people that.'

He was not amused. 'Mia, please.'

'I'll be careful.'

That was the closest she'd come to capitulation, he understood. 'Good night, Mia.'

A sober, wistful look flitted across her face. 'Good night, Reed.'

Wednesday, November 29, 10:05 P.M.

He'd finally come back. It had certainly taken him long enough.

He'd thought his target would wait inside Flannagan's for fifteen minutes, but he'd waited an hour. During which he'd hidden in the back floorboards of the man's car, biding his time.

The first part had been so easy and fast. He'd been early, waiting in the shadows. He'd watched as the man locked his car, which was a total joke. He'd been able to pop the lock with his trusty slim-jim in fifteen seconds. Then he'd gone flat in the backseat, pulling on the ski mask and waiting, visualizing in his mind what had to be done.

It wouldn't be pretty, but it would be fast. And painless. Because his target was his friend and didn't deserve to writhe in agony, like Mrs Dougherty would tonight. But first things first. *Focus.* They'd been driving for fifteen minutes. It wouldn't be long now.

He wanted to sigh, but kept it in. He'd never killed someone he liked. There was a first time for everything, but he wasn't relishing the task.

He eased up on his elbow and stole a look out the opposite window. Good, they were on a small road, one lane each way. There was an all-night shopping center nearby where he could steal a car when he was finished. He drew his knife.

He'd sharpened the blade yet again. He wanted it to be quick. Springing to a crouch, he whipped the knife around and held it to his friend's throat. 'Pull off at the next light,' he instructed, keeping his voice low.

His friend's eyes whipped up to the rearview, wide with terror, but he knew he'd see nothing but the black ski mask. 'If you want the car, I'll give it to you. Just don't hurt me.'

He thought it was a carjacking, which was exactly what he'd hoped his friend would think. No use in risking identification, should the plan go south. They were off the main road now. The area was a little too populated for his liking, but it would do.

He grabbed his friend's hair and yanked his head at an angle. 'Slow down. That's right. Nice and slow. Pull off onto the shoulder. Farther. Now stop.'

'Don't kill me. Please.' He was sobbing. 'Please don't kill me.'

He frowned. He'd expected him to go with more backbone. What a girl. Maybe he wouldn't make it so painless after all. But his knife was sharp. It would slice deep given the smallest pressure. 'Put it in park. That's right. Now roll down the window.'

Cold air rushed in, feeling wonderful against his overheated skin. 'Take the keys from the ignition.' His target hesitated and he put more pressure on the knife. 'Do it.'

The car's engine went silent. 'Now throw the keys out the window.'

The keys hit the snow with a muted jangle.

'You won't get away with this,' his target said, desperation in his voice.

How clichéd. He'd choose his friends more wisely when he started his next life.

'I think I will,' he responded in his normal voice and had one moment to savor the look of wild recognition before he yanked straight back and brought the blade across the man's throat. Hard.

Blood gushed. Spurted. Filled the car with its metallic odor. He wobbled the head side to side and found he'd nearly severed it. Cool. He'd never done that before.

He let go of the hair and climbed out of the backseat. With a handful of snow he cleaned his knife, then picked up the keys. Keys made a nice souvenir.

His jacket would have to go. His sleeve was covered in blood. He'd have to get a new jacket at some point. Perhaps when he got to the shopping center, he'd find a car with a coat in it. He'd walk to the shopping center, steal a car and have plenty of time for a nap before the Doughertys. He wanted to be fresh after all.

Wednesday, November 29, 11:15 P.M.

The house was quiet. Beth was asleep and Lauren was on her own side of the duplex. Reed sat on the edge of his bed and shuddered, torturing himself with the fantasy yet again, imagining what would have happened had he not needed to leave. Her mouth had been soft and sweet and hot and urgent all at the same time. Better than he'd imagined. And that was only a few short kisses. When he got her to bed . . .

She wanted him. He'd have her. Another shudder shook him. God. It hurt, he wanted her so much. He drew the chain from around his neck and held it up, the ring at the end shining softly. He'd worn the ring on his hand for the five happiest years of his life, then another two as he grieved. It was only at the worried insistence of his family that he'd finally taken it off, but it hadn't gone far. He'd worn it on a chain around his neck ever since. Knowing it was there was like keeping a little piece of Christine to himself. Just like Christine's poetry, it kept her alive in his heart. But tonight it wasn't dreams of Christine that crowded his mind. Mia was there, firmly entrenched. She'd stay there until he'd ridden this thing out, wherever it took them. Whatever it cost.

He set the ring swinging, like a hypnotist's coin. He could go over there right now. And have her. The blood was pounding in his head, drowning out all the reasons he shouldn't. He lowered the ring until it hit the nightstand and let the chain pool inside it.

He picked up the phone, hit Lauren's speed dial. 'I need you to stay with Beth.'

She yawned. 'Give me two minutes. I'll be there.'

He hung up, guilt for the deception eclipsed by a need that left him trembling. She'd wanted him, even though she hadn't wanted to. He'd find out why.

Wednesday, November 29, 11:50 P.M.

Mia blinked. She'd read that name before. Her eyes were tired. It was time to stop.

She sat back in the hard chair and twisted, stretching her neck muscles. She'd made it through a month of Burnette's case files, specifically the month before Manny Rodriguez was sent to Hope Center. She'd carefully cataloged every name, every place mentioned on every case Burnette had supervised or been associated with.

It was a nasty list. She didn't envy Burnette his Vice clientele. But other than being a nasty list, there was nothing useful or unusual about it. Not a single name or place popped. It was a tedious task, and she still had tons of paper to wade through.

But, as tedious tasks went, it had been a halfway decent way of pushing Reed Solliday and his intriguing mouth to the back of her mind. Well, not the back of her mind, really. More like . . . dead center. Front row. Hell.

She'd kissed him. And now she knew how he tasted. How his lips felt against hers. How it felt to press against that solid wall of muscle he called a chest. And now, having tasted him, she wanted to taste him again. She wanted it a very great deal.

Goddamn hamburger. She blamed Dana for this. She'd been happily miserable until she'd started craving hamburger. So what would happen when Solliday wanted to go upscale? Move from hamburger to filet? She'd get her heart broken, that's what.

And maybe break his, too. It was a sobering thought. But not enough to squelch the craving. She didn't just want to kiss him. Now that she'd taken the plunge . . . well, if he walked in this minute, he'd be a very happy man. At least for the short term. She was fairly good at sex, Mia knew. Sex itself had never been the problem. Intimacy was.

She stood up, stretched her back again. She was still sore from Solliday's tackle last night but she wasn't sleepy. There was too much caffeine in her system for her to sleep. So now she would lie in bed, stare at the ceiling, and wish she was getting laid.

Damn that Dana. She probably was getting laid, right this minute. It wasn't fair.

She paced restlessly, wondering if Solliday was sleeping. She certainly hoped not. She hoped he was—

A heavy knock at her door made her jump. Cautiously she drew her weapon from the shoulder holster she'd draped over a chair. Holding the gun down at her side, she stood on her toes and peeked through the peephole in the door.

She huffed out a relieved breath. She opened the door to Reed Solliday, who stood on her welcome mat wearing a forbidding frown. 'You scared me to death,' she said, bypassing any greeting, then got worried. It was almost midnight. 'What's happened?'

'Can I come in?'

Immediately she stepped aside and let him in. He stalked in, his stride almost belligerent. She closed the door and leaned against it. 'What's happened?'

He took off his trenchcoat and dropped it on her sofa. He'd shed his suit coat and tie at some point. His shirt was unbuttoned so that a glimpse of coarse dark hair teased. Her heart started a slow pounding in her chest. The pounding got harder when he took the gun from her hand and returned it to her holster. And when he approached her with a hard, predatory cast to his face, the pounding spread low. And deep.

Not taking his eyes from hers he flattened his palms against the door on either side of her head. She was caged in, but there was no fear. Only excitement and the dark thrill of arousal. When he lowered his head and took her mouth it was savage and greedy and left no doubt as to why he'd come back. She let herself be swept away. Just his mouth on hers. She moaned and he jerked his head back. She stood, eyes closed, the door bearing her weight. His breath beat her hair and she knew if she lifted her hand to his heart, she'd feel it thunder against her palm.

'I couldn't sleep,' he whispered harshly. 'I could only think of you. Under me. I have to have you. But if that's not what you want, tell me now and I'll leave.'

Her heart physically hurt. Her body was throbbing. He was what she wanted. This was what she needed. Now. 'Don't go.' She lifted her eyes to his. Then lifted her hands to his face and pulled him down for another bruising kiss that made her knees go weak. He ran his hands down her sides, over her breasts, shaping and reshaping. Flicking his thumbs across her nipples and she shivered. Violently.

It had been too long since she'd had a man's hands on her. Too long since she'd had her hands on a man. She reached for his shirt and pulled at the buttons, yanking at the fabric until she pulled it free. For a full minute she ran her hands over yards of muscle, then raked her fingers through the coarse hair that covered his chest.

With a muttered curse he grabbed her rear end and lifted her off her feet until their bodies aligned and supporting her weight, thrust against her. He was hard and hot and just where she needed him to be.

No, not exactly where she needed him to be. Not yet. His mouth left hers and kissed a path down the side of her neck. The hard ridge no longer throbbed against her as he lifted her higher, pulling her legs around his waist.

She opened her mouth to protest, when his mouth closed over her breast and sucked. Hard. She cried out, the protest disintegrating to a moan. She threaded her fingers through his hair and held him there, suckling. He pulled away, moved to the other breast and she let her head drop back against the door and . . . absorbed.

Abruptly he straightened and startled, she grabbed his shoulders. 'Grab my coat,' he said and she blinked at him.

'What?'

He carried her to the sofa. 'Grab my coat.'

She clutched one of his shoulders and leaned over to do what he asked. 'Why?'

He was already heading back to her bedroom. 'Condoms in the pocket.'

She dug in one pocket, then the other and pulled out a white plastic drugstore bag. She let his coat fall to the floor and leaned in to nip at his lips. 'Got 'em.'

He knelt at the foot of her bed, lowered her carefully to the mattress. He stripped her pants down her legs before she could blink and, unwilling to sit on the sidelines, she pulled off her shirt. She was reaching behind her for the hooks of her bra when he set his mouth to her, right through the silk triangle of her thong. She fell back against the pillow, clutched the bedspread in both fists, and once again, simply absorbed.

'You're wet,' he muttered. 'So wet.' He lifted his head and his eyes glittered. 'I was hoping you would be.'

'I was thinking of you.'

His brow lifted and he looked like the devil himself, but the image enticed. 'What were you thinking?'

Reflex had her lifting her hips, wanting him back where he'd been, doing what he'd been doing. Never before had it felt so incredibly good. 'Solliday, please.'

'First you talk.'

She lifted herself up on her elbows. 'That's extortion.'

He grinned and licked her through the silk. 'Sue me.'

She could play the game. 'I was thinking about last night. How you felt against me.' She lifted her brows. 'You're . . . incredibly well endowed, Solliday.'

His eyes narrowed. 'Take off your bra.'

Her hands steady, she did, pulling her chain and dog tags off with it.

He drew a breath. 'So are you.' He pulled the thong aside and dragged a guttural moan from her throat with his mouth.

'I thought about your mouth the first day,' she said, panting. Then his tongue stabbed at her and she closed her eyes. 'Please.'

'Tell me if I do something you don't like.'

'I don't like when you stop,' she muttered and he laughed. Then got busy again, dragging her higher, winding her tighter, tauter. She bucked her hips and he pressed her into the mattress and sucked and she arched like a bow. The orgasm shot through her like an electric shock, hard and complete, leaving her weak and gasping.

He slapped a condom in her hand. 'Do it,' he bit out, pushing his pants to the floor.

Mia's eyes widened. Sated for now, she could admire him. 'Oh. This is gonna be good.'

'Mia, please. I'm not going to be able to hold back much longer.' Gently, she touched him with her fingertips and he jerked. 'Mia,' he said between his teeth.

So she covered him, then gasped again when he slammed into her with one solid thrust of his hips. He held himself still as if he, too, absorbed. 'Did I hurt you?' he asked.

'No. I was just . . . No.' She ran her hands over his shoulders. 'Don't stop now.'

He grimaced. 'I'm not sure I could.' He started to move inside her and she did her part, locking her ankles around his waist, meeting each thrust. But his pace quickened, and the thrusts became harder, faster. Deeper. And she felt herself climbing again until she came, this time on a wave that seemed to go on and on until once again she collapsed back against the pillow, weak and gasping.

Above her, Reed went still, his head tilted back, his teeth bared, the muscles in his chest and arms quivering. Beautiful, was all she could think. He was simply beautiful. His head fell forward, and slowly he lowered his weight to his forearms and sighed.

She ran her finger along the line of his goatee, breathing too hard to speak. It had been incredible. Earth-shattering.

Not hamburger. She closed her eyes, too tired to worry. That would come later. For now, she'd try to take in as much as she could. Store it away for when she had it no longer. He kissed her forehead, her cheek, her chin. 'We have to talk,' he said.

She nodded. 'Not right now, though.' She'd have this, at least. Unspoiled.

'Later, then.' He rested his forehead against hers. 'Mia. I can't stay all night.'

'I know.'

'But . . . I'd like to stay a while longer.'

Don't run from him. See where this takes you. 'I'd like that, too.' Her mouth curved. 'You stopped by the drugstore. You must have been pretty sure of yourself.'

He lifted his head, met her eyes, and she saw that he spoke truth. 'I wasn't. All I knew was that if I didn't have you I'd explode. I hoped you'd say yes. I'm hoping you'll say yes again.'

She nodded soberly. 'Yes. Again.'

COUNT TO TEN

Thursday, November 30, 12:30 A.M.

He was ready. He felt the energy flow through his body, like a fine hum. He'd worked through his plan. Their hotel room couldn't be located any better. All the room doors opened to the outside, but theirs was on the first floor, parking places only yards away.

He gently shouldered his backpack. It held three eggs. One was for the Doughertys' bed. He'd studied and now knew exactly how he'd bypass the sprinkler in their room. He'd investigated stairwells and exit paths and laundry rooms and knew exactly where he'd place the two other bombs for maximum burn, turning the whole hotel into hell. There would be mayhem as people streamed out in their pajamas, crying and terrified. Since there'd be no gas for an explosion, a little mayhem was only fair. The fire department would send three, maybe four trucks. There would be ambulances and flashing lights. The newspeople would come, film would roll. They'd frantically check to be sure everyone was out. Then they'd find two bodies.

His system was revved, still charged from before. He'd killed once tonight. He was on a roll. He'd bagged the bloody coat hours before. He now wore a pair of coveralls he'd stolen from the hotel's laundry room. Master key cards were useful things.

He stood at the Doughertys' motel room door, confident no one would give him a second look. Not that it would matter if they did. Thanks to a wig and a little padding, he looked like a different man. His right hand gripped his very sharp knife. In his left was Tania's master key card. He swiped it and gently tested the door, frowning when it caught. The Doughertys had used the swing bar for extra security. But no worries. He had considerable experience with these devices. Nothing was truly secure if you knew how to get around it. Sliding the thin blade of his knife through the narrow opening of the door he dislodged the swing bar and slipped in the room, carefully closing the door behind him. It was quiet except for the sound of gentle snoring coming from the bed. He stood still, allowing his eyes to become accustomed to the darkness.

And became instantly aware of two things. There were no flowers in this room. And there was only one person in the bed. A young woman, not more than twenty-five. A spear of panic went through him. He had the wrong room. *Run.*

But the woman opened her eyes and opened her mouth to scream. He was too quick. Too powerful. He yanked her head back as he already had once that evening. He held the knife at her throat. 'You will not scream. Do you understand?'

She nodded, a whimper of terror escaping.

'What's your name?'

'N-N-Niki Markov. Please . . .'

His hand tightened in her hair. 'What room number is this?'

'I – I don't kn-know.' He yanked harder and she let

out another whimper. 'I can't remember. Please. I have two kids. Please don't hurt me.'

His blood was pumping, pounding in his head as he fought to contain the sudden rush of fury. Damn women. None of them stayed with their kids. 'If you have two kids, you should be home' – he yanked again – 'with your two kids.' He switched on a light and looked at the phone. The room number was the right one. 'When did you get here?'

'T-tonight. Please, I'll do whatever you want. Please don't hurt me.'

They were gone. Goddammit they were gone. He'd missed them. Fury bubbled. Boiled. Spilled over, eating like acid. 'Come on,' he snarled. She stumbled when he dragged her toward the bathroom.

'Please,' she was sobbing now, hysterical.

He yanked at her hair, bringing her up on her toes. 'Shut up.' Another whimper crawled from her throat. He couldn't ruin any more clothes, he thought. But he couldn't let her live. She'd tell. He'd be caught. Which was not going to happen.

So he pushed her in the tub, held the tip of the knife to her throat as he turned on the shower, full blast, which was really a piss-poor trickle. He grabbed her hair again, twisting her to her stomach. Then he pulled the knife across her throat savagely.

And stood, watching as the trickle carried all her blood down the drain.

As her blood drained, his rushed. Rage seethed until

he trembled from the force of it. He'd been denied his satisfaction. He'd been robbed of his revenge.

The Doughertys had managed to elude him once again. He'd find out where they went but he was running out of time. His jaw clenched as he waited for the woman in the tub to bleed out. He'd had plenty of time, until the cops showed up.

Because of Brooke Adler. Because of her stupidity, he would be discovered. It was a matter of time. He didn't have the Doughertys, but by God, he'd have his satisfaction. He still had three eggs in his backpack and he'd be damned if he'd let them spoil.

First, he needed to take care of this one. If he left her here, she'd be discovered by noon tomorrow. The police weren't so stupid as to not make the connection between a dead woman who just happened to occupy the Doughertys' old room and a dead woman who just happened to occupy the Doughertys' empty house. She had to go.

He could drag her out, but she was big enough to make it awkward. So he'd have to make her smaller. He held his knife under the miserly stream of water and washed it clean before testing it against his thumb. Good. It was still sharp enough for what he needed to do.

Chapter Fourteen

Thursday, November 30, 3:10 A.M.

What the hell are you doing?' Startled, Brooke looked up from the computer. Her roommate stood in the hall, her iPod in her hand. 'It's three A.M.,' Roxanne said.

'I don't know what to do,' Brooke murmured.

Roxanne sighed. 'You can't do any more tonight, Brooke. Go to sleep.'

'I tried. I can't. All I can think of are bills and loans and debts. I can't sleep.'

Roxanne's expression softened in sympathy. 'It'll be okay. You'll find another job.'

'I don't think so. I've been searching all night. There's nothing open around here.'

'You'll find something. Now go to bed, Brooke. You'll just make yourself sick with worry and then you really won't be able to find a job.'

'You're right. I know you're right. But without a recommendation from Bixby, it's going to be close to impossible to find anyone who'll even consider me.'

'I still think you should sue the bastard, no matter what Devin's lawyer friend thinks.'

Devin had called his lawyer friend from Flannagan's, but the friend had told him that her claim would be hard to prove and it would take a long time. She didn't have a long time. She only had forty-two dollars in the bank. 'I might. But that doesn't help me now. I'm almost broke.' She closed her eyes. 'You may need to find another roommate.'

'We'll cross that bridge when we get there. I've got to get to sleep. Bach's lullabies work. You should try it.' Pressing the earphones to her ears, she headed to her room.

It'll take more than Bach to relax me, Brooke thought. She went into the kitchen and found the brandy she saved for special occasions. It wasn't gourmet, but it was strong enough to do the trick. She downed a glass, then poured herself another and sat at the kitchen table. She sipped at the second glass, despair overwhelming.

She had no money. She couldn't call her parents. They were living on next to nothing as it was. Hate surged. Bixby was a bastard. *I did nothing wrong.* She gulped more brandy, bitterly resigned. It didn't matter. She'd be out of a job just the same.

She wasn't sure how long she'd sat brooding when she heard it.

Click. She looked up, trying to place the noise. Then walked to the kitchen doorway to stare at the front door. It was opening. With a key. *Somebody has my key.*

Call 911. Where was the cordless? She stumbled to the counter, pulled a butcher knife from the block. *Oh God.* She ran to the living room. *Where was the phone?*

Then her mouth fell open as the man came through the door. He held a knife. Recognition was instantaneous, but she had no time to even say his name before his hand flattened over her mouth and he twisted her wrist. Her butcher knife fell to the floor.

Eyes wide with horror, she saw the metal of his long, thin blade before it swept down and pressed against her throat. *He's going to kill me.* She struggled and the blade pressed a little harder. Abruptly she stopped struggling and he chuckled.

The hand left her mouth, but the knife continued to press and a stifled sob rose in her throat. 'I've cut two throats wide open tonight,' he said. 'Say one word and I'll make it three.' He yanked, making her walk on her toes to her bedroom. He threw her down on the bed, drove his knee into her ribs and shoved a ball of cloth into her mouth.

She fought him when he grabbed one wrist and tied it to her headboard, then cried out when he slammed his fist into her jaw. But her cry was muted, she could barely hear it herself. He leaned into her body with his knee, tying her other wrist.

'You've ruined my work, Brooke,' he hissed in her face. His eyes were wild, crazy. He couldn't be the same man she knew. But he was. 'Now I'll have no time to finish and you'll pay for that. I told you to let it go, but you wouldn't listen. You'll listen now.'

He came to his feet and she kicked, hoping to make a noise Roxanne would hear. He bent to his backpack and when he straightened, he held a pipe wrench in his hand.

No! She screamed it, but nobody heard. When the first blow struck she moaned. With the second she wished she was dead. With the third, she knew she would be.

Grimly satisfied, he zipped the used condom in a baggie, just as he'd done with Penny Hill. He recalled how Hill's eyes had glazed over from the pain and halfway through she'd closed them, robbing him of the pleasure of seeing her suffering.

He stood over Brooke, sweat dripping down his face. He slapped her cheeks hard and a muffled moan escaped her throat. Good. She was still conscious. He wanted to be sure she had felt everything he did to her, and that she heard every word. 'You ruined my work. I may never get my justice. So tonight you'll take her place.'

He worked quickly, applying the gel to her body as he'd done to Penny Hill. He placed the egg between her knees, ran the fuse past her feet. There wasn't any gas in this house – only electric, so he'd have to compromise.

He'd already decided to place a second egg at the apartment's front entrance. Just another little hoop for the firemen to jump through. He ran a second fuse and laid that egg next to his knife on the night table. Then pulled out his lighter and leaned down to Brooke's face. 'You're like the others. You say you care, but you betray their trust. You say you want to help those boys, but the first chance you get, you give them to the police. You're just as deceitful and just as guilty. When I light this fuse, start counting.'

Her eyes flickered, focusing over his shoulder. He turned, a split second before a violin would have come crashing on his head. It struck his shoulder instead, splintering into pieces. A woman stood, eyes wide, breasts heaving as she panted. She held the neck of the shattered violin in her fist, then she swung it at him again. He caught her forearm, but she twisted free. He barely dodged the little chair she swung at him.

He grasped his knife from the nightstand and in one fluid motion plunged it into the violinist's gut and ripped, his eyes locked on hers. Her face contorted and she dropped to the floor on top of her splintered instrument. His heart was pounding, his blood rushing. He felt alive. Untouchable. Invincible. He flicked the lighter, lit the fuse at Brooke's feet, then leaned over her ear. 'Count to ten, Brooke. And go to hell.'

He grabbed his backpack, the knife, and the other egg, and ran from the apartment, down the stairs. He lit the second fuse and placed the egg in the corner of the lobby. The carpet was threadbare, but it would burn quickly. Then he bolted out the front door.

And nearly had heart failure. Two police cruisers

were turning into the complex, lights flashing, sirens blaring. *The violinist had called the cops. Fucking bitch.* He ducked behind the building and ran to the parking lot behind the next row of apartments. At least he'd had the good sense to case the place when he'd first arrived. Keeping to the shadows, he chose the easiest car to steal. A minute later he was driving away.

He'd almost been caught. He struggled to catch his breath and smelled the violinist's blood. It covered his coat, his gloves. She hadn't been in the plan, but . . . Wow. It was an incredible feeling, taking a life like that, looking into her eyes as he stole her very soul. He chuckled. The English teacher had rubbed off on him.

Then he sobered. And wondered how much of him had rubbed off on the English teacher. The fire would be going by now, but without the gas, it might not be enough to destroy everything. He'd used a condom. He'd worn gloves. But he might have dropped a hair. Still, in order to use it against him, they'd have to find him first.

He didn't have much time and he still had to find Laura Dougherty. Then there were four more. They were the worst. They hadn't been merely involved in Shane's death. *They'd killed him.* One was in Indy. He'd find the other three, then he'd be finished.

He'd roll into a new life just as he'd rolled into this one, make new friends, find another woman to serve his needs at home. He'd have to think about his next job. He'd never thought about doing the one he had now. It had been the right time and place, so he'd snatched the opportunity. But he'd been good at it.

Who needed a college degree? He was the master chameleon. *Like in that movie where the guy impersonates a doctor and a lawyer and a pilot.* Maybe he'd try his hand at one of those jobs next time around.

Thursday, November 30, 3:50 A.M.

'Holy shit.' The words wheezed from Mia's chest as she lay limp and lax and sated.

Beside her Solliday chuckled. 'I love your way with words, Mia.'

She pushed up on her elbow and smiled down at him. 'You know we're going to be wrecks tomorrow. Today,' she corrected, glancing at the clock next to her bed.

'I know, but it was worth it. I don't think I realized just how much I needed this.'

She slid her palm across his hard belly, feeling the muscles quiver. 'How long has it been?' she asked quietly.

His eyes flicked up to hers. 'Six years.'

Her brows went up. 'Holy shit,' she said and he laughed. She raked her fingers through the coarse hair on his chest, sobering. 'I needed it, too.'

He studied her for a long moment. 'I want to know why you didn't want to want this.'

'And I'll tell you.'

'Just not now?' She nodded, her eyes solemn. 'Tonight?' he pressed and again she nodded wordlessly. 'It'd be better if you could come to me, after Beth's in bed. That way I don't have to ask Lauren to watch her like I did tonight.'

'Somehow I didn't get the impression that she'd mind,' Mia said wryly and his expression changed. He hadn't told Lauren where he was going. His sister thought he'd been called to a fire. The realization stung a little. 'You don't want her to know.'

'Not yet.' He sat up and she rolled to her back. The night was officially over.

'Tomorrow,' she started. 'Today, I mean. We're colleagues. Nothing more.'

The look he sent her was level. 'Nothing more.' Then he surprised her by leaning down and kissing her with a hunger that stole her breath. 'Tonight, though, much more.'

He was buckling his belt when his cell phone rang. 'Solliday.' He got down on one knee to find his socks. 'Was there a gas explosion . . . Fine then. I'll proceed to 2026 Chablis Court. Thanks, Larry. I should be there in fifteen to twenty.'

'It's way past midnight,' Mia observed and he threw a look over his shoulder.

'There was no gas explosion, so it's probably not our guy. It's an apartment fire, so they've called four companies to the scene – Larry's is one of them.' He slipped his feet in his shoes. 'There's no reason for us both to lose sleep. I'll check it out and call you. Can you give me a hand with the buttons on my shirt? It would be faster that way.'

She helped him, making quick work of the buttons. 'I do hot dogs, too.'

He lifted one eyebrow and now she could admit that had turned her on from the beginning. 'You are a very bad girl, Mia.'

'Mustard, Solliday.' She smacked his ass as he walked away. 'Think *condiments*.'

'Very bad girl.' He was almost to the front door when it struck her – *2026 Chablis*.

'*Reed, wait*.' She ran after him. 'Did you say 2026 Chablis Court, like the wine?'

He frowned. 'Yeah, why?'

Her heart skipped a beat, visualizing the records check she'd run yesterday. 'That's Brooke Adler's address.'

His expression went grim. 'Meet me there,' he said. 'Hurry.'

Thursday, November 30, 4:15 A.M.

The fire was contained to one apartment building, the end of a row of five. To the untrained eye it might seem chaotic but it was under control. People stood on the edge of the parking lot, huddled in small groups. Many were crying, child and adult alike. The apartment fire he'd worked last year came back and with it the horror for the victims.

And while every one of them was important, one victim was at the front of his mind. Reed found Larry Fletcher and immediately knew it was very bad. 'What's happened?'

'We were still en route when you called back, told us about the Adler woman.' Larry's voice was flat. 'The 186 was doing search and rescue in the building, but Mahoney and Hunter wanted to go in. Wanted to win this time. Chief of the 186 said it was my call, so I let them. Now I wish I'd said no.'

'They're hurt?'

'Not physically. They pulled out Adler and her roommate. It was bad, Reed.'

Reed looked over his shoulder. Mia was turning in from the main road. 'Alive?'

'One was DOA. The other's on her way to County.'

Ten cruisers surrounded the perimeter, uniforms controlling the crowd and passing out blankets to the victims. 'What about the cops who were first on the scene?'

Larry pointed to the cruiser farthest away. 'Jergens and Petty.'

'Thanks.' He jogged over to the cruisers. 'Solliday, OFI. Jergens and Petty?'

'I'm Jergens, this is Petty,' the officer on the left said. 'We were first on the scene.'

Mia was walking toward him. Reed gestured for her

to hurry and she closed the distance at a run while he took out his recorder. 'This is Detective Mitchell.' He turned to her. 'Two women pulled out of the fire, one dead, one en route to County.'

'This is the guy that did Burnette's kid,' Jergens said, his mouth flattening. 'SOB.'

'Which woman is dead?' Reed asked and the two shook their heads.

'Both were burned pretty badly. The neighbors said they were both about the same size, both brunettes, but nobody would make an ID. That's the DOA.' A gurney was being rolled toward the ambulance, the body bag zipped.

Mia motioned the MEs to stop. 'Well, let's find out.' They cringed then exhaled in unison as the ME unzipped the bag. The burns were bad. 'Not Adler,' she murmured, then turned back to Petty and Jergens. 'Did the neighbors at least provide a name?'

Jergens checked his notes. 'Roxanne Ledford. She called in the 911.'

'Tell us what happened,' Mia said calmly. 'Start from the 911.'

Jergens nodded. 'Rape in progress was called in at 3:38. The 911 operator told her to vacate the premises, but she didn't. We got here at 3:42.

'We could see flames upstairs and in the lobby when we got here. Petty radioed for the fire department. I grabbed the extinguisher from the cruiser and tried to go in, but the fire in the entry was already too big.

Another cruiser was behind us. I went to see if the perp was still on the grounds and Petty and the other two started evacuating.'

Mia lifted her eyes. 'But you didn't find anyone?'

'No. I'm sorry, Detective. There was nobody around.'

'The last time, he drove off in the victim's car. I want you to find out which cars belonged to Adler and Ledford and see if they're still here. If not, put out an all points.'

'What else?' Petty asked. 'We really want this SOB.'

Mia looked around. 'Any of these guys the super?'

'That one.' Petty pointed. 'Tall, big guy wearing the fuzzy pink slippers.'

'Find out if the building's got security cameras. I want any and all tape from the last week. Oh, and what are we doing for these people? We gotta worry about exposure.'

'Two buses are on the way,' Jergens said. 'We're going to put them in the elementary school down the street until we can set up a shelter.'

'We'll need statements from everyone. I want to know if there was anybody around here that anybody didn't know.' She shot them a hard smile. 'Thanks. I appreciate it. So will Roger Burnette.' She looked up when the officers moved off to follow her orders. 'We need to get to Brooke. Maybe she can tell us something.'

'Hunter and Mahoney pulled them out.'

She shot him a look of disbelief, then started toward the trucks at a run. 'They went in *again*? There are four companies here. Why Mahoney and Hunter for God's sake?'

He remembered the look of honest affection she'd given Hunter at the Hill fire. A nasty voice whispered in his ear, but Reed dismissed it. Whatever had happened between Mia and Hunter in the past, Reed had been the one to leave her bed tonight.

'They wanted to go in. After pulling corpses, it really makes you feel good to pull out a live person. The other chief understood that and let Larry's guys go in for the rescue.'

'Like Howard and Brooks let me have DuPree.'

'Yeah. Just like that.'

Hunter and Mahoney sat on the back of the truck. Both looked shell-shocked.

Mia put her hand on Hunter's shoulder. 'David. Are you two all right?'

Hunter nodded, his eyes flat. 'Fine,' he murmured.

Mahoney grimaced. 'Yeah. Sure. We're just fine.' But the sarcastic words were filled with pain. He closed his eyes. 'I really hate this guy.'

'What happened?' Reed asked quietly. 'Tell us everything you saw.'

'We went in the front,' Mahoney began. 'He'd started a fire there, too, but the 186 knocked it down. Smoke was heavy in Adler's apartment, but the stove was in place.'

'Where did you find them?' Mia asked.

'In the back bedroom.' Mahoney shook his head,

cleared his throat. 'The bed was in flames, all the walls, carpet, everything.' His voice broke. 'There were two women in the room. One was on the floor. I picked her up and started out. Called for backup for Hunter. When I got her out, the EMTs said she was already dead. She was wearing flame-retardant pajamas, so her body wasn't burned so badly, but her face and hands were. She'd been stabbed. Ripped open.' He pursed his lips and turned away.

'And the second woman?' Reed asked quietly.

Hunter swallowed. 'She was tied to the bed. Nude. Her body was on fire. I grabbed a blanket and rolled her up in it. Her legs were broken. Bent at angles.'

Mia suddenly stiffened, her eyes swerving to the road where a woman with a blond braid approached. Two officers turned her away. 'Goddammit.'

Carmichael again. 'She was following you,' Reed commented and her eyes flashed up to his. He knew she was thinking the same thing he was. Carmichael had been waiting outside her apartment. She'd seen Reed leave just before Mia had. That he'd spent the night would be all over the front page. *Shit*.

But Mia's attention was already back to Hunter. 'What happened next, David?'

'I had to cut the ropes to get her out of there. But I didn't touch anything else. I picked her up and carried her out. She was burned.' His jaw trembled and he clenched it. 'Badly. The EMTs weren't sure if she'd make it.'

Mia squeezed Hunter's hand. 'If she does, it will be because of the two of you. You have to hold on to that, David.' She let go and looked up. 'I have to talk to Brooke.'

Reed looked up at the building. The fire was nearly out. 'I'll stay here and go in as soon as I can. Foster and Ben should be here any minute. Can you call Jack?'

'Yeah.' She kicked at some gravel at her feet. 'Dammit, we missed him again.'

Thursday, November 30, 4:50 A.M.

'I'm Detective Mitchell. You just took in a Brooke Adler. Rape and burn victim.'

The ER nurse shook her head. 'You can't see her.'

'I have to talk to her. She's the only one who's seen a killer. She's his fourth victim.'

'I wish I could help you, Detective, but I can't let you see her. She's sedated.'

A doctor walked up, brows crunched. 'She's heavily sedated, but somehow still lucid enough to mutter. She has third-degree burns over ninety percent of her body. If I thought she'd survive, I'd make you wait. Hurry. We were just about to intubate.'

Mia fell into stride beside the doctor. 'We need to do a rape kit.'

'Already noted on my chart. She looks bad, Detective.'

'I saw his first two victims in the morgue, Doctor. They looked bad.'

'Just tryin' to prepare you.' He handed her a mask and surgical drape. 'After you.'

Mia came to a stumbling halt. Acid rose to burn her throat, choke her air. *Dear God*, was all she could think for the first five seconds. 'Oh, sweet Christ.'

'I tried to tell you,' the doctor murmured. 'Two minutes. No more.'

The nurse standing at Brooke's side glared. 'What's she doing here?'

'She's the bad cop,' the doctor said blandly. 'Let her through.'

Mia shot him a sharp look. 'What?'

He shrugged. 'That's what she kept calling you. The bad cop.'

'She's muttering something about "ten," ' the nurse said.

'Like the number?'

'Yes.'

'Hey, Brooke, it's me, Detective Mitchell.'

Brooke's eyes opened, and Mia saw wild fear and excruciating pain. '*Ten.*'

Mia lifted her hand, but there was no place to touch her. 'Who did this, Brooke?'

'Count to ten,' Brooke whispered. She moaned in agony and Mia's heart clenched.

'Brooke, tell me who did this. Was it someone at Hope Center? Was it Bixby?'

'*Go to hell.*'

Mia flinched. The woman had been afraid to talk to them. They'd forced her to speak, she and Reed. *I'll have to live with that.* And though she knew this wasn't her fault, she understood Brooke's anger. 'I'm so sorry, Brooke. But I need your help.'

'Count to ten.' She labored for a breath and machines started beeping.

'Pressure's dropping,' the nurse said with grim urgency. 'Oxygen level's dropping.'

'Push one amp of epi,' the doctor commanded, 'and start an epinephrine drip. Get ready to intubate. Detective, you have to leave.'

'No.' Brooke struggled, pathetically. 'Count to ten. Go to hell.'

The nurse was injecting a syringe into Brooke's IV. 'Get out, Detective.'

'One more minute.' Mia leaned closer. 'Was it Bixby? Thompson? Secrest?'

The doctor leaned over Mia with a growl. 'Detective, *move.*' Mia backed away, helpless, horrified, while the doctor and nurse battled for Brooke's life.

Thirty grueling, endless minutes later, the doctor stepped back. His shoulders sagged. 'I'm calling it. Time of death oh-five-hundred twenty-five hours.'

There had to be a word for what churned inside her. But that word wouldn't come. Mia lifted her eyes to the doctor's weary gaze. 'I don't know what to say.'

The doctor's mouth tightened. 'Say you'll catch who did this.'

Roger Burnette had demanded it for Caitlin. Dana had demanded it for Penny Hill. 'We will. We have to. He's killed four women. Thank you, for doing what you could.'

Grimly he nodded. 'I'm sorry.'

'So am I.' She got to the door and stopped. Forced herself to turn around and look at Brooke Adler one more time. Then crossed herself and backed out of the room.

Thursday, November 30, 5:45 A.M.

The child watched from his hiding place. He was outside again. He didn't know what the man buried, but he knew it had to be very, very bad. Because he was very bad. *Doesn't anybody else know? Am I the only one that sees how bad he really is?*

He thought of his mother, tossing and turning in her bed and he was suddenly, fiercely angry. She had to know. She had to see. She knew he disappeared in the night. But she got up every morning and put on her best face. Made him bacon and eggs and smiled like they were normal. They *weren't* normal.

He wished he would just go. Leave them alone. He wished his mother would throw him out. Tell him to never come back. But she wouldn't, because she was scared. He knew that. He knew she had a right to be. *So am I.*

Thursday, November 30, 7:20 A.M.

'Daddy?'

Reed looked up from buttoning his shirt, buttonhook in one hand. 'Yes, Beth?'

She stood in his doorway, her brows drawn together in worry. 'Are you okay?'

No. He was sick at heart. Two more. 'Just tired, honey. Just really tired.'

She hesitated. 'Dad, I need more lunch money.'

Reed frowned. 'I just gave you lunch money on Monday.'

'I know.' She made a face. 'I owed some library fines. I'm sorry.'

Feeling unsettled, he gave her another twenty. 'Return the books on time, okay?'

'Thanks, Dad.' She slipped the money into her jeans. 'I'll go put your coffee on.'

'I could sure use it.' Wearily he sat on the edge of his bed. Mia had been right. He was a wreck this morning. He wondered where she was, imagined her back in her apartment, alone. He should have held off, waited until they could establish the ground rules. No strings. But he hadn't been able to. His mind had been too full of her, his body at the edge of control. He had to stay in control because he didn't want to hurt her.

He looked around his bedroom. Everything here was as Christine left it, elegant and tasteful despite the passage of time. Mia's room was a hodgepodge of clashing colors, orange and vivid purples. Striped blankets and plaid curtains. All rummage sale stock.

But the bed had served its function quite well. Sex with Mia could become addicting if he allowed it. But he didn't allow addicting behaviors. He was stronger than that. Absently he rubbed his thumbs over his numb fingertips. He'd stopped himself from drinking when it got out of hand, something his biological mother had never done. A disease, she'd said. A choice, he knew. She'd loved the liquor more than she'd loved him, more than she'd loved anything. He grimaced, pushing the thought of his mother out of his mind. He'd thought about her more this week than in years.

He had to stay in control. Not let this thing with Mia distract him from what was important. The life he'd built for Beth. For himself. He lifted the fine gold chain from his nightstand and put it around his neck. A talisman, perhaps. A reminder, most certainly.

He had to get moving or he'd be late for morning meeting.

Chapter Fifteen

Thursday, November 30, 8:10 A.M.

'Count to ten and go to hell?' Spinnelli sat at the head of the table, frowning. Jack was there, along with Sam and Westphalen. Spinnelli must have been shoring up the troops because Murphy and Aidan Reagan had joined them. Mia had taken the chair farthest away where she sat alone, eyes shuttered. But Reed knew her emotions churned. She'd called him when she'd left the hospital, her voice heavy with despair.

'Those were her dying words,' she said, blandly now. 'Literally.'

Westphalen was watching her closely. 'What do you think it means, Mia?'

'I dunno. I thought at first she was telling me to go to hell.' She huffed once, sardonically. Painfully. 'God knows she had the right.'

'Mia,' Spinnelli started and she held up her hand, straightening in her chair.

'I know. It's not our fault. I think it's what he said to

her, Miles, right before he lit her on fire. I've never seen anything like that before. I know I never want to again.'

'Then let's get busy.' Spinnelli went to the white-board. 'What do we know?'

'Well, Manny Rodriguez couldn't have done it,' Mia said. 'He was in holding.'

'You were right about him,' Spinnelli agreed. 'Now it's even more important to find out what he knows and isn't telling. What else? What about the victims?'

'Brooke Adler and Roxanne Ledford,' Mia said. 'Both were schoolteachers. Brooke, English; Roxanne, music. Roxanne was twenty-six. Brooke just turned twenty-two.'

Spinnelli's expression became one of grim resignation. 'Cause of death?'

'Cause of death for Adler was cardiovascular collapse secondary to overwhelming burns,' Sam said. 'Cause for the second victim was the stab wound to her abdomen.'

'The blade?' Mia asked tightly.

'About six inches long. Thin. Sharp. He plunged it into the abdominal cavity and' – he made a horizontal slicing motion – 'cut her, approximately five inches across.'

'The knife is consistent with his sexual assault on his victims,' Westphalen said. 'Many believe the knife is an extension of the penis.'

'I'd like to take a knife to his extension,' Mia muttered.

Reed cringed. He wasn't alone. 'Smoke inhalation?' he asked.

'None. Ledford died within a few minutes at most. Well before the fire started.'

Spinnelli wrote it on the whiteboard, then turned. 'What else?'

'Adler's car is gone.' Mia checked her notes. 'We have an APB, but nothing so far.'

'He repeated that part of the MO,' Spinnelli said thoughtfully. 'What else is the same?'

'The device was the same,' Reed said. 'I found remnants in Brooke's bedroom and at the front entrance of the building.'

'Adler's legs were broken like the first two victims,' Sam added. 'But she wasn't cut like the Hill woman. If she had been, she probably wouldn't have lived long enough to have been rescued. Ledford had only the stab wound and the burns caused by the fire.'

'I think it's safe to say Roxanne Ledford surprised him,' Jack said. 'We found pieces of her violin around where firefighters found her body. I think she hit him with it.'

'After she called 911,' Mia murmured.

'And we can be thankful for that,' Spinnelli pronounced. 'If she hadn't, Adler wouldn't have lived as long as she did and a lot of other people may have been hurt.'

'Thirty people lived there,' Reed said. 'Ledford may have saved their lives.'

'I'm sure that came as a great comfort to Roxanne's family,' Mia said harshly.

'You told them?' Westphalen asked gently.

'About two hours ago. They didn't take it well.'

Neither had Mia, Reed thought.

Murphy squeezed her forearm. 'It sucks, kid,' he murmured around his carrot stick.

She chuckled bitterly. 'Y'think?'

Reed wished he could touch her too, hold her hand, but he knew that was out of the question. He fixed his eyes on the board. 'There was no gas explosion. The apartments only had electric. There was also a difference in the egg fragments.' He pushed a glass jar holding a lump of melted plastic to the table. 'I found this a few feet from Brooke's bedroom door. I think the egg came apart before the fuse burned through. It never shattered.'

Spinnelli's mustache bent down. 'Interesting. Theories?'

'Well, if I'd set the device, I would have put it on the mattress itself. It would have caught fire faster and have been closer to Adler's body. But I don't think it was there.'

Aidan Reagan was scratching notes on a pad. 'Why not?'

'Because if it was on the mattress, she wouldn't have been alive when Hunter and Mahoney got to the bedroom – she would have looked like Penny Hill and Caitlin Burnette. Also, the burn patterns indicate the fire started on the floor close to the door, so it took a few minutes to spread to the bed.'

'It would explain the severe burns on the second victim – the Ledford woman,' Sam said. 'Even though her body had no accelerant, she was closer to the origin.'

'And finally, I found what looked like ammonium nitrate deposited deep in the carpet fibers. Somehow the egg ended up on the floor, with enough force to break it open.'

'She kicked it?' Mia asked and Reed shrugged.

'It's possible.'

Sam shook his head. 'Her legs were broken. It's hard to believe she kicked it.'

'The doctor said it was hard to believe she was still muttering after being sedated,' Mia said. 'She was in excruciating pain, yet she kept asking for me.'

'She tried to stab him,' Jack commented. 'We found a butcher knife on the living-room floor with Adler's fingerprints on it. Unfortunately, no blood, so she didn't get him.'

'I think Brooke Adler was a lot stronger than I gave her credit for yesterday.' Mia's smile was bitter. 'Again, that came as a great comfort to her parents.'

'Mia.' Westphalen's mouth bent in sympathy. 'You told both families back-to-back?'

'I'm sure it hurt them a hell of a lot more than it hurt me. But, speaking of hell, I'm thinking he said "go to hell" as some kind of symbolic tie to the fire.'

'Makes perfect sense,' Westphalen agreed. 'So the

people he's killed have done something that he's condemned them to hell for doing. What about "count to ten"?'

'His fuse,' Reed said. 'Penny Hill's neighbor, Mr Wright, said that he heard the tires squeal, saw the car driving away and a second later the house blew. Now assuming Wright is ... well, right, and assuming Hill's killer ran as soon as he lit the fuse, he would have had about ten to fifteen seconds to get away. I tried it.'

'But why "ten"?' Westphalen mused. 'It has to have some significance besides a Clint Eastwood-esque belligerence.'

Mia's face tensed. 'I hope it's not the number of people he plans to kill.'

There was a half beat of silence. 'Well, that's an uplifting thought,' Jack muttered.

'Let's have some encouraging news,' Spinnelli said pointedly. 'Jack?'

'We ran prints all day and night. Theoretically, all the prints in the art room and the science lab should be accounted for. Everybody at Hope Center has been printed, staff and residents. But one set of prints was unmatchable to any of the prints on record. And although it's redundant at this point, they don't belong to Manny. Also, the prints don't match anything in AFIS, so our guy doesn't have a record.'

'Someone's had access to the school without being printed,' Spinnelli mused.

'Maybe.' Mia met Reed's eyes and he could see her wheels turning. 'But Secrest didn't seem like a slouch. He's a secretive SOB, but he knows what goes on at that place. I can't see him letting just anyone stroll through. Bixby had print cards on every teacher and juvenile, past and present. Every print should have been accounted for.'

Reed thought he knew where she was headed. 'So Secrest missed somebody or one of the print cards Bixby gave us was wrong. Either through design or oversight.'

Spinnelli's jaw tightened. 'Print everybody at that school. If they balk, haul 'em in.'

Mia's smile was sharp. 'My pleasure.'

'Have you found any connection between Burnette's and Hill's files?' Spinnelli asked.

'Um, no.' Her composure slipped for an instant and Reed couldn't help but think about what she'd been doing instead of reading files. But they were entitled to some time of their own. He wouldn't feel guilty about it. He hoped she wouldn't either. She cleared her throat. 'We'll keep looking. Did the news shows give the women's names?'

'I caught two of the local broadcasts,' Aidan offered. 'Both Channel Four and Seven said they were withholding the names of the victims until their families were notified.'

'I saw Channel Nine news,' Westphalen added. 'Same thing.'

'And the fire started after press time for all the papers,' she said.

Reed followed her train of thought. 'So, we may be able to assume that Bixby and his friends haven't heard about the murder yet, unless they're somehow involved.'

She nodded, brows lifted. 'I think we'll go back to Hope Center this morning. I want to see if the Axis of Evil can look us in the eye.'

Reed's lips curved. 'The Axis of Evil? Bixby, Thompson, and Secrest. It works.'

She smiled back, then her mouth was grim again. 'And I want to tell Manny that Brooke is dead. Maybe that'll unsettle him enough to tell us what he's hiding.'

'Wait until I've talked with him,' Westphalen requested. 'I'm afraid if you push him any harder, he'll break and we won't get anything from him. I'll be done by lunchtime.'

'All right. But no later. I don't want him having time to get his story right.'

'What about Adler's apartment?' Murphy asked. 'Any cameras?'

'No,' Reed said. 'This was a no-frills place and what they had wasn't maintained properly. A couple of the units didn't even have working smoke detectors. We're going to have to question all the residents the old-fashioned way to see if anybody saw him.'

'Murphy and Aidan, you get the statements,' Spinnelli said. 'Anything else?' he asked as everyone stood up. 'Then let's meet back here at five. I want a suspect with a name, Mia.'

She sighed. 'One can hope.'

Thursday, November 30, 8:15 A.M.

He had to squint as he scanned the headlines. He was tired. He'd debated calling in sick, but that would have looked somewhat suspicious. Under the circumstances.

But what circumstances they'd been. He'd been on a roll last night. Four. Zapped. Gone. That had to be a record. It was for him anyway. *My personal best.* He chuckled and flipped to the next page of the *Bulletin*. They seemed to be the fastest with new stories, so he'd started with their paper. But there wasn't anything new about him on page one. Just recycled hash from the press conference the day before. He sat a little straighter. He'd rated a press conference. *Cool.*

He scanned the other news. And stopped at the bottom of page three when he saw two familiar names. Joanna Carmichael and none other than Detective Mia Mitchell.

Apparently Mitchell had been shot at on Tuesday night. A gunman had fired shots in her neighborhood, at 1342 Sedgewick. Well, that was something you didn't see every day. A cop's address printed in the paper. That had to be fate or karma or something. He was becoming a firm believer in fate. Apparently this gunman had some kind of grudge against the good detective, related to another shooting almost three weeks ago. Apparently the gunman was a piss-poor shot and ran away.

He tore the article and meticulously trimmed the edges. Mitchell was a busy lady. Lots of enemies. She'd come too close yesterday. With Brooke Adler dead, she'd have every reason to come closer. If she got shot, they'd just put on more cops. But they'd be looking for this guy. He ran his finger under the name of the gunman. *Melvin Getts*. If Mitchell happened to die, they'd look even harder for the poor bastard. It would be distraction and that's all he really needed now. Just a little distraction to buy a little time.

He shoved the article in his book, along with the others. He could sleep when it was over. Now, he had a loose end to tie up, then a sad face to put on. Poor Brooke was dead. He'd be devastated. And quick to offer his personal assistance to the cops.

It was the least he could do.

Thursday, November 30, 8:35 A.M.

A giant yawn nearly split Mia's head in two. 'I'm tired.'

'Me, too.' Solliday was typing at his computer with a slow methodical rhythm.

He looked crisp and professional and not tired in the least and for a second she allowed herself the luxury of remembering what he'd looked like sprawled in her bed after the third bout of the best sex she'd ever had. 'What are you doing?'

He didn't look up. 'I think that before we go back to Hope Center, we should have a little background on the actors.' His lips quirked up. 'I mean the Axis of Evil.'

'I should have done that already,' she muttered and forced herself out of her chair.

'Well, you didn't,' he said mildly. 'That's why you have a partner, Mia, so you don't have to do everything yourself.'

She leaned a hip against his desk and drew in a breath, smelling his aftershave. His face was smooth around the goatee, which had tickled her inner thighs. She let out a breath. 'So *that's* why I have a partner?' she murmured, loud enough for only his ears.

His fingers paused on the keyboard, then resumed their steady pace. 'Mia,' he warned under his breath, through his teeth.

'Sorry. You're right.' She shook herself and paid attention to the screen. He knew his way around law enforcement databases. She'd never thought of fire marshals using them. She was learning a great deal about fire marshals lately. 'What did you find?'

He tapped a few keys and read the screen with interest. 'Secrest is an ex-cop.'

'Lots of cops go into private security after they retire. Doesn't surprise me.'

'No, but this does. He quit and went to work for Bixby

four years ago, just two years before he would have retired from CPD.'

'Lost out on a hefty pension,' Mia murmured. 'I wonder what happened.'

'Maybe you can talk to some of his old friends and find out.'

'I'll ask Spinnelli to do it. He can weasel info I can't. What about Thompson?'

'Our helpful school psychologist,' he muttered. 'No record in this database.' He Googled him. 'Thompson's a PhD from Yale.'

Mia frowned. 'What's a Yale boy doing in juvie? The pay's gotta suck.'

'He's authored a book. *Rehabilitation of Juvenile Offenders*. I checked Manny's Hope Center file. He's been in therapy with Thompson for some time.'

She lifted her brows. 'I wonder if Dr Thompson's planning a sequel.'

'It would explain his temper tantrum when we took Manny in. Can we get into his files?'

'Probably not based on what we've got, but we can ask. So what about Bixby?'

He kept his eyes on the screen. 'He's authored a few articles on education.'

'Two of the articles are on using education in rehabilitation,' she noted.

'Again, I wonder why he's not going for a higher salary.'

'We'll find out. Check on Atticus Lucas, the art teacher.'

He did. 'He's had exhibits before.' He scanned the page then looked up at her. 'Prestigious galleries. Again, I wonder why he's there.'

'What about Hope? It'll be a nonprofit, right? Do you know how to check finances?'

The look he shot her was overly patient. 'Yes, Mia.'

The look she shot him was dry. 'Then see if you can find anything while I check my voice mail. Then we should get going. All the teachers should be there by nine.'

A newspaper landed on her desk. Murphy stood glaring. 'What?' she said.

'You're in the news again, glamour girl. Page three of the *Bulletin*, bottom right.'

For a moment she wondered if Carmichael had already reported on her wild night with Reed, but dismissed it. Press time was one A.M. at the *Bulletin*. Reed didn't leave until almost four. Her eyes dropped down and she felt the blood drain from her face.

It was worse. Way worse. Temper spilled over and she fought the pagan urge to wrap her hands around Carmichael's neck. 'I want to . . .' *Kill that woman*. She bit the words off and looked up at Solliday, whose eyes were worried. 'Carmichael. She found out about Getts shooting at us on Tuesday night. She printed my home address. First Wheaton, now this. I have no privacy anymore. You know, I really hate reporters.'

'What about Wheaton?' Murphy asked and she sighed.

'She noticed the mystery blonde yesterday. She tried to use it to get Reed to give her confidential information on this case.'

'But you didn't, Solliday.' Murphy's fingers drummed a beat on her desk.

Reed flicked him an impatient glance. 'Of course I didn't.' He picked up the paper calmly, but his jaw was clenched and his eyes flashed fury. 'She needs to be stopped.'

'She'll hide behind the First Amendment.' Mia ran her tongue over her teeth. 'She's off my Christmas list, Reed. I don't care if she did give me DuPree on a platter.'

His eyes still flickered with anger. 'That'll fix her for sure. Mia, you can't stay at your place. Every scum-sucking toad in town will be hanging out on your doorstep.'

She grinned. 'Scum-sucking toad? I think I'm starting to rub off on you, Solliday.'

'I'm serious, Mia. You have to find a new apartment.'

'He's right, Mia,' Murphy added. 'It's like she painted a bull's-eye on your ass.'

'I'm not moving and I'm not talking about this right now. I'm going to listen to my voice mail then do my fucking job.' She grabbed her phone, ignoring the two glowering men. Then frowned. 'I got a message from Dr Thompson last night.'

'Which one of the Axis of Evil is he again?' Murphy asked, still mad at her.

'The school psychologist. He said he needed to see us. That it was urgent.'

'I don't trust a word that comes out of his mouth,' Reed gritted.

'Me either. But let's go find out what he wants.'

Thursday, November 30, 9:15 A.M.

'Solliday and Mitchell here to see Dr Bixby and Dr Thompson,' Reed said.

Marcy's mouth tightened. 'I'll call Dr Bixby.'

Secrest was with Bixby, but Thompson was not. Neither knew about Brooke Adler's death, Reed decided. Or if they did, they were damn good at hiding it.

'Can I help you?' Bixby asked formally.

'We asked for Dr Thompson as well,' Mia told him. 'We'd like to speak to him.'

Bixby frowned. 'You can't. He's not here.'

Reed and Mia exchanged a glance. 'Not here?' Reed asked. 'Then where is he?'

'We don't know. He's usually at his desk by eight, but he hasn't come in yet.'

Reed lifted a brow. 'Does he normally just not show up?'

Bixby looked irritated. 'No, he always calls.'

'Did anybody call his house?' Mia asked.

Secrest nodded once. 'I did. Nobody answered. Why do you need to see him?'

'He called me. I thought it might have something to do with Brooke Adler's murder.'

For a moment, neither man moved. Then Secrest's jaw cocked to one side and Bixby's face drained of color. Behind him, Reed heard Marcy gasp.

'When?' Secrest demanded. 'How?'

'Early this morning,' Reed said. 'She died of injuries sustained in a fire.'

Bixby looked down, still dazed. 'I can't believe this.'

Mia lifted her chin. 'I can. I was there when she died.'

'Did she say anything before she died?'

Mia smiled darkly. 'She said a great many things, Dr Bixby. For the record, where were you this morning between three and four?'

Bixby blustered. 'I can't possibly be a suspect.'

Secrest sighed. 'Just answer her question, Bix.'

Bixby narrowed his eyes. 'At home. Asleep. With my wife. She'll confirm it.'

'I'm sure she will,' Mia said blandly. 'And Mr Secrest? Same question.'

'At home. Asleep. With my wife,' he answered with the barest hint of sarcasm.

'She'll confirm it.' Amused, Mia smiled. 'Thank you, gentlemen.'

Reed nearly smiled. She was taunting the men and enjoying it. 'We'll need to talk to your staff and see their personnel files. If you could prepare a room for us to use?'

'Marcy,' Bixby snapped. 'Set up conference room two. I'll be in my office.'

Secrest just leveled them a long bitter look before following his boss.

'I wonder if we'll hear paper shredders in the next few minutes,' Reed murmured.

'Patrick said we didn't have enough for a warrant for all their files,' Mia murmured back, disgusted. 'But maybe we'll have enough for Thompson's if we can show he's skipped town. Let's make some calls.' She frowned at Marcy. 'Outside, I think.'

Outside, she pulled her phone from her pocket. 'I'll call Patrick and see if we can get a warrant for Thompson's computer and file cabinets both here and at home. Can you call Spinnelli? Ask him to send a unit to Thompson's house. Find out if he's there.'

'I'll also ask for units to cover the exits here. I don't want anybody slipping away.'

They made their calls, then pocketed their phones at the exact same time. Mia sucked in one cheek. 'Soon you're going to be finishing my sentences.'

Something inside him cringed, uncomfortable at the implied intimacy. The last person who'd finished his sentences was Christine. 'You get a warrant?' he asked brusquely and she blinked. Instantly he felt guilty. There was intimacy between them now, at least the physical kind. He hoped he'd read her right and she was a no-strings woman. If not, she'd be hurt. 'I'm sorry. I didn't mean to snap at you.'

She shrugged it off. 'Patrick's going to try for a warrant. You get Spinnelli?'

'I did. He'll call us when the cruiser gets to Thompson's house. He also said Jack's on the way with a fingerprint tech and somebody to sweep for bugs.'

She frowned. 'I've been agonizing over whether to take the staff downtown, but that would take forever. I want to talk to these people now.'

'Then we sweep and see.' He made himself smile. 'Ready to go kick some Axis?'

She laughed and the sound eased him. 'Let's go.'

Secrest was waiting to escort them, a stack of files in his hands. It was the room Bixby had had them wait in yesterday. It seemed like a million years ago.

'Please have the staff come to us one at a time,' Mia said when they'd settled in on the hard wooden chairs. 'We want to talk to the people first who knew Miss Adler best.'

Secrest dropped the stack on the table. 'Yes, *ma'am*.'

Reed winced when Secrest walked away. 'Ouch.'

'Excuse me.' A man stood at the door, looking very, very pale. 'You're the detectives.' He cast a glance over his shoulder. 'I need to talk to you.'

Mia looked up at Reed. 'Should we wait for the sweeper?' she murmured.

'He looks nervous. You might not want to give him time to back away. Besides, if Bixby really wanted he could listen at the door even if the place is clean.'

'You're right. We'll keep the questions straight-forward, then take anybody that sounds interesting downtown.' She nodded at the man. 'I'm Detective

Mitchell and this is Lieutenant Solliday. Please come in and sit down.'

'I'm Devin White.' He slid the textbook he carried to the table and sat down, his eyes shocked and grieved. 'I just heard. I can't believe it. I saw on the news that there had been a fire, but I never dreamed it could be Brooke.'

'We're very sorry for your loss, sir,' Mia said gently. 'We need to ask a few questions.'

He moved his hands nervously and glanced at the door. 'Yes, yes of course.'

Reed placed his recorder on the table. 'You knew Miss Adler well?'

'No. She hadn't been here that long. I'd just gotten to know her in the last week. I mean, I'd seen her around the campus, but this week we talked for the first time.'

'How long have you taught here, Mr White?' Mia asked.

'Five months. Since the beginning of last summer.'

'When did you see her last?'

'Last night.' He let out a sigh, then leaned forward. 'Look, Detective, I have to say I'm nervous to even be talking to you at this point.' He said it under his breath.

'Why?'

'Because Brooke talked to you and now she's dead,' he snapped. He lowered his voice to a whisper. 'Brooke had an argument with Bixby yesterday. I only heard the end of it, but he threatened to fire her. He demanded Brooke resign. She threatened to go to the press. She was so upset, worrying that she'd go bankrupt. I took her to

Flannagan's to calm her down. It's a bar where a lot of us go to hang out after work.'

'When did you say good night?' Reed asked.

'Seven thirty,' he said, his voice at normal volume. 'Brooke had a beer too many, so I drove her home and walked her up. Then I went straight home. Brooke said she'd have a friend drive her to work and I could take her to Flannagan's after school to get her car. But she didn't show up this morning. I thought maybe she'd folded and resigned.'

The killer hadn't taken Brooke's car after all, so there would be no evidence that might point to his identity should they find it. 'Flannagan's is close?' Reed asked.

'About a mile from here. She was so worried about that damn book she'd assigned. *Lord of the Flies.* She worried she'd pushed Manny into setting fires. He scared her.'

'Was she afraid of anybody else?' Reed asked and White shrugged.

'Jeff DeMartino gave her the shivers, but he gives everybody the shivers.'

Mia wrote down his name. 'He's a student?'

'Yeah. Smart kid. Big trouble. Julian said he was a sociopath.'

'Anybody else?' she asked.

'Bart Secrest made her nervous. But that's all.'

'One more question.' Mia caught the man's eyes and held them. 'Where were you last night between three and four A.M.?'

He blanched. 'I'm a suspect? I guess I'd have to be. I was at home. Asleep.'

'Anybody to verify that?' she asked pleasantly.

'My fiancée.'

Mia blinked at him. 'But I thought you and Miss Adler . . .'

'Friends. I helped her out when she was scared. But there was nothing romantic.'

Mia gave him her card. 'Thanks. Please call me if you remember anything else.'

White stood and tucked his book under his arm. 'You'll watch Bixby, right?' he whispered. 'I never thought the man could be . . . evil, but now I'm not so sure.'

She didn't respond to White's dire assessment of Bixby. 'Thank you, Mr White. We appreciate your information.' She opened the door to find the dour-faced Marcy waiting. With a shaken sideways look, White slipped away and Marcy frowned.

'There's a Sergeant Unger waiting outside. He says you're expecting him.'

'Yes. Can you give us another room? Sergeant Unger will be redoing fingerprints of all staff and students.'

Marcy's back snapped straight. 'Dr Bixby didn't approve that.'

'Dr Bixby doesn't have to,' Mia told her mildly. 'You are required to be fingerprinted by the state. We have reason to believe . . . mistakes were made in your records. Please find the sergeant a room. He'll need a table and an electrical outlet.'

Reed leaned back in his chair. 'I think Dr Bixby should be the first one they print.'

'I agree.' She sighed. 'No wonder Bixby wanted to know what she said before she died. That was a bomb-shell. We'll keep talking to the teachers while Jack gets set up.' She poked her head into the hall. 'Whoever's next, please come in.'

Thursday, November 30, 10:15 A.M.

'Please sit down, Miss Kersey.' Jackie Kersey had been crying hard, her face red and puffy. 'I'm Detective Mitchell and this is my partner, Lieutenant Solliday. We're very sorry for your loss, ma'am, but we need to ask you some questions.'

They were the same words she'd said to the math teacher, the history teacher, and the librarian they'd just finished interviewing, but in no way did her words sound any less sincere. Kersey nodded shakily. 'I'm sorry, I just can't seem to stop crying.'

Mia squeezed her arm. 'It's okay. Now what do you teach here, Miss Kersey?'

She sniffled and drew a huge breath. 'I teach geography to the middle school.'

'What can you tell us about Miss Adler?'

Jackie Kersey wrung her hands. 'Brooke was young. So full of . . . optimism. You lose that pretty fast around here. She wanted to do the right thing, to reach these kids.'

'Any kids in particular?'

'She was worried about Manny.' She frowned. 'She was afraid of Jeff.'

Four out of four teachers had mentioned this Jeff, Reed thought.

'Are you?' Mia asked softly.

'Let's just say I'm glad he's in lockup. When he turns eighteen I'll say yes.'

'How well did you know Miss Adler?' Reed asked.

'About as well as anyone. She'd just started to come out of her shell. I convinced her to go to Flannagan's after work on Monday. Devin was going, and she liked him.'

'Did he like her?' Mia murmured.

'Devin likes everybody.' She managed a watery smile. 'He likes you more if he can sucker you into his football pool. But yeah, he liked her.'

'Like as in a girlfriend?'

'I saw him staring at her chest more than once, so I think he was attracted to her, but to my knowledge they didn't see each other outside of school. Look, we all know you were here yesterday. Somehow Brooke was involved and now she's dead. I don't mean to be crass, but are the rest of us in any danger?'

Mia hesitated long enough to make Jackie Kersey pale. 'Don't go anywhere alone.'

'Oh my God,' Kersey whispered. 'This place is a nightmare. I knew it.'

Reed frowned. 'You knew what, ma'am?'

'I came here because my old school closed and I needed a job. But it's never felt right. I can't tell you any more than that, because it's only a feeling.'

Mia squeezed Kersey's hand before giving her a business card. 'Trust your instincts, Miss Kersey. That's why you have them. To keep you alert and safe.'

When she was gone, Mia came around to Reed's side of the table and leaned one hip against its edge. 'Kersey didn't know White had a fiancée already,' she murmured.

'I know.' Reed pulled out Kersey's personnel file. 'She's only been here eight months.' He looked up, thoughts connecting. 'Have you noticed that all the teachers in this school have been here less than two years? But the school's been here for five. As have Bixby and Thompson. Secrest has been here four.'

'Huh.' He could see that she hadn't thought of it but unlike earlier this morning, she wasn't annoyed that he had first. 'You're right. Lucas, Celebrese, the history teacher, the librarian, White, Kersey, Adler. All less than two years.' She ran her thumb down the stack, counting. 'About two dozen. Let's take a look before we talk to any more teachers to see if this is true for all of them.' She gave him an impressed nod. 'Nice.'

Her simple praise shouldn't make him feel like turning cartwheels, but it did. Pushing the feeling aside, he opened the first file. 'I'll read, you write?'

She waved her pen. 'Let's roll.' They'd checked three of the files, all three staff employed less than a year, when Jack knocked on the door.

'This is Officer James. He's here to sweep. Officer Willis is almost ready to take the prints. I just came along to make sure everything was perfect. By the frickin' book. I don't want to have any questions about that unmatched print when we're done.'

Reed and Mia followed Jack to another conference room where an officer was plugging a scanner into a laptop computer. 'You'll have to get Thompson's print from his office,' Reed said. 'He's AWOL.'

'Interesting. I'll take his prints and Willis can get started on the staff.'

'Did Spinnelli send the units to cover the exits?' Mia asked.

'I didn't see them when I got here,' Jack said.

Willis looked up. 'They pulled in just after me. I was a few minutes behind.'

'Willis stopped for a yellow light,' Jack sneered.

Willis gave Mia a knowing wink. 'It was red. I would've had to give myself a citation.'

'What is the meaning of this?' Bixby stood in the doorway, glowering. 'Coming in here and fingerprinting us like we're all common criminals. This is outrageous.'

'No, it's not,' Reed said, losing his patience. 'We have four dead women in the morgue, Dr Bixby. One is your former employee. I'd think you'd want to know who is responsible. I would think you might even be a little afraid for yourself.'

Bixby paled a shade. 'Why should I be afraid for myself?'

'I can't imagine you have no enemies,' Reed said quietly. 'So do yourself a favor and stay out of the way. Better yet, take Sergeant Unger to Dr Thompson's office and let him do his job.'

Bixby nodded stiffly. 'This way, Sergeant.'

Mia was smiling at him. 'Nice,' she said again, just as her cell phone rang. 'It's Spinnelli,' she murmured. 'This is Mitchell . . . Uh-huh . . .' Her eyes widened. 'Aw shit, Marc. You're kidding.' She sighed. 'Not yet. Willis is just about to start. Thanks.' She snapped her cell phone closed. 'Well, looks like we found Thompson.'

Reed leaned back and looked at her frustrated face and knew. 'How dead is he?'

'Very, very. Somebody slit his throat. Some guy on his way to work found him. He saw a car on the side of the road with what looked like mud caked on the windshield. The mud turned out to be blood. Car's registered to Dr Julian Thompson. Let's go.'

On their way out Mia found Secrest's office. 'We need to step out for a little while.'

'Forgive me if I don't cry,' he said sarcastically, arms crossed over his chest.

'Don't you even want to know why?' she demanded.
'Should I?'

Mia blew out an angry breath. 'Goddammit, what kind of cop were you, Secrest?'

His eyes flashed. 'A former one, Detective.'

'Thompson's dead,' she said and he flinched, then his face returned to stone.

'When? How?'

'I don't know when and can't tell you how,' she snapped. 'While we're gone, Sergeant Unger will fingerprint the staff and students.'

He stiffened. 'Why?'

Reed cleared his throat. 'Because we found a discrepancy in your records, Mr Secrest,' he said calmly. 'Your cooperation would be appreciated.'

He nodded. 'Anything else, Lieutenant?' and Reed nearly winced at the civility in his voice, a marked contrast to the derisive tone he'd used with Mia.

Mia tilted her head, ignoring the slam. 'Yeah. Nobody, nobody comes in or goes out of this complex. Anyone attempting to will be taken to the precinct. You're all on lockdown until we settle the issue of fingerprints. Are we clear, Secrest?'

'Crystal.' He bared his teeth in a parody of a smile. 'Ma'am.'

'Good,' she said. 'We'll be back as soon as we can.'

Chapter Sixteen

Thursday, November 30, 10:55 A.M.

'Hell.' Mia grimaced as she walked up to Thompson's Saab.

It was the first word she'd said since leaving Hope Center. He'd pissed her off, stepping in to smooth and soothe again. But they'd needed Secrest calm and Mia was not making that happen. Thoughts of Secrest vaporized when he saw Thompson in the driver's seat. His head lolled, like a rag doll missing stuffing. Blood was everywhere.

Gingerly Mia stuck her head in the window. 'Oh God. He went all the way to bone.'

'Head's hanging on by a patch of skin about three inches wide,' the ME tech said.

'Wonderful,' she muttered. 'He's still wearing his seat belt. Kept him upright.'

The ME tech was making notes. 'They say seat belts save lives. Didn't help him.'

'That's not funny,' Mia snapped. 'Goddammit.'

The ME gave Reed an is-it-PMS look. Reed shook his head. 'Don't,' he mouthed.

'Time of death?' she demanded acidly.

'Between nine and midnight. Let me know when I can move him. I'm sorry,' he added. 'Sometimes a joke's a way to take off the edge when we find a body like this.'

Mia took a deep breath and let it out, then turned to the young ME tech with a rueful smile. She squinted to see his badge. 'I'm sorry, Michaels. I'm tired and frustrated and I snapped at you.' She stuck her head back in the car. 'Anybody see his keys?'

'No.' A woman with a CSU jacket rose from inspecting the other side of the car. 'We haven't touched him yet. The keys could be under him.'

Mia opened the back door on the driver's side. 'He sat back here. Grabbed him by the hair and yanked his head back and slashed. Any sign of struggle or skid marks or dings on the car? Was he forced over?'

The CSU tech shook her head. 'I've checked all around the vehicle. Not a scratch. This car was brand-new. Pretty expensive car not to steal.'

'Luxury car on a juvie salary,' Mia murmured. 'Move him when you're ready.'

The ME techs did, immobilizing Thompson's head to keep it from completely ripping from his body. 'He's wearing a ring,' Reed noted.

Mia lifted Thompson's hand. 'Ruby. I'm betting it's real. Not a robbery, then.'

'Did you think it was?' Reed asked and she shook her head.

'No. Wallet's still in his back pocket. Cell phone's in his front.' She took it out and punched buttons. 'He made six calls yesterday afternoon.' Her eyes narrowed. 'Four to 708-555-6756, one was to me, and one to . . . This is the number for Holding.' Rapidly she pulled out her own cell and dialed. 'Hi, this is Detective Mitchell, Homicide department. Did a Dr Julian Thompson visit last night?' Her brows lifted. 'Thanks.'

She dropped her phone in her pocket and looked up, meeting Reed's eyes for the first time since they'd left Hope Center. 'He visited Manny Rodriguez,' she said. 'He signed out on the visitor sheet five minutes before he called my voice mail last night.'

'Can you trace the other number?' Reed asked.

'I'm betting from the exchange that it's a disposable cell,' she said.

Michaels looked up from securing Thompson's head. 'You could call it.'

She smiled at him. 'I could, but then he'd know we'd found Thompson. I'm not sure I want to tip my hand yet. But thanks.' She patted the young man's shoulder. 'And, um, Michaels? That crack about the seat belt? It was kind of funny. In a real juvenile, break-the-tension kind of way.' She huffed a tired chuckle. 'Wish I'd thought of it.'

Michaels's face was full of empathy. 'Feel free to borrow at any time, Detective.'

Thursday, November 30, 11:45 A.M.

Solliday parked his SUV. 'If I make a juvenile joke, will you speak to me again?'

She looked up, brows furrowed. He'd broken her train of thought. 'What?'

'Mia, you've given me the cold shoulder for the last two hours. I'm ready to grovel.'

Her lips quirked. 'The ride over was the cold shoulder. The ride back I was just thinking. But a little groveling wouldn't hurt.'

He sighed. 'You were making Secrest mad on purpose. You didn't need to.'

She tucked her tongue in her cheek. 'But it felt so good.'

'We might need him.'

'Oh, all right. But I'd feel a lot better if I knew why he quit CPD early.'

'I'd feel a lot better if he respected you.'

She shrugged. 'I got that all the time from my old man.' She slid down before he could ask the questions he so obviously wanted to. 'Let's see what Jack's been up to.'

Secrest waited for them at the front door. 'Well?'

'He's dead,' Mia said. 'Throat slit. We'll need to contact his next of kin.'

This time Secrest's flinch was more pronounced. He opened his mouth to speak, then cleared his throat. 'He was divorced,' he murmured. He looked away, his face grown pale. 'But I know his ex-wife. I'll get you her number.'

'Bring it to where we're doing the printing,' she said, trying to be nice. 'Thanks.'

Officer Willis was printing Atticus Lucas's beefy fingers when they walked in. 'Mr Lucas,' Mia said. 'Thanks for cooperating.'

'I got nothin' to hide.' He ambled out and Mia shut the door behind him.

The mobile fingerprinting unit was a digital system, ink-free. Once a print was scanned, it could be immediately compared to the database. Jack looked up from his laptop screen. 'Both rooms are clean. No bug concerns. What did you find?'

'Thompson's dead. Throat slit. He visited Manny Rodriguez last night.'

Jack blinked. 'Interesting.'

Solliday pulled up a chair and looked at Jack's screen. 'Well?'

'I've printed all the staff but one. I asked the desk dragon to go get him. She just paged him on the loudspeaker. When we get his prints, we'll start on the students.'

Mia's lips twitched. Marcy the Desk Dragon. She liked it. But she sobered, taking in the stack of print cards. 'So do we have any obvious differences?'

'Sorry, Mia. Everybody's prints match the ones in the state's database.'

'And the fingerprint cards Bixby gave us?' Solliday asked.

'Just a nice souvenir the printing agency gives, really.

The official print I go by is what's in the state's system. And none match the odd print we found in the art room.'

'Who's the teacher you haven't printed?' Solliday asked.

There was a knock on the door and Mia opened it to Marcy, aka the Desk Dragon.

'I've looked everywhere for Mr White. I can't find him anywhere in the building.'

Secrest came up behind her, looking grim. 'And his car isn't in the parking lot.'

Mia's brain started to churn. 'Shit. Aw, shit.'

'He can't be gone,' Jack said. 'There's been a unit out front all morning.'

'He was standing here when Marcy announced you'd arrived, Jack,' she remembered. 'He must have heard we were getting ready to fingerprint. Willis was a few minutes behind and that's when the units got to the front gate.'

'Thompson,' Solliday said through gritted teeth. 'The cell phone number. He called White last night.'

Solliday rushed for the teachers' personnel files he'd left in the other conference room. She ran to look over his shoulder. 'Please say White's cell isn't 708-555-6756.'

'It is.' He looked up, her frustration mirrored in his eyes. 'It was White. He's gone.'

She clenched her hands into fists at her sides, her chin dropped to her chest. 'Shit, damn, fuck.' A wave of weary despair washed over her. 'He's slipped right through our fingers.' Brooke Adler's face flashed in her mind, as she'd been a few hours ago, burned and in blinding pain. The woman had clawed and clung to life long enough to give them important information. *Count to ten. Go to hell.*

They'd use it to find the bastard. 'Let's go find him. Before he kills anybody else.'

Thursday, November 30, 12:30 P.M.

'Beacon Inn, River Forest. This is Kerry. How can I help you?'

He kept his back to the pay phone, eyes scanning the street, ready to run. 'Hi. Can you connect me with Joseph Dougherty, please?'

'I'm sorry, sir, but the Doughertys checked out yesterday.'

I kind of figured that out on my own. 'Oh dear. I'm calling from Mike Drummond's Used Cars. We heard about the loss of their home and wanted to offer them use of one of our cars until their insurance supplied them with another one. Could I possibly get a forwarding address or telephone number?'

'Let's see . . .' He heard the clacking of a keyboard. 'Here. Mr Dougherty asked deliveries be forwarded to 993 Harmony Avenue.'

'Thank you.' He hung up, well satisfied. He'd head

on over there right now to make sure they were there. He wouldn't let them slip through his fingers a third time.

He got back into the car he'd stolen. He was boiling mad on the inside, but freezing on the outside. He'd had to walk out of Hope Center with nothing more than the clothes on his back and the book in which he'd stuffed all his articles. And not a minute too soon. He'd been halfway down the block when a cruiser pulled up to the front gate. Another minute and he'd have been trapped. He'd quickly abandoned that car and stolen another in case they detected his absence right away.

Damn bitch cop. She'd gotten to the print discrepancy sooner than he'd expected. He'd thought he'd have another day at least. *Shit*. For the time being he'd have to travel light. He'd run back to his house, taking time only to leave a surprise for the lady of the house and to grab his seven remaining eggs. He had to make sure the woman who'd cooked and cleaned for him all these months wouldn't give him up to the cops, because he had big plans for his little bombs. And when everything settled down, he'd go back to the house for the rest of his things. His souvenirs of the life he was leaving behind. Then he'd go on with a new life, all sources of anger eliminated from existence. He'd finally be free.

Thursday, November 30, 2:45 P.M.

'You gonna eat those fries?' Murphy asked and Mia gave him the Styrofoam box.

They were sitting around Spinnelli's table, Reed and Mia, Jack and Westphalen, Murphy and Aidan. Spinnelli paced, his mustache bunched in a scowl.

'So we have no idea where he is?' Spinnelli said for the third time.

'No, Marc,' she said, irritated. 'The address on his personnel sheet was fake. He told us he had a fiancée, but nobody at the school knows her name. He has no credit cards. He's cleaned out his bank account, the address on which is a PO box in the main post office with about a million other people who don't want to be found. We have an APB on his car, but so far it hasn't turned up. So, no. We don't know where he is.'

Spinnelli glared. 'Don't get sarcastic with me, Mia.'

She bristled. 'I wouldn't dream of it, Marc.'

'What do we know about Devin White?' Westphalen inserted in a way that made Reed think the old man had calmed those two down before.

'He's twenty-three,' Reed said. 'He taught math at Hope Center starting this past June. Before that he was a student at Drake University in Delaware. According to the résumé in his personnel file, his degree is in math education and he played on the school's golf team. The registrar's office at the university confirms he was a student there.'

'He had to live somewhere,' Spinnelli said. 'Where did they mail his checks?'

'Direct deposited,' Reed said.

'We lifted prints from the coffee cup in his classroom,' Jack said. 'They matched the ones I'd been looking for so I didn't bother reprinting the students.'

'How did he get through the background check?' Aidan asked.

Jack shrugged. 'I talked to the company that does Hope Center's fingerprinting. They swear they printed him and that they uploaded his prints into the system.'

'I used to work with ex-cons in a rehab program,' Westphalen said. 'On drug test days, they'd pay people for their urine. We had to change our system. One of us had to go in the toilet with these guys and watch them give their sample.'

Everyone grimaced. 'Thank you for that picture, Miles,' Spinnelli said dryly.

Westphalen smiled. 'My point is, if White didn't want to be in the system, there are ways to avoid it if the security at this printing company was lax enough.'

Spinnelli sat down. 'How reputable is the company?'

Again Jack shrugged. 'It's a private firm. It does employee fingerprinting for a lot of companies in the area. I suppose it's possible White got somebody to take his place, but why would he? His prints aren't in AFIS.'

Murphy's mouth bent speculatively. 'Maybe he was worried they were.'

'He could have been arrested for a misdemeanor,' Mia mused. 'But he still would have shown up on a records check. Unless . . . this guy has no credit cards, and all the addresses he's given are fake. He's flying really low under the radar. What if Devin White's a fake?'

'The university confirmed he'd gone there,' Reed said. Exhausted, he dragged his palms down his face. 'Graduated with honors.'

'Yeah, they confirmed Devin White went there.' She tilted her head. 'Can we get a picture from the university? A yearbook picture or something?'

Aidan stood up. 'I'll check. Murphy, you fill them in on what we found.'

'We found a neighbor who remembers seeing a guy meeting White's description with Adler last night,' Murphy said. 'He was helping her up the stairs to her apartment.'

'That's consistent with White's story. The bartender says she drank three beers. Her car was still at the bar. We knew that already. What else?' Mia said impatiently.

Murphy shook his head. 'Testy today. While we were going door to door, a woman came screaming at us, saying someone had stolen her car. Ten-year-old Honda.'

'His getaway car,' Reed said.

'But it gets better.' Murphy's brows went up. 'It had GPS. Installed aftermarket.'

Mia sat up. 'No way. He probably picked an old car thinking it wouldn't have GPS. So where did you find it?' she demanded.

'Parked in a 7-Eleven lot near Chicago and Wessex.'

Reed frowned. 'Wait.' He pulled the list of White's bank transactions from the pile of paper in front of him. 'That's a block from where he wrote some of his checks to "Cash." '

Mia's grin was Cheshire-cat slow. 'It's where he lives. The bastard murdered two women then drove to his neighborhood, probably walked home and went to sleep.'

Spinnelli stood up. 'I'll get uniforms canvassing that area with pictures of White.'

'We can go to the press,' Westphalen said and Mia gave an exaggerated wince.

'Do we have to?' she whined.

Spinnelli shot her an understanding look. 'It's the most direct way.'

'Not Wheaton or Carmichael, okay? How about just to Lynn Pope? We like her.'

'Sorry, Mia. This one I'd have to give to all the networks. But I'll try to avoid Miss Wheaton.' He left to organize the search.

'Damn.' Mia turned to Westphalen. 'Did you talk to Manny today?'

'I did.'

'Thompson went to see Manny last night. Right before he called me. A few hours before he died.'

Westphalen took off his glasses and polished them. 'That makes sense. He said that his doctor had told him not to talk to anybody. Not to "cops, lawyers, or shrinks." '

'So he didn't talk to you?' Reed asked.

'Not a lot, no. He was genuinely terrified, but not of Thompson. He did tell me that cutting out the articles wasn't his idea. That they were given to him, but he wouldn't say how or by whom. I asked him where he got the matches, and he claimed he didn't take them, that they'd been planted there. When I asked why someone would do that to him, he shut up. Didn't say another word, no matter how I pried.'

Mia's brows furrowed. 'Is he paranoid?'

'Hard to say without more observation. I will say that he's every bit as fascinated with fire as you indicated, Lieutenant. Even when he wouldn't speak, his eyes became glazed over when I showed him video of a burning house. It was like he couldn't control himself. I think that if he'd known the matches were in his room that he wouldn't have been able to resist using them. Do you know exactly where they were found?'

Reed was annoyed. Like Manny couldn't control himself. The kid liked fire. The kid made bad choices. The shrink was showing his true colors. And because he was so annoyed, he bit his tongue and said nothing.

'Secrest said they found them in the toe of his high-tops,' Mia answered.

Westphalen nodded. 'Not exactly the most discreet place to hide something.'

She looked perplexed. 'Are you saying you believe somebody actually planted matches in his shoes? Why would somebody do that?'

'I don't know. You're the detective. Your lieutenant is very annoyed with me, Mia.'

Reed kept his voice calm. 'Yes, I am.'

'Why?' Westphalen asked.

Reed controlled the exhale that would have been a frustrated huff. 'Manny Rodriguez is not a radio-controlled hypno-zombie,' he replied. 'He's a kid who's made some bad choices. Every time he lit a match, he knew it was wrong and yet he chose to do it anyway. Maybe he didn't steal those matches. I don't know. But to suggest that using them would be out of his control is not only ludicrous, it's danger-ous.'

Westphalen's amusement had fled. 'I agree.'

Reed's eyes narrowed, not trusting the sudden capitulation. 'You're setting me up.'

One side of Westphalen's mouth lifted. 'No, I'm not. Really. Reed, I don't believe that anybody's decision to break the law makes them less accountable. They should still be punished. But their ability to control their impulses is sometimes hampered.'

'By upbringing,' Reed said flatly.

'Among other things.' Westphalen studied him. 'You don't buy that, either.'

'No, I don't.'

'And you're not going to tell me why.'

Reed relaxed his face, made his mouth smile. 'It doesn't really matter, does it?'

'I think it matters a great deal,' Westphalen murmured. 'What I'd be looking for now is Devin White's trigger. What made him start now? Why? We can assume Brooke was retaliation, but what role did the other victims play in his life to make him hate them so?'

Mia sighed. 'So we're back to the files.'

Westphalen smiled at her paternally. 'I'd say so. Call me if you need me.'

Mia watched him go, then turned to Reed, questions in her eyes. But she left them unasked. 'Let's go talk to Manny, then back to the files.'

Thursday, November 30, 3:45 P.M.

Reed waited until the boy was seated across from him. Mia was standing behind the glass, watching. 'Hi, Manny.'

The boy said nothing.

'I would have come to see you earlier today, but we've been very busy.' Nothing.

'It started at four this morning when Detective Mitchell and I were called to the scene of this really big apartment fire.' Manny's chin stayed stoically rigid, but his eyes flickered. 'Big flames, Manny. Lit up the whole sky.'

He paused, let the boy get his salivation under control. 'Miss Adler is dead.'

Manny's mouth fell open. 'What?'

'Your English teacher is dead. She lived in the apartment that was set on fire.'

Manny's eyes dropped to the table. 'I didn't do it.'

'I know.'

Manny looked up. 'I didn't want her to die.'

'I know.'

He sat there for a moment, just breathing. 'I'm not going to talk to you.'

'Manny.' He waited until he had the boy's attention. 'Dr Thompson is dead.'

Manny paled, shock flattening his face. 'No. You're lying.'

'I'm not. I saw his body myself. His throat had been slit.'

Manny flinched. 'No.'

He slid Thompson's morgue photo across the table to Manny. 'See for yourself.'

Manny wouldn't look. 'Take it away. Fuck you, take it away.' The last was a sob.

Reed slid it back and turned it facedown. 'We know who did it.'

Doubt flickered in his eyes. 'I'm not talking to you. I'll end up like Thompson.'

'We know it was Mr White.'

Manny slowly met his eyes. 'Then why do you need to talk to me?'

'Dr Thompson called Detective Mitchell right after he left here last night. He said it was urgent. He then called Mr White. A few hours later he was dead. We want to know what you told him that he needed to tell us.'

'You don't have White.'

Reed shook his head. 'No. And we may not unless you're straight with us.'

Manny shook his head. 'Forget it.'

'Okay. Then about the matches. How do you think they ended up in your shoe?'

Manny's expression soured. 'You won't believe me anyway.'

'How can I? You haven't told me anything. Were the shoes in your room all the time?'

The kid was considering the question. 'No,' he finally said. 'I had them with me all that day. It was my group's day to use the gym.'

'When did you use the gym?'

'After lunch.' He sat back. 'That's all I'm gonna say. Let me go back to my cell.'

'Manny, White can't hurt you in here.'

Manny's lips curved. 'Sure he can.'

Thursday, November 30, 4:45 P.M.

'You rang?' Mia asked as she and Solliday stopped at Aidan's desk.

Aidan looked up. 'I did. I called the registrar's office at White's university in Delaware, but they were gone for the day – they're an hour ahead of us. But I did get in touch with the secretary in the education department. Very helpful lady.'

Mia sat on the edge of his desk. 'What did the nice lady say?'

Aidan handed her a black-and-white photo on plain paper. 'She faxed this twenty minutes ago. It's a picture from a department newsletter, taken at a university golf benefit last year. She circled Devin White. It's grainy but you can see his face.'

Solliday looked over her shoulder, so close that if she turned her head she could kiss him. The longer the day dragged on, the more she was anticipating the evening. But they'd made a deal and Aidan was watching her intently.

'It's close, isn't it?' Solliday murmured. 'Same height, same coloring.' He straightened and she finally drew a breath.

'But not the man we talked to this morning,' she said. 'The face is wrong. But most people only notice size and coloring unless they're really looking. He picked a good ID to steal. I'm betting the real Devin White is dead. Did the secretary have any numbers for his family or contacts or anything?'

'Said he'd left his family section blank. She didn't think he had any relatives living. His mother was dead and he'd never known his father.'

'Well, did the helpful lady give any more helpful information?'

'She said that Devin was one of her favorites,' Aidan said. 'That he'd promised to call her when he got settled. But he never did and she assumed he'd gotten busy in his new life. He'd been headed from Delaware to Chicago for a job interview, but he was planning to stop in Atlantic City for a few days. That would have been early last June.'

Energy started to percolate through her veins. 'We can check the hotels, see if White stayed at any of them.'

'Already started,' Aidan said and handed them each a sheet of paper. 'These are the main hotels in Atlantic City. If we split it up, we can get through them faster.'

Mia took the paper to her own desk, then stopped with a frown. A video-sized brown padded envelope lay on top of the stack of Burnette's files. In block letters it was addressed to her. There was no return address. 'What's this?'

Aidan looked over and slowly came to his feet. 'I don't know. It wasn't there when I went to the fax machine earlier. We could ask Stacy.'

Mia pulled on a pair of gloves. 'We saw her leaving when we came in.' She shook the video from the envelope. Solliday still had the TV/VCR on his desk, so she slid it in.

Holly Wheaton's face appeared, sad and grave. 'In light of the recent, tragic murder of the child of a local police officer, we wanted to take a look at the toll police work takes on their families. Often they pay a high price for their family's public service. Some, like Caitlin Burnette, are targets of revenge for their parents' stand against crime.'

'Bitch,' Mia muttered. 'Using Roger Burnette's suffering for her damn ratings.'

'More,' Wheaton continued soberly, 'find the expectations of being the child of a cop too great to handle and go the other way.' The camera panned back and Mia felt her stomach simply drop. She opened her mouth but no words came out. Solliday gripped her arm and pushed her into a chair.

His hands covered her shoulders and shook gently. 'Breathe, Mia.'

She covered her mouth with her trembling hand. 'Oh my God.'

Wheaton gestured to the brick building behind her. 'This is the Hart Women's Correctional Facility. Sentenced here are women who've committed crimes from drug possession all the way up to murder. Sentenced here are women from all walks of life, from all kinds of families.' The camera zoomed to Wheaton's pained expression. 'Even families of cops. One such inmate is Kelsey Mitchell.'

'What is this?' Spinnelli demanded from behind them. 'Oh God. Mia.'

She waved him to quiet as Kelsey's arrest photo filled the screen. Kelsey looked haggard, old, strung out from drugs. 'She was only nineteen,' Mia whispered.

'Kelsey Mitchell is serving a twenty-five-year sentence for armed robbery. She's both the daughter and sister of a cop. Her father died recently, but her sister, Detective Mia Mitchell, is a decorated homicide detective, and ironically, is responsible for several women being detained in the very same cell block as her sister.'

'They're going to kill her.' Mia could barely hear her own voice. 'They're going to kill Kelsey.' She lunged to her feet, her heart beating wildly. 'She can't show this tape. This is a damn threat. She wants her damn story and she doesn't care who gets hurt.'

'I know.' Spinnelli ejected the tape. 'I'm going to call Wheaton's producer right now. Try to calm down, Mia.' He headed back to his office, his expression grim.

Mia reached for Solliday's phone. 'I'm going to call that fucking bitch myself.'

Solliday grabbed her shoulders, twisting until she faced him. 'Mia. Let Spinnelli take care of this.' She tried to pull away, but Solliday held firm.

Pain throbbed in her shoulder and she flinched. 'You're hurting me.'

Instantly he loosened his grip, but he didn't let go. 'Promise me you will not call Wheaton. You will not threaten her. You will let Spinnelli handle this. Promise me, Mia.'

She nodded. He was right. Suddenly too weary to fight it, she lowered her forehead to his chest and rested against him. His hands tightened then opened wide, hesitating before moving to her back and bringing her close.

'Somehow it'll be all right,' he murmured into her hair.

She nodded, fighting the tears that rose in her throat. Cops didn't cry. She should know. Bobby had told her so. Often. 'They'll kill her, Reed.' He said nothing, just held her until she felt control of her emotions return. She pulled away, calm now. 'I'm okay.'

'No, you're not,' he said quietly. 'The last three weeks have been hell. You've held up better than anyone could have expected.' He tilted her face up. 'Even you.'

His eyes were filled with both sympathy and respect and she took comfort from both. Then stepped away to find Aidan watching her and she felt her cheeks heat.

Wanting to shift the focus from what had obviously been a public embrace, she narrowed her eyes at Aidan. 'You know, I think that Jacob Conti had a point after all.'

For a second Aidan's eyes widened, then he grinned before he could stop himself. He sobered himself, giving her a proper glare. 'Mia Mitchell. You should be ashamed.'

Solliday looked confused. 'Who is Jacob Conti?'

Mia sat down in her chair with the list of Atlantic City

hotels. 'Bad man. Very bad.' Conti was a very bad man who'd dealt his own brand of justice to a TV reporter who, through stirring things up to make news, put Conti's son in the sights of a killer. Conti's revenge for his son's death had been effective and final. Unfortunately for him, illegal as well. Mia would have to take more conventional routes of revenge.

'Old case,' Aidan said. 'Back when my sister-in-law Kristen was being stalked.'

Solliday sat down at his desk and tapped at the keyboard with his methodical pace. Then he looked up, eyes wide. 'He was a bad man.'

He'd looked up the old case, then. 'Told you.'

'And Reagan's right. You should be ashamed.' But there was a sudden sparkle in his eye. 'You are a very bad girl, Mia.'

She laughed softly, remembering the last time he'd said those same words. Then, the respite was gone, dread returning with a vengeance as she looked over at Spinnelli's door. If Wheaton's piece ran, Kelsey's life would be in certain danger. But she'd let Spinnelli handle it. For now. 'Let's call these hotels, then call it a night.'

Thursday, November 30, 5:30 P.M.

The Doughertys' big truck had finally pulled into the driveway at 993 Harmony Avenue. For a while he thought the girl at the hotel had lied. That would've been bad.

He'd been listening to the radio. Nobody reported Tania missing. And nobody had mentioned Niki Markov, the woman who should have been home with her two kids, but had instead had the bad luck to be sleeping in the Doughertys' hotel bed. If women stayed where they were supposed to be, they wouldn't get into such trouble. Now Niki Markov was dead and buried, her own suitcases providing her final resting place. He grinned to himself. *Places*, that was. Plural. The cops would never find all of her.

The Doughertys got out of the truck and headed straight around the back of the house, bags from JCPenney in their hands. They'd been shopping to replace clothes, most likely. Seeing as how all theirs were gone. Too bad they wouldn't need them.

After he finished here tonight, he'd be done in Chicago. He'd drive south on his way to the last few names on his list. His stomach growled, reminding him he hadn't eaten since breakfast. He pulled the car from the curb knowing that when he returned it would be time to act. And old lady Dougherty's time to finally die.

Thursday, November 30, 5:55 P.M.

'Mia, can you come here for a minute?' Spinelli stood in his office doorway.

Throwing a worried look at Solliday and Aidan, she approached. 'What?'

'Inside. Shut the door. Reporters are the lowest forms of life on the planet.'

Her heart sank. 'They're going to run the piece.' Her stomach followed. 'Oh, Marc.'

'Relax. I talked to Wheaton. She insists the video you got was a mistake. She meant to send you a copy of the press conference as you'd obviously been watching someone in the crowd.' His lip curled in distaste. 'She just wanted to help.'

'Marc,' she gritted through her teeth. 'What about Kelsey?'

'I said relax. Wheaton hinted about an exclusive on this case. I turned her down flat and suggested that threatening a police officer was a felony. She got huffy and said there was no intended threat. The piece with your sister was scheduled to air Sunday night with or without any words from us. It was an ultimatum with a deadline.'

Her heart was hammering, but trust in Spinnelli kept her feet glued in place. 'And?'

'I can't stop her from airing that piece, Mia, but I'll be damned if that . . .' He drew a breath, editing himself. 'I called Patrick. He's pulling some strings to have Kelsey moved to another facility tomorrow morning. She'll be brought in under another name. It'll be done very discreetly.' He lifted a shoulder. 'It's the best I can do.'

Mia swallowed hard, a wave of relief and gratitude

overwhelming her. 'A lot of people wouldn't have done that much.'

'You've sacrificed for this department, this city countless times. I'll be damned if I'll let Wheaton or anybody else use this department to threaten you or your family.'

She closed her eyes, moved. 'Thank you,' she whispered.

'You're welcome,' he said softly.

His voice returned to its normal briskness. 'Murphy's still sweeping the area where they found the car White used to get away from Brooke Adler's apartment, but he hasn't turned anything up yet. They'll keep canvassing for the next hour, then resume in the morning. I had math teacher White's picture faxed to the local news teams and the newspapers. It's the best way to find him.'

'I know.'

'You guys find the real White at any of those Atlantic City hotels?'

'Not yet. We'll keep going until we do.'

Spinnelli tilted his head, studying her. 'Where are you going to stay tonight?'

Her eyes narrowed. 'What?' He couldn't possibly know about her and Solliday. The words 'it was just a supportive hug' were on the tip of her tongue.

'Your address was in the paper, Mia. Find another place to live. That's an order.'

'You can't tell me where to live. Last I looked, I'm a cop. I can take care of myself.'

'Last I looked, you were a cop and I was your boss. Find another place, Mia. I don't want to worry about you all night.' When her mouth set stubbornly, he exploded. 'Goddammit, Mia. For days I sat next to Abe's bedside wondering where the hell you were. I thought I might lose two of my best people. Don't *put* me through that again.'

She looked down, feeling suddenly small. 'Well, when you put it like that.'

He sighed. 'It's just for a little while. Howard and Brooks are close to pulling Getts in. They've closed off about all the rat holes he can crawl down.'

'He already knew my address.'

'True, but now every punk wannabe does, too. You worry about Kelsey on the inside. There are a lot more on the outside that would love bragging rights to you.'

'I have a gun. Kelsey doesn't.'

'And you both have to sleep sometime.'

She ran her tongue across her teeth. 'I don't want to admit that you have a point. But,' she hurried on before he could say more, 'who would you have me put in danger? Dana? She's got kids. Abe? He's got Kristen and the baby.'

Spinnelli's door opened and Solliday filled the doorway. 'She can stay at my house.'

Mia's mouth dropped open. '*What?*'

Spinnelli just blinked. 'What?'

He shrugged his wide shoulders. 'It makes sense. I've got a duplex. My sister rents the other side. Lauren's on my side taking care of my daughter more than she's on her own side, anyway. Detective Mitchell can stay in the other side, have her own place.'

Mia found her voice. 'You were *spying* on me. *Again.*'

He shrugged. 'I was waiting to talk to Spinnelli. It's not my fault I have good ears.'

She glared at him. 'I'm *not* staying with you.'

'Not me.' He smiled innocently. 'At Lauren's. It makes sense, Mia. And we can keep going through Burnette's and Hill's files after dinner. That should speed things up.'

She just bet it would. The very thought of what would speed up sent new color to her cheeks. And Solliday just stood there, smiling like a damn choirboy.

But if Spinnelli had any inkling of Solliday's ulterior motives, he gave no indication. 'It does make sense, Mia. And you never have time to study those files during the day.'

She drew a breath. 'I want to formally state my opposition to this stupid plan.'

Spinnelli nodded. 'Formally noted. Do it anyway.'

'What about Solliday's kid? I'm putting her in danger, too. They'll follow me.'

'Mia, if you can't lose a tail by now . . .' Spinnelli gently pushed her out the door. 'Finish calling hotels, then break for dinner. After you eat, you can get back to the files.'

'Aren't you kind?'

His mustache bunched and his eyes darkened, a sure

417

sign his patience was spent. 'We have to get a connection between White, Burnette, and Hill or we have nothing more than circumstantial evidence. We can't place him at any of the three scenes, so we have to at least have a strong motive. Find one. Stop worrying about your apartment and concentrate on what matters. Find White before he kills again.'

She knew when she was beaten. 'All right. You'll make sure they move Kelsey.'

'You have my word.'

'Fine. Then I'll stay on Lauren's side of the duplex.'

Spinnelli's chest moved in a small sigh of relief. 'Thank you. And thanks to you also, Reed,' Spinnelli said. 'I appreciate you offering up the house.'

Mia looked at Solliday, her jaw cocked. 'Yeah. Thanks a lot, Solliday.'

Something flickered in Solliday's dark eyes and she knew he knew she was pissed. 'You're welcome,' he told Spinnelli. Then he muttered under his breath, 'I think.'

Thursday, November 30, 6:15 P.M.

He'd nearly finished his dinner when the face on the TV screen threatened to bring it all back up. The face was his. In horror his eyes froze to the screen. He knew they'd be looking for him. Somehow he never thought they'd put his face on TV.

As he fought to control his shock, his temper began to

boil. The bitch. This was the work of the Mitchell woman. Now he couldn't move around the city without people knowing who he was. Today it was Chicago. Tomorrow, CNN? He'd be recognized wherever he went from sea to goddamn shining sea.

He had to get out of this restaurant. Now. With a casualness that came only through superior self-control, he rose, threw the contents of his tray in the trash, strolled through the restaurant door and to his car.

She had to go. He patted his pocket where he still carried pretty Caitlin's gun. Mitchell had to go. With her gone, the focus would be shifted to the gunman who'd tried to kill her once before. Melvin Getts was his name. It would be Getts's face on the news.

A cop killer trumped an arsonist any damn day of the week.

Chapter Seventeen

Thursday, November 30, 6:45 P.M.

Reed hung up the phone. 'Found him.'

Both Mia and Aidan quickly hung up. 'Where?' Mia demanded.

'The Willow Inn in Atlantic City. Their computer shows Devin White checked in on June first and checked out June third. Paid cash. Guy at the desk didn't remember him.'

'We don't know if it was the real Devin or Math Boy,' Mia said. 'Now we know where he stayed, but we still don't know which casino he went to. So many people go through the casinos. It's hard to think anybody would remember a college kid.'

'But all the casinos have cameras,' Reed said. 'We know the days he was there. We should be able to find him on video. At least to know if it's Devin White or . . .' He winced a little. 'Or Math Boy. Can't we find a different pet name for him?'

'It works for now.' She frowned. 'There are a

dozen casinos. Where do we start?'

'You familiar with Atlantic City?' Aidan asked.

'Never been there,' Reed answered and Mia shook her head as well.

'Tess and I went to the Jersey shore on our honeymoon just a few weeks ago. One of the days we drove to Atlantic City and did some of the casinos, so it's still fresh in my mind.' Aidan brought a map to their desks and the three of them stood, studying it. 'Willow Inn is down here, close to the Silver Casino. Harrah's and Trump's Marina are way up here and all the other big casinos are way over here, on the beach.'

'He probably went to the Silver Casino at least once or twice since it was close,' Mia said.

'And it's one of the smaller casinos, so it should be easier for them to locate him.'

Reed looked at the grainy picture. 'The university has a better photo of the real Devin. We could ask Atlantic City PD to search tonight with this, or wait until tomorrow morning.'

'Four women are dead,' Mia said. 'I don't think we can afford to wait.'

'I agree,' Aidan said. 'Besides, if they don't find him before morning, then we give them a better picture and ask them to start again.'

'I'll send pictures of White and Math Boy to Atlantic City PD. Maybe somebody filed a missing person on the real Devin. Thanks for the help, Aidan. You guys go on home.'

Aidan quickly complied, waving good-bye on his way out. But Reed remained, watching her. 'You're coming home with me, Mia.'

She looked up, eyes narrowed. 'That was a dirty stunt to pull, Solliday.'

He inclined his head, his own dander up. 'What? That I want to keep you alive?'

She turned to her computer, her lips a thin line. 'You could have asked me first.'

He backed off. 'Yeah. And I probably should have. I'm sorry.'

'Yeah. Well, fine. Go home, Solliday. I'll meet you later. After Beth goes to sleep.'

'You could come for dinner.'

Her eyes were locked on her computer screen. 'I promised Abe I'd have dinner with them. Besides, you need time with your daughter. Go home. I'll see you later.'

He leaned against her desk, closer than was wise, but dammit, he could still feel her trembling as he'd held her. She thought she was superwoman. But she was a hell of a lot more human than she wanted to admit. 'Mia, I was there the other night, remember? I saw how close you came to not having a head anymore. Doesn't that scare you?'

She looked up, eyes flat. 'Yes. But that's my job and my life. I'm not going to run every time a bad guy waves a gun in my face. If I did, I'd be useless to anyone.'

'If you're dead, you're useless to everyone,' he shot back.

'I said I'd meet you later.' Her eyes closed. 'I promise. Now go home to your kid.'

Mia waited until he was gone, then called the Atlantic City police department, explained what she needed, answered all the questions she could. They said they'd coordinate a search with the management of the Silver Casino. She came back from faxing the photos to find Roger Burnette standing at her desk.

He was not pleased. He may have been a little drunk. His eyes were filled with pain and a reckless wrath that made her steps slow. Instinctively she put the photos on the first desk she passed so that when she approached him, it was with empty hands. No sense in giving a grief-ravaged parent the identity of their child's killer. Especially when the parent was a cop. 'Sergeant Burnette. Can I help you?'

'You can tell me you know who murdered my daughter.'

'We believe we do, sir. But we don't have a legitimate identification or location.'

He took rapid breaths. 'In other words, you know jack shit.'

'Sergeant.' Carefully she came closer. 'Let me call someone to take you home.'

'Dammit, I don't need anybody to take me home. I need you to tell me you know who killed my Caitlin.' In a rage he knocked the stack of file folders from her desk.

Papers flew all over the floor. 'You sit here and read all damn day. Why aren't you out there looking?' He grabbed her then, gripping her shoulders like a vise and for the second time in an hour pain speared her. She'd been wrong – Burnette was very drunk. 'You're no cop,' he hissed. 'Your father was a cop. He would have been ashamed of you.'

She shoved his arms away. 'Sergeant. Sit down.'

He towered over her, fists clenched. 'I'm burying my daughter tomorrow. Does that mean anything to you?'

She stood her ground even though she had to crane her neck to look up at him. 'It means a great deal to me, Sergeant. We're close, but we don't have him yet. I'm sorry.'

'*Roger.*' Spinnelli was out of his office and between them faster than Mia had ever seen him move. 'Just what the hell do you think you're doing?'

Burnette stepped back. 'Getting an update on my daughter's case. Not that there's anything to update,' he added in disgust.

'Detective Mitchell has been working this case nearly nonstop since Monday.'

'Then she's not very good at her job, is she?' he sneered.

'Roger, you're outta line,' Spinnelli barked.

Burnette turned on his heel, swatting at the air. 'Go to hell, all of you.'

Spinnelli searched her face. 'Are you hurt?'

'I'm okay, but he's drunk,' Mia murmured. 'Make sure he doesn't drive himself home.'

'Mia, go home.' He winced. 'Not home. To Reed's. With whatever her name was.'

'Lauren.' She pointed to Burnette, who'd stopped at the bullpen doorway, his shoulders hunched. 'Go help him, Marc. I'll see you tomorrow.'

Thursday, November 30, 8:05 P.M.

'Dinner was great, Kristen.' Mia smiled down at Kara Reagan's dirty little face as she struggled to take off a layer of spaghetti sauce without taking off a layer of the child's fair skin. 'You enjoyed it, too, didn't you, Sweetpea?'

Kara bounced on Mia's lap, a sly look in her eyes. 'Ice cream. Pleeease?'

Mia laughed. She loved this little girl like she was her own. Playfully she tugged one of Kara's red curls. 'You have to ask Mommy about that.'

'Mommy said no,' Abe said. His color was better, but his face was still too thin. 'But Daddy and Kara are hoping Aunt Mia being here will change Mommy's mind.'

Kristen's sigh was dramatic. 'Two against one. They gang up on me like this every night. I made up the spare room, Mia. You'll stay here tonight.'

Kara bounced. 'Stay,' she demanded. She smacked a wet kiss on Mia's cheek.

425

Kristen lifted the baby from Mia's lap. 'Bath time, baby. Then bed. Say good night to Aunt Mia.' Kara kissed her other cheek noisily, then Kristen carried her off, the two singing some silly bath-time song, Kara delivering the words with a sweet lisp.

'You have sauce on your cheeks,' Abe said wryly and Mia scrubbed it off.

'It was worth it.' She smiled wistfully after them, grateful the innocent child would never have to wonder if her parents loved her. 'I don't see how Kristen resists her.'

'She's really a marshmallow. Don't let the tough act fool you.' Abe sat back in his chair. 'You're not staying here tonight, are you?'

'No, but don't tell Kristen until after I'm gone. She threatened to tie me down.'

'Please tell me you're not going home.'

Mia rolled her eyes. 'Solliday has a duplex. I'm going to use the other side. I get my own room, my own kitchen, my own private entrance.'

Abe's lips twitched. 'Your own tunnel to the other side for midnight rendezvous?'

Mia sucked in a cheek. Abe was laughing now and she knew Aidan had spilled the beans about the office embrace. 'Your brother has a big mouth. It was nothing.'

'Aidan's always had a big mouth.' Abe chuckled. 'You should see your face. It's redder than Kara's covered in spaghetti sauce.'

She threw a napkin at him. 'And to think I've missed you.'

'I'll be back soon enough. Back to curry and sushi and vegetarian delights.'

She narrowed her eyes at him. 'Solliday lets me choose.'

'Choose what?' he asked with a grin and she felt her face flame even hotter. He leaned back, his face sobering. 'You'll let me know if he . . . if you need help.'

'What? If he's mean to me, you'll beat him up?'

'Or something.'

He was serious and Mia was touched. 'Other than being a little overbearing, he's a gentleman. But he does piss me off. Trying to outmaneuver me.'

'Sounds like he's succeeded.' He shrugged when she scowled. 'You aren't in your apartment right now. I see that as a plus. Maybe he can maneuver you into moving.'

Mia stared at him. 'You, too? Abe, it's my place. You wouldn't sell this place. If I moved every time I made some bad guy mad, I'd be a nomad in a fucking tent.'

'This is bigger than one bad guy. What is Spinnelli doing to curb Carmichael?'

'What can he do? She didn't say that was my address. She said shots were fired and that I was the target. She leaves it up to the reader to infer. She broke no laws.'

'Mia, how did Carmichael know where to find Getts and DuPree?'

'She said one of her sources had told her.'

'What if she's the source?'

'You mean, what if she was there that night you got shot?' He nodded and she considered the possibility. 'She could have followed them then. But that would mean she knew where they were the whole time and said nothing.'

'It would mean she waited until the day you came back to share the information.'

Mia could hear her temper pop. 'Dammit. She wanted the story of me taking them down and I gave her half of what she wanted when I took DuPree.'

'And it was a front-page story when you did. Don't trust her, Mia.'

'Shit.' She stood on shaky legs. 'This day has sucked all the way around.'

'Stay a little longer. You look tired.'

She blinked hard. 'I am tired. But I've got to get through Burnette's files. We don't have . . .' She hesitated, then shrugged and used Burnette's own words. 'We don't have jack shit in terms of physical evidence. We've got to find the link.'

'But if you don't know his real name, then what are you looking for?' he asked.

She rubbed her aching forehead. 'You're trying to trick me with logic,' she grumbled. 'I'll get some sleep, then hit the files.' She headed for the front door.

He followed, moving slowly but steadily. 'Bring me some of them. I can help.'

She shrugged into her coat, wincing at her shoulder.

She'd be lucky if Burnette hadn't left a bruise. 'You're on disability, pal.'

'I can sit and read. I'm going nuts here all day.' He tilted his head. 'Pleeease?'

She laughed. 'Now I know where Kara gets it. If Spinnelli approves it, consider yourself hired. I'll call tomorrow. Thank Kristen for dinner and kiss Kara for me.'

As she pulled away from his house, she could see him standing in the window, watching, just as Dana had watched her drive away the night before. Once again, she felt the unwelcome tug of jealousy mixed with resentment. But she didn't resent Abe and Dana. Not really. It was the closeness they had with their new families. This she could admit to herself. It was coming home to a noisy house, with people who loved you no matter what. It was not having to drive away alone.

And even though the location had changed, she'd still be alone tonight. She'd be staying in Lauren's house, while Reed's family gathered on the other side. She thought of her own family. Kelsey in jail. Her mother . . . after the funeral they hadn't spoken. Annabelle had ordered her not to return, which wasn't hard to obey. She thought of the mystery blonde, wondered who she was and if she had a family. If *she* liked *her* mother.

She still hadn't run those license numbers. When everything died down, she would. *When everything dies down. When everything settles.* They were the words she used to put off things. To put off buying new furniture, painting her bedroom. To put off moving in with Guy last year when he'd asked. Marrying him. When everything settles down . . .

And when will that be, Mia? How old will you be when that happens?

Out of sorts, she pushed the thoughts from her mind. She had more important things to worry about now. She was going to her apartment to pack a bag, so she had to have her mind clear, her attention sharp in case nasty people with guns lurked about. She'd think about all the angst later. She laughed aloud, the sound brittle and bitter to her ears. *When everything settles down.*

Thursday, November 30, 8:15 P.M.

'Good dinner, Lauren,' Reed said, helping her clear the dishes from the table.

Lauren looked at him shrewdly. 'I'm surprised to hear that. You looked like you were punishing the food the whole time.'

More like he'd been punishing himself. He'd completely mishandled that whole thing with Mia. 'Sorry. I have some things on my mind.'

'I guess you do.' She squeezed his arm and took the plates to the sink.

'Whoa!' He stopped Beth, who was leaving the room without a word. 'Where do you think you're going?'

Beth gave him the look. 'Upstairs,' she said, like he was mentally infirm.

She'd been silent through dinner, a petulant scowl on her face. Once again she'd asked to go to this sleepover on the weekend. Once again he'd said no. It was getting old. 'Get back here and help your aunt. I just don't know what's gotten into you, Beth.'

Setting her teeth, she started tossing silverware onto plates with a clatter. 'Beth!'

She looked up and he was shocked to see tears in her eyes. '*What?*' she said through her teeth.

'Beth, honey, what's wrong?'

Viciously she wiped crumbs from the table. 'Nothing you'd understand.' Throwing the crumbs at the trash can, she ran from the room, leaving Reed staring, dumbfounded.

'What was that?' he asked.

Lauren took the broom and swept around the base of the trash can, where most of the crumbs had fallen. 'Something's been bothering her this week. Maybe it's a boy.'

Reed closed his eyes and shuddered. 'She's fourteen, Lauren. Don't say that.'

'She's fourteen, Reed. Get used to it.'

'I'll go talk to her.'

'Give her time to pull herself together.' She leaned on the broom and gave him an appraising stare. 'You haven't been with it the last few days, either. Need to talk?'

Reed looked over at her. Of all their siblings, he and Lauren were the closest. He loved the others, but he and Lauren had always shared a bond. 'I don't know.'

She smiled. 'When you decide, you know where I live.'

'Ahh, that.' He rubbed the back of his neck awkwardly. 'I kind of volunteered your house. For a worthy cause.'

She nodded, eyes narrowing. 'You volunteered my house. Why?'

'Mitchell needs a place to stay for a few days. I offered the other side of the duplex. I figured you wouldn't mind staying in the spare room since most of your stuff is here.'

She considered this in silence for a moment. 'Why can't she just share with me?'

He opened his mouth. Closed it again. He'd thought of that after he'd made the offer to Mia, then pushed the thought aside. He wanted her alone. He wanted her naked. He wanted to hear her cry out when she came. Without worrying about his sister overhearing or leaving his daughter alone. Understanding filled Lauren's eyes and heat filled Reed's cheeks.

'You're finally taking my advice.'

'No, I'm not.'

'But—'

'Lauren, it's none of your business, but now that you know, it's temporary. Just like the partnership.'

Her eyes shadowed. 'Do you know what you're doing, Reed?'

He blinked. 'Excuse me?'

'I don't mean technique-wise. I assume you have that down pretty well.'

'Lauren,' he warned, but she ignored him.

'I meant this . . . thing. With Mia. Just remember that slinking around in secret doesn't make it less important. Telling yourself it's temporary doesn't make it true. And even though she seems like a tough cookie, the woman's got feelings.'

He knew that. 'I don't want to hurt her.'

'If wishes were horses.' She whisked the crumbs into the trash. 'I'll get her room ready.' Her expression pained, she ran her finger down his shirt, tracing the chain he wore beneath it. 'You took it off last night.'

'You were in my room?'

'Looking for some aspirin. It was on your night table in plain sight. Be careful, Reed. No woman wants to live in another woman's shadow. Even temporarily.'

He didn't know what to say and the ringing of his cell phone saved him from saying anything. He didn't recognize the number. 'Solliday.'

Lauren shook her head and with a backward look, left to prepare Mia's room.

'This is Abe Reagan. Mia's partner.'

Reed's guard went up. 'Nice to meet you. Just curious, how did you get my cell?'

'Got it from Aidan who got it from Jack. Mia just left here. She said she was staying at your place, but I know she's stopping by her apartment first. If I could, I'd go cover her.'

'I'll go. Thanks for the heads-up.' Reed pocketed his cell phone. But first, he'd talk to Beth. He took the stairs two at a time, then knocked on her door. Loud music played inside and he couldn't hear her answer. 'Beth? I need to talk to you.'

'Go away.'

He jiggled the door, found it locked. 'I need to talk to you. Open the door. Now.'

After about a minute, the door opened and she stood there staring up at him, belligerence in her dark eyes, still red and puffy from crying. 'What?'

Gently he reached out to push some wet hair from her cheek. She flinched and pulled away, which hurt him more than her words had. 'Beth. Please tell me what's wrong. I can't understand if I don't know.'

'It's nothing. I'm just tired.'

Helpless and frustrated, he frowned. 'Are you sick? Do we need to see a doctor?'

Her smile was bitter and far too adult. 'Are you asking me if I need a shrink? Don't think so, Dad. You're the one who's always saying what a crock they are.'

He winced, her aim true. 'I have said that. Maybe I shouldn't have. Maybe there are lots of things I should do differently. I can't know unless you talk to me, baby.'

Her eyes flashed. 'I'm not a baby.' Then her eyes went sad, but he could see the slyness beneath. 'You could let me go to the sleepover. That would make me happier.'

He stepped back, the hair on the back of his neck standing straight up. This wasn't his child. This manipulating stranger belonged to somebody else. 'No. I said you were on restriction and nothing you've said makes me change my mind. In fact, just the opposite. I don't know what's so important about this sleepover, but no, you cannot go. Starting now, I don't want you going over to Jenny's anymore.'

Her nostrils flared, her breath deliberate. 'You're blaming her. She said you would.' She stepped back, her hand on the door. 'Are you finished ruining my life?'

He shook his head, having no words. 'Beth. I have to go out for a few minutes. We'll finish this when I come back.'

'Don't bother,' she said coldly. 'I'll be asleep when you come back.' Then she closed the door in his face.

He shoved his hand through his hair, cupping the back of his head as if to hold it in place. What was wrong with his child? Was it just a temper tantrum? Or could it be more? Something . . . worse? But he couldn't believe that. Beth was a smart girl. A good kid. She was only fourteen. But he knew what fourteen-year-olds could get involved in, from personal experience. But this was Beth. She wasn't the kid of an alcoholic drug-addict who cared more for her next fix than feeding her son.

Beth was lucky. *She has me.* He sighed. *And right now, she hates me.* He didn't know what to do. He felt like breaking down her door, but knew that wouldn't solve a thing. He needed help. He'd call her guidance counselor first thing in the morning.

Now he had to see a woman who would probably make him feel as welcome as his daughter just had. 'You should just give it up, Solliday,' he muttered as he walked down the stairs and grabbed his coat. He passed Lauren coming across the front yard as he walked out. 'I have to go out,' he snapped. 'Beth's in her room.'

'Did you talk to her?' Lauren asked, a canvas book bag over one shoulder.

'For all the good it did. I'm calling her school counselor tomorrow.'

'That's a good idea.'

'I'll be back later.' He stalked toward the SUV, churlish and embarrassed for it.

'Reed?'

He stopped. Didn't turn around. 'What?'

'Take off the chain before you get there.'

Without looking back he climbed in the SUV, pulled out of the driveway and around the block. Then he slowed down and pulled the chain from around his neck, stared at the ring in his palm, then carefully laid it in the console next to his seat. 'Shit.'

Thursday, November 30, 8:45 P.M.

There she was. He came to his feet in the alley across the street, slinging his backpack onto his back. It paid to travel light. If he had to run, he had everything he needed. The car he'd taken was parked a block away, close enough to get to once he'd done the deed. Then Melvin Getts would be on the news. *Not me.*

Mitchell was getting out of her car across the street, a briefcase on one shoulder. She stood for a moment, alert, scanning the area, but he was tucked out of her sight in the shadows. She was a perfect target, her head in just the right position. His hand steady, he pointed the gun. From this distance, he couldn't miss. He aimed—

An SUV pulled up beside her, blocking his shot. *Dammit.* Lieutenant Solliday.

Solliday lowered his window and they were talking, but not loudly enough for him to hear what they were saying. Solliday sat back, scanning the street as she had done.

Shit. She was going up to her apartment. Who knew when she'd come back down? It could be two minutes or twenty. Hell, it could be all night. He had places to go. Doughertys to kill. He couldn't stay here waiting for her. *Dammit.* It was now or never. It was now. He stepped out of the shadows and raised the pistol. And fired.

'Police! Drop your weapon.'

He lurched back. The shout hadn't come from Mitchell or Solliday. Mitchell was nowhere to be seen and Solliday was out of his vehicle, his own gun drawn. *Shit.*

He backed up, one step, then two. His heart stopped when Solliday spotted him.

'Stop.' Solliday was coming at a run. A fast run.

Get away. He turned and fled.

Mia pushed herself to her feet, her radio in one hand, weapon in the other. 'Shots fired at 1342 Sedgewick Place. Plainclothes officer in pursuit. Request backup ASAP.'

She stood in the street, making her mind focus through the adrenaline blur. Someone had yelled, right after the shot was fired, but the street was empty. She pressed the radio to her forehead, then back to her mouth. 'Solliday.' When he didn't answer panic began to grip her throat and she began to run. '*Solliday*.'

'I'm here.' His voice came crackling across the radio and she stopped, breathing hard, light-headed with relief. 'I lost him,' he growled. 'Get an APB out on White.'

She froze. 'What?'

'White. Math Boy. Hurry, Mia. He's still on foot around here somewhere.'

He tried to kill me. 'This is Detective Mitchell, Homicide. We are in pursuit of a Caucasian male, approximately twenty-three years of age. Five-eight, one hundred fifty pounds. Blond hair, blue eyes. Suspect is armed and wanted in connection with four murders. Goes by the name of Devin White. Repeat, suspect is armed.'

'We read you, Detective,' Dispatch said. 'Do you need medical attention?'

'No. Just send backup. We need to seal off this entire neighborhood. He escaped on foot, so send a unit to the El station two blocks south of here.' She looked up to see Solliday emerging from the alley at a jog. He stopped short, eyes going fierce.

'You're hit.'

She lifted her hand to her cheek, wiped at the blood there. 'Grazed me. I'm fine.'

He lifted her chin, nodded once, then let her go. 'Who yelled "Police"?'

'Don't know.' She turned in a circle, looking. 'That was Math Boy? You're sure?'

He nodded, still breathing hard. 'Yeah. Fast little bastard. I almost had him and he darted around some trash cans and knocked them into my path.'

'You were pretty fast yourself.'

'Not fast enough. He's given us the slip again.'

'We'll set up roadblocks.' Her instinct said someone was still there. 'But the El is only two blocks from here. He could be there now. He could still be here. Dammit, I feel like somebody's watching . . .' A noise behind her had her spinning around, her weapon in a two-handed grip. 'Come out with your hands up.'

'I'll be damned,' Solliday murmured and Mia blinked.

From out of the shadows, near where White had escaped, walked . . . *her*. Her blond head was covered with a black beret and instead of the dark suit she'd worn at the press conference, she wore a black leather jacket, identical to the one Mia had been wearing the night Abe was shot. Her lips were curved in a self-mocking smile. In one hand she held a pistol, but flat against her raised palm. The other hand held a badge.

Mia blew out a breath. 'God, this day just keeps getting better and better.'

Thursday, November 30, 9:15 P.M.

He got off the El two stops later and walked right to a little Ford, his slim-jim in his hand. A wiggle and a pop later he was behind the wheel and thirty seconds after that, driving down the road, his backpack on the seat beside him.

Once again out of the public eye. He'd sat on the train, wondering who was watching him, comparing his face to the photo they'd shown on the news. He'd been coolheaded, not shrinking into his seat but not meeting anyone's eye. Normal.

Had he got her? Was Mitchell dead, brains splattered all over the pavement? He wasn't sure. His bullet had come close. But *he'd* come too close to getting caught, that was for damn sure. Solliday had seen him. Recognized him. His ruse had failed.

So step back. Stay out of public for a while. Do what you need to do tonight and tomorrow, hightail it out of town. *Find the last four, then you're done.*

COUNT TO TEN

Thursday, November 30, 9:15 P.M.

'Just put the gun down slowly,' Mia said.

The woman did, placing her weapon gently on the sidewalk. 'You got hit,' she said.

Mia holstered her own service piece. 'A scratch.'

Two cruisers pulled up and Mia looked over her shoulder. Four more followed.

'I'll take care of it,' Solliday said. 'I'll get them organized in a roadblock.'

'Thanks,' she murmured, then turned back to the woman. 'Let's have it.' She took the woman's badge and held it up to the light. 'Olivia Sutherland. Minneapolis PD.'

Sutherland's mouth curved, that same self-mocking smile. 'Hey, sis.'

Mia gave her back her badge. 'Why didn't you just come talk to me? Why have you been following me around for weeks? Are you trying to make me fucking nuts?'

'I wasn't trying to make you . . . nuts. I didn't know if I wanted to talk to you. I didn't know if I wanted to know you. I kind of thought I wouldn't.'

Mia waited a half beat before inclining her head. 'And that would be *because*?'

She shrugged. 'He wanted you. Not me. Your mother. Not mine.'

Mia blinked. Then laughed. 'You're kidding, right?'

441

The mocking smile disappeared. 'I wouldn't dream of it.'

Obviously someone had painted this woman a much rosier picture of Bobby Mitchell than he deserved. 'Let's start again. Olivia Sutherland, thank you for saving my ass.'

The little smile came back. 'I was hoping you'd noticed.'

'Why did you?'

She shrugged. 'I didn't want to like you. I wanted to hate your guts. But I watched you and realized I might have a few things wrong. I was set to leave this afternoon when I saw your address published in this morning's paper.' She frowned. 'You need to do something about that woman, you know. That Carmichael woman is poison.'

'Yeah. I kind of got that. So . . . you've been hanging here all day?'

'Off and on. Mostly on. I thought if you came home, I'd say hi and good-bye. But you don't come home very often.'

'I know. I usually hang at friends' houses.'

'The redhead at the funeral?'

'She's one. Look, I want to talk to you, but I've got to take care of this.' She gestured over her shoulder to where Solliday had a map spread out on the hood of one of the cruisers, setting up the roadblocks.

Sutherland smiled. 'When things settle down, we can talk.'

When things settle down. Suddenly the phrase smacked Mia in the face. She'd lost too many things because she'd waited for things to settle down. Now here was an opportunity that might not come again. 'No, because they never will. How old are you?'

Sutherland blinked. 'Twenty-nine.' Then she smiled. 'You're rude to ask.'

Mia smiled back. 'I know. Can you stick around for a few more days?'

'No. I had some time saved up, took some leave, but my captain is after me to come back. I have to go home.'

'Just another day. Please. I didn't know you existed until three weeks ago. We obviously have a few things in common, besides Bobby. Where are you staying?'

Sutherland studied Mia's face, then nodded. 'Mother moved to Minnesota after I was born, but my aunt still lives here. I'm staying with her.' She scrawled an address and a phone number on the back of her card. 'I know where you live.'

'Not for a few days. I'll be on the move most likely. But here's my cell.' She gave Sutherland a card, watched her pocket it, then thoughtfully raise her eyes.

'I lived my life wishing I was you. Hating you. You're not who I thought you'd be.'

'Sometimes I even surprise myself,' Mia said wryly. 'Now we're going to have to take your statement. The guy you scared off has killed four women.'

Her blue eyes widened and it was like looking into a mirror. 'Then that's . . . ?'

Little sister read the papers. 'Yeah. Come on. Let's get to work.'

Thursday, November 30, 10:00 P.M.

Math Boy was gone. Reed silently fumed as he watched the police go door to door. So close. He'd come so close. He could see the bastard's leering face. His triumphant grin when he knew he'd gotten away. If he'd been another step faster . . .

'If you keep frowning like that, your face will stay that way,' Mia said and leaned against his SUV next to him.

'I had him in my hands.' He gritted his teeth. 'Dammit. I almost had him.'

' "Almost" only counts in hand grenades and horse-shoes,' she said. 'We're wasting our time, Reed. He's not going to stick around here. He's gone.'

'I know,' he said bitterly.

'I'm wondering why he did this at all. Why me?'

Reed shrugged. 'We're getting close and he knows it. Besides, if he knows your address, he also knows you were shot at Tuesday night.'

She lifted her fingers to her cheek where an EMT had placed two stitches to close the skin the bullet had grazed. 'A distraction.'

'Mia!'

As one they turned to find Jack by the door of her

apartment building. He held a bullet in the palm of his hand. 'If he'd been a fraction of an inch more on target . . .'

As it had multiple times in the last hour, Reed's blood went cold. A fraction of an inch more and the bullet would have plowed into the base of her skull rather than skim the surface of her cheek. A fraction of an inch and he might have lost her.

'Yeah, yeah,' she said. 'I'd be dead. Thanks, Jack.'

'Actually,' Jack said dryly, 'it probably would have bounced off your damn hard head. Sometimes I wish you weren't so lucky. You're starting to think you are bulletproof. And you're not.'

No, she wasn't. Reed swallowed back the fear that rose in his throat every time his mind replayed the scene of her dropping to the pavement. 'Jack, we're beat. Can Mia pack her bag and get out of here?'

Jack eyed him shrewdly and Reed knew the phone calls between Abe and Aidan and Jack hadn't just been about trading phone numbers. 'Yeah. Watch her back until she gets . . . to where she's going.'

They all looked around at that, each one realizing that the walls potentially had ears.

'I will.' Reed held open the door to her apartment building. 'Let's get your bag packed.' He waited until she'd unlocked her front door, then pushed her inside and up against the door, his heart pounding. He covered her mouth with his, too hard and too desperate. But in a second it didn't matter because her arms were around his neck and she was kissing him back, just as hard and just as desperate.

He pulled away, breathing as hard as he had when he'd chased the scum-sucking murdering asshole toad. 'Thanks. I needed that,' she whispered.

He rested his forehead on hers. 'Dammit, Mia. I was so . . .'

She drew a breath. 'Yeah. Me, too.'

He stepped back and she looked up at him, awareness in her eyes. 'Pack fast. I want you out of here.' Then, unable to resist, he cupped her cheek and gently traced his thumb below the stitches. 'I want you, period. Come home with me.'

'I don't seem to have a choice.' One side of her mouth tipped up. 'That was a lousy thing to do, manipulating me like that. Putting Lauren out of her own house.'

His thumb moved to her lower lip, fanning back and forth. 'Technically, it's my house. She just rents.' He paused a half beat. 'The guest room on that side has a really comfortable bed. King size. Firm mattress.'

'Mine's firm enough,' she said blandly, but her eyes darkened. 'What else?'

'Well . . . There is the firepole. And the trapeze. And the trampoline.'

She laughed. 'You win. I'll pack.'

He followed her back to her bedroom. It looked like a tornado had gone through, sheets and blankets in a tangled mess on the floor. Just as they'd left them early this morning. He eyed the bed, then her. She was eyeing it, too. Then shook her head.

'No,' she said. 'Not with half of CSU combing the street outside my window.'

Hurriedly and without fuss she stuffed a duffel bag with the things she'd need, then hesitated, her hand on a small framed photo. Two teenage girls smiled brightly for the camera, but even though they stood close, they didn't touch. 'You and Kelsey?'

'Yeah.' She shoved it in the bag. 'I need to tell her about Olivia, but I'm afraid to visit her in the new place. I'm afraid to even know where it is.'

'So . . .' He hooked a finger under her chin, lifted her face. It was the first time she'd mentioned the woman other than to take her statement and wish her a pleasant evening. Jack had figured out who she was, but Reed knew Mia wasn't anxious to broadcast the woman's identity to every uniform within earshot. 'Tell me about Olivia.'

She shrugged. 'You know everything I do. We're going to try to get together for an hour tomorrow night and talk.' She started to shoulder the bag, but he took it from her.

'Let me. Please,' he added when her eyes flashed. It was so hard for her to accept help in any form. Tough. She'd have to learn to accept his.

For how long? That would depend on the conversation they'd have as soon as he got her back to his house. That would depend on her expectations. Right now, he was praying he hadn't misjudged her need for independence. And strings.

She nodded, walked to her front door, then stopped. 'Fuck,' she muttered, then wrenched open the closet door. Sitting all alone were the small box and trifolded flag. Teeth clenched, she grabbed the box and shoved it in the bag as well. 'Let's go.'

Chapter Eighteen

Thursday, November 30, 10:40 P.M.

'Olivia Sutherland?' Dana's tone was thoughtful as it came across the phone line.

Mia sat at Lauren's kitchen table. Reed's sister had prepared the guest room with matching towels and perfumed soap. Mia had almost pushed the soap aside, but was glad she hadn't. The scent was calming and, ridiculous as it sounded, feminine.

She'd thought of Reed as she'd used it, wondering if he'd like it, knowing he would. Knowing that was probably Lauren's intent all along. Sisters. Reed's and now . . . *mine.*

'She wore a jacket just like mine, but somehow looked better in it.'

'You want Ethan to check her out?'

'That's okay. She gave all her info when we took her statement. If she doesn't check out, we'll know soon enough. She hated me. Before anyway.'

'It had to be hard growing up without a dad,

knowing he'd chosen someone else.'

'And I grew up wishing *I* could be someone else.'

'You're not going to let this chance slip away, are you? Please tell me you won't.'

'No, I won't. I thought about what you said. About filet mignon and hamburger.'

'That was with respect to men,' Dana said dryly. 'Not women and especially not women related to you. That's just wrong, Mia.'

'Shut up. I meant, I thought about making do versus having it all. I've already missed too much by waiting for my life to settle, to be normal. Maybe Olivia and I can have a relationship, maybe not. She made the first step. I'll make the next one. And if nothing else, at least I can cure her of her misinformed view of her father.'

Dana was silent, then asked, 'How much will you tell her, Mia?'

'I don't know. Not all, I guess. Too much information and all that.'

'Do you want me to come with you?'

Mia smiled. If nothing else, she had a good best friend. 'I'll think about it.'

'Did you think any more about what I said about hamburger with respect to *men*?'

Mia lifted her eyes to the ceiling. 'Yes.'

'And?'

She blew out a breath. 'The man's no hamburger, Dana.'

'Oh?' There was a cagey delight in Dana's voice. 'Tell me.'

'Prime rib.' She thought about the way he'd felt. The way he'd made her feel. 'Way prime.' And as if she'd conjured him, there he was at the back door. 'Oops. Gotta go.'

'Wait,' Dana protested. 'You never told me where you were tonight.'

Reed was making faces outside the window. 'I'm safe,' she said and leisurely came to her feet. 'And I'm about to . . . consume sustenance.'

'Call me tomorrow and be prepared to be a little more forthcoming with the details.'

Mia hung up and let him in. He'd also showered and changed, dressed in a pair of worn jeans and an old jersey, his feet sockless in a pair of gleaming leather loafers. The man did love his shoes. He shivered. 'I misplaced my key to this side.'

They stood, measuring each other in the quiet of his sister's kitchen. Then she tilted her head. 'You lied. There's no firepole and no trapeze.'

He didn't smile. 'But there is a trampoline out in the backyard.'

All of a sudden she didn't feel like smiling either. 'So spill it, Solliday.'

He didn't pretend to misunderstand. 'We need to set some ground rules.'

Rules. She could deal with rules. She had a few of her own. 'Okay.'

He frowned. Looked away for a minute, then back. 'Why are you single?'

The question raised her hackles. 'Hectic schedule,' she said sarcastically. 'Never found time to pencil in the fitting for my wedding gown.'

He exhaled. 'I'm serious.'

Trouble was, so was she. Still, she found another answer, equally true. 'I'm a cop.'

'Lots of cops marry.'

'And lots get divorced. Look. I'm a good cop. Being married is difficult enough under ideal circumstances. I don't think I could be good at both things at the same time.'

The answer seemed to relax him. 'Have you been?'

'What, married? No.' She hesitated, then shrugged. 'Engaged once, but no cigar.' She regarded him evenly. 'Why have you never remarried?'

His eyes locked on hers, sober and intent. 'Do you believe in soul mates?'

'No.' But her mind pricked. Dana and Ethan were. Abe and Kristen were. Bobby and Annabelle . . . were not. 'For some people, maybe,' she amended.

'But not you?'

'No, not me. Why? Was Christine your soul mate?'

He nodded. 'Yes.'

His conviction was unassailable. 'And you only get one?' she asked.

'I don't know,' he said honestly. 'But I've never met

anyone else like her and I'm not willing to settle for second best.'

She couldn't stop the wince. 'Well, that's direct.'

'I don't want to lie to you. I don't want to misrepresent myself to you. I like you. Respect you.' He looked down at his shiny shoes. 'I don't want to hurt you.'

'You just want to have sex with me.' It came out flatter than she'd intended.

He looked up, wary. 'Basically. Yes.'

Irritation jabbed. 'So why not pick up some woman in a bar?'

His dark eyes flashed. 'I don't want a one-night stand. Dammit. I don't want to get married, but that doesn't mean I'll settle for . . . Never mind. I was wrong to start this.'

'Wait.'

He paused, hand clenched on the doorknob, and said nothing.

'Let me get this straight. You want sex with someone you respect, whose company you can enjoy on a limited basis. You do not want marriage or any semblance of formal commitment. I think the term for this is "no-strings affair." Is this correct?'

He drew a breath, exhaled on his answer. 'Yes. And my daughter doesn't find out.'

Mia found herself wincing again. 'We certainly wouldn't want to set a bad example.'

'She's too young to understand. I don't want her

thinking that it's okay to have indiscriminate sex. Because that's not what this would be.'

Mia sat at the little table and raked her hand through her hair. 'So this is a mutually beneficial, physical relationship with some pillow talk and no strings.'

He stood where he was. 'If you're willing.'

She lifted her chin. 'And if I'm not?'

'I go home and sleep alone.' His eyes flickered. 'I really don't want to sleep alone.'

'Hmm. And you've had these "no-strings" relationships before?'

'Not often,' he admitted.

His long abstinence now made sense. 'Which is why it'd been six years.'

'Essentially. Did you want strings, Mia?'

There it was. The offer. It was filet mignon on a hamburger bun. All the taste, without the fuss of silver and fine china and waiters to tip. Twenty-four hours ago, in Dana's kitchen, it was what she'd insisted she'd wanted. Now, in Lauren's kitchen, she recognized this was what she was destined to accept. There would be no hearts to break, no children to ruin. It would be for the best. 'No. I don't want strings, either.'

He was silent as he stared down at her. He didn't believe her, she thought. She wasn't sure she believed herself. Then he stretched out his hand. She put her hand in his and he pulled her from the chair. Slowly at first, he yanked her the rest of the way, banding his arms around her. Then he was kissing her, his mouth warm and hard and . . . necessary. The need unleashed within her was instantaneous, too powerful to deny.

She slid her arms around his neck, her fingers into his hair, and took what she needed. His hands cupped her butt, lifted her into him, rubbed her against the hard ridge in his worn jeans. He sent uncontrollable shivers through her body and she arched against him. *More. Please.* The words echoed in her mind, never passing her lips, but she told him what she wanted with her body. With the way she kissed him back.

He tore his mouth away, kissed down her neck, hungry. Ravenous. 'I want you.' It was a growl, deep in his throat. 'Let me have you.' His mouth closed over her breast, wringing a desperate cry from her lips. 'Say yes. Now.'

She arched her back, abandoning herself to the feel of him. 'Yes.'

He shuddered, hard, as if he hadn't been sure of her answer. Then he carried her through the kitchen and up the stairs to where the big bed waited. 'Now.'

Friday, December 1, 2:30 A.M.

The car at which he'd been scowling for the better part of two hours pulled away from the curb. Finally. He didn't think those teenagers would ever stop making out in the back of that Chevy. And once they did, the boy walked the girl to the door at 995 Harmony Avenue, just one house away from the one he wanted, only to spend the next half hour with his tongue down her throat at the front door. But now the girl was inside and the boy gone.

He slipped around the back of 993 Harmony Avenue, the ski mask once again in place. The homeowner had added on a suite with its own kitchen and separate entrance. He didn't know why Joe and Laura Dougherty were there. He didn't care. He just wanted to kill them so he could get on with things. He jimmied the lock on the back door with ease and slipped inside.

And a patch of white caught his eye. It was the same cat he'd put outside the night he'd killed Caitlin Burnette. Quickly he scooped up the cat, gave it one stroke head to tail, then put it outside again. He turned to study the kitchen, frowning at the electric coils on the stove. No gas again. No explosion again. He huffed a frustrated breath.

It couldn't matter anymore. He'd have to take comfort in making Laura Dougherty writhe in enough agony while she lived. Then he'd set her on fire, just like he'd done to the others. Quietly he crept to the bedroom. Good. Two people slept in the bed this time. He had them. They wouldn't get away again.

He tapped his back, made sure the gun was secure there, which it was. He didn't plan to use it, but he'd be prepared in case of the unexpected. He should have used it on the fire marshal tonight, he thought darkly. That he hadn't was as much an embarrassment as almost getting caught to begin with.

Solliday had rattled him. He hadn't expected so much speed from such a big guy. But for the minutes he'd run for his life, he hadn't thought about his gun. He liked knives much better anyway.

He approached the bed. Joe Dougherty lay on his stomach and Laura lay curled on her side. Her hair was darker than it had been all those years ago.

It annoyed him when women tried to stay young when they weren't. But he'd get to her later. First he had to deal with Joe. And he did, thrusting his knife into the man's back with stealthy skill, in just the right place that he died instantly. Just a little gurgle of air escaped his lungs. Old lady Dougherty was probably too deaf by now to hear it.

But she stirred. 'Joe?' she murmured. He was on her before she could roll over, pushing her face into the pillow, pushing his knee into her kidneys. She thrashed with surprising strength. He pulled the rag from his pocket and shoved it in her mouth, grabbed her hands and secured them behind her back with thin twine.

Then he flipped her over and sliced the flannel nightgown from her body before lifting his eyes to her face. His heart skipped a beat. *It wasn't her.*

Goddammit to hell, this wasn't her. Teeth clenched, he put the tip of the knife to her throat. 'If you scream, I'll butcher you like a pig. Got it?' Eyes wide with terror, her head moved in a little nod so he pulled the rag from her mouth. 'Who are you?'

'Donna Dougherty.'

He was breathing hard. *Control.* 'Donna Dougherty. Where is Laura?'

Her eyes widened farther. 'Dead,' she croaked. 'Dead.'

He grabbed her hair and yanked. 'Don't lie to me, woman.'

'I'm not,' she sobbed. 'I'm not. She's dead. I swear it.'

He felt an animal roar fight to escape his chest. 'When?'

'Two years ago. H-heart attack.'

The rage nearly overwhelmed him. He turned over the man lying next to her. Blood dribbled from the corner of his mouth and Donna moaned.

'Joe. Oh no.'

'Fuck.' The man was too young. This had to be Joe's *son.* Joe *Junior.* The woman had to go. She'd seen him. Viciously angry he'd been cheated *yet again*, he flipped her over to her stomach and holding her by her hair, slit her throat in one hard slice.

He laid the egg on their bed, his hands shaking. He should have taken the hint the first time they weren't home. Should have accepted this as fate. She wasn't as important as the others, but she'd been a missing piece in a finished puzzle, bothering him as long as she was alive. But Laura was dead. Long dead. And out of his grasp.

He lit the fuse, this time not to punish or to celebrate, but to hide.

COUNT TO TEN

Friday, December 1, 3:15 A.M.

Reed knew the moment she woke up. Spooned against him, her tight body stretched and arched back into him. 'Hey,' she mumbled.

His face was buried in the graceful curve of her shoulder, his hand busy in the warm, moist heat between her legs. 'Did I wake you?' he asked.

She sucked in a breath when his thumb found her most vulnerable spot. 'I wondered how you'd manage this,' she said. 'I mean, given the whole . . .' She jerked back against him with a hard shudder. 'Dexterity thing. Damn.'

'I manage just fine,' he said, stroking her, enjoying the way her body felt as she undulated. 'I woke up wanting you again.' He'd woken reaching for her, his heart easing when his hands grasped her flesh instead of empty air.

She tried to roll over, but he held her firmly in place.

'No.' He pulled her leg back over his hip. 'Let me. Let me.' She yielded completely, moaning when he pushed into her. 'Let me, Mia.'

She grabbed him around his neck as she worked her hips like pistons. 'I am.'

She was. She'd let him do everything, responding with an intensity that made him feel like he'd conquered a continent. This time was no different and she came hard around him, pulling him into his own climax with enough force that it was a wonder his heart didn't stop.

459

They lay panting and her laugh filled the room. 'You woke me up.'

He pressed a lazy kiss to the side of her neck. 'Should I apologize?'

'Would you mean it?'

'No.'

She laughed again, softer this time. 'Then don't.' He held her to him, stroking the length of her thigh when he noticed the bruise on her arm in the dim glow from the streetlamp outside. Appalled, he switched on the light. 'Did I do that?'

'What? Oh, that. No. I bumped into something on my way out of the office tonight.'

'Good. I didn't mean to be rough with you.'

'You weren't. It was just right.' She sighed, content. 'I think we've both got a lot of need stored up. It hasn't been six years, but it's been a while for me, too.'

She'd been engaged. Suddenly he needed to know why she hadn't gone through with it. 'Mia, why didn't you get married?'

She was quiet for so long he thought she wouldn't answer. He was kicking himself for asking when she sighed, this time pensive. 'You want to know about my ex.'

'What I really want to know is why you said you didn't want to want this.' He pressed a kiss to her shoulder, made his tone light. 'You're so good at it, after all.'

But his teasing tone did nothing to lighten hers. 'Sex

has never been my problem, Reed. Guy never complained about that.'

His name was Guy then. A French name. He couldn't see Mia with a French guy named Guy. She wasn't the roses and romance type. Still, jealousy speared at him and Reed pushed it away. Guy was gone after all. 'What did he complain about, then?'

'My job. The hours.' She paused. 'His mother complained, too. She didn't think I was good enough for her baby.'

'Mothers often don't.'

'Did your mother think Christine was good enough for you?'

He remembered their relationship fondly. 'Yes. Yes, she did. Christine and Mom were friends. They went shopping and did lunch and all those things.'

'Bernadette and I never had that kind of relationship.' She sighed. 'I met Guy at a party. He was fascinated with my job. The whole *CSI* thing. And I was interested in his.'

'What did he do?'

She flipped to her back and looked up at him. 'He was Guy LeCroix.'

Reed had to admit he was impressed. 'The hockey player?' LeCroix had retired the season before, but he'd been magic on the ice. 'Wow.'

Her lips curved. 'Yeah. Wow. I got great seats, right behind the penalty box.' The smile faded. 'He liked introducing me as his girlfriend, the homicide cop.'

'So why did you get engaged to him?'

'I truly liked him. Guy's a nice guy and while he was playing, things were good. He wasn't home enough to make demands. Then he retired and things changed. He wanted to get married and I got sucked into the flow. Then Bernadette got involved. She had very specific ideas about how weddings, and wives, should be.'

'I take it you didn't fit her requirements.'

'No,' she said wryly. 'Anyway, I'd canceled one too many fittings for my dress and Bernadette threw a fit. I found out about it the next night when Guy took me to this fancy place downtown with linen and crystal and waiters who hovered.' She grimaced.

She'd hate a place like that. He stroked her chin with his thumb. 'And?'

'And Guy informed me that I'd canceled seventy-three percent of the appointments his mother had set for the wedding and then he got stern and added that I'd broken sixty-seven percent of our dates. That our dates came second was telling. Anyway, he insisted I "improve my performance." Yeah, I think that's how he phrased it.'

'And did he have any coaching tips on how you should do this?'

Her lips quirked up in amusement. 'Of course.' Again the smile faded. 'But the biggest gist of it was that I was to transfer to another department. Or better yet, quit altogether. I wouldn't be able to work once I was pregnant anyway.' She stared straight up at Reed, defiant challenge in her eyes. 'I'd been honest about that all along. I didn't want kids. He'd conveniently forgotten that fact or thought he could maneuver me into changing my mind. I reminded him and we had one major argument. And when it was done, I'd given him back his ring. He didn't think I'd do it in a public place like that with the china and linen.'

He felt a stir of pride at her stand. 'He was wrong.'

'Yeah, but I hurt him. I didn't want to and I didn't mean to, but I did. He wanted a home and a wife and in the end he got a homicide cop.'

It was too much of who she was to change, but he could feel some sympathy for LeCroix. 'I should say I'm sorry.'

One corner of her mouth lifted. 'Would you be?'

He ran his fingertip under the fullest part of her breast, watched her areolae pucker and her nipples stand erect. She had incredible breasts. 'No,' he said huskily.

Her eyes darkened in response. 'Then don't. Anyway, I think Guy was less impacted by the whole breakup than Bobby was.'

Ah. Now they were getting somewhere. 'Bobby. Your father.'

Her smile was brittle. 'My father. He liked the thought of having Guy LeCroix as a son-in-law. I think in his mind it was the best thing I'd ever done.'

He frowned at the bitter hostility in her voice. 'Better than being a cop?'

'I was never a cop to him. I was just a . . . *girl*.' She spat it, like the worst of epithets. 'Good for marriage. If he got good hockey seats out of the deal, all the better.'

Reed reached over her, pulled the old chain with its dog tags from the nightstand where he'd dropped them earlier. He'd thought it odd that she'd worn them as she'd never been in the military. He held them up to the light. *MITCHELL, ROBERT B.* 'They're his. Why do you wear them if you hate him?'

Her brows crunched. 'Your mother . . . did everyone know she was abusive, or did she have a nice face she let everyone on the outside see?'

The need to know that had spurred him on suddenly froze. 'Mia, did your father . . . ?'

Her eyes shifted, then came back to him, shadowed and full of guilt. 'No.' But he didn't believe her and his stomach rolled at the images his mind stirred up. 'No,' she repeated, a little more forcefully. 'He mostly just hit. When he got drunk.'

His first impulse was to draw away, afraid of breaking her, but he didn't. Knew he couldn't. He swallowed back the queasy bile that burned his throat. Because he thought she needed it, he pressed his lips to her temple and held them there. 'You don't have to tell me any more, Mia. It's all right.'

But she kept going, her eyes now glued to the dog tags he still held in his hand. 'When I was a kid, I used to think that if I was fast enough, smart enough, good enough . . . that he'd stop drinking. Be the father to us that he pretended to the rest of the world that he was. I was the star athlete in high school. I thought it would make him care. When I realized that he wasn't going to change, the sports became my ticket out.'

'You went to college on a soccer scholarship,' he remembered. 'You got out.'

'Yes. But Kelsey was still home, getting wilder and wilder.' Her lips pursed and he wondered what it was that she wasn't letting out. 'It was her way of punishing Bobby. She couldn't make him stop, but she could embarrass the hell out of him, and once Kelsey got something in her mind, she wouldn't let it go.'

A family trait, he thought. 'She got in trouble.'

'Oh, yeah. Took up with this addict named Stone. I tried to stop her, but she . . . wanted nothing to do with me. By the time she was seventeen she was hooked. By nineteen, she was in prison. For the first three years she was in, she wouldn't even see me. Then she did and . . .' She let the thought trail. Swallowed hard. 'She's all I have left. If Marc can't get her transferred . . .'

'Has Marc Spinnelli ever lied to you?'

'No. I trust him more than any man I've ever known. Except maybe Abe.' She drew a breath and let it out. 'And I suppose, you. I've told you things I shouldn't have.'

Something inside him shifted. 'I won't tell. I promise.'

'I believe you. I think tonight put me on edge more than I'd like to admit. I really hate getting shot at.' She flicked the dog tags in his hand. 'But I never answered your question. The day I got my badge my father took me out with his cop friends at their bar. I was one of them then. A part of . . . something. Do you understand what that means?'

He nodded. To be a part of something close-knit and supportive when you'd been alone for so long. He'd had that with the Sollidays, then with the fire department. Then with Christine. 'It was like being in a family. Finally.'

'Yeah. Anyway, Bobby was in his element, showing off. It was a big day, he said. And in front of everyone he gave me the dog tags. Said they'd kept him safe in Nam and hoped they'd keep me safe on the force. What was I going to do? I'd grown up with most of these guys but none of them ever knew what really went on in our house.'

'Or they chose not to,' he murmured and she shrugged.

'Who knows? Anyway, I put them on, intending to take them back off, but before I made it home I was in an accident. My car was totaled and I walked away without a scratch. I thought maybe the dog tags had some luck after all. And over the years, I've been lucky more times than I want to count.'

He pressed a kiss to her shoulder where a puckered scar had formed. 'Murphy told me about the other time. When your first partner got shot. He said they almost lost you.'

'I was lucky then, too. Bullet hit me right here.' She

touched her abdomen. 'Went straight through, missed every major organ. It was then I found out that I was missing a kidney. I'd been born without one, so there was nothing there to hit. The bullet sailed through and I was good as new.' She looked away. 'And Ray died. After that I had to add on the medic alert tag because of the kidney. A few times I almost took the dog tags off, but never did. I guess there's enough superstition in me to keep them on.'

She'd put the engraved medic alert tag behind her father's dog tags. He wondered if she even knew she'd done so. 'Or maybe a part of you still needs to please your father,' he said and her eyes went flat. Carefully she slipped the chain around her neck.

'You sound like Dana. And you could be right. Which, Lieutenant Solliday, is the real reason I want no strings. I'm too fucked up not to hang myself with them.' She rolled away and sat on the edge of the bed, alone, and his heart wanted to break.

'I'm sorry, Mia.'

'Really?' Her voice was harsh.

'This time, yes. I am. I—' Her cell phone started to ring. 'Dammit.'

She grabbed her phone from the nightstand. 'It's Spinnelli.' Eyes on Reed's, she flipped it open. 'Mitchell.' She listened and the air rushed out of her lungs. 'I'll call him. We'll be there in under twenty.' She snapped her phone shut. 'Get dressed.'

He already was. 'Another one?'

'Yeah. Joe and Donna Dougherty are dead.'

His eyes shot up, his hands paused on his belt buckle. 'What?'

'Yeah. Apparently they moved out of the Beacon Inn.' She pulled her shirt over her head and her eyes flashed. 'Apparently they were the original targets after all.'

Friday, December 1, 3:50 A.M.

He hadn't come home. The child lay in his bed, curled into a ball, listening to the muffled sounds of weeping down the hall. It wasn't the first night his mother had cried in her bed. And he knew it wouldn't be the last. Unless he did something.

He hadn't come home, but his face was on the news. He'd seen it himself. So had his mother. That's why she'd cried all night. *We have to tell, Mom*, he'd said, but she'd grabbed him, her eyes wild and scared. *You can't. Don't say a word. He'll know.*

He'd stared at her throat, the top of the mark showing above her dress. The slice was long and deep enough to leave a scar. *He'd* done that to his mother, the very first night. And threatened to do worse if they told. His mother was too scared to talk.

He tucked himself harder into the ball, shaking. *So am I.*

COUNT TO TEN

Friday, December 1, 3:55 A.M.

The front of the house was intact. Two firefighters were coming from around the back, pulling the hose. The odor of fire still hung in the air. Mia made her way past the fire truck to where two uniforms stood talking to the ME tech. It was Michaels, the guy who'd processed Dr Thompson's body less than twenty-four hours before. Behind him were two empty gurneys, each with a folded black body bag.

'What do you have, Michaels?' she asked.

'Two adults, one male, one female. Both about fifty. Male's been stabbed in the back with a long thin blade, woman's had her throat slit. Both were in bed at the time. The bed was ignited, but ceiling sprinklers put out most of the flames so the bodies are burned, but not charred. I left the bodies in the bed until the fire marshals had a chance to look around. I understand they're on their way.'

'I called Lieutenant Solliday as soon as I got the word. In fact,' she said, looking over her shoulder, 'that should be him right now.'

Solliday's SUV pulled to the end of the line of cars. He grabbed his tool bag before making his way to the fire truck. He stopped to talk to the company chief, flicking occasional glances up at the house. Once, he lifted his hand in greeting, as if she hadn't just come from his bed. As if she just hadn't told him her damn life story in the most embarrassing and humiliating of ways. *What was I thinking?* What was he, now?

His was the best way to handle it, she supposed. She turned back to the uniforms. 'Who ID'd the couple as the Doughertys? Last we heard they were in the Beacon Inn.'

'The homeowner. She's sitting in the cruiser,' one of the uniforms said. 'Her name is Judith Blennard.' He led Mia to the cruiser and bent down, speaking in an overly loud voice. 'Ma'am, this is Detective Mitchell. She'll want to talk to you.'

Judith Blennard was about seventy years old and didn't weigh many more pounds. But her eyes were fierce and her voice boomed. 'Detective.'

'You'll have to speak up, Detective. They carried her out without her hearing aid.'

'Thanks.' Mia crouched down. 'Are you all right, ma'am?' she asked loudly.

'I'm fine. How are Joe Junior and Donna? Nobody will tell me.'

'I'm sorry, ma'am. They're dead,' Mia said and the woman's face crumpled.

She covered her mouth with a thin, bony hand. 'Oh dear. Oh my.'

Mia took her hand. It was ice cold. 'Ma'am, why were they staying with you?'

'I've known Joe Junior since he was five years old. No better people in the world than Joe Senior and Laura Dougherty. Always volunteering with charities, taking in lost boys. When I saw what had happened to Joe Junior and Donna, it seemed right I should return the favor and take them in. I offered to let them use my addition for as long as they needed it. They refused at first, but . . . This was no coincidence, Detective.'

Mia squeezed her hand. 'No, ma'am. Did you see or hear anything?'

'Without my hearing aid, I don't hear much of anything. I go to sleep by ten and I don't wake up till six. I'd still be asleep if that nice fireman hadn't come in to get me.'

It wasn't David Hunter's company, Mia had noticed right away. As the firefighters packed up their gear, Reed finished talking with the chief and started toward them, talking into his little recorder. He stopped at the cruiser and Mia motioned him down.

'This is Mrs Blennard. She owns the house. She knew Joe Dougherty's parents.'

Solliday crouched down beside her. 'The fire took out the addition only,' he said loudly. 'Somebody was smart enough to build with firewalls and sprinklers.'

'My son-in-law is a builder. We built the addition for my mother. We were afraid she'd leave a burner on or something, so we installed extra sprinklers.'

'It saved your home, ma'am,' he said. 'You can probably go back in a few days, but we'd like you to stay somewhere else tonight if you don't mind.'

She gave them a sharp look. 'My son-in-law's coming to get me. I'm not a foolish old woman. Somebody killed

Joe Junior and Donna tonight. I'm not sticking around for him to come back for me. Although it would be nice to get my hearing aid.'

'I'll send someone in for it, ma'am.' Solliday gave the request to one of the officers, then motioned to Mia. 'The sprinklers wreaked havoc from an evidence preservation standpoint, but the bodies weren't burned.'

'That's what Michaels said. Can we go in?'

'Yeah. Ben's already inside and I'm waiting for Foster to get here with his camera.'

'And I called Jack. He's sending a team.' She followed him around the back and inside where Ben Trammell was setting up the field lights.

'The fire only burned the bedroom, Reed,' Ben said. 'And not that much. We could get lucky this time and get something to tie our guy to this scene.'

'Let's hope,' Solliday said, shining his flashlight up at the ceiling. 'Nice installation. The sprinklers wouldn't have been noticeable to White.' The field lights came on and everyone stared at the bed. Mr Dougherty lay on his stomach looking sideways and Mrs Dougherty lay facedown in the pillow. Blood soaked the bedding.

'He died immediately,' Michaels said from behind them. 'Blade went right through his heart. She's got defensive wounds.' He lifted her gown to show a large darkening bruise on her lower back. 'Probably his knee.'

'Did you cut her nightgown?' Mia asked and Michaels shook his head.

'We found her that way. The fabric's sliced clean through.'

'Do a rape kit, okay?'

He shot her a glance. 'Doesn't appear to be any evidence of force, Detective. This lady bruised pretty easily and there are no bruises on her thighs. But we'll do the kit.'

'Thanks. Can he take them?' she asked Solliday and he nodded. Frustrated and sad, she stood with Reed at the foot of the Doughertys' bed as Michaels took them away. Then shook herself back into focus. 'He killed Mr Dougherty first,' she said.

'Because he would have tried to protect his wife.'

'Right. He died painlessly. But Mrs Dougherty . . . He tied her up, shoved a knee in her back and at some point flipped her over and cut away her nightgown.'

'But then it looks like he didn't rape her. I wonder why. I can't see him as merciful all of a sudden.'

'He could have gotten disrupted. Then he flipped her back over and slit her throat from behind. Spooked and run. Why?'

'I don't know. Why the Doughertys to begin with?'

'It doesn't make sense,' she agreed. 'The Doughertys didn't even know Penny Hill.'

'And we've been looking for ties that didn't exist all week,' he added grimly.

But more than the wasted hours reading files, Mia was thinking about Roger Burnette and the grief in his eyes when he'd confronted her about their lack of progress. 'We need to tell Burnette. He needs to know he's not responsible for Caitlin's death.'

'Do you want me to go with you?' he asked.

She thought about the drunken rage in Burnette's eyes. Having Solliday along probably would be smart. 'If you would.'

'When I'm done here we'll go.'

'I'll call Joe Dougherty's father in Florida.' She was headed for her car when she heard her name. It was one of the officers and he held a white cat.

'Detective? We found this cat outside and Mrs Blennard says it belonged to the Doughertys. She can't take it with her to her daughter's house.'

Mia stared at the cat. 'What do you want me to do with it?'

He shrugged. 'I can call animal control or . . .' He smiled engagingly. 'Want a cat?'

Mia took the cat with a sigh. The ID tags on his collar looked remarkably like her dog tags. 'You're a lucky cat, Percy. You dodged a bullet twice this week.' The cat blinked up at her. 'Kind of like me,' she murmured. 'You can sit in my car for now.'

Friday, December 1, 5:05 A.M.

He felt her behind him before she spoke. 'Anything?' Mia asked.

Reed shook his head. 'No. He didn't use gas, because

there isn't any. He didn't coat Donna Dougherty's chest with the solid accelerant like Penny and Brooke.'

'He did use an egg with a fuse,' Ben said from the corner where he was sifting through debris. 'That's about the only thing he did that was the same.'

'I notified Joe Senior and did some door-to-door.'

Reed could see how much it cost her. 'Did you ask him how Joe Junior and Donna were linked to Penny Hill?'

'I tried. After I told him about their deaths, he stopped talking.' Her brows crunched. 'I called the local sheriff and they found him passed out on the floor, still holding his phone. They rushed him to the hospital. They think he had a heart attack.'

'This just keeps getting better,' Reed said. 'That poor man.'

'I know. I wish I'd known he had a heart condition. I'll get next-of-kin information on Donna Dougherty from her office when it opens in a few hours. On the plus side, I did get a description of a suspicious-looking car that sat on the street for about two hours tonight. A girl and her boyfriend were making out in the boyfriend's backseat and every time they came up for air they saw this car. Light blue Saturn.'

'Did they get a plate number when they were coming up for air?' Jack asked wryly.

'Only half. Oh, and he let the cat out again.'

'Where is Percy?' Reed asked.

'In my car. He's clean this time. If you're ready, I still want to go to Burnette's.'

'Let's go.' He waited for her to leave, then groaned. An *Action News* van sat on the side of the road, a well-groomed Holly Wheaton standing in the street. He felt Mia tense next to him. 'Don't say anything,' he murmured. 'Please. No matter how much you want to rip off her face. Don't mention Kelsey or her story. Let me say "no comment." '

Holly walked up to them, a feral gleam in her eye. 'This is the fourth fire the arsonist has set this week. What are the police doing to keep the people of Chicago safe?'

'No comment,' Reed said and walked faster, but Holly was not to be deterred.

'The victims here were Mr and Mrs Joe Dougherty, the same couple whose house was destroyed last Saturday night.'

Mia stopped and Reed wanted to protest. But he'd cut her off at the knees the last time the two dueled. This time he'd keep his mouth shut. As long as he could, anyway.

'We don't release the names of victims until their families have been notified.' She looked directly at the camera very soberly. 'It's our department policy and it's the humane thing to do. I hope you agree. Now, if you'll allow us to get back to our jobs.'

'Detective Mitchell, Caitlin Burnette will be buried today. Will you be there?'

Mia kept walking and Reed started to draw an easy breath.

'Detective Mitchell, some have said the murder of Caitlin Burnette was related to her father's career. Do you think a child should be punished for the sins of her father?'

Mia paused, her body snapping rigid. Her head turned, her mouth opened to spit out what would no doubt have been a scathing retort on Burnette's behalf. Then Reed felt the abrupt change as her shoulders relaxed. She stepped up her pace. 'Follow me,' she said, her voice low so that only he could hear. 'Holly might have something.'

Chapter Nineteen

Friday, December 1, 5:40 A.M.

Mia met him at the curb. 'I'm sorry. I didn't want her to follow us here.'

Reed looked around. It was a well-kept neighborhood. 'Where is here?'

'Blennard's daughter's house. Something Wheaton said about the sins of the father made me think.'

'Wheaton was just trying to get a rise out of you, Mia.'

'I know.' She started walking up the front walk. 'But what if the Doughertys were killed because of the sins of Joe Junior's *parents*? And based on the way Donna Dougherty died, the sins of his *mother*? Blennard said the Doughertys were always taking in boys.'

Realization dawned. 'Foster parents. And they're both Joe Dougherty. Joe Junior never even needed to change the name on the mailbox. He killed the wrong couple.'

'I think so. I tried calling to confirm with Joe Senior,

but the cops in Florida say his heart attack was really bad. He's intubated, so he can't talk. But maybe Blennard remembers something.' She rang the bell and a man came to the door. 'I'm Detective Mitchell and this is my partner, Lieutenant Solliday. We need to talk to Mrs Blennard.'

'Clyde, who is it?' Mrs Blennard came to the man's side, the hearing aid now in her ear. Her eyes widened. 'What can I do for you, Detectives?'

'Ma'am,' Mia started. 'You said the Doughertys "took in lost boys." Did you mean they were foster parents?'

'Yes. For ten years or more after Joe Junior moved away and got married. Why?' Her old eyes sharpened. 'The other woman killed, Penny Hill . . . she was a social worker.'

One side of Mia's mouth lifted in respect. 'Yes, ma'am. Do you remember any trouble they had with anyone? The boys? Their families maybe?'

She frowned, thinking. 'It's been a long time. I know they took in a lot of boys. I'm sorry, Detective, I can't remember. You should ask Joe Senior. I'll get you his number.'

'It's all right. I called him.' Mia hesitated. 'Ma'am, he didn't take the news well.'

The old cheeks went a shade paler. 'His heart's been bad for years. Is he dead?'

'No, but he's not good.' She tore a page from her notebook and scrawled a name. 'This is the officer I talked to in Florida. Now, we have to go. Thank you.'

'He spared Joe Junior and stopped in the middle of his revenge against the woman he thought was Laura Dougherty,' she said when they were outside.

'Because he realized he had the wrong woman. It makes sense. Nice job.'

'Would have been nicer if I'd figured it out sooner.' She stopped at her car where the white cat lay curled on her seat. 'Now we have to find a list of all the kids Penny Hill placed with the Doughertys.'

'And figure out which kid is connected to White.'

'Or whatever his name is. Move over, Percy.' She got in, shoved the cat to the passenger seat. 'But first, I have to talk to Burnette.'

'I'll follow you there.'

Friday, December 1, 6:05 A.M.

Mia was waiting at the curb. 'The house is dark,' he said. 'They're probably asleep.'

Mia turned only her head, leveled him a sober look. 'Reed, he's going to bury his daughter today. Burnette thinks he's responsible. If it were Beth . . . Could you sleep?'

Harshly he cleared his throat. 'No. I couldn't.' They walked up the sidewalk to the door where the picture of the turkey still hung. Such a small thing, but it made his chest hurt. Time had stood still for this family. For a week, a father had lived with the knowledge that he'd been a tool in his child's brutal murder. If it had been Beth . . .

Mia knocked. The door opened to Roger Burnette, his face haggard and worn.

'Can we come in?' Mia asked and he nodded wordlessly and led them inside.

In the living room, Burnette stopped with his back to them and Reed couldn't help noticing that the room which had been so neat and tidy before now . . . was not. Mostly there was clutter. But in one wall there was a hole, waist-high and fist-sized and Reed could picture a father tormented by grief and rage and guilt putting it there.

Burnette slowly turned. 'You caught him.' It was barely a murmur.

Mia shook her head. 'Not yet.'

Burnette's chin lifted, eyes cold. 'Then why are you here?'

Mia met the man's eyes without wavering. 'We found out tonight that the real target at the Doughertys' house was the previous homeowners. Joe Dougherty's parents.' She paused, let it sink in. 'Not Caitlin. And not you.'

For a moment Burnette stood, rigid and unmoving. Then he nodded. 'Thank you.'

She swallowed. 'Try to sleep now, sir. We'll see ourselves out.'

They'd turned for the door when Reed heard the first sob. More like the cry of a wounded animal than a man.

But it wasn't the expression on Burnette's face that stabbed Reed's heart the deepest. It was the expression on Mia's. A naked, desperate longing that before last night Reed would not have understood.

Roger Burnette had loved his child. Bobby Mitchell had not.

Shaken, Reed took her arm and gently pulled. 'Let's go,' he murmured.

'Detective.'

Drawing a deep, shuddering breath, Mia turned back. 'Sir?'

'I'm sorry, Detective. I was wrong.'

Reed frowned, but Mia seemed to know what he meant. 'It's all right,' she said.

'No, it's not. I said some terrible things. You are a good cop. Everyone says so. Your father would have been very proud and I was out of line to say anything different.'

The nod she gave Burnette was harsh. 'Thank you, sir.'

Under Reed's hand, she trembled violently. 'We'll be going now,' Reed said. 'Again, our condolences.' He waited until they stood at the curb. 'What was that?'

She wouldn't look at him. 'He came by last night. After you left. He was not pleased that we had not caught the man who mutilated and killed his child.'

Fury took him by surprise. 'The bruise on your arm?'

'It was nothing. He's a grief-stricken father.'

'That didn't give him the right to put his hands on you.' Reed's own hands clenched.

'No, it didn't.' She started walking. 'But at least he cared.'

'And your father wouldn't have. I'm sorry, Mia.'

Her hand faltered on the car door. 'Yeah. Well.' She sniffed at her sleeve. 'I smell like a stale fireplace. I'm going back to Lauren's for a shower before morning meeting. Do you think she'd mind if I brought Percy with me? He's had kind of a hard week.'

The subject of Bobby Mitchell was closed. For now. 'I'm sure she wouldn't mind at all.'

'Fine. I'll meet you at Spinnelli's at eight.'

He stood frowning as she drove away. She'd pulled away and he didn't want to admit that it stung. But it did. This, he supposed, was the flip side to no-strings. He could walk away when he wanted to. So could she.

It was what he wanted. What she'd said she needed. Now he had to wonder if either of them truly knew what they were doing.

Friday, December 1, 7:10 A.M.

'There,' Mia muttered as she poured kitty litter into the plastic box as Percy watched. 'Don't say I never bought you anything.' She opened a can of cat food and dumped it in the bowl that said CAT she'd thrown in the Wal-Mart cart on impulse on her way back to Lauren's.

She put the bowl on the floor and sat as Percy chowed down.

'I'm an idiot,' she murmured aloud to no one at all, cringing as she thought of all she'd told Reed last night. But in his arms it had seemed a natural thing to do. He was a good listener and . . . hell. She'd become a typical female, spilling her guts in pillow talk after mind-blowing sex. She rolled her eyes, mortified now.

'I'm an idiot.' She'd laid herself bare to a man who'd been honest enough to say he only wanted her for mind-blowing sex. This morning, standing in Burnette's living room, Reed Solliday had seen and understood way too much. And he'd pitied her.

The thought rankled, burned deep. She'd wanted him on equal terms. Sex. No strings. Pity completely fucked that up.

She looked around Lauren's kitchen. She didn't belong here. That he'd manipulated her into coming here proved they'd never really been on equal terms. She should just pack her bag and leave. She eyed the cat. Maybe Dana would take him.

Dana owed her that much, with all that damn talk of hamburger and having it all.

She stood up. Dana would take the damn cat. Then tomorrow she'd find a new place. Give Lauren back her house. And as for Solliday . . . She had to be honest. No need to throw out the baby with the bathwater. She still wanted mind-blowing sex. So first, she had to get them back on equal terms. No more pillow talk. No more pity.

Friday, December 1, 8:10 A.M.

'Well, at least we finally have the connection,' Spinnelli said grimly.

'By noon we should have a list of names,' Mia said from the opposite end of the table, where she'd very deliberately placed herself. 'Social Services is going through all the files from the period when the older Doughertys were foster parents.'

'Before we only took Penny Hill's files for the last two years,' Reed added, trying not to focus on the fact that she hadn't looked at him once. 'We never would have found them listed. Once we get names, we can start matching them to his picture.'

Spinnelli went to the whiteboard. 'Okay, we've got some irons in the fire now. I want to know who the hell this guy really is and where he lives.' He was making notes on the board as he spoke. 'I want to tie him to the first two fires with something more than access to the plastic eggs and I want to know why the hell he's doing all this.

'Murphy, you and Aidan find out where he lives. Continue showing the teacher's picture in the area where we found the car he used to get away from Brooke Adler's. Find somebody who knows this guy outside of Hope Center. Jack, have we found anything physical tying him to either the Doughertys' house or Penny Hill's house?'

'There's nothing left in the houses that we haven't sifted through,' Jack said.

'We never found Penny Hill's car,' Reed said. 'Maybe he left something there.'

'Penny's boss gave us a list of the gifts she got at the retirement party.' Mia rubbed the back of her neck wearily. 'If somebody found her car, they may have hocked them.'

'I'll have someone check the pawnshops,' Spinnelli said. 'Mia, anything from Atlantic City PD?'

'Not yet. I'll call them to see if they found either of our guys on their tapes.' She squinted at the board. 'We're missing something. We need to know why he's doing this but also why *now*? Miles said that something triggered this to happen *now*.'

'What do you recommend?' Spinnelli asked.

'I dunno. But I still get a very strange feeling from that school. He taught for six months, then all of a sudden goes on an arson and murder spree. Why?'

'You talked to the teachers about Brooke,' Spinnelli said. 'Ask them about White.'

She nodded. 'Okay.'

'I want to know how he knew where to find the Doughertys last night,' Reed said. 'They checked into the Beacon Inn on Tuesday. Judith Blennard said they came to her house Wednesday afternoon. He found them Thursday night. He couldn't have been waiting all day for them to leave because he was at Hope Center teaching.'

'The hotel must have told him,' Mia said. 'We should go by on our way to Hope.'

'Aidan, you take Atlantic City PD. Mia and Reed will cover the hotel and the school.'

Aidan wrote it in his own little book. 'Will do.'

'Anything else?' Spinnelli asked.

'Caitlin Burnette's funeral is at ten,' Mia said. 'Do you think he'll go? Should we?'

'I'll handle that,' Spinnelli said. 'Jack's got video surveillance planned and I'll be in the congregation. I honestly don't think he'll be there. Caitlin was an accident, but I'll watch. You're all dismissed. Call me with any news. I have a press conference at two this afternoon and I'd like to look reasonably capable. Mia, stay for a minute.'

Reed waited outside the door, but he could still hear.

'Kelsey got moved at oh-seven-hundred this morning. She's safe.'

Reed heard her tired sigh of relief. 'Thank you.'

'You're welcome. Oh, and Mia, try to catch a few hours' sleep. You look terrible.'

Her chuckle was wry. 'Thank you.'

Reed fell into step alongside her when she came through the door. 'I think you look pretty damn good,' he murmured.

He'd hoped she'd laugh, but the look she sent him was almost grave and sent a sudden shaft of panic through his heart. It was the first time she'd really looked at him since leaving Burnette's house. 'Thank you,' she said quietly.

He said nothing until they were sitting inside the SUV. 'What's wrong?'

'Just tired. I have to make some time to go apartment hunting tomorrow.'

He felt the breath leave his lungs. 'What?'

She smiled at him, but it was cool. 'I never expected to put Lauren out for more than a night or two. Reed, staying at your place was temporary. We both knew that.'

Temporary. He was beginning to dislike that word. But she was right. He hadn't planned to oust Lauren from her side of the duplex forever. *So for how long had you planned to have Mia stay? Until your craving was satisfied? Until you got tired of her?*

Yes. No. *Hell.* 'And us?'

She was perfectly calm and his heart was pounding which irritated the hell out of him. 'For as long as we want to continue. Let's get to work. Beacon Inn, please.'

Jaw tight, he pulled into traffic and made it to the next light when her cell phone rang.

'This is Mitchell . . . Yeah, put him through. Mr Secrest, what can I do for you?' She bolted upright. 'When? . . . Have you touched anything? . . . Fine. We'll be right there.'

Reed pulled into the left lane to do a U-turn back toward Hope Center. 'What?'

'Jeff DeMartino is dead.'

Friday, December 1, 8:55 A.M.

'He didn't respond to the morning wake-up call so the guard called the nurse,' Secrest said. 'The nurse called me and I called you.' The boy lay on his back, skin waxen, lifeless eyes staring up at the ceiling. CSU was already snapping pictures.

'When was the last time anybody saw him alive?' Mia demanded.

'The guards check every room in this unit every thirty minutes during the night. He was here in his bed.' Secrest looked frustrated. 'The closest anybody can remember seeing him walking, talking, and breathing was last night at nine thirty. That's his group's assigned shower hour.'

'Excuse me.' Sam Barrington stepped inside the room, filling it further.

'We got the big guns this time,' Mia murmured and Reed hushed her.

'Nobody's touched him, Sam,' Reed said.

'Where's the nurse? I want his medical history five minutes ago.'

Secrest held it out. 'She pulled his file right after she called me.'

'Where is she?' Sam repeated, pulling on gloves. 'I want her *here*.'

Secrest gave the folder to Mia with a scowl. 'She's in the infirmary. I'll call her.'

Sam crouched close to examine the boy. 'Spinnelli asked me to come. The victim's been dead at least ten hours. No obvious wounds or trauma . . . except . . .'

Reed stepped to Sam's left, Mia to his right. 'Except what?' she asked.

'This.' Sam held up the boy's hand. 'He's got a cut on his thumb and it's fresh.'

'Before-dead fresh or after-dead fresh?' she asked.

'Before. *Just* before.' Sam stared down at the boy. 'Let me see his file.' Mia passed it to him and Sam scanned. 'He was healthy. No heart issues, no asthma.'

'Just a little cut,' Mia mused. 'Where's the blood from the cut?'

'There's a smudge on the blanket,' the CSU tech said. 'Right on the edge.'

'On the middle of the bed,' she said. 'Like he was sitting there and wiped it. You see a knife?'

The tech shook his head. 'It could be under him.'

'You done with the pictures?' Sam asked the tech. 'Then let's roll him. Gently.' Sam and Reed lifted and Mia crowed.

'There it is,' she said. 'Jackknife with the blade pulled out.' It lay flat on the bed.

'Don't touch it,' Sam snapped when she reached a

gloved hand under the body. 'If it's what I'm thinking, you don't want to touch it.'

Mia's brows went up. 'Poison?'

'Yeah.' Sam crouched down, shone a flashlight at the boy's bare back. 'From the lividity and the bruising, I'd say he was lying on the hilt of the knife before he died.'

'He fell on it,' she said thoughtfully. 'Now, where would Jeff get a knife?'

'Same place Manny got matches?' Reed countered.

'Looks like Manny may have been telling the truth. Did you look at those matches?'

Reed shook his head. 'No, but I want to now.'

Sam looked from Reed to Mia. 'You're thinking they were booby-trapped.'

'Yeah.' Reed nodded and turned to where Secrest stood watching from the doorway. 'Do you still have the matches you found in Manny's room?'

Secrest nodded. 'In my office. I'll get them for you.'

Mia held up her hand. 'Mr Secrest, just a minute, please. Who were the boys in Jeff's group? The ones who shared the shower hour?'

'Jeff, Manny, Regis Hunt, and Thaddeus Lewin. The boys call Thad "Faggeus."' An uncomfortable expression tightened Secrest's face. 'Thad was taken to the clinic Thanksgiving night.'

'For?' Mia asked.

'He complained of a stomach-ache,' the nurse said. 'But he'd been assaulted.'

Secrest moved so that the nurse could get through.

She stood looking at Jeff with a curious mixture of contempt and . . . satisfaction that made Reed frown.

'Assaulted how?' Reed asked and she looked up, met his eyes.

'Thad was sodomized. There was rectal tearing. He denied it happened.'

'And you think Jeff did it,' Reed said quietly.

She nodded. 'But Thad wouldn't talk. All the boys were afraid of Jeff.'

'Which is why you're glad he's dead,' Mia said and the nurse's eyes went hard.

'I'm not glad he's dead.' She shrugged. 'Per se. But he was a vile, angry, mean boy. We were terrified of what he would do when he was released next month. Now we don't have to be afraid anymore.' Suddenly she snapped her gaze up to Secrest. 'Thad had a visitor Thanksgiving night. Devin White. Thad called him.'

'Your trigger,' Reed murmured.

'You're right,' Mia murmured back, then cleared her throat. 'I'd like to take Thad and Regis Hunt downtown for a chat. Line up your advocates and have them meet us there.' She looked around. 'Where's Bixby? I would have thought he'd be here for this.'

Again Secrest looked uncomfortable. 'He hasn't arrived yet.'

Mia rolled her eyes. 'Wonderful. I'll get a unit to his house and an APB for his car.'

COUNT TO TEN

Friday, December 1, 10:10 A.M.

The manager at the Beacon Inn was irritable. 'Excuse me,' Mia said.

He didn't look up. 'I'm sorry, ma'am, but you'll need to wait your turn.'

The customer at the counter smirked. 'End of the line's down there,' the man said.

'Want me to teach him some manners?' Reed murmured behind her and she huffed a chuckle, ignoring the shiver that raced down her spine. This was why she didn't do cops and why it was against regulations to do partners. Even temporary ones. It was too damn hard to concentrate. She'd pulled off being cool and collected when he'd asked 'about us' but it had taken everything she'd had. Now she focused on the hotel manager, who'd made the unfortunate choice to ignore her.

'No, let me.' She slapped her shield on the counter. 'Take a break, pal.'

The manager's look was murderous as his eyes lifted. 'What now?'

Mia frowned at him. 'What do you mean, "What now?" You, wait over there,' she said to the customer who was no longer smug. 'I'm Detective Mitchell, Homicide. This is my partner, Lieutenant Solliday, OFI. What do you mean, "What now?"'

'Homicide? I was afraid of that.' His eyes filled with weary resignation. 'I'm sorry. Half my staff is out with the flu and my assistant manager never showed up for her shift this morning. I'm Chester Preble. How can I help you?'

'First, tell me what's happened here,' she said, softening her tone.

'Officers in uniform came by this morning, checking out a missing person report. Niki Markov. She checked in Wednesday and her husband called Thursday morning. Said she wasn't answering her phone. I told him perhaps she'd stepped out.' He shrugged uneasily. 'People come here to get away from their spouses, if you know what I mean. We try to be discreet.'

'But the husband filed a missing person report,' Mia said, instinct sending a new shiver down her spine. 'And she hasn't come back.'

'She wasn't due to check out until today. Her clothes are still hanging in her closet.'

'What room is she in?' Mia asked.

'Room 129. I can take you to it if you give me just a minute to check out the people who have planes to catch.'

'Sir,' she said sharply, 'this is a homicide investigation. These people have to wait.'

'You found her . . . body, then?' he asked, some of the color draining from his face.

'No. I'm investigating another homicide. A couple who checked out Wednesday were killed last night. Joe and Donna Dougherty. Can you see what room they were in?'

He tapped a few keys, then all his remaining color drained away. 'Room 129.'

'Hell,' Solliday murmured.

Mia raked her fingers through her hair. She had a headache brewing. 'Yeah.'

Friday, December 1, 10:50 A.M.

'You rang?' Jack asked and came into room 129 with his CSU team, all wearing white coveralls.

'Niki Markov, reported missing. This was Joe and Donna Dougherty's room until Wednesday,' Mia said.

'You think he came, thinking they were still here,' Jack said. 'And found Markov.'

'Her clothes are in the closet,' Solliday said. 'But all her suitcases are gone. Those are her sales materials stacked there on the bed.'

Jack grimaced as he grasped what she and Solliday had already surmised. 'Oh God.' Then he gave a brisk nod to his team. 'Start checking this room,' he said. 'I'll check out the bathroom.' Quickly, capably, he removed the trap from the tub. 'We'll check it for hair and ... other stuff.' He then treated the shower tiles with Luminol. Thirty minutes later, he turned out the lights.

Every surface glowed. For a few beats, the three of them just stared.

'That's a hell of a lot of blood,' Jack finally said.

'Given the suitcases are gone, I think a reasonable assumption is—'

'That he dismembered her,' Mia finished grimly. 'Good God. I'm losing count.' She pressed her fingers to her temples. 'Caitlin, Penny, Thompson, Brooke and Roxanne . . .'

'Joe and Donna,' Solliday added quietly. 'Jeff and now Niki Markov. That's nine.'

She looked at him. 'Count to ten?' she asked and he shrugged.

'Maybe. Although he had nothing against this woman.'

'She was an accident,' she murmured. 'Like Caitlin. Wrong place, very wrong time.'

'I'll see what I can find,' Jack said. 'In all this mess, he had to have left something.'

'And I'll get the information on her next of kin. I got the number for Donna's from her boss on the way over.' She sighed, dreading the task as she dreaded no other. 'Then I'll tell Markov's husband and Donna Dougherty's mother that they're dead.'

'I'll tell them,' Reed said. 'You don't have to do that alone, Mia.'

She nodded wearily, surprising him. 'All right. Call us when you find something, Jack. We'll see if he took Markov's car. Hopefully we'll find her body.'

Friday, December 1, 11:50 A.M.

Jenny Q slid her tray next to Beth's and sat down. 'So what are you gonna do?'

'I don't know. I do know I'm not missing this, Jenny. He's being so damn stubborn.'

Jenny sighed. 'And I had my sister all ready to cover for us. Cost me, too.'

Beth squared her jaw. 'I'll just . . . leave,' she said and Jenny laughed.

'No, you won't. You're not going to just walk out with him screaming behind you.'

'No,' Beth agreed. 'I'll find another way.'

Friday, December 1, 1:30 P.M.

'I'd hoped for a suspect in custody,' Spinnelli said quietly. 'Not two more bodies.'

They had regrouped. Mia sat between Murphy and Aidan, and Reed had been joined by Miles Westphalen. Sam sat at the far end of the table and Jack was still at the Beacon Inn, processing the Markov crime scene. Reed brooded, still depressed from breaking the news to two families that the people they loved were never coming home.

He didn't deal with death often in his role as a fire investigator. The apartment fire last year was the biggest loss of life he'd dealt with in his career. He couldn't fathom how Mia dealt with the families day after day for all the years she'd been with Homicide.

Across the table, she sighed. 'We don't know where he is, but we're getting closer to motive. It had something to do with the kid's, Thad's, assault. We've got Thad Lewin and Regis Hunt in separate interview rooms. We'll talk to them when we're done here.'

'I found the solid accelerant on the matches Secrest found in Manny's shoe,' Reed said. 'If Manny had lit one he would have been severely burned.'

'Secrest checked the security tapes for White's classroom for Tuesday, the day they searched Manny's room,' she said. 'He saw White pause next to Manny's desk. He might have dropped the matches in his shoes then, or not. But he did find White on video dropping the knife into Jeff's open backpack.'

'Did they check the third boy's room? Regis Hunt?' Aidan asked.

'Secrest found another knife in Hunt's room,' Mia said.

'Coated with D-tubocurarine,' Sam said. 'Both knives were coated with it. And I found it in the victim's urine tox.'

Reed frowned. 'Tubocurarine? Are you sure?'

'I did the rush urine tox myself,' Sam answered. 'I never saw a curare victim before and I was interested. My initial take is that the victim died of respiratory failure.'

Mia's eyes widened and a chuckle of disbelief

escaped her lips. 'Curare? Like in Amazon jungle tribes and poison darts? You're joking.'

'No, I'm not,' Sam said. 'Today it's used in surgery. It's available in hospitals, veterinary clinics . . . All your guy would have had to do was steal a vial and cook it down in a glass pot on the stove.' He stood. 'Thanks for lunch. I have to get back now.'

'Aidan?' Spinnelli said when Sam was gone. 'Anything from Atlantic City?'

'Yeah. The Silver Casino found the real Devin White on their tapes. He was an inept gambler until his luck suddenly changed. Not enough to kick him out, but enough that they watched him. Security remembered him because at the end of his stay, he met with a certain well-known card counter who *had* been thrown out of the casino.'

'Math Boy,' Mia murmured.

'Yeah. He went by the name Dean Anderson, but they found the real Anderson died two years ago. Casino security said our guy had a gift. Could calculate odds in his head like a computer. But the casino people weren't the only ones who remembered him. The police have had him on their short list for the last year.'

'Do I want to know why?' Spinnelli asked.

'Rape,' Aidan said succinctly. 'A string of rapes for the six months before last June. They'd been watching Anderson but they think he made them. Then in June the assaults stopped. They had no idea where he'd disappeared to.'

'He met the real Devin White, helped him win, won his trust.' Mia shook her head. 'Then he took his life and . . . took his life.'

'It would explain why he faked his prints for the school. He knew he was wanted and didn't want to get traced back,' Murphy said thoughtfully.

'That's what I figured. And,' Aidan added, 'most of the rape victims had broken legs so they couldn't run or kick. When we find him, New Jersey wants a bite.'

'They'll have to stand in line,' Mia muttered.

'We have to catch him first,' Spinnelli said, 'and we still don't know the bastard's real name. Murphy?'

'We've covered about half the search area. Nobody's seen him.'

A thought poked through the dark cloud in Reed's mind. 'Did you check pet shops?'

'No,' Murphy said. 'Why?'

'Because this guy likes animals and he's had access to a surgical pharmacy. Some of the big pet shops have vet offices in them now. I just took my daughter's puppy to one for his shots. One-stop shopping. It's worth a try.'

'Yeah, it is,' Murphy agreed. 'I'll go when we're done.'

Spinnelli stood up, tugged at his uniform. 'I've got to get to that press conference. We've had about three hundred calls on the photo the news services have been broadcasting. Stacy's weeded out the obvious crackpots. Aidan's eliminated some of the others. I've left the list on your desk, Mia.'

She turned to Westphalen who'd been silent. 'What are you thinking, Miles?'

'I'm thinking there are patterns here as well as an understanding of human nature.'

'Okay,' she said. 'What about the patterns?'

'Numbers. He says "count to ten" and does mental statistics to help him gamble. He's been very precise in everything he's done. And think about this. He stole Devin White's identity, but he didn't have to take his job. He likes math. He likes numbers.'

'He managed the football pool at Hope.' Mia pulled the stat sheets they'd taken from the computer in his classroom and frowned. 'He lost often.'

Reed went around the table to look over her shoulder. 'But he lost only when the Lions lost. He picked the Lions even when his own statistics said they'd lose.'

She looked up at him, a smile playing on her lips. 'Home team sentiment?'

He nodded. 'Our boy's got ties to Detroit.'

'Let's send his picture to Detroit PD. See if anybody recognizes him.'

'Send it to their Social Services,' Miles suggested. 'I'll bet he's been in trouble before. And he knows the way these kids' minds work. Look at the traps he set for Manny and Jeff. He tempted them with the things he knew they'd be powerless to refuse.' He waved his hand before Reed could say a word. 'That they'd choose not to refuse,' he amended.

'Thank you,' Reed said dryly. 'But you're right. He

did pick the best temptation. And even if Manny didn't light the matches, he was caught with contraband. He knew the first thing Jeff would do would be to test the sharpness of the blade, to see if it was real. And even if he didn't, he'd be caught. Sent to real jail. You're right. He knows the drill. He's spent time in juvie or knows someone who has.'

'Thank you,' Miles said, just as dryly. 'One other thing. The way he focused on the Doughertys. He missed them twice and went back for them a third time.'

'He had to finish,' Mia said. 'They're super important or he's super compulsive.'

'I'm thinking some of the first, more the second,' Miles said. 'Maybe his compulsive personality is something we can use.'

'But like Spinnelli said, we have to find him first,' she sighed.

Murphy tapped the table with his ever-present carrot stick. 'Mia, you said you'd have the list of the kids Penny Hill placed with the Doughertys by noon.'

'You're right. I should have had the list by now. I'll call them. Aidan, can you keep helping us with the three hundred phone calls?'

'Sure.'

She stood up. 'Then let's go.'

Chapter Twenty

Lido, Illinois
Friday, December 1, 2:15 P.M.

He'd forgotten how much he hated the sight of corn. Miles of corn. As a boy it had mocked him, swaying so gently, as if everything were all right with the world. This place, this house, this corn . . . had become Shane's grave.

They'd rebuilt the house on the same foundation. The new place was bright and cheerful. A kid's tricycle was in the yard and a young woman moved around inside. He could see her when she passed in front of the window as she went about her chores.

Chores. He'd hated the farm chores. Hated the man who'd brought him here so that he could have another pair of hands for slopping pigs. He hated the woman who'd known what was going on under her own roof and wouldn't help. He hated the younger brother for being a coward. He hated the older brother for . . . He pursed his lips as a shiver of rage singed his skin. He hated the older brother. He hated Penny Hill for being too stupid to see the truth from the beginning and too lazy to ever come back and check on them.

Penny Hill had paid for her sins. The Young family was about to get the same. He got out of his newest car as the young woman came out the front door, a toddler on her hip. She stopped the minute she saw him, afraid.

He smiled his most pleasant smile. 'I'm sorry ma'am. I didn't mean to startle you. I was looking for a friend. He lived here and we lost touch. His name is Tyler Young.'

He knew exactly where Tyler Young was. In Indianapolis selling real estate. But he didn't know where the other Youngs were. The woman stayed where she was, her hand on the knob of her front door, ready to flee. Smart woman.

'We bought this place from the Youngs four years back,' she said. 'The husband had died and the wife didn't want the farm anymore. I don't know about the boys.'

The rage fanned hotter. Another dead before he could mete out his revenge. Still he kept his face calm, slightly disappointed. 'I'm sorry to hear that. I'd like to visit Mrs Young, pay my respects. Do you know where she is?'

'Last I heard, she had to go in a nursing home in Champaign. I have to go.' She slipped inside. He could see her fingers on the window blinds as she watched him.

He got back in his car. Champaign was less than an hour away.

Chicago, Friday, December 1, 4:20 P.M.

'My eyeballs are going to fall out.' Fatigue and a headache made Mia petulant.

'What did you come up with?' Solliday asked, stifling a yawn.

'Of the twenty-two kids Penny placed with the Doughertys, three are dead, two in jail and six are still in foster care. Of the others, I've got current addresses on two.'

He ran a thumb down the side of his goatee. 'Any come from Detroit?'

'Not that any of the birth records show.' She stood and stretched, then dropped her arms to her sides when she saw his eyes following her movements. 'Sorry.'

'Quite all right,' he murmured. 'Don't stop on my account.'

She wouldn't let herself smile. Equal terms. She came around his side of the desk. He'd been checking phone records for the Beacon Inn. 'What did you find?'

'The hotel gets a hell of a lot of phone calls. None trace to Hope Center, but I didn't think they would. I figured if he called for the Doughertys, it would have been on a disposable cell or from a phone locally. These are the numbers I'm still working.'

Mia ran her finger down the list. 'This one's from where Murphy's searching.'

He typed the number into the reverse lookup screen.

'You've got a good eye, Mia. It's a pay phone.' He dialed the hotel and put it on the speaker.

'Beacon Inn, this is Chester. How can I help you?'

'Chester, this is Lieutenant Solliday with the OFI. Detective Mitchell and I are here with another question for you. We're showing a phone call to your front desk at 4:38 P.M. Tuesday. It may have been someone trying to get the Doughertys' room number.'

'No one would have given it out,' he said. 'It's against our policy.'

'Chester, this is Detective Mitchell. Can you find out who took the call?'

'Tuesday afternoon would have been Tania Sladerman. You can't talk to her. She didn't show up for . . .' He trailed off. 'Oh my God. She didn't show up for work today.'

Solliday's glance was sharp. 'Give us her address. Now.'

Friday, December 1, 5:35 P.M.

'Hell, Reed.' Mia stood in Tania Sladerman's bedroom, staring at the dead woman as the ME techs lifted her to the gurney and zipped the bag. 'This is ten.'

The assistant manager for the Beacon Inn had been raped, her hands and feet bound. Legs broken. Throat cut. 'I hope that's what he was counting, Mia, because then he'd be done. But I don't think so.'

'She's been here since Wednesday morning. Why didn't anyone miss this woman?' Emotion made her voice unsteady and she cleared her throat. 'Check on her?'

He wanted to put his arm around her, but couldn't. 'Let me take you home.'

She straightened her spine. 'I'm okay. I'll get a ride back to the precinct with CSU. You go home, Reed. You've got a daughter who wants to see your pretty face.'

He frowned. 'I don't think so. She and I had a pretty big argument yesterday.'

'About what?'

'A party this weekend. Jenny Q's. I didn't like her attitude, so I said she couldn't go.'

'Tough love. Go home, Reed. Spend some time with her. I'll call you if anything comes up.' He hesitated and she gave him a little push. 'I mean it. Go. It would make me feel better to know you and Beth were working things out. She needs her father.'

She started walking toward Tania's front door and he knew she was dismissing him. He wasn't ready to go yet. 'What about you and Olivia?' he asked, very quietly.

'We've been trading voice mails. I think we're going to try to get together tonight. I'll call you either way. I promise.' She leaned a little, teetering on her feet and he wanted nothing more than to take her in his arms, give her comfort. Take a little comfort back.

He dropped his voice. 'I found my key to the other side.' Her eyes flashed with awareness and memory.

Satisfied he'd sufficiently enticed her into keeping her promise, in his normal voice he said, 'All right. I'll see you tomorrow.'

Friday, December 1, 6:20 P.M.

Aidan was gone when she got back, but Murphy was there, typing his report in his slow hunt-and-peck way. 'Reed was right,' Murphy said. 'There were three pet stores in the area. Two of them had vet offices either inside or nearby. Petsville was my last stop – and guess what their supply closet was missing?'

'D-turbo-whatever-stuff. Amazon jungle poison,' she said and he grinned.

'You get the prize. After threatening them with a subpoena, I finally got a list of employees and just finished mapping their addresses. These people live in a one-mile radius of where we found the car he abandoned after he killed Brooke and Roxanne. He could have easily walked to any of them.'

'Fourteen households. I should be able to hit five or six still tonight.'

Murphy stood up. 'We should.'

'Murphy . . .'

'Mia . . . You can't go alone. What if you find him?'

She thought about the bodies she'd seen this week. 'You're right. If I go alone, I might kill him myself. I should call Solliday, but he's with his kid.'

'And you and me have no ties.'

She frowned at that. No ties. No strings. 'Murphy, do you ever want them?'

He paused in zipping his coat, shot her a grin. 'What, ties? Got a closet full of 'em.'

She shook her head, her mouth curving despite herself. 'I'm serious.'

He sobered. 'It's starting to get you, isn't it? All your friends pairing off.'

Abe, Dana, Jack and Aidan. Now it was down to her and Murphy. 'Yeah. You?'

He nodded. 'Yeah. But I've been married before.' He slung a brotherly arm around her shoulders. 'And you know what they say. Fool me once, shame on you.'

'Fool me twice, shame on me.'

'Come on. Let's go.'

Friday, December 1, 6:55 P.M.

The knock at their door broke the silence. His mother looked up, fear in her eyes.

'It's not him, Mom. He has a key.' That she'd given him. Why, he didn't understand. But once she had, it had been too late.

She got up, smoothed her hair. And opened the door. 'Can I help you?'

'We're sorry to bother you, ma'am. My name is Detective Mitchell and this is Detective Murphy. We're searching the neighborhood for this man.'

He sneaked around the corner and peeked. All he could see were legs. A pair of shoes and a pair of boots. Smaller. But he could hear them. The lady sounded . . . nice.

'Is that the man I saw on TV?' his mother asked, her voice small and scared.

'Yes, ma'am,' the lady detective said. 'Have you seen him?'

'No. I'm sorry. We haven't.'

'Well, if you see him, could you please call this number? And don't open your door to him. He's very dangerous.'

I know he's dangerous. I know. Please, Mom. Please tell them.

But his mother nodded and took the flyer the detective offered. 'If I see him, I'll call,' she said and shut the door. She stood for a minute, still except for her fist that crumpled the paper into a ball. Then she went to the sofa, crumpled herself into a ball and cried.

He went to his room, closed the door, and did the same.

Mia leaned against her car, her eyes on the tidy little house. Murphy leaned beside her. 'She knows something,' he said.

'Yes, she does. And she's terrified. She's got a kid.'

'I know. I saw him, peeking around the corner.'

'I did, too.' She blew out a breath. '*He* could be in there, right now.'

'Looked like the dinner table was only set for two. If he's there, he's hiding. She's a pet store employee, so technically she wouldn't have had access to the vet's office. Just a terrified face probably isn't enough to get us a warrant to search her place.'

'Let's check the houses on this street. Maybe somebody saw him. If so, that could be enough for a warrant.' She pushed away from the car, when a movement caught her eye. 'Murphy, look up at the window.' Little fingers were pulling at the blinds.

'The kid's watching us.'

Mia smiled warmly and waved. Immediately the little fingers disappeared and the blinds went flat. Her smile faded. 'I want to talk to that kid.'

'Then we need to get inside the house. Let's start knockin' on doors.'

Friday, December 1, 7:30 P.M.

'Well?' Murphy asked. 'I got bubkes.'

'Nobody's seen him. Nobody even knew her. One person remembers seeing the kid riding his bike to school. You know, when I was a kid, everybody knew everybody else. You were afraid to do anything bad, scared it would get back to your parents.' Mia jangled her car keys in her pocket. 'Okay, now what?'

'Now you go home, sleep. I'll stay here and watch. I'll call you if anything pops.'

'I shouldn't let you do that, but I'm too tired to argue with you.'

'Which says a lot,' Murphy said mildly. 'Mia, are you okay?'

They'd been friends a long time. 'Not really.' To her mortification, tears stung her eyes and she blinked them away. 'I must be more tired than I thought.'

He caught her arm. 'If you need me, you know where to find me.'

Her lips quirked up. 'Yeah, here, freezing your fool ass off all night. Thanks, Murphy.' Murphy was a good friend. Tonight, she wanted more than a friend. Tonight she wanted . . . more. *Strings*, the voice in her mind taunted. *Go ahead and admit it.*

Fine. She wanted strings. But God knew she didn't get everything she wanted.

Friday, December 1, 8:15 P.M.

Mia recognized the car waiting at the curb and wanted to groan. Hell, she wasn't up for a heart-to-heart with little sister tonight. Olivia met her on the sidewalk in front of Solliday's duplex, holding a pizza box. 'So you found me.'

'I pulled a few strings, got your partner's address. Hope you don't mind.'

Yes, I mind, she wanted to scream. *Come back when things . . . settle down.* But they wouldn't settle down and Olivia had to go home soon. And Bobby's other child needed to know the truth. Or some of it anyway.

'No, I don't mind. Come on in.' Lauren's place was quiet and dark, but next door she could hear the TV and music. Reed was there. But she'd get through this first.

Reed heard her come in. He'd been sitting in front of the TV, watching something that meant nothing, just waiting for the slam of the door on the other side. Beth was sulking in her room. Lauren was studying. He was alone. And, he admitted, lonely. But Mia was there, on the other side of the wall and even if it was watching her eat leftover meat loaf, he wouldn't be alone when he was with her.

He grabbed the glass bowl from the oven with mitts and slipped out the back door. Cradling the warm bowl under one arm like a football, he reached for the doorknob and stopped. She wasn't alone. The other voice belonged to Olivia Sutherland.

He should go home. Give her privacy. But he remembered her eyes as she'd bared her secrets in the night. And how she'd rolled away from him. Alone.

They were two people, wandering through life alone. And he wondered why two intelligent people would insist on making that choice.

*

Mia led Olivia to the kitchen and took the pizza. 'It's stone cold.'

'I waited awhile.'

Mia sighed. 'I'm sorry. This case . . .'

'I know.' Olivia unzipped her jacket and slipped the scarf from her head, looking a little like an old-time movie actress. Elegant and a little unsure. And so young.

And unspoiled. A shaft of resentment poked her heart and Mia was ashamed. It wasn't Olivia's fault she'd escaped Bobby Mitchell. She slid the pizza onto a pan and into the oven. 'So . . . Minneapolis PD. You're a detective, too.'

'I earned my shield last year,' she said. 'You've been doing this longer.'

Mia sat down and nudged the other chair with her foot. 'I'm considerably older.'

Olivia sat down, her movements graceful. 'You're not even thirty-five.'

'I feel like seventy today.'

'It's a bad case, then.'

Ten faces flashed through her mind. 'Yeah. But if you don't mind, I don't want to think about it for a while.' She looked at Olivia's hand. 'You're not married.'

'Not yet.' She smiled. 'Trying to build my career first.'

'Hmm. Don't wait too long, okay?'

'Sisterly advice?'

Mia blew out a breath. 'Hardly. I did a pretty lousy job of it the first time around.'

'You mean Kelsey.'

Something in Olivia's eyes made Mia's hackles go up. 'You know about her.'

'I know she's in prison. Armed robbery.' Her tone was mildly judgmental.

Mia clenched her teeth. 'She's paying her debt.'

'All right.'

But it wasn't. It wasn't all right. Nothing was all right today.

'You, on the other hand,' Olivia continued, 'are a decorated cop and were engaged to a hunky hockey player.'

Mia blinked 'You've been watching me?'

'Not until recently. I didn't even know about you until recently.'

'But you said you hated me all your life.'

'I did. But I didn't have a name or face to go with you until he died.'

'What did your mother tell you?'

'For years, nothing. We didn't talk about my father and I kept dreaming he was out there, that he'd come for me. When I was eight, Mama told me the truth, or most of it.'

There was pain there. Mia wondered just how the truth had come out. 'Which was?'

'My mother was nineteen when I was born. She met my father in the bar where she waited tables in Chicago. She said that my father was a good man, a policeman. They started talking and one thing led to another. She thought she was in love, then found out she was pregnant. When she told him, he told her he was married. She hadn't known.'

'I believe that,' Mia said quietly and watched Olivia's shoulders sag. 'You didn't.'

'I wanted to. I didn't want to believe my mother would play around with a married man. But knowingly or not, that's what she did. He said he'd leave his wife, marry her.'

'But he didn't.'

'No. She said after I was born, he came to her and said he couldn't leave his wife and daughters. That he was sorry.'

Bobby was sorry she'd been born Olivia and not Oliver, Mia thought, but nodded. 'And that's when your mother took you to Minnesota.'

'Shortly thereafter. She'd burned some bridges with her own parents. They'd wanted her to give me up for adoption, but she kept me. It was a while before I had a relationship with my grandparents, but eventually things smoothed over. I'd come to Chicago on my summer vacations and look at every cop and wonder, was that him?'

'You didn't know his name?'

'No, not until he died. Mama wouldn't tell me and nobody else seemed to know.'

'Is your mother still living?'

Pain flashed in Olivia's blue eyes. 'No. She died last year. I thought my father's identity had died with her, but my mother had told her sister. Aunt Didi called me the day his obituary appeared in the paper. I drove straight from the airport to the cemetery.'

She sighed. 'And then I saw you, standing next to your mother, in your dress uniform. Your mother gave you his flag, then you saw me. You didn't know about me.'

'No. It was . . . quite a shock.'

Olivia looked down. 'I imagine it was. The first time I saw your name was in the obituary. It didn't mention Kelsey.'

'That was my request. The official department obituary had her listed, but I asked them to remove her name. I didn't want anybody to make the connection.'

'That makes sense. It can't be good for your career, having a sister in prison.'

Mia stiffened. 'It's not good for her health having a sister who's a cop. Don't judge Kelsey, Olivia. Not until you know her.' *Not until you know everything.*

'All right. When I saw you, I was shocked. There's some . . . family resemblance.'

'I noticed that,' Mia said dryly. 'Why didn't you come and talk to me?'

'I was so shocked at first, I didn't know what to do. You were the one I'd hated my whole life. You were the one who got a father. Who got a home. A family. Mama and I, we had nothing. No one. And then to see you, dressed as a cop, looking at me. Looking *like* me. Afterward, I went to Aunt Didi's house and got on the

Internet and found out everything I could about you.'
She stood up and checked the pizza. 'You forgot to turn
on the oven.' She hit the knob impatiently.

'I'm not a culinary kind of person.'

Olivia turned, her eyes now flat. 'What kind of
person are you?'

'You did the research, kid. You tell me.'

She considered it. 'I've checked you out thoroughly
this week. You're a cop first.'

'Last and always,' Mia finished, her voice now as flat
as Olivia's eyes.

'But you have compassion. Dedication. The reporters
hate you, so you must be doing something right.' Mia
huffed a chuckle at that and Olivia's lips curved. 'You
have a few close friends, you're intensely loyal. You've
had a few boyfriends, and one fiancé. He was hot by the
way.'

'Thank you.'

'You've just started a relationship with Lieutenant
Solliday and you don't want anyone to know. But I
think most people do.'

Mia frowned. 'What do you mean?'

'It's hard to miss. Big flashing neon sign over your
head. "I like him. Stay back. He's mine." Oh, I've finally
hit a chord. You're blushing. He's hot, too, by the way.'

Mia rolled her eyes. 'Thank you.'

Olivia sobered. 'You're welcome.' She turned to the
fridge, opened it and stared inside, closed it again. 'I'm
impressed and resentful and jealous, all at once.' She

turned back around and met Mia's eyes. 'Honest enough for you, big sister?'

Mia nodded. 'Yeah. But I'm not sure you're going to like it when I return the favor.'

Olivia drew a breath calmly. 'All right.'

'Your father is not the man you wish he was.'

Her eyes flickered. 'Nobody's perfect.'

'No, but Bobby Mitchell swung to the far left of the bell curve. He drank too much and he hit his kids.'

Her eyes narrowed. 'No.'

'Yes. You know what I thought when I saw you tonight? That I was impressed and resentful and jealous all at once. You may have had nothing, but nothing was better than what we endured in that house.'

'How can nothing be better than something?' Olivia asked bitterly.

'I'm a fast healer, which is a good thing, because Bobby had big fists and he used them often. Not so much on me. Mostly on Kelsey. Stitches and broken bones and lies to doctors all over town.' Olivia's eyes were horrified. 'And that's the truth.'

'That's . . .'

'Horrible? Unbelievable? Irreconcilable?'

'Yes. He can't have . . .'

'Been that bad? I'm *lying*?'

She shook her head. 'That's not what I meant. Kelsey was a wild kid. Maybe . . .'

Mia lurched to her feet. 'Maybe she *deserved* it?'

Olivia's chin lifted. 'She is in prison, Mia. On a plea.'

'Yeah, she is. She ran away from home when she was sixteen. Got mixed up with some bad people. She wasn't lily white, but she wasn't like them.'

'But she did it. Look, she's your sister. Of course you'd feel compassion for her.'

Mia's throat closed and her eyes filled. 'You don't know what I feel.'

'You've been a cop long enough to know that people make choices. She chose to run away. And having a father beat her wasn't justification for pulling a gun on a store clerk while her boyfriend killed two people. A father and a little boy are dead and Kelsey is responsible. Surely you can't excuse that.'

The blood was pounding in Mia's head. Yep, little sister did read the papers, even the really old ones. 'No, I don't, and neither does Kelsey. You might be surprised to learn she hasn't actively petitioned for her parole. She'll serve her time until she's done. And when she's done she'll have spent more than half her life behind bars.'

Olivia looked surprised, but her jaw was still hard. 'It's what she deserves.'

Mia's lips curled. 'You have no idea what she *deserves*. You know *nothing*.'

Olivia's eyes flashed fire. 'I know she had a family. A house to live in. Food to eat. A sister who loved her. Which was more than I had and I didn't turn out that way.'

Something snapped. 'Yeah, and *you* didn't have a father who traded sex for protection, either.' As soon as the words came out of her mouth, Mia wished them back. 'Goddammit,' she hissed.

Olivia stood there, every ounce of color drained from her face. 'What?'

'Hell.' Mia grabbed the edge of the sink and hung her head but Olivia yanked her arm until she looked up.

'What did you say?'

'Nothing. I said nothing. We're done. I can't do this anymore.'

'Is that what Kelsey *told* you?'

Everything went still, the implied accusation of Kelsey's lie hovering between them. 'Yeah, that's what she told me.' She swallowed. 'And it's what I know.'

Olivia's eyes were dark against her pale face. 'That can't be true.'

'It's true. Believe what you want about *your* father, but it's true about mine.'

Olivia took a step back, trembling. 'Then why did you become a cop? Like him?'

Like Olivia had, Mia realized and felt the pain of her loss as keenly as if it had been her own. 'Not like him,' she said wearily. 'I was raised around cops. Good, decent men. They had a sense of family I didn't have. I wanted that. And, I suppose I wanted to save kids like Kelsey since I couldn't save her. There are so many out there like Kelsey. You're a cop. You've seen them. I started helping kids like her, runaways. Then I got good at catching the bad guys who hurt them. Now, it's what I am. It's all I am.'

'I'm sorry.' Tears slid down her cheeks. 'I didn't know.'

'You couldn't have known and I didn't want you to. I thought I could make you understand what kind of man he was without knowing. But I didn't want you to grieve a man who wasn't worth spit on his grave. Or feel inferior because he didn't choose you.'

'I need to go.' She backed up, grabbed her coat and scarf. 'I need to go.'

Mia watched her run out the front door. Flinched at the slam. Then pulled the pizza from the oven. She wanted to throw it. But it wasn't her kitchen. It was Lauren's kitchen with the pretty framed cross-stitched teapots and flowers with the 'CS' in the corner. Made by Reed's wife. Whom he'd never found anyone good enough to replace.

Including me. Trembling, she carefully placed the pan on the stovetop and turned on the water, then the garbage disposal. Then under the cover of noise, let herself cry.

Reed stood at the window, his heart thundering in his chest. *Dear God.* His life before the Sollidays had been dark and dank and dismal. He'd been hungry and afraid. His mother had used her fists. But *this.* He'd been afraid of *this* last night. She'd denied it too forcefully. Her father had molested his daughters. Rage bubbled with hate and Reed would have liked nothing more than to resurrect Bobby Mitchell so he could kill him again. But that wasn't what Mia needed. He watched her shoulders heave as she cried and his own eyes stung. She'd do this. Cry so that nobody would hear. Nobody would come. Nobody would help.

She'd accept his help tonight. He opened the door, set the glass bowl on the stove, turned off the disposal and the water, then turned her into his arms. She stiffened, tried to pull away, but he held her firmly until her fingers curled into his shirt, hanging on.

Gently he pulled her across the kitchen, sat down and pulled her into his lap where her arms came around his neck and she clung, weeping so pitifully he thought his own heart would break. He held her tight, rocked her, kissed her hair until her tears were spent. She sagged against him, her forehead pressed against his chest so her face was hidden. It was her last defense and this he'd leave her.

She was quiet for a long time. 'You were listening again.'

'I came to bring you meat loaf. I can't help it that the walls are thin.'

'I should be mad at you. But I don't seem to have enough mad left.'

He ran his hands up and down her back. 'I'd kill him if he weren't already dead.'

'You don't understand.'

'Then tell me. Let me help you.'

She shook her head. 'We made a deal, Solliday. This is way too many strings now.'

He lifted her chin, made her look at him. 'You're hurting. Let me help you.'

She held his eyes. 'It's not what you think. He never touched me.'

'Kelsey?'

'Yeah.' She stood, walked to the back door and stared out the window. 'I remember the day I understood that Bobby would never change. I was fifteen and he was drunk. Kelsey had done something and he'd already belted her once. I begged him not to hurt her anymore and he made me a deal.' She paused, then sighed. 'He put his arm around me . . . Somehow I *knew*. He said if I did it, he'd leave Kelsey alone.'

Reed swallowed hard. 'You didn't.'

'No, I didn't. Instead I busted my ass to get a scholarship by day. I took one of his guns and slept with it under my pillow at night. He'd been so drunk, I didn't think he even remembered he'd said it, but I was taking no chances. I tried to tell Kelsey to be careful, to watch out, not to antagonize him but she wouldn't listen. She hated me then. Or so I thought.' She turned abruptly. 'Do you know the meaning of sacrifice, Reed?'

'I don't know how to answer that.'

Her mouth curved bitterly. 'Wise answer. See, I always thought I escaped the big beatings because I was faster than Kelsey. Because I was somehow better. Smarter. I didn't antagonize him. He left me alone. What Kelsey didn't tell me until a few years ago was that he'd made the same proposition to her.' She lifted her brows and said no more.

'Oh my God,' he breathed, unable to fathom it. 'Oh, Mia.'

'Yeah. All the time I was telling her to straighten and fly right, to stop provoking him . . . all that time . . .' Her voice broke. 'She did it. For me. Until I was gone to college. Then she ran away with a punk named Stone and ruined her life. Now she's in prison. Olivia was right. Kelsey did it. But I have to ask if she would have if things had been different. If the tables had been turned, would she be the cop? Would I be in jail?'

'You wouldn't have. You couldn't have.'

'And you don't know that,' she said, fury giving her voice a hard edge. 'I've listened to you debate nature versus nurture with Miles all week and I'm here to tell you it's not that easy, Reed. Sometimes people go wrong, when if things were different they would have gone right. You said yourself you nearly ended up in a place like Hope Center. What if you had? What if the Sollidays hadn't taken you in? Where might you be?'

'I never broke the law,' he said tightly. 'Even when I was hungry, I never stole a penny. What I am, I made.'

'And the Sollidays had nothing to do with that.'

'They gave me a home. I did the rest.'

She looked at him, something close to contempt in her eyes and he felt compelled to make her understand. 'I'd been a runaway for three years, off and on. I met up with some kids who stole purses. I never did. Then one day one of them did and threw the purse to me. The lady screamed I'd done it and called the cops. I almost got hauled in, but a bystander went to bat for me. She'd seen the whole thing and swore I was innocent. Her name was Nancy Solliday. She and her husband took me.'

'And I'm grateful to them,' she said quietly, her eyes calmer now. 'But Reed, realistically, how long would you have lasted on the streets?'

'I would have found any other way.'

'Okay. Look, I appreciate the shoulder, but I need some time to myself right now. I haven't run in days, so I'm going around the block a few times.'

She'd closed the subject again. 'What about your dinner?' he asked.

'I'll heat something up later.' She kissed his cheek. 'Thank you. I mean that. I'll call you when I'm back.'

Reed sat while she ran upstairs to change her clothes. She went straight out without saying another word, leaving him to stare at the kitchen walls. Christine had decorated this room, like she'd decorated all the others. Beauty, elegance with enough hominess to balance the effect. Left up to Mia, the room would have a microwave, a toaster oven for her Pop-Tarts, and a stack of paper plates.

He got up to put away the food, wondering how much more a man really needed.

Friday, December 1, 9:15 P.M.

Mia rounded the block, headed for Solliday's house for the second time. When she looked at apartments tomorrow, she'd look in nice old neighborhoods like this. At least three dog walkers had smiled and waved as she ran by. It was in marked contrast to her own neighborhood, where no one made eye contact, or the neighborhood where little boys peeked out their blinds and no one had any idea who their neighbors were. Which made her remember that she'd forgotten to tell Solliday that his hunch on pet shops may prove profitable after all. She pulled out her cell phone to check on Murphy's status when she saw something strange.

One of the bedroom windows in Solliday's house slid up and a dark head poked out and looked both ways. Then a body followed the head and shimmied down the tree outside her window as if it were a firepole. Looked like Beth Solliday was going to her party after all. Kelsey used to do that, she recalled. Climb out the window and meet God-knew-who and do God-knew-what. *But Beth, honey, you will not.*

Beth straightened her coat, pulled on her gloves and took off at a run across backyards, taking fences like a pro. Keeping her distance, Mia followed.

Friday, December 1, 9:55 P.M.

'You're late,' a girl with a ring in her nose hissed and pulled Beth inside. 'You almost missed your slot.' That, Mia supposed, would be the infamous Jenny Q.

Mia had followed Beth downtown on the El to some kind of club called the Rendezvous. The kid had been damn hard to keep up with. She should be running track.

Beth took off her coat. 'I had to wait. My dad went next door and I kept thinking he'd come back, but he didn't. I guess he's there for the night again.'

Again? So much for discretion, Mia thought. Solliday thought his daughter was innocent. Well, she hadn't gone to a party but she'd sneaked out. Mia wasn't sure what this place was. It wasn't a bar, because no one was carding. It had a stage and about fifty little tables where a diverse group lounged. Jenny and Beth disappeared into the crowd, but when Mia tried to follow a man tapped her arm.

'Ten bucks, please.' His badge said he was security. He didn't look like a druggie.

She dug in her pocket, pulled out her emergency twenty. 'What's going on here?'

He made change and handed her a program. 'It's competition night.'

'And who's competing?'

He smiled. 'Anybody who wants to. You want me to see if there's any slots left?'

'No. No thank you. I'm looking for someone. Beth Solliday.'

He checked his sheet. 'We have a Liz Solliday. You'd better hurry. She's on now.'

Feeling like Alice in Wonderland, Mia hurried in. The lights dimmed and a spotlight lit center stage. And out walked Beth Solliday in a leather miniskirt amid polite applause.

'My name is Liz Solliday and the title of my poem is "casper," ' she said.

Poem? Mia held her program up to the red glow of the exit sign and blinked. Whatever the hell Slam Poetry was, Beth had made the semifinals. As soon as Beth opened her mouth, Mia understood why. The girl had a presence on the stage.

did I mention that I live with a ghost?
we'll call her casper
she follows me
staring at me
her eyes my eyes her eyes
she's stolen my eyes
my dad, he's the one who invited her in
sometimes when he looks at me he winces
like he sees her when it's only me
and i'm willing to bet he wishes
he could make a trade if only for one day

Casper was Christine. Mia's throat closed, but Beth's

voice was strong. Like music. And as she spoke, her words touched the very place Mia hurt the most.

i'm just the doppelganger
reminding the world of the better version that once
    was
flitting through my father's life
almost invisible
her eyes darker
every day mine fade a little more
every day my purpose less certain
until i wonder who's the ghost
and who just deserves better

The spotlight dimmed and Mia let out a breath. Wow. Grateful for the darkness, she wiped her cheeks dry. Reed's daughter had a gift. A beautiful, exquisite gift.

Mia stood up. And Reed's daughter was in trouble. One hell of a lot of trouble. She pushed in her chair and went to find *Liz*, who had a great deal of explaining to do.

Friday, December 1, 10:15 P.M.

He was still out there, the man cop. The lady had driven away hours ago. He didn't know what to do. Yes, he did, but he was so scared.

But police were your friends. His teacher had said so.

If you're in trouble, you can go to the police. He turned from the window and sat on his bed. He'd think about it. He could tell the cops and maybe he would come back and hurt them. But maybe he would anyway. The lady on the news said he'd killed people, which he believed.

I can wait for him to come and get me and be afraid for the rest of my life, or tell and hope the police really are my friends. It was a scary choice. But at seven years old, the rest of his life was a really long time.

Friday, December 1, 10:45 P.M.

Beth edged closer to the window as the El carried them home. *I am so dead.* Her stomach rolled every time she thought about what her father would do. She chanced a glance at Mitchell, who sat quietly, arms crossed. Beth could see the bulge of her holster through her sweat jacket. She had a gun. Well, she was a cop.

She still couldn't believe the woman had followed her. *Followed her*, for God's sake. It had been the moment she'd dreamed of, stepping off the stage to all that applause. And not polite applause, either. The real thing. Jenny Q and all the group had been there, jumping up and down and hugging her. And then she'd looked up and seen Mitchell standing off to the side, brows lifted. She'd said nothing, but Beth's heart had dropped into her feet. It was still somewhere down around her gut.

I am so dead. Her choice had been clear. Leave quietly or the cop would cause a scene. So here she was, chugging on the El toward home and certain doom.

'Believe it or not, that was the first time I ever did anything like that,' she muttered.

Mitchell looked at her from the corner of her eye. 'What, slam poetry or shimmying down a tree to gallivant all over town when your father told you to stay home?'

'Both,' Beth said glumly. 'I am so dead.'

'You could have been, going downtown by yourself this time of night.'

Beth's eyes jerked to Mitchell's face. 'I'm not a kid. I know what I'm doing.'

'Uh-huh. Okay.'

'I do.'

'Okay.'

Beth rolled her eyes. 'I mean, yeah, the 'Vous isn't in the best part of town.'

'Nope.'

'Will you say something that's not monosyllabic?'

Mitchell turned to look at her, eyes cool. 'You are an idiot. A very talented idiot. Is that enough syllables for you? Although technically, "okay" is disyllabic.'

Beth sputtered even as the compliment warmed her. 'I'm not an idiot. I'm a straight-A student. Honor roll.' She shook her head, disgusted. Then sighed. 'But you liked it?'

Mitchell's eyes changed. Went from cool to devastated. 'Yes. I liked it very much.'

'I wouldn't have taken you for a poetry fan.'

One side of the woman's mouth lifted. 'I wouldn't have, either. "There once was a lady from Nantucket" is more my speed.'

Beth huffed a chuckle. 'The limericks crack me up, too.' She sobered and drew a breath. 'So, are you going to tell my dad?'

Her blond brows went up. 'Shouldn't I?'

'He's gonna freak.'

'As well he should. He's a good father, Beth, and he loves you.'

'He keeps me locked up like a prisoner.'

Mitchell's eyes flickered. 'Believe me, you're no prisoner. Do you love your dad?'

Beth's eyes stung. 'Yes,' she whispered.

'Then why didn't you tell him about the slam thing?'

'He's not into this kind of stuff. He's into sports. He wouldn't understand.'

'I think he would have tried.' She sighed. 'Look, I don't want to get between the two of you. I'll give you until tomorrow to tell him. If you don't, then I will.'

Chapter Twenty-one

Indianapolis, Friday, December 1, 11:00 P.M.

There it was. Tyler Young's townhouse. He sat in a car down the street, watching the neighborhood. He'd need to wait a little longer for this crowd to be in bed.

He was nearly calm. He'd had to get hold of himself back in Champaign. He'd waited too long to exorcise his ghosts, because now they were all dead. Laura Dougherty and now Bill Young and his wife, Bitsey. The wife had just passed on, the nursing home said sadly. And our records are confidential, they'd added mournfully, so no, we can't give you next of kin.

He'd nearly lost it. He'd held back only after seeing the flicker of suspicious fear in the nurse's eyes. So he'd respectfully excused himself, gotten in his car, driven to the middle of nowhere and set a cornfield on fire. Just a random act of kindness.

So he was down to two. Tyler and Tim. It was like Tim Young had dropped off the face of the earth. He could let Tim go. But Tim had been big enough, strong enough then. Just not brave enough to stop Tyler. He had to find them both. To finish this.

If Tyler knows where his brother is, by God, he'll tell me. Because this time, I hold the power. I'll hear him beg. Then I'll see him die. You count to ten, you fucking bastard. Then go to hell.

Chicago, Friday, December 1, 11:05 P.M.

Mia closed the door to Lauren's place. It was dark and quiet. 'Reed?'

But no one answered. She wandered through the house, half hoping she'd find him asleep on the sofa or better yet, in the bed, but the house was empty. *Just me.*

She should be tired, but she was still buzzed. She held Lauren's keys up to the light. There were two keys; one was for the other side. She could slip in, find him. Beth was safe in her room, having shimmied back up the tree despite Mia's objections.

She actually considered going up the same tree to Reed's room, but chucked the idea with a grin. She'd probably fall on her ass and break something. She fingered the chain around her neck. Or not. She seemed remarkably resilient these days.

Or not. She thought about sitting on his lap, crying her eyes out, then once again telling him things she had no business telling him. But he was easy to talk to and she'd wanted him to know. For the first time she'd wanted to throw her faults out there.

Maybe it was a test. To see if he'd throw her back. He hadn't yet.

She slipped into Reed's side of the duplex. It was quiet. She crept up the stairs, her heart pounding. If the house was a mirror image to Lauren's, the last door on the right was the master bedroom. There he was, sprawled on top of the bedspread, sleeping deeply with the light still burning. Still dressed down to his shiny shoes.

He'd had a long day, too. She'd get him comfortable, then go back to her own room on the other side. Then tomorrow, she thought, she'd find a new apartment as close to this house as she could. Because there was no way in hell she was having sex in this room. It was Christine's, down to the lace on the bedspread.

She frowned at the picture on his nightstand. Christine. Of course he'd have a picture of his wife. He loved her. Still. *He's never found anyone quite as good*, the little voice reminded her. Beth felt the same. It was when Mia went to loosen his belt that she saw the book. Carefully she slid it from his fingers and curious, peeked at the title, but there was none. It was a notebook, and every page inside was handwritten.

She glanced at his face. He still slept. She should put the book right down. Right now. But he'd listened to her conversations. This only seemed fair. She flipped to the front page. It said simply 'My Poems, by Christine Solliday' but the next page tightened her throat. 'To my darling Reed. I promised you my heart. Here it is.'

Poems. Every page was poems, in Christine's own hand. So Beth came by her talent naturally, she thought. And how wrong the girl had been about her father's understanding. Every page was worn, some dog-eared. This book was well read and well loved. It was Christine's heart. And Reed's.

The words blurred as she read and Mia blinked away the stupid tears. He'd been honest after all. He'd said no strings. *And like a fool I believed that would be enough.*

Hands trembling, she put the book on the nightstand and went to work on his shirt. A fine gold chain appeared, glistening in the dark hair of his chest. He hadn't worn it when they'd made love, but vaguely she remembered feeling it against her cheek earlier, as he'd held her and let her cry. She wouldn't cry now. Not yet. She'd put him to bed, then go back and . . . She got to the bottom of his shirt and her fingers went still.

At the end of the chain was a ring. A plain gold band. *He still wears his wedding ring.* Her heart squeezed painfully, but her hand was bent on self-torture and lifted the chain. The ring dangled, reflecting the light from the lamp.

With a jerk Reed woke, one hand closing over the ring while the other closed over her wrist with enough force to make her flinch. 'You're hurting me,' she whispered.

Immediately he released her arm, but his hand stayed wrapped around the ring. His face was hard and angry. 'What are you doing here?'

Mia took a step back. 'Obviously making a big mistake. Good night, Reed.'

She made it out of his room, down the stairs and out the front door. Her hands shaking, she managed to get the key in Lauren's front door and bolted inside. She stood, breathing harder than if she'd run a mile. She thought he'd follow her. Obviously that was a big mistake, too. Her whole body was shaking now. Badly.

Stupid. She hadn't eaten in . . . She couldn't remember the last time. She downed a slice of cold pizza, her stomach churning. When she was on her second slice the front door opened. Reed's face was pained, his shirt buttoned. If he still wore his ring, at least he had the decency to hide it from her. No, that wasn't fair. The ring was his business. *He told you from the beginning, Mia. No strings.* 'We need to talk, Mia.'

She shook her head. 'It's all right. Go back to bed, Reed.' He didn't move and her patience snapped. 'You know, I've had a really foul day. I would like to be alone now.'

He came closer, cupped her cheek in his palm. 'I'm sorry. I didn't mean to hurt you.'

'Don't be.' She swallowed back the lump that rose in her throat. 'You told me what you wanted from the start. I'm the one who keeps crossing the line. I can't play by your ground rules, Reed. I can't do an affair with no strings. I was wrong to try.'

He went still. 'Then maybe we can change the ground rules.'

Hope lit a little fire in her heart. Then she slipped her hand inside his shirt and pulled out the chain where the plain gold band dangled and the fire in her heart fizzled. 'You know, I spent most of my life competing with a dead boy I never knew existed for the love of a man who wasn't worth slime. I'm not going to compete with your dead wife, Reed, even though the prize would be . . . very worthwhile. I think I deserve better than that. Now, I think you should go. I'll be out of here tomorrow.'

She thought he'd argue, but he stood, his expression haunted and desolate. 'I guess I'll see you at work tomorrow.'

'Eight o'clock. Spinnelli's. I'll be there.'

She didn't see him to the door. She turned to the backyard, wishing things were different. That she was different. Then something brushed at her leg and she jumped.

Percy looked up at her, accusation in his eyes. 'Meow.'

With a weak laugh she picked him up. 'I'd forgotten about you. At least you can ask for your dinner, unlike poor Fluffy.' She rested her cheek against his soft fur, felt his purr. 'Let's eat, Percy, then bed.'

Indianapolis, Saturday, December 2, 2:15 A.M.

You'd think a realtor would have better home security, he thought as he let himself in through Tyler Young's patio

539

door. *His loss, my gain.* Shouldering his heavy load, he crept up the stairs, listening, but there was no sound except for the pounding of his own heart. *Finally.*

He would finally face the one who'd killed Shane, as an adult now, not the helpless kid he'd been. Two people slept in the bed, one a woman. A ceiling fan turned above the bed and along with Tyler's snores, covered his steps as he moved to the woman's side. One stab of his knife and she painlessly gurgled her last.

Tyler still snored heavily and this close, he could smell liquor on his breath. Good. Drunk people made such easy targets. Tyler would be that much easier to subdue.

He had dreamed of this as a kid, in the Youngs' house of hell. Every night he'd fantasized his revenge as Tyler . . . He swallowed, the memory making his stomach churn even now, ten years later. As Tyler did what Tyler did. The fantasies had kept him sane then. Now, those fantasies were about to come true. Now *he'd* do what Tyler did. Every single step. Quietly he fixed the chain he'd brought to the head of the bed, down at the floor. At the end of the chain was a cuff and with a click he snapped it around Tyler's beefy wrist. And held his breath.

But Tyler's snores continued. The rag for Tyler's mouth was soaked in urine, another little trick he'd learned from the man who was now his captive. But he had his own tricks now. With great care he took out the third of the knives he'd treated with his curare paste.

How easy to do, and how . . . exotic. His gun in his left hand, he quickly opened one of Tyler's veins with his right. Tyler's eyes surged open, but the gun was already aimed between the man's eyes. Horror filled Tyler's eyes by degrees as he took in the gun, the chain, his bleeding arm.

But there was no recognition and that pissed him off. 'It's Andrew.' He knew the moment Tyler remembered and laughed softly. 'In about two minutes you won't be able to move, but you'll feel every little thing I do.' He leaned in close. 'This time *you'll* count to ten, Tyler. This time *you'll* go to hell. But first, you'll answer to *me*. I'm going to take out this rag. If you scream, you will die. Understand?'

Tyler nodded, sweat beading on his forehead.

He removed the gag with distaste. 'Where is Tim?'

Tyler licked his lips nervously. 'If I tell you, will you let me go?'

He hadn't even asked about his wife. 'Sure.'

'New Mexico. Santa Fe.' He drew back a fraction of an inch. 'Now let me go.'

Before Tyler could react, he shoved the rag back in his mouth. 'You grew up stupid, Tyler. Let me help you. One, two, three . . .' And as he counted Tyler's body went stiff and rigidly still. 'Ten. It's showtime.'

He knew he didn't have much time. Under normal circumstances, Tyler would lose consciousness in under ten minutes. But after ten years, he wanted more than ten minutes and he wanted Tyler Young fully aware. He wanted Tyler Young to feel pain. He wanted Tyler Young to pay.

So he'd planned ahead. Placing his gun on Tyler's nightstand, he unpacked his kit. As usual he carried his sharp knife and lead pipe and his remaining plastic eggs, but tonight he'd brought a little extra along. He pulled an oxygen tank and mask from his pack. He'd be able to extend Tyler's conscious minutes by three times by forcing oxygen into his lungs. Tyler might just pass out from the pain first.

The thought made him smile.

'So, Tyler,' he said conversationally, placing the mask over the man's frozen face. 'How y'been? Molested any children lately?' Tyler and his wife had no children, at least no children that lived with them. He'd checked all the bedrooms before finding the master, and there were no children in this house. No pets either. So he could fully concentrate on his work. 'Can't talk? Too bad. You'll just have to listen to me. Don't worry, I'll keep you informed, every step of the way. First, I'll break your legs, just because I can.'

And he did, enjoying the way Tyler's eyes crossed with pain. He then rolled the pipe from one hand to the other. 'Normally I'm finished with the pipe by this point,' he said, still casually. 'But I have another use planned for you. See, I don't like men. Just women. But I'd hate to let that keep me from giving you the same pleasure you gave me.' He could tell Tyler understood. 'Excellent. Oh, and the knife? Normally I just slit throats

with it, but again, I have a special use planned for you.'
He grinned down at his victim, kept alive because he
wished it. Tyler would die when he wished it. 'You
called us dickless pussies back then. I guess you'll get to
find out what that term really means. So let's get this
show on the road, Tyler. Before the oxygen runs out.'

Chicago, Saturday, December 2, 6:35 A.M.

Murphy watched as Mia approached his car. He was
alert, but eyed the coffee cups in her hand with appreciation. He got out and stretched, then took one. 'Thanks.'

She leaned against the car, looking up at the house.
'Anything?'

'White never came back, but the kid's been watching.
There he is now.'

Once again the blinds bent and little fingers
appeared. Once again Mia gave him a warm smile and
a wave. Once again the kid disappeared. 'I say we try to
get a warrant. We've certainly gotten them on less
before.'

'I'll call a cruiser to watch while we're in meeting.
We'll coordinate with the others.'

The others. Which would include Reed. She would
do her job.

'Spill it, kid,' Murphy ordered in his mild way. 'What
did pretty boy Solliday do?'

She smiled, surprised she could. 'Nothing. He made

no promises, Murphy, and broke none. And I got a couple of nights of really good sex out of the deal.'

Murphy winced. 'Rub it in, why don't you?' He tilted his head. 'Let me know and I'll mess up that pretty face of his for you.'

'My hero.' Abruptly she sobered. 'Look what we have here.'

The front door opened and the kid came out, dressed for church in a dark suit and a clip-on tie. He paused on his front porch, then sucked in a breath and started walking, not stopping until he'd crossed the street to where they stood. He was holding the flyer they'd given his mother. It was flattened, but someone had crumpled it. His swallow was audible.

He was only about seven or eight. Reddish blond hair was carefully wet and combed. Freckles covered his face. She'd always been a sucker for freckles. Soberly she held out her hand. 'I'm Detective Mitchell. This is Detective Murphy.'

He shook her hand. 'I'm Jeremy.'

'Jeremy Lukowitch?' Murphy asked and the boy nodded.

'Where's your mom, Jeremy?' Mia asked.

'Still asleep. I think we should go to the station,' Jeremy said gravely.

'And maybe we will,' Mia said, then went down on one knee. 'Tell me, Jeremy, have you seen the man in this picture?'

'Yes.'

'When?'

He swallowed again. 'Lots of times. He lives here sometimes.'

Oh, sweet bingo. 'Do you remember the last time you saw him, honey?' she asked.

'Thursday morning before I went to school, but he came home late that morning.'

'Do you remember what time?'

'Five forty-five. I looked at my clock.' Jeremy lifted his chin. 'You should get a warrant to search our backyard.'

Mia's heart was knocking, but she kept her voice calm. 'What will we find?'

'He buried stuff there.' Jeremy started counting on his fingers. 'Thursday, Tuesday, Sunday and last Friday.'

Mia blinked. 'Last Friday?'

Jeremy nodded soberly. 'Yes, ma'am. Now I'll agree to testify if you give me and my mother witness protection. We'd like to change our names and move to . . . Iowa.'

Mia looked up at Murphy, who was unsuccessfully trying to bite back a smile, then back at Jeremy. 'You watch a lot of TV, don't you, Jeremy?' she asked.

'And I read,' he said. 'But mostly TV.' Then his chin trembled, spoiling his facade. 'I have to have the protection for my mom. He hurt her once. Really bad. She's afraid.' Tears filled his eyes. 'And she cries all the time. Please, lady, please don't let him hurt my mom.' He stood there, so brave and alone as tears ran down his freckled cheeks and Mia had to bite the inside of her cheek to keep from crying with him.

Crying would hurt Jeremy's expectation of cops. But she did gather him in her arms and hug him tight. 'We'll protect your mom, Jeremy. Don't worry, honey.'

Murphy already had his radio out, calling for support.

Mia backed away and wiped Jeremy's cheeks with her thumbs. 'You hungry, kid?'

He nodded, sniffling. 'We didn't finish our dinner last night.'

'I've got a breakfast burrito in my car. I'll split it with you while we wait for CSU.'

Jeremy nodded sagely. 'They should bring X-ray and metal detectors.'

Mia's lips twitched. 'I'll tell them you said so.'

Saturday, December 2, 7:15 A.M.

Reed stopped behind a line of cruisers and CSU vans. Nothing was happening yet. He supposed they were still waiting for the warrant. Mia was leaning against her department car. He approached, not knowing what to say, or how she'd respond.

He didn't know what he felt. Or what he wanted. It had been a sleepless night. She looked over and gave him a friendly smile that didn't come close to brightening her eyes. 'Lieutenant Solliday,' she said formally. 'I have someone here you should meet.'

Inside the car was a little boy, with strawberry blond hair and freckles.

'Lieutenant, this is Mr Jeremy Lukowitch,' Mia said. 'Jeremy, this is Lieutenant Solliday. He's a fire investigator.'

Fear shadowed the boy's eyes. 'Detective Mitchell says she'll protect my mom.'

'Then she will. She's a good cop.'

Mia swallowed, but her smile didn't falter. 'Jeremy, you wait here in my car where it's warm, okay? I'm going to trust you not to touch anything.'

'I won't.'

She started to walk away, then stuck her head back in the window. 'Jeremy, we won't go inside until we have a warrant, but will your mom come out?'

'She's probably still asleep. Sometimes she takes sleeping pills.'

Mia nodded briskly. 'That's fine. I'll be back soon.' She backed away from the car slowly, but her expression had grown grim. 'Are you EMT trained, Reed?'

'Yeah. You think she OD'd on pills?'

Mia was jogging now, going around the back where Jack Unger was poised for action, waiting for the warrant. 'Not knowingly, maybe. But she saw White. She lived with him. He's not gonna let her live.'

'We get the warrant?' Jack asked.

'Not yet. I think the mom took some pills. We're

going in.' She threw her shoulder into the back door and it cracked. But she winced and hissed. 'That hurt.'

'Y'think?' Reed said. 'Move.' And with one heave the door splintered. Both of them drew their weapons and he followed her in.

'Mrs Lukowitch, this is the police.' She ran back to the bedroom where a woman lay curled in a fetal ball. 'Aw, shit. Aw, hell. I smell cyanide.' She holstered her gun and felt for a pulse. Then stepped back. 'She's dead, Reed. Rigor's already setting in.'

Reed sighed. 'Eleven.'

'You were right. Bodies weren't what he was counting.' She closed her eyes. 'Now how do I tell that baby his mother is dead?'

'With me. I'll tell him with you.'

She nodded. 'Okay. Let's go.'

Saturday, December 2, 8:10 A.M.

Mia and Reed shielded Jeremy with their bodies as the ME wheeled his mother out in a body bag. But the boy wasn't watching. He was looking straight ahead, at nothing at all. Mia crouched down when the ambulance had driven away. 'Jeremy, sweetie, I have to work on your house.'

'What will happen to me?' he asked so softly she had to lean forward to catch the words. 'My mom is dead. My dad is gone. Who will take care of me?'

Me, Mia wanted to say, but didn't. This was a boy, not a cat. 'I've called a social worker. They'll put you in a temporary home until we can get something worked out.'

'A foster home,' he said dully. 'I've seen them on TV. Kids get hurt there.'

Reed shot her a look and she stepped back. He crouched down in front of Jeremy. 'Son, I know what you've seen on TV. But you need to understand, those are only the bad ones and they're rare.' The boy wasn't buying it, so Reed tried again. 'Jeremy, you're a very smart boy. How many airplanes do you think fly in America every day?'

Jeremy turned his head. 'Thousands,' he replied flatly.

'That's right. How many times do you hear about plane crashes on the news? Not many. You hear about the one or two bad planes, but never the thousands of good ones that reach their destinations safely every day. Same with foster homes. Bad ones happen, but they're rare. I grew up in a good one, so I know.'

Jeremy's shoulders sagged. 'Okay.' He looked up at Mia. 'Can I still see you?'

Her heart squeezed. 'You bet. Now we have to do our jobs, Jeremy. You sit tight and don't leave without me, Lieutenant Solliday, or one of these officers.'

His look was far too wise for seven years old. 'I'm not stupid, Detective Mitchell.'

She ruffled his hair. 'I know.'

Murphy waved to them. 'Got the warrant.'

'That was good, what you said to him,' she murmured as they walked. 'Thanks.'

'Mia . . .'

'Not now, Reed. I can't.' She hurried off, leaving him watching her back. Confused and torn he jogged after her to watch what buried treasure Jack would dig up.

Saturday, December 2, 10:30 A.M.

It was a good day to be alive. Things were finally looking up. Put on a happy face. He grinned as the ridiculous phrases flitted through his mind. He'd left Tyler alive and burning. Immensely satisfying. He'd nearly started straight for Santa Fe, but the adrenaline high had quickly ebbed. Exhausted, he found a cheap roadside motel and went to sleep. When he woke, he was clear-minded once more. He'd drive to Santa Fe, sticking to back roads. Once there, and once finished, Mexico seemed the best idea for lying low. Eventually his picture would be old news and he could return.

He had to go under. Hide like a girl. Because Mitchell had his picture everywhere.

Rage for the woman bubbled up and he pushed it back. He'd tried to get her once. He needed to learn from Laura Dougherty. Listen to fate. *Let it go*.

Control returned and with it the logistics of his plan. Even when he emerged from Mexico, he would not return to Chicago. He'd settle somewhere south, where it was warm. So he needed to get his things. His memories. It was another eight hours of his life, from Indy to Chicago and back south to where he'd started that morning. But he'd waited ten years. What was another eight hours? He wanted his things.

His instinct was alerted blocks from the house. He turned two blocks too soon and slowed to a stop. He could see cruisers and vans and men with shovels. At his house.

Mitchell had found his house. *She'd taken his stuff.* Coldly he turned his car around. To hell with fate. The woman had to pay. She'd dodged a bullet twice this week. Lucky bitch. But her luck was about to run out.

Saturday, December 2, 11:45 A.M.

Mia rocked back on her heels, fists on her hips. The table was covered with the items they'd recovered from the Lukowitches' yard. And they'd needed both the X-ray and metal detectors. Jeremy would be proud of that at least. 'This is remarkable.'

Spinnelli was examining each item. 'We've got Caitlin's purse, a necklace from Penny, fourteen sets of keys . . . shoes, more necklaces . . . My God.'

'These keys belong to Dr Thompson,' Reed said. 'These are Brooke's. We think he took them Wednesday night when she'd had too many beers. These belong to

Tania from the hotel, these are Niki Markov's, the saleswoman. The rest we don't know.'

'Now we can tie him to the Burnette and Hill murders,' Spinnelli said with satisfaction. 'I still want forensics, but this is a hell of a lot better than what we had.'

'Atlantic City is sending someone to look at this stuff,' Aidan said. 'The women he raped there say he took their keys, his way of saying he could come back anytime.'

'Sonofabitch,' Reed muttered.

'I think we'll all second that emotion,' Spinnelli said. 'Sam called. He said the urine tox on Yvonne Lukowitch showed Valium laced with cyanide, not the Ambien in her prescription.'

'We found a receipt from a photography shop,' Jack said. 'He bought the cyanide there. It's used in film developing. Sam said she never would have felt a thing.'

She sighed. 'Later on it will mean something to Jeremy that his mother didn't commit suicide. Now it's not much comfort to a terrified seven-year-old. Jeremy said his mother met White when she was leading a dog training class in the park last June. His mother came home talking about this new man she'd met. White brought her wine and roses. She asked him to move in within three weeks.'

'That's fast,' Jack said.

'She was lonely,' Mia returned. 'We found a scar on her body, collarbone to breast, from a knife slice. Jeremy said White did it the first night he moved in. He told her if she told, he'd do worse and to Jeremy. Jeremy and his mom have been living in terror since the end of last June.'

'And we still don't know his name,' Murphy said bitterly.

Spinnelli looked hopeful. 'I may have something for you. I got a call this morning from Impound. They recovered a car that was reported stolen on Thursday. It was found in the area Murphy was searching. Impound found a book under the seat.'

Reed sat up. 'A math book?'

Spinnelli's smile was sharp. 'Algebra One. Somebody should be bringing it in the next few minutes. Until then, what will we do next?'

'I'm following leads from the photo on the news,' Aidan said. 'And I'll be the liaison to Atlantic City PD. I sent the photo to Detroit PD, but we don't have anything yet.'

'Keep calling,' Spinnelli said. 'Mia?'

'We have the list from Social Services of all the kids Penny Hill placed with the elder Doughertys. We're going to follow up on that today. We've got nine names with no known address to track down and a few alibis from the known ones to verify.'

'Okay,' Spinnelli said. 'Did we get anything out of the two boys from Hope Center?'

'Miles talked to them,' Mia said. 'Thad admitted after he learned Jeff was dead that it was Jeff who assaulted him. He said Jeff and Regis did it and Manny watched the door. They threatened to gut him like a pig if he told. So, he didn't tell. Regis Hunt gets moved to adult prison pending an investigation and trial. Thad will transfer to another juvie facility. But Dr Bixby's still missing.'

'He's not home, dead or otherwise,' Spinnelli said. 'I've got an APB out for his car.'

'And it doesn't appear that his keys are in the pile,' Reed added.

'So he could be alive and hiding, or dead and hidden. What else?' Spinnelli asked.

'Just something Jeremy said,' Mia mused. 'Remember, Murphy, he said that White buried something in the backyard last Friday, the day after Thanksgiving. If he killed somebody then, we haven't found them yet.'

There was a knock at the door and an officer stuck his head in. 'Lieutenant Spinnelli? I'm from Impound. I have some evidence for you.'

'Thank you. We hope this is good.' Spinnelli handed the book to Mia when the officer from Impound was gone. 'Do the honors, Mia.'

Mia pulled on a pair of gloves and slid the book from the paper evidence sack. 'One math book. And inside . . .' She looked up. 'Newspaper clippings. Hill and Burnette.' She grimaced. 'And me. Here's the one of me taking down DuPree and here's the one with my address, thank-you-Carmichael, and . . . hello.' She grinned. 'One clipping from the *Gazette* in Springdale,

Indiana. THANKSGIVING NIGHT FIRE LEAVES TWO DEAD. It's dated the day after Thanksgiving.'

'The first time Jeremy saw White burying something in the backyard,' Murphy murmured. 'Who did he kill?'

Mia scanned the article, her heart picking up. 'One of the victims was Mary Kates. Kates is one of the names on the Social Services list.' Hurriedly she found the list. 'Two names. Andrew and Shane Kates. They're brothers. Andrew would be the right age.'

'This is good.' Spinnelli paced. 'Very good. Now that we know who the hell this guy is, we need to know where he'll strike next or where he'll hide or run. The four of you find out. I'm going to call the captain and tell him we finally made some progress.'

Mia felt invigorated. Renewed. She stared at the table with all his souvenirs, her heart pumping gallons. 'Andrew Kates. Your days are numbered, you sonofabitch.'

Saturday, December 2, 5:15 P.M.

The wig was making his head sweat. 'How much is the rent?' It was an empty apartment in Mitchell's building. The super held the key in her hand. He was waiting for the right moment to get the information he needed. If she couldn't tell him, he'd take her keys and investigate Mitchell's place himself.

'Eight fifty,' the old woman said. 'Due first of the month.'

He made a point of looking in the closets. 'And is the neighborhood safe?'

'Very safe.'

No more than a couple of shootings a week on the street outside. The woman lied like a rug. 'I read about that detective in the paper.'

'Oh, that. She's moved out. It'll be very quiet from here on out.'

Panic rose in his throat. But she was probably lying again. 'That was fast.'

'Well, the movers haven't come yet. But she's out of here. No need to worry.'

But there was every need to worry. He wanted Mitchell. He needed to get into her place before she moved all her things. Surely there was some clue to where she'd gone. He considered shooting the old bag where she stood, but the new gun in his back waistband would be loud. Tyler had built quite a gun collection. He'd wanted to take them all, but he still had to travel light, so he'd taken only two. A .38 and a .44, both of which would bring people running if he fired them. So he'd do it the old-fashioned way. From under his jacket he pulled his pipe wrench and smacked the old lady's head. Like a rag doll she crumpled, blood from her wound starting to soak the carpet. He bound her hands and feet and gagged her before stuffing her in the closet.

With her key he let himself into Mitchell's place. She

needed a good decorator. Methodically he checked the coat closet. Other than a trifolded flag on the shelf, it was empty. Her kitchen cabinet was filled with boxes of Pop-Tarts, her freezer with microwave meals. She needed a good nutritionist more than a decorator.

Her bedroom was a mess, blankets in a pile on the floor. But interestingly, a box of condoms sat open on the nightstand. Her closet was such a mess, there was no way to know if she'd taken clothes or not. Frustrated, he returned to the living room. A pile of mail covered a lamp table. Greedily he searched it. The only thing remotely personal was a postcard with a crab on the front. 'Dear Mia, wish you'd come with us. Miss you. Love, Dana.' Dana? A friend with whom Mitchell might stay?

He opened the lamp table drawer and pulled out a photo album with a grin. He'd struck gold. He lifted the cover and sighed. Mitchell was no more organized about her photos than she was about anything else. None of the photos were put into the plastic sleeves. It was just a pile, as if she threw everything in here with the plan to someday do it right. How had she ever managed to get as far as she did?

On the top of the stack was an obituary she'd ripped from the paper without even trimming the edges. He fought the urge to trim them himself and read it. Her father had died four weeks before. Interesting. He was survived by her mother. More interesting still. She'd come to heel if her mother were in danger.

He kept searching. Lots of kids' school pictures. And a wedding picture. Mitchell in pink with a tall redhead in white lace. On the back it said 'Mia and Dana.' Bingo. But Dana who? And where would he find her? Ask and you shall receive. Under the wedding photo was an invitation. DANA DANIELLE DUPINSKI AND ETHAN WALTON BUCHANAN REQUEST YOUR PRESENCE . . . It was completely intact. He smiled. She'd been a bridesmaid so there'd been no need to send in the RSVP. He pocketed the card and the obituary. Dana Dupinski lived a good half hour from here. He'd better hurry.

Saturday, December 2, 6:45 P.M.

'Talk,' Spinnelli said from the head of the conference table. They'd regrouped, Reed and Mia, Murphy and Aidan, and Miles Westphalen. 'What do we know?'

The table was again full, this time of paper. After more than seven hours of phone calls, faxes, and e-mails, they'd been able to put together a great deal of Andrew Kates's past. Reed was energized. They were closing in.

'We know where Andrew Kates has been,' he said, 'where he's likely to go, and importantly, why ten is the magic number.'

Mia stacked her notes. 'Andrew and Shane Kates were born to Gloria Kates. Aidan tracked Andrew to the Michigan juvie system, who faxed us copies of their birth certificates. No father listed for either boy. Andrew is older by four years and served time in Michigan juvie for stealing a car when he was barely twelve. Nobody there remembered him, but it's been about ten years.'

'Is that the count to ten?' Westphalen asked and Mia shook her head.

'Be patient, Miles. This took us seven hours. You can listen for ten minutes.'

'Sorry,' Westphalen mumbled, properly chastised and Reed swallowed his smile.

'Anyway,' Mia said. 'I talked to the head caseworker for the juvie facility. She didn't remember him, but she looked up his file. He was a model resident. Claimed he'd been forced to steal the car by his mother to feed her drug habit. Gloria Kates had a yellow sheet full of drug possession charges, so this was probably true.'

'Obviously he got out,' Spinnelli said.

'Yeah.' Reed took up the story. 'When Andrew got caught stealing the car, his mother, Gloria, skipped town, leaving him to hold the bag.'

'Which would explain his hostility against women,' Westphalen said. 'Why hasn't he gone after her?'

'Because she's dead,' Reed answered. 'Heroin overdose, a few months later.'

'So he has to go after substitutes,' Westphalen mused. 'Interesting.'

'It gets better,' Reed promised. 'When Gloria left, Andrew went to juvie and Detroit placed Shane with his maternal aunt, Mary Kates, in Springdale, Indiana.'

'The Thanksgiving night fire,' Spinnelli murmured.

'Yes,' Reed said. 'I talked with the sheriff and the fire chief there about the Thanksgiving fire. The chief said they found gas cans in the backyard, but no eggs or evidence of solid accelerant. Just a gas and match affair. No fingerprints, no nothing. The sheriff said the aunt and her common-law husband, Carl Gibson, were found dead in their bedroom, close to the window. Their legs were broken so they couldn't get away.'

'Same as the Atlantic City rape victims,' Aidan said.

'And some of our victims,' Reed agreed. 'Nobody in Springdale was sorry or surprised to see it happen and the locals are having trouble making any headway on the case. Gibson had a history as a child predator. He was out on parole.'

Westphalen nodded. 'Ah. This makes sense.'

'When was Gibson arrested?' Spinnelli asked.

'I checked out Gibson,' Murphy said. 'He had no complaints on his record when Detroit social services first placed Shane. The first charges were filed on behalf of Shane Kates. Gibson pled out, but later he was nailed for molesting two other kids.'

'That's the trigger,' Westphalen said. 'Gibson molested Andrew's brother, then nearly ten years later this boy at Hope Center, Thad, is molested. That same night Gibson and Andrew Kates's Aunt Mary die. But ten years is a long time for such rage to lie dormant.'

'That's because you got ahead of our story,' Mia said. 'Be patient, Miles.'

Westphalen grimaced. 'Sorry. Please continue.'

Reed nodded. 'Okay. Shane was molested by Gibson at some time during the year he was there. Based on Gibson's profile, probably multiple times. He's a sick bastard.'

'Was,' Mia corrected. 'Now he's a dead bastard.'

'Was,' Reed echoed. 'Shane would have been seven or eight at the time.'

'Same age as Jeremy Lukowitch,' Murphy noted and Mia nodded, troubled.

'I don't know what to make of that. Maybe that's why he didn't hurt Jeremy, just his mother. Sorry, Reed. Go on.'

'Andrew was in juvie a year. When he got out, he was placed with his aunt, but before the first sundown, Andrew took Shane and ran away. They were picked up by Indiana police a few days later, but Andrew told them what Carl Gibson did to Shane and since the aunt had permanent custody of both of them they were put in foster care in Indiana versus being sent back to Detroit. That's when the first charges were filed against Gibson.'

'It was hard to place two brothers together,' Mia said, 'especially with one of them having a juvie record. The local social services agency couldn't place them, so they transferred the case to Chicago, who had a lot more homes available. Penny Hill was their caseworker. She placed them with Laura Dougherty, who had developed a reputation for success with troubled kids. And she was willing to take them both.'

'What did Laura Dougherty do that was so bad that Kates tried to kill her three times?' Westphalen asked.

'That took a little more digging,' Mia said. 'The Social Services manager didn't know and Penny Hill didn't write it in the file. I finally had to drive out to see Mrs Blennard, their old friend. She remembered Shane. He was beautiful, blond and blue-eyed. At one point, Laura had considered adopting both boys, then Shane started in on one of the younger boys who was only five.' She looked resigned. 'Shane fondled him.'

'The abused became the abuser,' Westphalen said and held up his hands when Reed frowned. 'It happens, Reed. However you choose to explain it, it happens.'

'Well, it happened with Shane Kates,' Mia inserted when Reed would have responded. 'When Laura brought Penny Hill back to discuss it, Shane started breaking things on the sly. He blamed this younger boy, but Mrs Dougherty didn't believe him.'

'So who ultimately threw the boys out?' Westphalen asked.

'Mrs Blennard said Andrew begged Laura not to send them away. Nearly broke Laura's heart. Penny got them counseling, but Shane did it again, and that time Laura caught him in the act. So Laura told them they had to go.'

'So where did they go?' Spinnelli asked.

'It got harder to keep them together, but Penny Hill tried. She found a place in the country, a real rural area. She thought it would settle the boys, fresh air and chores.' Mia shrugged. 'Cows. This was Bill and Bitsey Young's house. They had two biological sons, older, high school age.'

'This is where the records start to break down,' Reed said. 'It answers questions for us, but it raises a whole host for Social Services. All of this information comes from Andrew's file. Nobody can find Shane's.'

Spinnelli's eyes widened. 'They lost the file?'

'So it would seem,' Mia said uneasily. 'The boys were placed with the Youngs about ten years ago, but there aren't any more entries in Andrew's file for a whole year. Not by Penny Hill or anybody else. They were essentially abandoned.'

'Abandoned by another woman,' Reed added.

'Penny Hill forgot about them?' Westphalen's gray brows shot up. 'That doesn't sound like the woman everyone described as dedicated to a fault.'

'No, it doesn't.' Mia frowned. 'Penny's daughter said she worried about dropping the ball, that a kid would get hurt. Maybe they weren't foundless worries. At any rate, the next entry in Andrew's file is a year later when he's transferred to another foster home. Andrew was noted as a quiet kid, very withdrawn. Straight A's.' She lifted a brow. 'Math club in high school. But after placement at the Youngs' there isn't another word about Shane in the state's social services files.'

'We don't know what happened in the Youngs' house.' Reed pulled a photo from his folder. 'But we do know the house ended up looking like this.'

563

'Burned to the ground,' Westphalen murmured. 'When?'

'After the boys had been there nearly a year,' Mia answered.

Murphy leaned over and picked up the photo. 'How did you find this?'

'The fire was documented in insurance records.' Reed shrugged. 'It was a hunch.'

Mia shook her head. 'It was better than a hunch. I found Shane Kates's death certificate listed in the county's database. Cause of death was respiratory failure.'

'From the fire,' Aidan said.

Mia nodded. 'Exactly. Reed looked up Shane's death date in his insurance database and cross-referenced the Youngs and found they'd filed a claim the following week for their house which had been destroyed in the fire.'

'This picture was from the local fire department,' Reed said. 'They're pulling together the firefighters that responded that day so we can get more information, but it was almost nine years ago.'

'So,' Westphalen mused, 'Andrew set the fire and his brother died.'

Mia nodded. 'The brother he'd gone to great lengths to protect.'

Westphalen's eyes had narrowed in thought. 'It's a significant trauma.'

'One a person might bury for nearly ten years?' Mia asked.

'Possibly. A compulsive personality might chew it to death or deny it entirely.'

Spinnelli frowned. 'I'm still missing something. Why is ten the magic number?'

'That looks like the easiest question to answer.' Mia slid two faxed pages to the middle of the table, side by side. 'Shane's birth certificate from Michigan and his death certificate from Illinois. I overlooked the death date in the computer the first time I searched because the numbers are nearly identical to his birth date. One digit off.'

'Shane Kates died on his tenth birthday,' Westphalen murmured.

'In a fire,' Reed confirmed.

Mia sighed. 'Count to ten and go to hell.'

'So what next?' Spinnelli asked.

'Track down the Youngs and their sons,' Reed said. 'He's done things in order as much as he can. It makes sense the Youngs are next.'

Spinnelli nodded. 'First thing in the morning I want you in . . . what's the town, Mia?'

'The Youngs lived in Lido, Illinois.'

'Get down to Lido and find them. Murphy and Aidan, you're on call. Dismissed.'

Chapter Twenty-two

Saturday, December 2, 7:25 P.M.

Mia was searching the Internet for the Youngs when Reed leaned his hip against her desk, closer than was wise. She'd keep it professional. 'The meeting went well.'

'Yes, it did. It's coming together. We should have him soon.'

'You go on home to Beth. I need to work a little longer.'

'You didn't go apartment hunting today.' His voice was a smooth murmur.

She gritted her teeth against the shiver that prickled her skin. 'No, but my bag's in my trunk. I'll stay with Dana. Percy has food till tomorrow. I'll come and get him then.'

'Use Lauren's place one more night, Mia. I won't bother you, I promise.'

From the corner of her eye she saw Murphy alone at his desk, watching in that quiet, shrewd way of his, then she looked up at Reed. She kept thinking she'd be prepared, but every time she looked at his face it still hurt. She kept thinking she could look at his chest without wondering if he still wore his ring on the chain. Without some small part of her hoping he'd take it off. That she'd be enough to make him want to.

Which was as pathetic as it was stupid. 'Reed, stop. It's not fair.'

His shoulders sagged. 'Call me when you get to Dana's, so I know you're okay.'

She waited until he was on his own side of the desk before speaking again. 'When you get home, make sure you talk to Beth.'

He frowned. 'Why?'

Mia hesitated. 'Just tell her you love her, okay?'

Uncertainly he nodded. 'I will.' He gathered his things and left.

'You're sure you don't want me to mess up his face?' Murphy asked.

'No.' She turned back to her computer. 'I'm going to find the Youngs, then call their local PD and warn them. For now that's all I can do.'

'You know, Mia, that little kid today. Jeremy. You were good with him.'

So was Reed, she thought. *We made a good team.* 'Thanks. He's a nice boy.'

'I bet he's feeling scared right now. I bet you could find out where they took him.'

She thought of Jeremy, scared and alone. 'I found out in case I got done early.'

Murphy came over and turned off her computer. 'There, you're done early. I'll look for the Youngs. You see Jeremy, then go to Dana's. I'll call you if I find something.'

'Thanks, Murphy.' Her throat closed up at the sympathy in his eyes. 'I have to go.'

By the time she made it down the stairs she was back in control. Which was a good thing, because a woman with a blond braid waited outside the main door. 'Do you want anything else, Carmichael?' she asked acidly. 'Like maybe my kidney?'

'I know where Getts lives.'

Mia stopped. 'Where?' *And how long have you known?*

Carmichael handed her a piece of paper on which she'd written the address. 'I didn't mean for your address to go in the paper. I'm sorry.'

Mia almost believed her, the girl was that good. She took the paper anyway. 'Stay out of my way, Carmichael. And you'd better hope you never need a cop.'

Carmichael's eyes narrowed. 'I'm serious. I didn't know. Mitchell, you're as close to a meal ticket as I could hope for. I would no more try to get you killed than fired.'

Now Mia's eyes narrowed. 'What? What do you mean, fired?'

'I was there the night of the Adler fire. I saw Solliday

come out of your place. It would make good gossip, but if you're fired my meal ticket's gone. I really didn't put your address in that story. My editor did. He thought it would spice it up. I am sorry.'

Mia was too tired to care anymore. 'Fine.' When she got to her car, she called Spinnelli, gave him the information. 'Have Brooks and Howard make the collar.'

'You don't want him?'

A week ago, it was all that mattered. Now . . . 'I think I need a vacation.'

'You've got the time. When this is over, take some. Go to the beach. Get a tan.'

She laughed even though she didn't want to. 'You're obviously thinking of somebody else's skin. Call me if they get Getts, okay?' She had important things to do.

Twenty minutes later she was knocking on the door of the emergency foster home in which Social Services had placed Jeremy. He was sitting on the sofa, watching TV.

'He hasn't moved all day,' the foster mother said. 'Poor thing.'

Mia sat down next to him. 'Hey, kid.'

He looked up at her. 'Did you get him?'

'Not yet.'

'Then why are you here?'

He sounded just like Roger Burnette. 'I came to see you. You okay?'

He nodded his red head, his freckled face sober. Then he shook his head. 'No.'

'I guess that was a stupid question. So, I'll try again. What's this show?'

'The history of jet aviation.'

She put her arm around his shoulders. 'Okay.' After a few minutes of rigidity, Jeremy put his head on her shoulder. And stayed that way until the show was over.

Saturday, December 2, 9:20 P.M.

Mia pulled into Dana's driveway, later than she'd wanted. She'd stayed longer with Jeremy than she'd planned. But after the week she'd had, it felt good to sit with a small boy who'd needed her to be there as much as she'd needed it herself.

She had her hand on the front doorknob when Dana and Ethan moved into view through the window. Dana was laughing and Ethan had his hand on her stomach. Then he leaned down and talked to Dana's middle and just like that, Mia understood.

To her consternation, there was no wave of joy. Just a huge empty sadness. And shame. Her best friend was pregnant and had been too concerned about her emotional state to bubble her happiness. *How selfish can I be?* Tonight, pretty damn selfish. Like a coward, she backed away and almost made it to her car when the front door opened.

'Mia?' Dana stood on the front porch shivering. 'Come in, for heaven's sake.'

Mia shook her head. Pursed her lips. Drew a breath and forced a smile. 'I just realized I'm late. I promised . . .' But no lie leaped to her tongue and Dana's face fell.

'I'm sorry. I wanted to tell you.'

'I know.' She swallowed hard. 'I'll come by tomorrow and get all the details.'

Miserably, Dana nodded. 'Where are you staying tonight?'

'With Lauren.' *When hell froze over.* 'Hey, do you have room for another kid?'

'Actually, we do. Social Services gave the kid that was coming back to his mom.'

'I have a kid that needs a good place. His mom was murdered last night.'

Dana's eyes filled. 'Hormones,' she muttered. 'What's his name?'

'Jeremy Lukowitch. He's a nice kid.' Who deserved better than what he got. *But then don't we all?* 'I have to go. Get some rest.' She grinned awkwardly. 'Boil water.'

He'd had to park on a side street far away not to be seen as he waited. But it was worth it. Through his binoculars he saw Mitchell talking to the redhead, then she got in her car and drove away. He followed her.

He hadn't even been waiting all that long, having made a stop on the way, wanting a backup. A check of the public records showed her mother's address. And on a lark, he'd looked for Solliday's as well. Sooner or later she would show up at one of those places. And if he got desperate, he'd planned to wait outside the precinct. But as luck would have it, none of those measures were called for. He'd found her. He'd follow her, and when her guard was down, he'd take her out. Sooner or later she had to sleep.

Abruptly she sped up when she got to the highway, slipping in front of a big truck. He floored it, his heart in his throat. But she was gone. She'd lost him.

I lost her. His temper was ice cold. Fine, he'd just make her come to him.

Saturday, December 2, 10:00 P.M.

They said misery loves company and that must have been true, because after ditching the pesky, lying Carmichael, Mia found herself parked in front of Fire Company 172, hoping she'd find David Hunter on duty. He was in the kitchen making chili.

'That's so clichéd,' she said and he turned around, eyes widening.

He shrugged. 'It's also good. You want some?'

'Sure.' She sat down at the kitchen table. 'Smells good.'

'I'm a good cook.' He put a bowl in front of her. 'You find him?'

'Not yet.'

'Then why are you here?'

Mia rolled her eyes. 'I swear I'll deck the next person who says that. I came by to see how you are. The fire at Brooke Adler's was . . . devastating.'

He joined her at the table. 'I'll be okay. I imagine you see worse on a regular basis.'

She thought about Brooke Adler, the burns and the woman's excruciating pain. 'No, I don't think so. That was bad, David. Don't feel bad if you need to talk to someone.'

He said nothing, leaving her to stare at his *GQ* face and compare him to Reed. She must be nuts, because Reed came out on top. She sighed. 'I wish I wanted you, David.'

The initial surprise in his eyes gave way to wry amusement. 'Same goes.'

'You, too?'

He laughed sadly. 'A few times I've wondered why one person does it for you and another doesn't. Sorry, Mia, but you don't. Although there are about five guys in this company alone who'd kill to be with you. That was an expression, of course.'

'Of course.' When she got over Reed, she'd ask David to introduce her to one of those five lucky guys. 'You're not over her, are you?' Dana, whom he'd loved for years and who had absolutely no idea how much she'd hurt him.

His gray eyes shuttered. 'Eat your chili, Mia.'

'Okay. Listen, my car got ambushed the other night. The department will fix the windows, but one of the bullets hit the hood. Will you take a look at it in your garage?'

His dark brows went up. 'Bullets hit your car. Your little Alfa.'

'Yeah.' Then she grinned. 'It was damn exciting.'

He threw back his head and laughed and for one moment she wondered if she and Dana were both blind and stupid. 'I'll bet it was.' He sobered. 'Why are you here, Mia?'

She should tell him about Dana and the baby because as hard as it had been for her, it would be worse for him. But not tonight. 'I'm at loose ends tonight.'

His eyes shadowed. 'Fair enough. We have a pool table upstairs.'

'Can I ride the firepole back down?'

He grinned, lightening the dark mood. 'Sure.'

'Then rack 'em up, Ace.'

Saturday, December 2, 10:50 P.M.

Lauren was on a date and Beth was sulking. It was eleven on a Saturday night and he was alone. He closed his eyes and let himself admit that he didn't want to be alone. He wanted Mia here, with him. He wanted her smart mouth, her rough edges and her soft curves. God, the woman had the softest curves. He remembered how it felt to sink into her, thrust against her, fill his hands with her. She'd been . . .

Perfect. He opened his eyes and stared at the wall, wondering if he was both blind and stupid. *Perfect*. She wasn't elegant and the home she made would be filled with take-out boxes and sheets that didn't match. But it could be a home. She made him . . .

Happy. He fingered the chain around his neck. He'd hurt her. Mia.

But it wasn't too late. It couldn't be. He got up and paced. He wouldn't let it be.

His computer beeped at him. He either had new e-mail or a hit on the search he'd scheduled to run three times daily. He sat in front of the screen and his breath caught. It was a new hit on the solid-accelerant search. The first four entries were his own. But the fifth had been logged just that afternoon. By a Tom Tennant of Indianapolis.

Reed found the number for the Indianapolis Fire Department. Ten minutes and three transfers later, he got through. 'Tennant.' It was a sleepy growl.

'Tom Tennant? My name is Reed Solliday. I'm with OFI in Chicago. You logged a solid-accelerant fire utilizing natural gas into the database this afternoon.'

'Yeah, I did. Hell of a fire. Nearly took out half a city block.' In the background Reed could hear the tapping of a keyboard. Tennant was checking him out.

'You'll find my four entries in the database already. This is likely related to a serial murder/arsonist in

Chicago. What was the name of the homeowner at the origin?'

'I can't give you that information right now.'

Reed blew out an impatient breath. 'Can you tell me if the last name was Young?'

There was a beat of hesitation. 'Yes. Tyler Young.'

One of the sons. Shit. 'Did he survive?'

Tennant hesitated. 'I need to check you out first. Give me your badge number.'

Reed rattled it off. 'Hurry. Call me back when you've verified.' They'd found one of the Youngs. Too late it seemed. They might be in time for the other three. He started to dial Mia, then canceled. He'd wait until Tennant called—

The shrill barking of the puppy broke the quiet. It sounded like Biggles was outside, but he hadn't heard Beth come down to let him out. Then the high squeal of the smoke detector added to the din. His heart jumped into his throat as he ran up the stairs, dialing 911. *Beth was upstairs.* Smoke already filled the hallway.

'Fire at 356 Morgan. Repeat, fire at 356 Morgan. People still in the house.'

'Sir, you need to get out,' the 911 operator said.

'My daughter's still in here.'

'Sir—' Reed snapped the phone shut, grabbed the fire extinguisher from the wall. *'Beth.'* He tried to open her door, but it was locked. She had her headphones on. She couldn't hear him. He threw himself into her bedroom door and wood cracked and splintered. For a split second he could only stare in horror as flames licked the walls and smoke filled the room. '*Beth!*' He ran to her bed and yanked the blanket, emptying the extinguisher at the base of the flames, but her bed was empty.

She wasn't here. *Wasn't here.* He ran into the hall, checked the bathroom, the spare room. *Nothing.* He touched the door to his own room and it burned his hand.

Back to the bathroom. Wet the towels. Cover hands and face. He was on autopilot when he pushed open his bedroom door. The wave of heat knocked him back, smacked him down. His bed was solid flames. He dropped to his stomach and tried to crawl into the room. *My baby.* 'Beth! I'm here. Call to me. Let me know where you are.'

But he could barely hear the sound of his voice over the roar and the hiss. Then hands were pulling at him and he fought. '*No.* My daughter's here. She's still in here.'

He was dragged from the room by firefighters in full gear. Breathers covered their faces. One of them lifted the mask. 'Reed? My God, man, get the hell out of here!'

Reed shook them off. 'My daughter. She's still in here.' Smoke filled his lungs and he fell to his knees, coughing until he couldn't breathe at all.

'We'll find her. You get out.' One of the men

pushed him out the front door into the grip of an EMT. 'This is Lieutenant Solliday. His kid's inside. Don't let him back in.'

Reed jerked away from the EMT, but another fit of coughing left him breathless. The EMT led him to the ambulance and strapped an oxygen mask to his face.

'Breathe, Lieutenant. Now sit. Sir.'

'Beth.' His body was limp. He could only stare as one of the windows shattered.

The EMT was bandaging his hands. 'They'll find her, sir.'

He closed his eyes. *Beth's in there. She's dead. They won't be in time.*

I didn't save my own child. Numb, he sat. And waited.

Saturday, December 2, 11:10 P.M.

The men had gathered around the pool table, and Mia guessed at least two of the guys were ones who'd kill to be with her. In the past she would have been flattered, but like she'd told Reed, the trouble never had been the sex. It was the intimacy. But the one man she'd been truly intimate with, sharing her deepest secrets, didn't want her.

Not the way it counted, anyway. She had no doubt that Reed Solliday wanted her sexually. She even knew down deep he wanted to want her emotionally. But he was afraid. As was she. And until she got past that fear, she'd come home to an empty place and be Aunt Mia to everyone else's children.

'I won.' Larry Fletcher laid his cue across the table.

'You cheated,' Mia corrected with a smile. 'It's been fun, but I gotta go.' Where, she wasn't sure. The two flatterers protested, then everyone went quiet at the radio call. When it was clear it wasn't for the 172, the chatter resumed, but Mia heard a phrase that made her heart stop. 'Quiet.'

'It's not us, Mia,' David said, but she was already running for the stairs.

'That's Reed's house,' she said over her shoulder and saw Larry's grim face.

He'd heard it, too. 'I'm coming with you,' Larry said, right behind her.

Saturday, December 2, 11:25 P.M.

Mia ran to the ambulance. 'Reed. My God.' His face was lifeless but for the tears streaking his cheeks. His hands were wrapped in bandages. An oxygen mask dangled from his neck. She dropped to her knees. 'Reed?'

'Beth is inside,' he said, his voice flat. *Dead*. 'I couldn't find my little girl.'

She took his bandaged hand in hers. 'Where is Lauren?'

'On a date,' he said tonelessly. 'It was just me and Beth.'

'Reed, listen to me. Did you check Beth's room?'

He nodded mechanically. 'She wasn't there.'

Little bitch, Mia thought, furious with the girl for causing her father such grief. Beth went out the window again. 'Larry, wait with him.' She stalked off to the side, radio in hand. 'This is Mitchell, Homicide. I need a cruiser to proceed at fastest safe speed with lights and sirens to the Rendezvous Café.' She gave the address. 'They're looking for Liz Solliday. Tell them to make a scene. And if she's there, scare her shitless.'

'Ah, understood, Detective Mitchell,' Dispatch said warily.

'No, you don't. Her house is burning down and her father thinks she's inside.'

'Unit dispatched, Detective.' Mia waited impatiently, tapping her foot, watching Reed grieve for nothing. Her anger faltered. What if she was wrong? What if Beth was in there? She could be dead. Kates had struck *here*, right in Reed's home.

After what seemed like an eternity of watching Reed stare at his burning house, the radio crackled, calling her name. 'Mitchell here.'

'Girl is safe, sound, and uh, scared shitless. You want them to bring her home?'

'Yeah. Make her ride in the back. And make sure everybody sees them.' Mia walked to Reed on shaky legs. 'Reed, Beth's okay. She wasn't in the house.'

His eyes snapped to hers. '*What?*'

'She went out the window. She probably hasn't been home for a few hours.'

His eyes darkened. 'Where is she?' His mouth precisely formed each word.

'At a slam poetry competition downtown. Place called the Rendezvous Café. I have a cruiser bringing her home, sirens and lights.' Her lips quirked. 'I told them to scare her.'

He came to his feet, trembling. 'You knew she'd gone there?'

'Not tonight. I knew she'd gone last night.' Warning alarms began to sound in her mind. He wasn't just angry at Beth. *He's angry at me.*

'You knew my fourteen-year-old had gone out the window and you didn't tell me.'

'She promised she'd tell you herself. I told her if she didn't tell you, then I would.'

'Well, you didn't.' He spat out the words and Larry Fletcher frowned.

'Reed, she's okay. Beth's fine. And Mia tried to help.'

Reed towered over her, fury in his eyes. 'That wasn't help.'

Mia stepped back, trembling herself now. 'I'm sorry. I thought it was the right thing to do. That's why I don't have kids.' She swallowed hard, then remembered Percy. The cat was as lucky as she was, but still her heart pounded. She found the chief in charge. 'The girl you thought was inside was somewhere else. She's being returned.'

The chief's eyes narrowed. 'I risked my men's lives for an AWOL kid?'

'Hey, she's not my kid. But my cat's inside on the other side of the duplex.'

'We've contained the fire to this side, but we'll go in for your cat when we can.'

'Thanks. Oh, and there was a puppy. Fuzzy dog, this big.' She gestured.

'Over there. We found him by the tree. Leg's broke. Otherwise he's fine.'

'Thanks. Tell me, is the house destroyed?'

'Mostly the top floor. Everything in the bedrooms.'

Mia remembered the book he'd held in his hand. *My darling Reed*. The book was gone. She closed her eyes on a wave of regret. She couldn't blame him for being angry. He'd had a giant scare. She should have told him about Beth. She'd had plenty of opportunities throughout the day. But she'd so hoped Beth would tell him herself.

She shook herself back into action. This was the work of Andrew Kates. He was close by. She called Jack and Spinelli, then noticed the four calls from Murphy, all within the last fifteen minutes. With all the noise, she hadn't heard her cell ring.

She called him back. 'Murphy, it's Mia. What's happened?'

'I can barely hear you, Mia.'

'That's because Kates burned Reed's house down. I'm surrounded by fire trucks.'

'Was anybody hurt?'

'No, but Kates found us. Reed was the target this time. What did you find?'

'Three of the four Youngs. The father and mother are both dead, natural causes. Tyler Young died in a fire last night in Indianapolis. I faxed Kates's photo to the PD.'

They'd been too late. 'Thanks, Murphy. I'll let Reed know.' Mia walked back to Reed, her posture apologetic. 'I'm sorry, Reed. I was wrong not to tell you about Beth.' He glowered and said nothing. 'Murphy found three of the Youngs. One of them was killed in a fire last night.'

His glower softened to a glare. 'I know. Indy OFI posted it to the database I've been searching all week. I was going to call you when I got confirmation, but this happened.'

'So we have one more target left to find.'

He nodded. 'Thanks for telling me. About the Youngs.'

'Reed, I didn't want to come between you and Beth.' She watched as the cruiser approached, its siren adding to the chaos of the scene. 'The prodigal daughter returns.'

'We won't be killing any fatted calves,' Reed said darkly and marched over to the cruiser. Beth got out, face stark with shock and horror. Reed glared, bandaged fists on his hips, then caught his daughter in a fierce embrace that made Mia's eyes sting.

Behind her, Larry cleared his throat. 'Mia, I've known

Reed Solliday a lot of years. He's a good man. He didn't mean to hurt you. He was just scared mindless.'

'I know that.' She also knew he'd keep hurting her until this was over. Wearily she wished it was. 'I'm going to get my cat and go to a hotel. Make sure he's okay, Larry.'

Larry gave her a shrewd look, reminiscent of Murphy. 'Which hotel?'

She laughed shakily. 'Probably the first one I come to. Good night, Larry.'

Beth sobbed. 'I'm sorry, Daddy. I'm sorry.' He held her tight, afraid to let her go.

'I thought you were dead,' he said hoarsely. 'Beth, don't ever do this to me again.'

She nodded, then pulled away, her eyes fixed to the house. 'Oh, Daddy. It's gone.'

'Not all. Just the top floor.' But it would take some time to put their house back together. He wondered how much time it would take to put their trust back together. 'Mia said you went to a slam poetry competition. Beth, why didn't you just tell me?'

'I didn't think you'd understand why it was important to me.' She lifted a childish shoulder, but her words were adult. 'Maybe I wanted something that was only mine.'

'Beth, everything I have is yours. You know that.'

She looked up, her eyes wet and very serious. 'No, Daddy. It's all hers. Mother's.'

He blinked. 'I don't understand.'

She sighed. 'I know.' She lifted his hands, her eyes filling again at the sight of the bandages. 'Oh, God, your hands. How bad is it?'

'Light burns. I'll heal.' He pushed a lock of hair from her face. 'I love you, Beth.'

His baby launched herself into his arms. 'I love you, too.' And as his arms closed around his child, he heard Mia's voice. *Just tell her you love her, okay?* And he knew the woman understood a great deal more than he'd ever given her credit for. He lifted his head, looking for her. But she was gone. He straightened abruptly. Mia was gone.

'What's wrong?' Beth asked anxiously.

'I need to find Detective Mitchell.'

'She went to a hotel,' Larry said from behind him.

'Which one?'

'She said the first one she came to.' His old friend's face was carefully nonchalant.

Reed's eyes narrowed. 'How did you two arrive together?'

Larry shrugged. 'She was playing pool with Hunter and me and the boys tonight.'

Jealousy pierced him, swift and sharp. Mia surrounded by men, one of them calendar boy David Hunter, with whom she'd had a past. Amusement filled Larry's eyes and one side of his mouth lifted. 'You want me to find which hotel she went to?'

'Yeah. Please.' Reed turned back to Beth, who was watching knowingly. 'What?'

'Detective Mitchell told me to tell you. She said you were a good dad and I owed you better. She was right. I'm sorry, Dad.'

'I don't know what to do about her, Beth. She's not . . . like your mother.'

'So? Dad, last I looked, my mother was dead.' She drew a breath. 'But you're not.'

And somehow, it was that simple. 'You're so much like your mother. She wrote poetry, too.' Which was gone forever. But he'd deal with the loss of it later.

'Really? Why didn't you tell me?'

'Maybe I wanted to keep something of her that was just mine, too.' He cupped her cheek, kept his voice gentle. 'You are grounded for the rest of your life.'

Her jaw dropped. She got ready to protest, then wisely closed her mouth. 'Okay.'

'Now, I think I heard something about Biggles needing attention. He's over there.' Reed pointed to the puppy. 'You see what needs to be done and I'll finish up here.'

Sunday, December 3, 3:15 A.M.

The history of jet aviation was better the second time around. Mia lay in the hotel bed, Percy curled up on her stomach. The History Channel was replaying its schedule and she'd already seen histories of ancient

Greece and Rome. She'd discuss them with Jeremy when he got to Dana's. The boy would be happy there and she could visit—

The knock on the door startled her. Grabbing her gun from the nightstand she peeked through the peephole. Her shoulders sagged and she opened the door. *Reed*.

He was freshly showered and shaved, a light bandage now only on the palm of one hand. The other held a plastic drugstore sack, the memory of which sent her senses pulsing. He looked handsome and . . . necessary. She could see the colors of the key card through the front pocket of his shirt. He was staying here. At this hotel. Proximity tempted, powerfully. But his shirt was open enough for her to see the glint of the gold chain around his neck and she squeezed her swollen heart back into its place. 'Reed.'

'Can I come in?'

'It's late.'

'You weren't asleep.' His brows crunched slightly. 'Please.'

Cursing her own stupidity, she stepped back and put her gun on the table by the door. 'Okay.' Words swirled in her head, but she kept them there. For all intents, Reed was married. And she didn't do married men. Or cops. Or partners. Or anyone.

He closed the door. 'I wanted to apologize. Beth told me what happened. You did exactly the right thing.' He looked down at his shoes, then back up with a boyish grin that made her chest hurt. 'The sirens and flashing lights were a nice touch. I don't think she'll be climbing out windows again any time soon.'

'Good. Because first slam poetry, then . . .' She sighed. 'What do you need, Reed?'

His smile faded. 'I think I need you.'

She shook her head. 'No. Don't do this to me. I want more than you can give me.' She laughed bitterly. 'And if you gave it, I wouldn't know what the hell to do with it anyway. So let's just stop this now. You said you didn't want to hurt me. So go.'

'I can't.' He ran a thumb over the two stitches under her left eye. 'I can't go.' He threaded fingers up into her hair, tilted her face up. Took her mouth in the sweetest, gentlest kiss she'd ever had. 'Don't make me go. Please, Mia.'

A shudder wracked her body. She'd never wanted anything so much. Of their own volition her hands reached, flattening on his chest before her arms wound around his neck and she kissed him back. For the first second it was tentative, then the kiss exploded, openmouthed. Demanding. She let herself be drawn in, let herself want. Desperately.

No. She broke the contact and stepped back. 'You can't be this cruel, Reed.'

He was breathing hard. 'I hope not.' His throat worked as he set the plastic sack on the table next to her gun. He pulled out two little black velvet jewelry boxes and snapped them both open. Both were empty. 'I thought we could do this together.'

She was losing her patience. 'Do what?'

'You take off your chain, I'll take off mine.'

Her mouth fell open. He stood there, face expectant. Eyes painfully uncertain. 'And then what?'

'I don't know. We play it by ear. One day at a time. But this time with strings.'

Her heart was pounding. 'I don't know how to do strings, Reed.'

He smiled. 'I do.' He slipped his finger beneath the thin tank top she wore and pulled out the old chain. Shook it so the dog tags clanked. 'So? What do you say?'

Mouth dry, she nodded. 'Okay.' And she was astounded when his shoulders settled. He'd actually thought she could say no. 'But I have to keep the medic alert tag.'

'Thought of that.' He pulled a cheap silver chain from the sack. 'This will do for now.' He put the chain in her hand. The price tag said five dollars. In that moment, it was worth more than all the diamonds in the world. He lifted the old chain from her neck. 'Change the medic alert tag now.'

Hands shaking, she did, then slipped the new chain on. 'It's lighter,' she said.

'Pays to dump a little excess weight every now and then.' He drew a breath and took off his chain. 'Let's do this, Mitchell.'

And they did, she closing her box with a satisfied snap, he closing his with a caress of his thumb. 'I'll put mine away,' he said. 'In my safe-deposit box.'

'I don't know,' she answered. 'Maybe I'll throw mine in Lake Michigan.'

He grinned. She grinned back. It felt good. 'So what else's in the sack, Solliday?'

His grin went sly. 'Big box,' he said and waggled his brows. 'Variety pack.'

She wrapped her arms around his neck. 'You were pretty sure of yourself.'

His hands ran up and down her back as he sobered. 'I hoped.'

Her heart turned over. 'Where is Beth?'

'In a room down the hall with Lauren.'

'And the puppy?'

'At an all-night veterinary clinic. In a cast and resting comfortably. My family is safe and accounted for.' He kissed her sweetly. 'Come to bed with me, Mia.'

She smiled up at him. It would be this easy then. 'Okay.'

Sunday, December 3, 7:15 A.M.

How had he managed to lose her again? He'd had her. She'd come to him. He'd been waiting for her at Solliday's house and she'd come. But with another man, not alone. And when she left, she'd checked into a hotel with very good security.

And when she came out this morning, it was with Solliday, who'd checked in a few hours after she did.

Solliday's arm was around her shoulders, hers around his waist. He remembered the box of condoms on her nightstand and it occurred to him that if he'd just waited, he might have gotten them both in Solliday's bed.

Now it was too late. He'd have to follow her. Sooner or later even Mitchell had to be alone.

Chapter Twenty-three

Sunday, December 3, 8:00 A.M.

Murphy tossed a copy of the *Bulletin* across the conference room table. 'Howard and Brooks picked up Getts last night. Page four, bottom corner.'

Mia flipped to the article with a smile. 'Go team.'

Reed studied her face. 'I thought you wanted in on that arrest.'

She lifted a shoulder. 'Abe and I figured Carmichael was there that night, that she knew where DuPree and Getts were hiding all along and that she was feeding us information to keep her stories front-page. She offered me Getts last night thinking I'd swallow the bait. Even tried to tail me. I decided not to play her game.'

Westphalen patted her hand. 'Our little girl's growing up.'

Mia just grinned at him. 'Quiet, old man.'

Spinnelli leaned back in his chair. 'So, Reed, how's your house?'

Reed grimaced. 'Now I'll know what it's like on the

paperwork end of an insurance claim. But it was Kates, no question. He came in through a window, went through the upstairs while I was downstairs on the phone. We think he grabbed Beth's puppy on the way back out her window, but dropped him halfway down the tree. Ben Trammell found residue and egg fragments in both bedrooms.' He paused, thinking. 'He used an egg at Tyler Young's Friday night. He's used nine now. Assuming he had access to a dozen of them in the art teacher's cabinet, he's still got up to three more.'

'What do we know about Tyler Young?' Spinnelli asked.

'His name was in the computer we took from Yvonne Lukowitch's house,' Jack said. 'Kates found Young's real estate website through a high school alumni site.'

'I called Tom Tennant from the Indy OFI this morning and got the rest of the story. He said Tyler and his wife died. Both bodies were charred, but the ME found organ damage in the wife consistent with the same stab wounds Joe Dougherty had. She was lying on her stomach, just like Joe Junior. But Tyler was chained to the bed, his legs broken.'

'He's getting good at that,' Mia murmured, troubled.

'I know. Their ME also thinks that Tyler received multiple stab wounds to the groin.'

'I think we know what happened in that house the year Andrew and Shane lived there,' Westphalen said. 'They were trapped and nobody came to check on them.'

'And Laura and Penny had put them there,' Mia said. 'Andrew must have cursed them every day. But they were there a year, then a big fire. Something must have happened on Shane's tenth birthday.'

'Maybe it was the first time Tyler assaulted them,' Aidan suggested.

Mia nodded slowly. 'Maybe. The other son might know.'

'Tennant said they found a number in Tyler's personnel file for his brother, Tim. Tim Young's a youth pastor in New Mexico. He works with underprivileged kids.'

Westphalen's brows went up. 'That's either an attempt at redemption or a kid in a candy store. We may find out which one depending on what he's willing to tell us.'

Reed had thought the same thing. 'Tennant informed Tim of Tyler's death yesterday. He's traveling to Indianapolis today. Tennant will call me when he gets here.'

'In the meantime,' Mia said, 'that leaves one person who knows what happened. Andrew Kates. We know he's in town. At least he was nine hours ago. He wanted Laura dead, so much he tried three times. He made mistakes with Caitlin, Niki Markov, and with Donna. And still he didn't get Laura. Ironically, he goofed with Penny, too.'

'What do you mean?' Spinnelli frowned. 'She left him there a year.'

'No. That didn't sit right with what everyone had told me about Penny. I went back and checked my notes and Reed, do you remember when we talked to Margaret Hill? Remember when she said she almost lost her mother when she was fifteen?'

'Yeah. She said her mother had been shot by a client. She almost died.'

'Margaret Hill is twenty-five,' Mia said. 'You do the math.'

'Oh,' Reed breathed. She was right. 'Penny Hill went into the hospital right about the time she placed Andrew and Shane in that home. She didn't forget about them. I bet her files got forwarded to other people and the kids fell through the cracks.'

Mia nodded. 'Then Shane dies and somebody says *Oh shit*. Andrew gets shuffled to another foster home and Shane gets swept under the rug.'

'And his file disappears,' Spinnelli said grimly. 'This is bad for the state. I'll work it.'

'That's fine. But back to Kates,' Mia said. 'Knowing how much he hates to miss his mark, what if he were to find out he'd goofed with Penny Hill? She never abandoned him. She wasn't even working the year he and Shane were at the Youngs'. Someone else dropped the ball with those boys. Someone else is to blame.'

'So someone else should pay,' Reed murmured, understanding her plan.

Spinnelli's smile started slow and grew. 'I like this. We could draw him out.'

'We'd have to set up some fake caseworker to take the fall,' Mia said. 'Social Services would have to cooperate.'

'Leave that to me,' Spinnelli said.

'And,' she added, her own smile starting to spread, 'it would have to get leaked to the press. By accident of course. And I wouldn't want to lie to any nice reporters.'

'Of course not,' Spinnelli repeated dryly. 'So Wheaton's going down?'

'Oh yeah. I'll have to give her a little factual information, like Kates is angry because he was lost in foster care. Wheaton will dig deeper. It could get ugly.'

'He's killed eleven people in my jurisdiction alone,' Spinnelli said grimly. 'Five more elsewhere, plus all those rapes. I want him stopped. Leak the story. Give his motive. Don't mention the dead brother or the lost file. We'll try to deal with that internally.'

'Wheaton said she'd run that clip of Kelsey tonight at six, Marc,' Mia said.

Spinnelli nodded. 'You think you can pull off the crawl-and-grovel act, Mia?'

'Oh yeah. Wheaton'll think she has the biggest exclusive since Deep Throat.'

'Then we wait for Kates to come to us,' Reed finished.

She gave a single, satisfied nod. 'And then we all live happily ever after.'

Sunday, December 3, 11:15 A.M.

Mia walked up to Wheaton's table, angry belligerence in every step. Wheaton had insisted they meet in the same place she'd met Reed a few nights before.

Wheaton looked at Mia's clothing with disapproval. 'I thought you'd dress.'

Mia took a deliberate look at Wheaton's low-cut blouse. 'I thought you would, too.'

Wheaton's smile was feline. 'Detective, that's hardly adult.'

'Neither was sending me that video. And we both know it wasn't a mistake so just cut the bullshit.' A lady at the next table gave her a glare.

'If you're done alienating the other diners,' Wheaton drawled, 'what do you want?'

Mia cocked her jaw. 'Don't run that piece on my sister.'

'Ah.' Buttering her toast, Wheaton smiled. 'I was wondering when you'd come to me. Well, that piece is set for tonight, opposite *60 Minutes*.'

She gritted her teeth. 'Airing that tape will put my sister's life in danger.'

'That can't be my concern. I'm a journalist.'

Mia let her eyes flash. 'Okay. Fine. What if you had an alternate story? One that would be bigger. More timely. That nobody else had. Yet.'

Wheaton was interested. 'Exclusive?'

Mia closed her eyes, made the word drag off her tongue. 'Yes.'

'What is it?'

'Tell me Kelsey's off the table.'

'Can't do that.' Wheaton leaned forward, rested her chin on her palm so that her perfect manicure showed perfectly. Her eyes sparkled. 'You go first.'

Mia drew a breath that was only part pretense. *I hate you. I really hate you.* 'The second victim, Penny Hill, was a mistake. He missed his real target.'

Wheaton's eyes narrowed. 'Who was the real target?'

Mia set her teeth. Hesitated. 'I . . . I can't do this. You go on the air with this and it paints a big bull's-eye on this person's head. I don't care what . . .' She got up. 'I can't.'

Wheaton sat back, eyes cool. 'I've got an updated picture of Kelsey. The old one didn't look like her at all. And we girls do like to look our best. Most of us anyway.'

Mia leaned forward as if fighting the urge to lunge, her hands curved into claws. But she calmed herself, stuck her hands in her pockets. 'You're evil.'

Wheaton shrugged. 'We can help each other here. Your call, Detective. Either way, I have a really good piece of film. So either way, I win.'

Mia closed her eyes. 'Milicent Craven,' she hissed through her teeth.

'Tell me why Kates is doing this.'

Mia opened her eyes, made her face ashamed. 'Penny Hill placed him in a foster home years ago. She got hurt, went on disability. His file was passed on to Craven, who dropped the ball, never checked him. Bad things happened to Kates in that home. This is about payback. But he paid back the wrong person.'

Wheaton was quiet for so long Mia started to think she wouldn't take the bait at all. Then she nodded. 'All right. If this pans out, your sister is off tonight's program.'

Mia jerked a nod and turned.

'Oh, Detective Mitchell?' Mia turned back to find Wheaton smiling like the cat who'd swallowed the canary. 'I'll see you again next week. Same theme song.'

The bitch. 'That's extortion,' Mia murmured, so low the other diners couldn't hear.

'That's such an ugly word. I prefer "partnership." Well?'

'All right.' Mia turned on her heel, walked out, then got in her car and after making sure she wasn't followed, pulled next to the police van parked a block away. She climbed inside and sat next to Reed. Jack had on headphones, watching the tape again.

'I almost didn't catch the extortion line,' Jack complained.

Mia pulled the wire from under her shirt. 'Sorry. I didn't want to scream it.'

Reed lifted his brows. 'I thought you were going to crawl and grovel.'

'She wouldn't have bought it. I hate her too much and it's not my style. So do you think that's enough for Patrick to get an indictment?'

'Hope so,' Jack said. 'If not, she's just going to up the ante, making reports that threaten cops and their families to get information. We don't know that she hasn't done it before, with other cops who might not have had the strength to say no.'

'Or the support,' Mia said quietly. 'I'm just glad they moved Kelsey.'

Jack started turning off his equipment. 'Well, it's Sunday. I'm going to run this tape into the office and go home to my wife and kids. It's been fun, but leave now.'

Mia smiled. 'Say hi to Julia for me and kiss that baby.'

Jack grinned. 'I'll kiss Julia, too. Now go. I got things to do.'

Mia and Reed climbed out and Mia looked up at the sky. 'It's sunny.'

'Perfect weather to clean up after a fire,' Reed said dryly.

Mia grinned up at him. 'I've got some things to do, but I'll come out and help as soon as I can. Then we have to get in position for tonight. This could be it.'

Reed watched her drive away, back in her tiny little Alfa. She'd gotten it back from the department garage just that morning, the windows replaced. There was still a bullet ding in the hood. She lived with danger every day and shrugged it off.

If the two of them really had something, if this became something, he'd have to learn to live with that danger. Now he knew how Christine had felt about him going into fires. He sighed. And, speaking of fires, he had one to clean up.

Sunday, December 3, 5:15 P.M.

'What have you done?' Dana came out of the house while Mia fought with the big box some helpful young clerk had tied into the trunk of her Alfa. Twine was everywhere.

'Friday was payday so I went shopping. Got a coat, some books, and this monstrosity.' She looked up at Dana. 'I'm sorry about last night.'

'Me, too. I wanted to tell you about the baby, but you've been kind of fragile lately.'

'Yeah. Well. Help me get this out.' Cutting at the string with her keys, she freed the box, carried it into the kitchen, and set it on the table. 'Open it.'

Ethan came to the doorway, barefoot, his shirt hanging open and Mia could only think that Reed was a thousand times better. Especially without the ring. That definitely helped his sex appeal. 'Hey, Mia,' he said as Dana ripped at the wrapping paper.

'Ethan. Hope I wasn't interrupting anything.'

Ethan grinned. 'Nope. Too many kids in the house. But I was trying.'

'Oh, Ethan, look.' Dana looked up, her eyes moist. 'Our first baby gift.'

Mia shifted, uncomfortable. 'It's a car seat, Dana. No need for the waterworks.'

'It's the hormones,' Ethan confided in a loud whisper, then kissed Mia's cheek. 'Thank you.' He smiled down at her and Mia knew he understood.

Dana wiped her eyes. 'Somebody's here you might want to see.'

Jeremy. 'Let me guess. He's watching TV.'

Ethan's smile faded. 'Documentaries on the History Channel, all afternoon. He hasn't said more than a few words. Understandable, given he's just lost his mom.'

'I was hoping he'd be here by now. I have something to give him. But first, keep your eyes open. The guy that killed his mom set fire to Reed's house last night.'

Dana and Ethan exchanged a look. 'Nobody hurt?' Dana asked.

'No. We're thinking it was either payback or a distraction, like when he shot at me. Either way, this guy probably won't bother with Jeremy, bu . . .'

Ethan nodded, jaw tight. 'I'll watch. Don't worry.'

'From a former Marine, that's good enough for me.' Mia went into the living room and sat next to Jeremy. 'Hey, kid.'

He turned only his head to study her. 'You came back.'

Her heart squeezed. 'Of course. I practically live here. Dana's my best friend.'

'You catch him yet?'

'Nope, and I'm here to see you. I brought you something.' She reached into the bag from the bookstore and handed him the large glossy book on jet planes.

His eyes widened and he took the book, but didn't open it. 'Thank you.' He turned back to the television. 'This show is about ancient Greece.'

'Yeah, I caught it last night.' She settled back against the sofa and put her arm around his shoulders. 'But I find I pick up a lot more the second time around.'

It was about time. He'd waited for Mitchell the whole damn day. He rolled his eyes. She'd been shopping. Somehow he'd thought more of a woman who filled her pantry with Pop-Tarts. But she was here. He crept through the wooded area that cut Dana's house off from the rest of the houses on the street. He wanted to get a look inside. To check the lay of the land in case she planned on staying there tonight.

He squinted through his binoculars. He could see in the living-room window, barely. Well. He lowered the binoculars, blinked hard, then raised them again. It was double or nothing and he'd hit double. Finally. For sitting next to Mitchell, his head on her shoulder, was Jeremy Lukowitch. If he wasn't with Yvonne, she must be dead or really sick, so the pill swap must've worked. If she was dead or really sick, the boy was the one who'd turned him in. *I should have killed the brat when I had the chance.*

A plan started to form. He had three eggs left and he knew exactly how to use them. His stomach growled. But first he had to get some food and some sleep.

Sunday, December 3, 6:15 P.M.

The mustache and wig afforded him some anonymity. Enough so that he could chance entering a diner and getting some food. Mitchell had made it so he couldn't show his face anywhere in Chicago. He scowled at the television behind the counter. His picture was on the news again. He fought the urge to see if anybody was looking at him, keeping his eyes on the screen. The reporter was talking about Penny Hill.

'*Action News* has learned today that Ms Hill was not the caseworker who handled Mr Kates's placement. An unfortunate accident placed her on disability for a year, during which time case manager Milicent Craven allowed the boy to go unmonitored. The boy was lost in an abusive environment, his cries for help unanswered. Now Penny Hill is dead. Ms Craven could not be reached for comment. Andrew Kates remains at large, another victim of an American social service system too bogged down by bureaucracy to adequately care for the children whose lives depend on them. We'll keep you up to date on this breaking story. This is Holly Wheaton, *Action News*.'

Fate had denied him justice with Laura Dougherty. He would not be deprived again.

But the timing was interesting. Mitchell had proved far more resourceful than he'd expected. It could be a trick. He'd check out Craven. If she was legit, then he'd act.

Sunday, December 3, 6:20 P.M.

Spinnelli switched off the television in the conference room. 'Good work, Mia.'

'And I'd like to thank the Academy . . .' Mia smiled. 'Okay, now what?'

'Now I want you to meet Milicent Craven.' Spinnelli opened the door to a woman, middle-aged and graying. She came in and sat at the table.

Reed leaned close. She looked fifty, but she was probably no older than Mia. 'When I'm fifty, can you make me look thirty again?' he asked and the woman grinned.

'I'll give you my card.'

Spinnelli smiled, too. 'This is Anita Brubaker. She's undercover, getting ready to come back to the real world. She's been living as Milicent Craven for two years at the address in the phone book. Her neighbors know only that she works for the state.'

'So you're the canary in the cage,' Mia said. 'You okay with this?'

'I am. I'll be in the house every evening through the night until we catch him. Then once we do, I won't need the undercover ID anymore anyway. Everybody's happy.'

'Except Andrew Kates.' Spinnelli sketched the neighborhood on his whiteboard. 'This is Craven's house. Mia, I want you and Reed here, Murphy and Aidan here, and Brooks and Howard here, in unmarked cars. I'll have cruisers in position. Social Services is alerted that if anybody calls for Milicent Craven they'll be connected to a voice mail we've just set up. If Kates or the press call, they'll get a confirmation of her existence.'

He looked around the room. 'Questions?' All heads shook no. 'Then get busy. This time tomorrow I want Andrew Kates in custody.'

Stacy stuck her head in. 'Excuse me. There's a man out here saying he needs to talk to whoever's in charge of the Kates investigation. He says his name is Tim Young.'

All eyes flew to Reed, who shrugged. 'Tennant was supposed to call me when Young got into Indianapolis. He never did.'

'Show him in.' Spinnelli stood, arms crossed over his chest. 'This should be good.'

Tim Young entered slowly, his step heavy. He was about twenty-five. His gray suit was wrinkled, his face dark with stubble. 'I'm Tim Young. Tyler Young's brother.'

'Please sit.' Spinnelli pointed to a chair. 'Stacy, call Miles Westphalen. Tell him to get down here as quickly as he can. Tell him why.'

When Stacy was gone, Spinnelli took the head of the table. 'This is a surprise.'

Young looked around the room, took in each face. 'I had to change planes in O'Hare. While I was waiting for my flight to Indy I saw the paper. I walked out of the airport and took a cab straight here. Andrew Kates is a name I've tried for ten years to forget.'

'Why?' Mia asked.

'Andrew and Shane were placed with my family ten years ago. Andrew was thirteen, Shane nine. I was fifteen and counting the days until I could graduate and leave. My father had a farm. He liked foster kids because they were an extra pair of hands. My mother went along with it, because she did everything he said. My older brother Tyler . . .' He let out a breath. 'Was bad.'

'He abused the boys,' Mia said softly. 'And you?'

There was pain in his eyes. 'Until I got big enough to fight back. He used to laugh that he liked his boys young enough to be flexible but old enough to put up a fight. He knew to back off when his prey got too big. Normally, none of the kids stayed that long.'

'Did your parents know?' she asked.

'I don't know. I never knew if they knew or if my father would have cared if he had. My mother would have looked the other way. I don't suppose you understand that.'

Mia's eyes flickered and Reed knew she understood too well. 'So what was Tyler's age of initiation?' she asked.

'Ten.' Young's lips curled. 'But he nearly made an exception with Shane. Shane was an attractive child and he'd had it before. Tyler could always tell.'

'He'd been abused by his aunt's husband,' Reed said.

'Like I said, Tyler could always tell. He teased Andrew that he'd make an exception for Shane, just to see Andrew try to fight back. Then he'd take Andrew. But Tyler had standards and methods. He'd hurt the older ones, then count to the younger ones. He'd count from one up to their age, then smack his lips and say, "When I get to ten, you'll be mine." Shane was nine. Tyler would count to nine, then taunt Andrew that soon Shane would be ten. "Count to ten, Andrew," he'd say. And laugh.'

'That connects a lot of dots,' Mia said. 'What happened when Shane turned ten?'

'Andrew was desperate. He'd tried to run away with Shane at least a dozen times, but the police always brought them back. He begged my mother to *do* something, but she told him not to make up stories. He hated her. I know Andrew had tried to set a few fires in the basement. Newspapers in the trash can kind of fires. He wanted to get caught. He wanted somebody from social services to come and take them away before Shane turned ten. Anyplace would have been better than our house.'

'What did you do?' Reed asked.

Young's laugh was mirthless. 'Nothing. I've lived with that for years. Not just with Andrew and Shane, but all the others. So many others. But you're interested in Shane.'

'For now,' Mia said. 'We'll sort through the others later. Tell us about Shane's tenth birthday. That was the day of the fire. The day Shane died.'

He let out a breath. 'The day Shane turned ten, Tyler . . . did his thing. First thing that morning. Shane was . . .' He shuddered. 'The look on that boy's face – I can still see it. He was just a kid. He was bleeding. But Tyler cleaned him up and our mother sent him to school. That afternoon, Andrew left school early. I saw him go.' He lifted a shoulder. 'Andrew was thorough. The house burned very well. But he didn't know Shane had left school early, too. Later the nurse said Shane had a stomach-ache. Later people said a lot of things. Nobody knew anything.'

'He set the fire in the trash can,' Reed said quietly and Tim Young nodded.

'In a trash can in the living room, then he ran away. He came back a little later, pretended to be shocked. He knew I knew. He thought I'd tell, but I stayed quiet about that like I did everything else. Then the firefighters found Shane. They carried him out, looking like a rag doll. He was dead. Andrew went numb, into shock. Catatonic even.

'The social workers came then. Took him away. A few cops asked me questions and I lied. I said he'd been at school. He couldn't have done it. The autopsy showed Shane had been sodomized. But nobody said anything. And eventually, life went on. We rebuilt the house. I graduated from high school and left town and never looked back.'

'And never heard from Andrew?' Mia asked, kindly now.

'No. Although barely a day goes by that I don't think about him or one of the others.'

'Andrew always saves the pets,' Reed commented. 'Do you know why?'

'Yes. We had a dog.' His smile was sad. 'Sweet old mutt. After Tyler was done with Andrew, Andrew would hide in the barn. A few times I found him, curled up against that old mutt. But he never cried. He just petted that old dog till it was a wonder he still had any coat. The day of the fire that old dog was in Shane's room. He died, too.'

'He never told the sheriff any of the times he was caught running?' Spinnelli asked.

Tim's smile turned sardonic. 'You mean Sheriff Young, my uncle?'

Spinnelli looked grim. 'I see.'

'I'm curious, Tim,' Mia said. 'You said you lied and gave Andrew an alibi that day, but didn't his teachers or some of the other kids notice he was missing?'

'Funny thing about that,' Tim drawled, his tone self-mocking. 'See, Tyler was a bully at school, too. All the kids knew it. The teachers did, too. Andrew's teacher at the end of that school day would have been Miss Parker. She was young and pretty and terrified of Tyler. Nobody "missed" Andrew that day.' He sighed. 'Maybe if we had, none of this would have happened.'

'I don't think you can know what would have happened, Tim,' Reed said quietly.

'Perhaps not. I've spent the years since I left home

trying to make up for what I did. And what I didn't do. Now I have to face my part in this. I can't be free until I've made some kind of restitution. Legally and morally. I'll do whatever you need me to do.'

Sunday, December 3, 8:35 P.M.

Mitchell thought she was smart. *I am smarter*. He approached Penny Hill's car, then reached in the backseat for her briefcase. He was glad now he'd left it behind. If he'd buried it in the backyard, Mitchell would have it by now.

Bitch cop, thought she could fool him. He'd found Milicent Craven's home address with ease. He'd called Social Services, was transferred to her voice mail. It was luck that he'd called again when the operator had been busy with another call. Well, not luck. That was instinct. He'd known it sounded too good to be true. When the operator was busy, calls were sent to the automated line. *Please enter the first few letters of the person's last name.* So he had. Three times. And all three times got the same answer. *No names match the letters you have entered. Please try again.*

So Milicent Craven was suspicious. Probably a fraud. But in the event he was wrong, he'd look at Penny Hill's belongings. She'd had a retirement party the night he'd killed her. There were presents and cards. If Milicent Craven existed, maybe she had signed one of them.

Maybe she'd be listed in Hill's Day-Timer. He needed to know.

He sat on the seat and started sorting through the contents of her briefcase. It was stuffed full of papers and files, but one labeled folder stood out. SHANE KATES.

After a moment his heart started beating again. He opened the folder and stared at the photo inside. He hadn't looked at his brother's face in nine years. He'd been such a beautiful little boy. Too beautiful. Too much of a temptation for perverts like his aunt's boyfriend and Tyler Young. They'd killed him. Every last one of them had killed Shane.

And they were all dead. Penny Hill was no innocent. She had Shane's file. She'd known where he was all along. All those months of hell in the Youngs' house.

Mitchell had lied. There was no Milicent Craven. She'd lied to lure him into the open. She was as conniving as the rest of the women. She should suffer for that.

She should die for that, just like Penny and Brooke and Laura and his aunt.

They'd be watching Milicent Craven's house. The minute he went in, he would have been dead. So he wouldn't go in. And he'd master their game. His original plan would stand. He'd draw Mitchell to him. And then he'd kill her. He'd see her burn.

First he'd get a good night's sleep. She'd wait for him outside Craven's house all night long. *She'll be tired tomorrow and I'll be fresh as a spring daisy.*

Monday, December 4, 12:45 A.M.

'Wake up, Reed.' Mia poked him in the darkness of the car. They were staked out, watching for Kates. Anita Brubaker was inside the house, armed to the teeth, while their unmarked cars watched from all directions. If Kates approached, they'd know.

'I'm not asleep,' Reed muttered, turning from the window. 'Wish I were, but I'm not.'

'Poor baby. You worked hard this afternoon, cleaning your house.'

He narrowed his eyes. 'You said you'd come help.'

'I did . . . just later. I went to see Jeremy.'

His eyes softened. 'You're getting attached to the kid.'

Her chin lifted. 'Is that so wrong?'

'No. Not if you don't plan to walk away. He'll have enough people walk away in the years ahead. The kid's got a long row to hoe.'

Her gaze swept the area and seeing nothing, returned to Reed. 'I wish I could take him home with me. But he's not a cat. I can't take him. I don't even have a home.'

'So you gave him to Dana. It's the next best choice. You did good, Mia.' He resettled himself in the seat, grimacing. 'Where did Spinnelli get this car? Yugoslavia?'

She chuckled. 'We couldn't use yours. Kates's seen it.'

'And five minutes in your car would put me in traction.'

'Hey, it's a classic. I can't help that you're too big.'

'I don't get it, Mia. You wait to buy a coat until you get paid, and it's a nice coat by the way, much better than the old one, but you have enough cash for a sports car?'

'Most of my money goes to Kelsey's lawyer. Every time we get close to parole, his billable hours go up, so I've been cash-strapped this month. Besides, the car wasn't that expensive. David got me a deal on a fixer-upper. I'd broken up with Guy and wanted something to lift my spirits, so I splurged. David fixed it up, keeps the engine happy.'

He frowned. 'Mia.' He hesitated. 'About Hunter.'

'Friends. Just friends. Always have been, never will be more.'

He looked unconvinced and she sighed. 'Look, I've told you all my secrets, but I won't tell you his. It would have been easier if we had wanted each other, but we didn't.'

'You were with him last night.'

She lifted a shoulder. 'I guess I wanted to be with someone else who couldn't have who they wanted.' She smiled. 'But things change.'

He smiled back. 'Yes, they do.'

'I never asked, did Beth win the slam poetry competition last night?'

'First in her age-group.'

'Did you hear her poem?'

He shook his head. 'We haven't made up quite that much.'

'You should ask her to . . . slam it for you, or whatever the right word is. It was good.'

He frowned and looked out the window at shadows. 'Christine was a poet.'

She thought about the poetry book she'd found. *This is my heart.* 'Really?'

'We met in college. I was taking a lit class and poetry was like ancient Greek to me. She saw me scowling, told me if I bought her a cup of coffee, she'd explain it all.'

'And she did.'

'She did. Then she read me her poems and it was like . . . listening to a ballet. She brought beauty into my life. I'd made myself disciplined through the army, gave myself a career with my degree. Made myself into a son the Sollidays were proud of. But I couldn't make beauty. Christine did that for me.'

Mia swallowed hard. 'I can't do that for you, Reed. I don't have that gift.'

'Not for ribbons and bows, no. But last night I realized you make me happy.' He turned his head. Met her eyes. 'And what's more beautiful than that?'

Moved, she had no words to give him back. 'Reed.'

His lips quirked up as he settled back into the seat. 'Plus you've got really nice breasts. So when I'm feeling lonely for ribbons and bows, I'll just look at those.'

She laughed. 'You're a bad man. Who makes bad rhymes.'

'I never claimed to be a poet.'

But he has the soul of one. Christine had been his soul

mate. She wondered if each person truly only got one. And hoped not.

After a few minutes he sighed. 'Mia, listening to Young had me wondering something. It's going to come out sounding bad, but I don't mean it that way. I just don't know how else to ask.'

She frowned. 'So just ask.'

'You grew up around cops. Why didn't you ever tell one of them about your father?'

'If you only knew how many times I've asked myself that same question, especially after Kelsey went to prison. When I was little, I was too afraid. Then when I was older, in high school, I didn't think anyone would believe me. He was a respected police officer. Then later, when I became a cop, I was . . . ashamed. I felt people would pity me if they knew, that I'd look weak and I'd lose respect. Then when Kelsey finally told me the truth, it was guilt. And now he's dead, so it doesn't seem to make much sense to tell now.'

'You told Olivia,' he said and she winced.

'And that went well, didn't it? I didn't want her to feel rejected. I should have just kept my mouth shut. When this is over, I'm going to Minneapolis to talk to her.'

'Do you want me to go with you?'

She studied his face. There was no pity there. Only support. 'Yes, I'd like that.'

He smiled. 'You accepted my help. Progress. Now, let's talk about your shoes.'

She grinned. 'Watch it, Solliday.' The grin faded. 'And thank you.'

His eyes became intense. 'You're welcome. I think we need to change the subject because it's becoming increasingly difficult not to touch you.' He shifted again and looked out the window. 'I wish the sonofabitch would come. I want this over with.'

Monday, December 4, 7:55 A.M.

Mia sat at her desk. 'I can't believe this.'

Reed yawned. 'He either didn't see Wheaton, or he made us.'

Kates hadn't taken the bait. 'Shit,' Mia grumbled. 'Now what?'

'We regroup. Then after morning meeting, we go back to the hotel and get some sleep. There's no way we'll find him if we're not sharp.'

'Maybe he's gone after Tim Young.'

'Santa Fe PD is watching,' he said, then sat up straighter. 'That's interesting.'

Mia twisted to look then shook her head. Lynn Pope from *Chicago on the Town* was walking her way, a distinctly hurt look on her face. *Crap.* 'Lynn,' Mia said.

'Mia. I'll be brief. You met with Holly Wheaton yesterday. Then last night Wheaton gets this great scoop. Why? You hate Wheaton.'

Mia met Pope's eyes. 'Yes, I do.' Head tilted, she

continued to hold Pope's gaze until the woman drew in a breath and cognition dawned.

'Oh. And it didn't work, did it?'

'Nope. Look, Lynn, when this is over, I'll call you.' One of her neurons fired unexpectedly, and the idea made her smile. 'Wait.' She walked to Solliday and whispered in his ear and he nodded. 'Lynn, check out a guy named Bixby. Runs an outfit called Hope Center. It's juvie. You might need to dig a little.'

Pope brightened. 'I will. Call me when this is over. And watch your neck.'

'I will.' Mia leaned on Solliday's desk. 'She'll do it right.'

But he wasn't listening. 'Now serving number two,' he said and again she twisted.

Margaret and Mark Hill must have passed Lynn Pope in the elevator. The brother and sister wore twin looks of grim resolve. 'Mr Hill, Miss Hill. How are you?'

'Have you caught him?' Margaret asked.

'No, but we're close. Why are you here?' It felt strange to be the one saying it.

Mark Hill drew an envelope from his coat pocket. 'Our mother's lawyer read her will on Saturday. He gave us this. We agonized yesterday over whether or not to give this to you. But we want our mother's murderer found and punished. So here.'

Mia took the envelope, read the letter inside. 'Oh boy.' She passed it to Reed, who shook his head silently. 'We'll try to keep your mother's name out of it. Thank you. I'll call you as soon as we catch him.' The Hills walked away, Mark putting his arm around his sister's shoulders. Margaret leaned against him. 'I guess they cleared the air.'

Reed stood. 'So it would seem. Come on, Mia. Let's get to morning meeting.'

Murphy and Aidan were already there. Spinnelli frowned when they came in. 'You're late.' Mia gave him the letter and reading it, he sat down. 'Oh boy.'

'What is it?' Murphy asked.

'A letter from Penny Hill,' Mia said, 'documenting what happened when she returned from disability, nine years ago. She went through her files, found Shane's buried at the bottom of some other records. No one had been assigned the boys. She then found Shane was dead and Andrew had been placed in another home. She went to her supervisor, who told her to destroy the file. She threatened to go higher, he convinced her she'd be fired if she did. She had medical bills, so she stayed silent.'

'This letter is dated six years ago,' Spinnelli said. 'She was experiencing a great deal of guilt, nightmares. She sealed the letter and gave it to her lawyer for safekeeping. I'll take care of this.' He blew out a breath. 'So where are we?'

'Either he didn't see the news or he made us,' Mia said.

'I figured that out for myself,' Spinnelli said darkly. 'What will you do next?'

'Follow him to Santa Fe?' Mia shrugged, frustrated. 'Set up Tim Young as bait?'

Spinnelli's brows went up. 'Tim Young it is.'

Mia shook her head. 'Wait, I was just . . . We can't use a civilian as bait, Marc.'

Spinnelli's mustache went down. 'He said he'd help. Kates must be stopped. And now we have one more victim. Mia, your super was found dead in the closet of an empty apartment in your building. Her keys were gone.'

As Mia's mouth fell open, Jack came in carrying a box. 'Kates was there. He left a mess in your bedroom, Mia. Blankets, pillows on the floor, clothes everywhere.'

Mia felt her cheeks heat even through the shock of her super's death. 'That doesn't mean he was in my place. I'm not much of a housekeeper. The bedroom was like that.'

'Did you leave your photo album out?'

Her heart started to pound. 'No. Hell.' Jack put the box on the table and Mia lifted the album to the table, sorted quickly. 'I'm not organized, but I know what was here. Bobby's obituary is gone.' Then her pounding heart stopped. She held Dana's wedding invitation in her hand. 'And so is Dana's reply card. He has her address.'

Spinnelli reached for the phone. 'I'll send a unit out there now.' But Stacy poked her head in with a frown.

'Marc, there's a Dana Buchanan on line one for either you or Mia. She's upset.'

Spinnelli put the phone on speaker. 'Dana, it's Marc Spinnelli. I'm here with Mia and others. Kates has your address.'

'Kates has Jeremy,' Dana said, her voice frantic. '*Mia.*'

Mia's blood went cold. She slowly rose, trembling. '*How?* How did he get Jeremy?'

'Let me talk to her.' The phone changed hands. 'Mia, it's Ethan. We're at Jeremy's school. We came in early this morning to get him enrolled. Jeremy went to his new class while we were still signing forms. The fire alarm went off right before school started and it wasn't a drill. Fire blocked one of the exits. It was chaos. We immediately started searching for Jeremy, but he was gone. How did he know Jeremy was here?'

'He had your address from my apartment. Marc, when was my super murdered?'

'Sometime Saturday afternoon.'

'I shook a tail when I left your place Saturday night, Ethan. I thought it was Carmichael. It must have been Kates. He must have come back yesterday and found Jeremy.' Her knees buckled and she sank into her chair. 'He was looking for me. He killed my super and now he's using Jeremy to get to me.' She drew a shuddering breath. 'Get Dana calm. This isn't good for the baby. We'll find Kates. And Jeremy.'

'Was anyone hurt in the fire at the school?' Reed asked.

'Just bumps and bruises. The teachers got control quickly. We weren't sure if we should push Jeremy back to school so soon, but we couldn't let him sit in front of the TV any longer. We wanted to get him back into a routine. Please find him.'

Mia rubbed her forehead. He'd taken Bobby's obituary. 'I think I know where he is.'

Chapter Twenty-four

Monday, December 4, 9:25 A.M.

Reed's hands fisted at his sides. 'You can't do this.' They had a SWAT team and every uniform and detective Spinnelli had been able to muster. They would wait, concealed in unmarked vans, a block away from Annabelle's house. They didn't want to spook Kates, so Mia would stroll inside alone, pretending to pay an ordinary visit.

Mia twisted at the waist. She wore a bulky sweater that hid the bulletproof vest and the weapon in her back waistband. 'Damn Kevlar itches,' she said, ignoring him.

'Mia, if he's in your mother's house, you're walking into a trap.'

'If he's still setting the trap, I'll get him first.' She met his eyes. 'He's got Jeremy.'

That a killer might also have her mother was absurdly absent. She was solely focused on the boy. And on Kates. After her initial shock, Reed had watched her training and skill take over. She was calm, while his heart was beating out of his chest.

'Reed.' Her voice was quiet. Sober. 'Let me do my job.'

You're not a cop. She'd said it that night he'd wanted to chase Getts. She was right. At the moment he didn't feel like a fire investigator, either. He was a man, watching the woman he cared for wrapping herself in Kevlar and arming herself like Rambo.

He turned to Spinnelli. 'You agree with this, Marc?'

'Not my first choice. But he didn't take the bait last night, so catching him before he's prepared is the best plan we've got. Mia's wearing a wire. She'll have backup.'

'Let me go in with her.'

Spinnelli shook his head and Reed could see the man understood all too well. 'No.'

'She's SWAT trained, Reed,' Murphy murmured beside him. 'Let her do her job.'

Reed drew a deep breath. 'Ben called. There were two points of origin at the school, so Kates used two more eggs, Mia. He may have one more.'

'I'm counting on it. No pun intended.' She flashed him a distracted smile. 'Don't take this wrong, Reed, but go away. I have to focus and I can't with you here.'

He cast his eyes up and down the street, looking at the utility markers. This neighborhood had gas lines. Mia could be walking into a fireball. *No, she won't.*

He couldn't go in at her side. So he'd shore her up

from below. Spinnelli and all the others were in deep conversation. Jack was pinning the same wire to Mia's sweater that she'd used with Wheaton yesterday. Nobody was watching him. He started walking.

'Going somewhere, Lieutenant?' The female murmur came from behind him.

He blew out a breath. 'Carmichael. Haven't you done enough?'

'I haven't done anything today. And I won't. I never even saw you.'

He turned, eyes narrowed. 'Excuse me?'

'You're going in.' She lifted a shoulder. 'Don't need to be a rocket scientist. I would appreciate a few words when you come out. Just watch Mitchell. Regardless of what you might think, I hold her in high personal regard. She thinks she's indestructible.'

'I know.' He started walking again. *Bulletproof*, Jack had said. *Lucky*, Mia believed. *All too human*, Reed knew. He slipped through backyards until he came to Annabelle Mitchell's. The main gas valve would be in the basement. A set of entrance steps went down into the ground. He crouched at the base of the stairs, prepared to break in. But one of the panes in the door was already broken. The door was unlocked.

Kates is here. Reed cautiously opened the door, slipped inside. *Now so am I.*

Monday, December 4, 9:35 A.M.

Mia let herself in Annabelle's front door with her key, her weapon pointed down behind her leg. The last time she'd been here was the day they'd buried Bobby. Now Bobby meant nothing. Getting Jeremy out unharmed and stopping Kates meant everything.

He was here already. She could feel it from the moment she walked through the door. There was an eerie stillness to the place. She crept to the kitchen doorway and drew a silent breath. Annabelle sat in a kitchen chair a foot from the stove. Hands and feet tied with twine. Mouth gagged. Dressed in only her underwear, she shivered violently. Her body gleamed, coated shoulder to hips with the solid accelerant Kates had used six times now. The stove was already pulled away from the wall, his intent clear.

Her mother's eyes met hers, terrified and . . . full of the furious contempt Mia knew so well. Her mother had always blamed them for Bobby's violence. Mia supposed this time her mother finally had it right. Kates was here, she was in danger, *because of me.*

No gas filled the air yet. Either Kates was still preparing or he was waiting to spring his trap. She scanned the kitchen, wondering where he'd put Jeremy. Her mother's eyes followed her narrowed, as Mia crept into the kitchen, opening the cabinets under the sink. It was the only place large enough to hide a small boy. But they were empty.

'Help me.' It was really two muffled grunts from behind the gag, but Annabelle's eyes left no question as to the translation.

Mia put her finger to her lips. Then she pulled a knife from the block on the counter and prepared to cut her mother's bonds. With one fewer hostage, she could focus on Jeremy. She'd taken a step toward the chair when a voice stopped her in her tracks.

'Put the knife down, Detective.'

Even though she'd mentally prepared herself for exactly this sight, Mia's heart froze. Jeremy stood trembling in front of Kates, one of Kates's gloved hands in his sandy red hair and Kates's long shiny blade at his throat. Jeremy's freckles jumped out from his white face. His eyes were terrified and . . . full of desperate trust.

'You've seen what my knife can do, Detective,' Kates said smoothly. 'So has the boy. Haven't you, Jeremy?' She watched his fingers tighten in Jeremy's hair, watched Jeremy's small jaw tighten as he struggled to control his own fear. 'Put down the knife.'

Mia set the knife down, hilt out so she could grab it quickly if the opportunity arose.

'And the gun.' He yanked Jeremy to his toes. 'Now. Kick it over here.'

Again she complied, and her gun went sliding across the kitchen floor.

'Mia.' It was Spinnelli's voice in the earbud she prayed Kates wouldn't suspect. The wire she wore gave Spinnelli and the others a view of the inside. The earbud was her link to the command center in the van. 'Get him into the living room. I have snipers with a clear shot through the front window. The boy is small. We'll aim high. Out.'

One flick of Kates's wrist and Jeremy would die. The snipers couldn't fire until Jeremy was clear. She had to get him to let Jeremy go first.

'Don't hurt the boy.' She didn't plead, didn't command. 'He's done nothing to you.'

Kates laughed. 'He has and we all know it, don't we, Jeremy? He told you I'd been there. Led you to my things.'

'No, he didn't. We found the house on our own. Jeremy said nothing.'

'Impossible.'

'Truth. We found the car you ditched the night you killed Brooke Adler. It had an aftermarket GPS you didn't see.'

His eyes flickered. He was annoyed with himself. Good. 'So?'

'You like animals. You let out the cat and dog before you set the houses on fire.'

His jaw cocked. 'I'll repeat the question. So?'

'And you had access to curare. We checked vet clinics and pet shops and their employees in a one-mile radius of the car we found. And we found Mrs Lukowitch.'

His mouth flattened to a line. 'And she told. I wish I'd killed the bitch myself.'

'No. She lied. But not well and that made us

suspicious. We found your stash the old-fashioned way, Kates. Good detective work and a search warrant. Jeremy said nothing. Let him go.' Kates stood still as stone. 'He's only seven. He's innocent.' She took a chance and prayed. 'Like Shane was before your aunt's husband.'

The hand that held the knife tightened on the hilt. 'Don't say his name.' Kates's chin came up, eyes narrowing. 'I don't recall seeing a single sweater like that in your closet. I only remember those clingy shirts that you wear to show off your breasts because you're a tease. You're wearing a vest. Take off the sweater, Detective. Now.'

'Mia, keep the vest on,' Spinnelli said with urgency, but Kates lifted his knife to the underside of Jeremy's chin and sliced, just deep enough to draw blood. Then the knife went back to the boy's throat.

'Take off the sweater or the boy dies right in front of your eyes.'

'Mia.' Spinnelli's voice held a thread of panic. 'Don't.'

Tears were welling in Jeremy's eyes. But he never wavered. Never whimpered. Kates's brows lifted. 'I cut Thompson's head nearly off his body. Jeremy is so much . . . smaller. You want that on your conscience, Mitchell?' He pulled Jeremy's head back and the steely look of determination in his eyes left Mia with absolutely no doubt he'd make good on his threat.

'All right.'

'Mia!' Spinnelli barked it. Mentally she tuned him

out. The camera was buried in the sweater's fibers below her left shoulder. If she could drape the sweater on the counter so the camera pointed out, Spinnelli would still have a clear view. Carefully she pulled the sweater over her head and put it on the counter. And prayed.

Kates's lips curved. 'Now the vest.'

'Goddammit, Mia. Do not take off that vest. That's an order.'

Her fingers were steady as she pulled at the Velcro. 'You protected Shane, Andrew. You sacrificed yourself to Tyler Young to keep him safe.' She was pulling at the Kevlar vest slowly, strip by Velcro strip, hoping to make headway before she was completely at his mercy.

'I told you not to say his name.' He straightened abruptly and Jeremy sucked in a breath as he stood on his toes.

Mia wanted to beg, but kept her voice calm. 'I'm sorry. I know it hurt you to lose him. I know you've been paying back that hurt all week.' Her fingers had paused on one of the last remaining Velcro strips. Kates's eyes were fixed on hers. She was getting through. 'But I also know that it all started when Jeff and Manny hurt Thad.'

Anger flashed in Kates's eyes. 'You don't know shit.' He clenched his teeth. '*Take off the damn vest.* Now, before this kid's blood runs like a river.'

Damn. Her fingers pulled at the last strip. The vest hung loosely on her body now. 'I know more than you think I do, Andrew. I know what it's like to be on the receiving end of the same sacrifice you made for your brother. My sister did the same for me.'

'You're lying.'

'No, I'm not. My father molested my sister and she didn't fight back so that I could have a normal life. I live daily with the guilt that I didn't protect *her*. So I understand more than you think, Andrew. You don't want to hurt this child. Your beef is with me. All along you've punished the people who've hurt you.' Except for his mistakes, but she'd keep him focused. 'You've never hurt a child before. Don't start now.'

He stood, uncertain. Sensing victory, she pressed.

'Your beef is with me, Andrew,' she repeated. 'I'm the one who found your real name, found you. I'm the one who took your stuff. I'm the one who's trying to stop you. Not the boy. Let him go. Take me instead.'

At the top of the basement stairs, on the other side of the door, Reed listened. His heart sank, even though it was what he'd expected her to do from the moment he'd heard the words 'Put down the knife, Detective.' He'd had his hand on the doorknob, ready to run to her aid when he heard Kates threaten the boy with his knife. Reed had stood, his own weapon in his hand, waiting for the right moment. She'd get him to release the child, of that Reed had no doubt. At what cost to herself, he didn't want to consider. Kates had been silent a long time, then he spoke.

'I could kill you both.'

*

Mia considered Andrew Kates carefully, made herself logically process all that she'd learned over the last week. 'You could. But I don't think you will.' He was a man who for ten years buried the fact that he'd killed his own brother. He would readily accept what he found more palatable than the truth. 'You spared Joe Dougherty a painful death. You spared the animals. You've punished those who deserved your anger. Penny Hill and Tyler Young deserved your anger, Andrew, but Jeremy does not.'

She took another tack. 'If you kill this child, I'll fight and kill you myself. None of the women you killed this week are trained like I am. You read the article in the paper. I took down a man twice your size all by myself a week ago today. You may kill me, but you won't walk away, either. I promise you that. Let him go and I won't fight you.'

'I don't believe you. It's a trick.'

'It's not a trick. It's a promise.' She lifted a brow. 'Call it paying my debt to my sister. Surely you can understand that.'

For what seemed like an eternity he stood thinking. 'You take off the vest all the way and I'll let the kid go.'

Mia peeled the vest from her body, down her arms. She shivered, only a thin T-shirt covering her upper half. 'I kept my end. It's your turn.'

In one motion he withdrew the knife from Jeremy's neck and pulled a .38 revolver from his back waistband.

Mia jerked her eyes from his new weapon to Jeremy, who stood shaking. 'Go, Jeremy,' she said urgently. 'Now.' Jeremy looked at her, his eyes miserable and her heart cracked in two. 'Go, honey. It'll be all right. I promise.'

Kates gave the boy a hard shove. 'She said go.' Jeremy ran.

The front door opened, then slammed.

'We've got the boy, Mia,' Spinnelli said in her ear. 'Get him to the window.'

Mia glanced at her mother, still tied to the chair by the stove. 'Let her go, too.'

Kates smiled. 'She wasn't part of the deal. Besides, she's rude.'

'You can't kill a woman because she's rude,' Mia snapped. 'For God's sake.'

'You obviously haven't found Tania Sladerman from the hotel yet. Your mother stays. If you welsh, she's dead. If anything goes wrong, she's my ticket out of here.'

'Living room, Mia,' Spinnelli hissed. '*Now.*'

Mia started toward Kates, trying to lead him to the window. 'So let's get started.'

Kates waved his gun. 'Sit down. We'll do this my way. Cuff yourself. Both wrists.'

She can't do that, Reed thought. She won't. The boy was safe. Now she'd make her move. He cracked open the door. It opened into a walk-in pantry. An open door led to the kitchen. He crept to the door and peered around. Annabelle Mitchell sat with her back to the stove, tied and gagged. Kates stood between the chair and the stove, a pipe wrench in his right hand, a knife in his left, the blade pressed against Annabelle's throat. Her eyes widened when she saw him and he shook his head.

His own eyes widened when he saw the .38 on the stove-top. Somewhere along the way Kates had upgraded from the .22 he'd taken from Donna Dougherty's nightstand.

Reed shifted, bringing Mia into view. She sat in a chair, wide-kneed, leaning forward. 'I'm wondering just one thing, Kates.' Her hands were between her knees, fumbling with her cuffs. Stalling. *Good girl.* Her backup piece was inside her boot. He should know. He'd taken it off her several times now. She was waiting for the opportunity to get to it.

'Just one?' Kates asked sarcastically. 'Hurry up with the cuffs,' he added impatiently. 'Or the old lady goes.'

'I'm trying,' Mia snapped back. 'My hands are shaking, okay?' She drew a breath. 'Yeah,' she answered him. 'Just one question. The fuses. Why were they so short? I have two theories.' She looked up, grimly mocking. 'My police shrink says your knife is an extension of your dick. I'm wondering if the short fuses were as well.'

Mia was baiting him. Trying to draw him into using the knife on her instead. And even as Reed saw the logic in her strategy, his heart clenched in fear. He set his aim at Kates's chest. The moment he took the knife from Annabelle's throat, he'd be dead.

Kates's face turned a florid red. 'You bitch. I knew you'd lie. Damn you.'

'Or,' she continued calmly, 'my second theory is that the short fuses are really your way of dealing with the person who really killed your brother. You.'

'Shut up,' Kates hissed. But his eyes flickered wildly. She was close, Reed knew.

'You killed your brother, Andrew,' she said. 'Every time you set a fire, a little part of you hoped it would take you out, too. Because you're the guilty one. You killed Shane.'

'You don't know shit and you're going to die.' Without taking his eyes from her, Kates knocked the gas valve right off the pipe. But instead of a steady hiss, there was only a gurgle followed by silence. *Count that, asshole*, Reed thought with satisfaction.

Stunned, Kates's eyes flicked to the pipe and Mia came to her feet, her backup piece in her hand. And before Reed could open his mouth to warn her, Kates hurled the wrench at Mia's head. She ducked and Kates grabbed the revolver.

Reed fired, the shot thunderous in the silence. Kates's knife clattered to the floor and a millisecond later, so did Kates. Reed rushed forward, his radio in his shaking hand, his fingers fumbling over the controls. He kicked Kates's gun from his hand. 'Kates is down. Mitchell's mother is hurt.'

Blood flowed from the wound at Annabelle's throat, but it didn't gush. It could be worse. He grabbed a terry towel from the counter and pressed it to Annabelle's throat. 'Mia.' He twisted to see her and . . . his hands froze.

'Goddammit, Reed, what the hell are you doing in there?' Spinnelli's furious voice crackled from the radio.

But Reed didn't answer. Couldn't answer. Mia lay on the floor in a heap, her white T-shirt already soaked with blood. Reed somehow made it to her side on his knees, his hands shaking. 'Mia. *Mia.*' He lifted her shirt and his pounding heart stopped. 'Oh God.' There was a huge hole in her side and blood gushed.

Her eyes struggled open, dazed with pain. 'Reed. Did you get him?'

He shrugged out of his coat and ripped at his shirt. He had to stop the blood. She'd bleed to death before they got her to the ER.

'I got him, honey. Stay still. Help's on the way.'

'Good,' she answered. A groan rattled her chest. 'It hurts.'

Hands shaking, he pressed his shirt to the gaping wound. 'I know it does, baby.'

She drew a hard breath. 'You should have let me keep the dog tags, Solliday.'

The front door flew open and EMTs charged in, followed by a swarm of uniforms led by Marc Spinnelli and Murphy. Murphy pulled Reed out of the way as the

EMTs lifted Mia to a stretcher. 'Her BP's dropping like a rock. Let's go!'

Numb, Reed watched them carry her out the door and into the waiting ambulance.

Another team carried Annabelle Mitchell out after her daughter. She was still alive, but unconscious. Spinnelli knelt next to Kates, pressed fingers to his throat. 'He's dead.' Spinnelli rose, heavily, his face pale beneath his bushy gray mustache. 'One shot to the chest, another to the shoulder. Different guns. Who fired the chest shot?'

'I did. Mia shot him in the shoulder.' Reed's knees threatened to give. 'He had a knife on Annabelle then pointed the gun at Mia. When he threw the wrench at Mia, she shot him, but her aim was off. Mine wasn't.' He leaned over and picked up his coat. 'I'm going to the hospital now.'

Spinnelli nodded unsteadily. 'Murphy, follow the bus to the hospital. Take Solliday with you. I'll finish up here and meet you there.'

Monday, December 4, 11:05 A.M.

'Daddy?'

Reed forced his eyes open. Beth hesitated at the edge of the surgery waiting room, one of his shirts in her hands, fear on her face. He made himself stand, even though his stomach roiled and his knees were still weak. 'I'm all right, Beth.'

She swallowed hard, then flew into his arms. 'I know. I know.' She was shaking. 'I heard about Mia and I thought it could have been you.'

Reed kissed the top of her head. 'It wasn't.' And it shouldn't have been Mia, either. *I should have shot the bastard when I had the chance.* But that would have risked Annabelle's life as well. Annabelle had been curiously absent from every painful secret Mia had shared. But he'd sensed no hate for her mother. He'd sensed nothing.

'How is she?' Lauren asked from the doorway.

'Still in surgery. We're waiting.' He looked around the packed room. Twenty faces were frightened and drawn, nearly all of them for Mia. 'We're all waiting.'

Beth sniffed. 'You smell like smoke. I thought there was no fire.'

'It's cigarettes.' Her wide eyes startled a small smile from him. 'Not mine.' Murphy had smoked a whole pack on the way over, abandoning the carrot sticks. Reed couldn't blame him. 'Thanks for the shirt.' He shrugged into it, saying nothing when Beth stepped up to do the buttons. There was no way he'd have been able to do it himself.

A doctor walked in, his face carefully expressionless, and Reed's heart stopped in his chest. She's *dead*. Beth squeezed his hand and Mia's friend Dana came to her feet, pale. Trembling. Her husband Ethan rose, holding her up.

'I'm looking for Detective Mitchell's family.'

'I'm her sister,' Dana said and pointed to Reed. 'He's her fiancé.'

The doctor nodded wearily. 'Then come with me.'

Ignoring the shocked looks, Reed followed the doctor and the Buchanans into a smaller room. The doctor gestured to some chairs, then shut the door. 'She's alive.'

'Oh, God.' Dana crumpled against her husband. Buchanan lowered his wife into one of the chairs and stood behind her, his hands on her shoulders.

'But?' Reed said. He was still standing. He owed Mia that much.

'The bullet did a lot of damage. There are a number of internal injuries, but the most serious one was to her right kidney. We had to remove it.'

Reed sat down now. He looked at Dana, her eyes huge against her pale face, and knew she understood the true meaning behind the doctor's words. But Ethan Buchanan did not. 'So? She has another. You only need one, right?'

'She only had one,' Reed said woodenly. He wanted to throw something. But he reined it in. 'So,' he said. 'What now?'

'She's not out of the woods yet. She lost a lot of blood and she's still unstable. We'll know more in a day. But if she survives, she'll need to consider the options.'

'Dialysis or donation,' Reed said. 'Test me. I'll give her one of mine.'

The doctor's look was kind. 'Family would have a better chance of being a match.'

Dana looked uncomfortable. 'Test me, but we're . . . adopted sisters.'

'And my wife's pregnant,' Buchanan added.

The doctor blew out a breath. 'I see.'

'She has a mother and a biological sister,' Dana said.

Now the doctor looked uncomfortable. 'Her mother refused to be tested.'

Reed's mouth dropped open. *'What?'*

'I'm sorry. Mrs Mitchell is conscious and has refused.'

But Dana looked sadly unsurprised. 'Her sister Kelsey is at Hart Women's Prison.'

'Not anymore. She was moved. Spinnelli knows where.' Reed met Dana's eyes. 'And there's Olivia.'

Dana nodded slowly. 'Let's check Kelsey first. Mia told me what happened between her and Olivia. She may not be receptive right now.'

'It doesn't have to be now,' the doctor inserted. 'She can survive on dialysis.'

'But she won't be a cop anymore,' Reed said flatly.

The doctor shook his head. 'Not a homicide detective anyway. Maybe a desk job.'

Reed swallowed. *It's what I am*, she'd said. 'I think she'd rather die.'

The doctor patted Reed's shoulder. 'Don't do anything drastic right now.'

The doctor left and Reed pressed his fingertips to his temples. 'I wish I'd shot the bastard when I had the chance. I was trying to save her mother, goddammit.'

'And now she won't even be tested,' Ethan murmured.

'She's a bitter woman,' Dana said quietly. 'But Mia wouldn't have wanted you to do anything differently, Reed. I'll get in touch with Kelsey. She'll donate. She loves Mia.' She drew in a shaky breath. 'I'm sorry about the fiancé thing. I figured you'd want to be able to see her and they wouldn't let you otherwise.' Her lips curved, but her eyes were devastated. 'It worked in the movies.'

Reed huffed a tired, mirthless chuckle. 'Congratulations on the baby. Mia told me.' As they'd sat on stakeout last night, waiting for Kates to appear.

Dana's eyes filled then. 'She has to get better. She's going to be the godmother.'

'She told me that, too. She can't wait.'

Dana blinked the tears away. 'Hormones,' she muttered. 'I have to go home for a little while to get things set up with the woman who's watching our kids. I'll be back later when Mia's awake. Don't let anyone tell her about this until I get back, okay?'

Reed felt like crying himself, but he nodded. 'Okay. For now we just tell the others that she's out of surgery. And we wait.'

She took his hands as she'd done the day they'd met. 'And we pray.'

Tuesday, December 5, 7:25 A.M.

'How is she?' Dana murmured. Reed started to get up, but she pushed him back into the chair at Mia's bedside in ICU. What seemed like a hundred tubes ran from her body and her face was as white as the sheets.

'The same.' She hadn't stirred since they'd wheeled her from recovery. 'The doctor says some of her not waking up may be exhaustion from the last week and from coming back to work too early after the last injury.'

Dana brushed at the hair on Mia's forehead lovingly. 'Our girl has a hard head. Can't tell her anything.'

The bullet would have bounced off your damn hard head, Jack had said. *Sometimes I wish you weren't bulletproof.* And she wasn't. 'The last thing she said was that I should have let her keep her dog tags. I'm not a superstitious man, but I'm wondering if she was right.'

'Remind me to smack you,' Dana said mildly. 'The dog tags needed to go and I'm grateful you convinced her of that. Reed, she's a cop. She put herself in dangerous positions every day. Superstition has nothing to do with this. Have you had any rest?'

'Some.' Dana's eyes were serene. Calming.

'Why will her mother not be tested?'

'Annabelle always blamed her daughters for everything. If they'd been sons, life would have been different, she thought. If they'd been sons, Bobby Mitchell would have found another reason to be abusive. It was who he was. Kelsey and Mia paid the price.'

'Does she love her mother?'

Dana lifted a shoulder. 'I think she feels obligated. You're trying to find some sense in a senseless thing. That if she loved her mother despite everything, that your actions would be somehow more justified. That's not how it works.'

'You sound like a shrink,' he muttered and she laughed softly.

'Go get some sleep, Reed. I'll sit with her and I'll call you as soon as she wakes up. I promise.' She waited until he'd heaved himself to his feet before handing him a bag from the bookstore. 'I found this in my living room. She brought a book to Jeremy on Sunday and left this behind. It's for you.' One side of her mouth lifted. 'It wasn't her normal reading material so I peeked inside. Make sure you read the note.'

He waited until he was back in his hotel room, alone for the first time since . . . since Saturday night, he realized. When he sat in his living room and realized she made him happy. She'd wake up. She had to. He couldn't believe anything else.

He drew the book from the bag and frowned. It was poetry. Hard-assed, sarcastic verse by a guy named Bukowski. It was titled *Love Is a Dog from Hell*. He drew a breath and opened to the note she'd penned. Like everything else, Mia's handwriting was open, sprawling and messy.

It's not my heart. More like my spleen. But my own words are awkward and this guy says what I feel. Maybe I like poetry after all.

Not her heart? *Oh.* He closed his eyes, remembering. The night she'd seen the ring around his neck. He'd been reading Christine's book of poetry. When he woke, it was on his nightstand. Mia must have read Christine's inscription. Now Christine's book filled with lyrical beauty was gone and in his hands he held a new book of raw, passionate, sometimes angry words. But the sentiment touched him deep and as he sat reading the book she'd chosen, he finally let the tears he'd held back for days fall.

She'd be okay. Mia was too hardheaded to accept any other outcome. *So am I.*

Chapter Twenty-five

Monday, December 11, 3:55 P.M.

A nurse stuck her head in the room. 'You have a visitor, Detective.'

Mia wanted to groan. Her head hurt. She'd had a steady stream of visitors since being moved into her own room. She could have told the nurses to make them stop, but every person was someone she loved. And someone who loved her. A headache was a small price to pay. 'Sure, send him in.'

Jeremy peeked around the corner and Mia smiled. 'Hey, kid.'

'Hey.' He approached the bed. 'You look better.'

'I feel better.' She patted the mattress. 'How's school?'

He gingerly climbed up beside her. 'My teacher made a mistake today.'

'She did? Tell me.'

And he did, telling her about his teacher's mispronunciation of the name of some Babylonian king Mia had never heard of, speaking very gravely as Mia had learned was his way. As he talked, the headache eased and she put the worry over the states of her body and her career from her mind. This child was safe. She'd done something important.

Now she wanted Jeremy to be more than safe. Occasionally he smiled and once in the last week he'd even laughed. He seemed content at Dana's, but somehow that wasn't enough. She wanted him to be happy, not just content.

He finished his tale and after a long pause and careful study of her face said, 'You made a mistake that day.' He frowned. 'Actually, you lied.'

Which day didn't need to be specified. 'I did?'

He nodded. 'You told Kates I never said a word about him. You lied.'

'Hmm.' So the teacher story was merely a clever segue. 'I suppose I did. Would you have preferred I told the truth?'

He shook his head. 'No.' He bit his lip. 'My mom lied, too.'

Ahh. 'You mean when she said she hadn't seen him? She was protecting you.'

'So were you.' He straightened abruptly. 'I want to live with you.'

She blinked. Opened her mouth. Denials and reasons why not sprang to her mind, but none would pass through her lips. There was only one answer she could give this child who'd been through so much. 'Okay.' And she'd find a way to make it happen if she had to move heaven and earth. 'But I have to warn you, I'm a bad cook.'

'It's okay.' He snuggled down beside her, the remote in his hand. 'I've been watching cooking shows. It doesn't look too hard. I think I can cook for us.'

She laughed and kissed the top of his head. 'Good.'

Monday, December 11, 5:15 P.M.

Dana had come for Jeremy and Mia was again alone. She had much to ponder. She'd gained a cat and a boyfriend and a kid. And she'd lost a kidney and a career, all in two weeks' time. Kates was dead, by Reed's hand. Jeremy was alive. And so was her mother. She'd have sacrificed nearly anything to save Jeremy, but the saving of her mother had sacrificed her career and that seemed a high price to pay.

I should have killed Kates when I had the chance, she thought. When he'd held the knife to her mother's throat, it was as if it were a stranger sitting there. She'd saved her mother, risking her own life. But she'd risked her life for strangers many times.

A stranger would be more likely to give her a kidney, though. It was hard not to be bitter about that. *I'll live.* And pragmatically that was the important thing. But her career was over unless a donor could be found. Kelsey wasn't a match, nor was Dana or Reed or Murphy or any of her friends who'd stepped up to the plate without being asked. Apparently even Carmichael had been typed, but no cigar.

Olivia was a solid fixture in her mind, but it wasn't something Mia felt she could ask. They were strangers. Maybe, someday, they'd be friends. If so, Mia wanted it to be for the right reasons, not because she'd cultivated a relationship in the hopes of begging a kidney. That seemed . . . cheeky.

So it seemed a career change was in the near future. *So what will I be?* It was an interesting question and not a little terrifying. But she didn't have to think about that now. Now she was taking the break Spinnelli had promised. But not at the beach and her skin was going the opposite way of a tan. *But I'll live.*

'Hey.' Reed came in, carrying a newspaper in one hand and a big plastic bag in the other. 'How are you feeling?'

'Headache, but other than that, okay. I swear, Solliday, if you have a box of condoms in *that* sack, then you'd better find another woman.'

He sat on the edge of the bed and kissed her gently. 'I never thought I'd miss your smart mouth.' He handed her the paper. 'Thought you'd want to see this.' The headline read LOCAL NEWSCASTER INDICTED FOR EXTORTION. The byline was Carmichael's.

Mia's lips twitched. 'This is much better than any of that pain reliever you keep shoving down my throat.' She scanned the page and looked up with a grin. 'Holly Wheaton's going to be broadcasting from a cell. I never thought that threat would be a reality.'

'You know, you told me why she hated you. You never told me why you hated her.'

'It seems so unimportant now. Remember I told you about how I fought with Guy in that fancy restaurant and gave him back his ring? Well, somebody had tipped Wheaton off that we were there and fighting. She'd been demoted from headline news to the society gossip stuff because no cops would let her near a crime scene. Anyway, Wheaton was waiting outside the restaurant with a camera. Asked me if it was true that Guy and I had broken up. It wasn't even good gossip. It was just spiteful.'

She sighed. 'And that's how Bobby found out his free hockey tickets were gone. He made sure I knew he wasn't happy. I shouldn't have cared. I guess it was a stupid reason to hate her.' She grinned. 'But I'm still happy her ass is going to jail.'

Reed laughed and kissed her again. 'Me, too.' He moved to the chair. 'Beth entered another poetry slam competition. I got invited. So are you, if you're out in time.'

Mia sobered. 'Did you ever ask her to do "casper" for you?'

Something moved in Reed's dark eyes, intense and profound. 'Yes. And then I told her I loved her, just like you said I should.'

'She's got a gift.'

'Yes, she does. I had no idea she felt that way.' He swallowed. 'To think that she'd thought I'd trade her to have her mother back. I never meant to hurt Beth that way.'

'So, what will you do about it?'

He smiled. 'I met with the contractors about the house. I approved the structural plans, but I'm going to let Beth and Lauren decorate. You get input on my bedroom.'

She lifted her brows. 'I do?'

'You're going to be living there when you get out of here.'

He said it with an uncharacteristic belligerence. Her brows stayed up. 'I am?'

'You are. At least until you're recovered. Then you can leave if you want to. You got something to say about that, Mitchell?'

He was nervous. It was sweet. 'Okay. But I only get input?'

He relaxed. 'I don't want stripes and plaid. Beth has a good eye. You can input.'

'Okay.' She laced their fingers together. 'Jeremy came to see me today.'

'And you watched TV,' Reed said dryly.

She chuckled. 'History of cheese or something.' Then she sighed. 'Reed, something's been on my mind.' She stared down at their hands. 'I don't want Jeremy growing up in foster care, even a good home like Dana's.'

'You want to adopt him, then.'

'Yeah. He asked if he could come live with me when

I get out. I said yes and I'll do whatever I need to do to keep that promise. I wanted you to know that.'

'We have a spare room. He can stay there. But he shouldn't have his own TV. That kid watches too much TV as it is.'

It was such a small thing to him, taking in a child. Mia was nearly floored by both the generosity and the ease with which he committed himself. 'We're talking a kid, here, Reed. Another person. I don't want you to make this decision lightly.'

His eyes darkened. 'Did you?'

'No.'

'Neither did I.' He drew a breath. 'I've had something on my mind, too. Do you remember when I asked if you believed in soul mates?'

Her heart quickened. 'Yes.'

'You said you believed that some people might have them, maybe.'

'And you said a person could have only one.'

'No, I said I didn't know.'

'Okay. Then you said you'd never found anyone to replace Christine.'

'And I never will.'

She blinked. It was not the direction she'd expected the conversation to go. 'Why did you ask me to stay with you, Reed? Because if it's only pity, I'm not interested.'

He lifted his eyes to the ceiling with a frustrated sigh. 'I'm not good with this. I wasn't good the first time, either. Christine actually proposed.'

Mia's jaw dropped. 'You're . . . you're not proposing.'

He shot that boyish grin that never failed to charm her. 'No. But you should see the look on your face.' He brought her hands to his lips and sobered. 'I couldn't replace Christine. She was an important part of my life. She gave me Beth. But what I realized is that I don't need to replace *her*.' He looked down at their hands. 'I loved Christine because she made me more than I'd been on my own. She made me happy.' He looked up and smiled. 'You make me happy.'

Mia tried to swallow the lump in her throat. 'I'm glad.'

He lifted one brow. 'And?'

'And you make me happy, too.' She grimaced slightly. 'Now I wonder when the other shoe's going to fall.'

'It's not a crime to be happy, Mia. So. Do you believe in love at first sight?'

It was a trick question. 'No.'

He grinned. 'Me, either. Especially since at first sight you looked insane.'

'And you looked like Satan.' She rubbed a finger over his goatee. 'But it's growing on me. Reed, I might not be normal . . . ever again.'

His grin faded. 'I know. We'll cross those bridges when we come to them. For now, concentrate on getting well. We'll keep searching for a match.' He cleared his throat. 'I brought you something.' He reached into a big plastic bag and brought out the board game Clue. 'I thought you should keep your detecting skills sharp.'

Mia's eyes stung. 'I go first. And I'm any piece except the revolver or the knife.'

He set up the board. 'You can be the candlestick. And just because you've got a hole in your gut is no reason for special favors. You'll roll to go first, like everyone else.'

Mia was ready to guess Colonel Mustard in the library with the pipe when the voice at the door caught her by surprise. 'Miss Scarlett in the conservatory with the rope.'

Mia's eyes widened. 'Olivia?'

Reed looked considerably less surprised, but more worried. 'Olivia.'

Olivia came to the foot of the bed and drew a breath. 'All right.'

Mia's imagination combined with the thin thread of hope. 'All right, what?'

Olivia looked at Reed. 'You didn't tell her?'

He shook his head. 'I didn't want to get her hopes up. And, you said no.'

'No, I just didn't say yes.' Olivia met Mia's eyes. 'Reed called me the day after you were shot and told me what you needed. He also told me your mother refused to be tested. You win, big sister. Your family is much worse than mine.'

Mia was speechless. 'You're willing to be tested?'

'No, I *was* tested. I never say yes to things right away. I had to get the facts. Get tested. Get a leave of absence.'

'And?' Reed asked impatiently.

'And I'm here. I'm a match. We're going to do this thing next week.'

Reed's breath came shuddering out. 'Thank God.'

Mia shook her head. 'Why?'

'Well, not because I love you. I don't even know you.' Olivia's brows furrowed. 'But I do know what you'd be giving up if I didn't. You're a cop. A good one. If you don't get a kidney, you lose that and Chicago loses you. I can keep that from happening. So I will.'

She searched Olivia's face. 'You don't owe me anything, Olivia.'

'I know. Kind of.' Her eyes shadowed. 'Then again, maybe I do. But what I do or don't owe you doesn't really matter. If a cop in my department needed this, I'd do it. Why not for my own blood?' Her brows winged up. 'Now if you don't want my guts . . .'

'She wants it,' Reed said firmly. He took Mia's hand. 'Let her help you, Mia.'

'Olivia, have you thought this through?' Mia wouldn't let herself hope. Not yet.

Olivia shrugged. 'My doctor says I'll be back to full duty in a few months. My captain has approved my time off. I'm not sure I could have agreed otherwise.'

Mia narrowed her eyes. 'Once you give it to me, I'm not giving it back.'

Olivia laughed. 'Okay.' She pulled up a chair on the other side of Mia's bed, sobering. 'I wanted to apologize to you. That night we talked . . . I was so shocked. I ran. I ran all the way back to Minnesota.'

'You needed time. I never meant to drop it on you that way.'

'I know. You'd had a bad day. Nice save on the Kates case, by the way.' She smiled. 'I read the *Trib*. I boycott the *Bulletin* on principle.'

Mia smiled back. 'Me, too.' Then she sobered as Olivia's smile faded.

'Mia, I'm sorry. I judged when I didn't understand. I understand better now. And I appreciate you trying to keep me from feeling . . . shunned. You were right. I was luckier. I wish my mother were alive for me to tell her so.' She stood up. 'I'm going to get a hotel room and go to sleep. I pulled a double shift before I got here.'

'I'd offer to let you stay with us, but we're still in a hotel, too,' Reed said.

'It's all right. Your doctor has my health records. He'll redo the typing a week before the scheduled day. Then it's a done deal. He says the procedure will be done laparoscopically on both of us. I'll be released in a day or two. You could be home by Christmas.' She looked at Reed. 'I assume this meets with your approval.'

Reed's nod was shaky. 'It does. Thank you.'

Then she was gone, leaving Mia staring after her. She turned to Reed, her eyes wet. 'You did this for me.'

'I tried. I didn't think she'd agree.'

'The first day we met, you gave me your umbrella.'

His lips curved. 'I remember.'

'Today you gave me back my life. An important part of it, anyway.' But not all, she realized. *Not anymore*. She was more than a cop. She had a cat. And a kid. And a man who sat looking at her as if he'd never let her go. 'How can I thank you for that?'

His dark eyes gleamed. 'I think we can come up with something.'

Epilogue

'Stop it, Reed.' Mia pushed his hand from its groping quest. 'Look.'

'I was trying,' he grumbled.

'I meant look at the news. Lynn Pope from *Chicago on the Town* told me not to miss this morning's show.'

With a sigh for the morning sex that was not to be, Reed sat up in bed and put his arm around Mia's shoulders. She leaned against him easily now, but the thrill was still brand-new. As was the gratitude he experienced every time he woke up to her face.

She was a phenomenal woman. A good cop. She'd returned to duty from her surgery after only four months. Her first day back he'd watched her strap on her holster, fear clutching his heart, but he'd said nothing. In the first week she and Abe Reagan had put away two murderers. Now he watched every day as she strapped on the holster and fear still clutched his heart. But she was a good cop, even better now with the added appreciation of her own mortality. She was careful. She had too much to lose not to be. She'd have to watch her health and take her meds for the rest of her life, but she *had* a life and for that Olivia Sutherland was on their permanent Christmas list.

Mia was a good mom, which he knew she'd be, but he knew it surprised the hell out her. Jeremy was thriving, having found an affinity for soccer. Mia was training him for the peewee leagues. But he still found time to watch the History Channel.

She wasn't a daughter anymore. Annabelle Mitchell had been incensed that Mia had told 'lies' about Bobby when she'd been negotiating for Jeremy's release. And 'when every cop could hear every word from her wire,' which Reed suspected was the real sin. Not the 'lie' but the disclosure, which had not brought the pity Mia had feared. She'd earned far too much respect in her career. She was a good cop.

He kissed the top of Mia's head. And she was a good wife. On the day of their wedding Beth had informed him it was the first day of spring. It hadn't been his plan, but it seemed appropriate. Beth thought Christine would approve. Reed agreed.

'What's this?' he asked as a picture of an awards ceremony filled the screen.

'Lynn Pope was up for the Newscasters Award for the story she did on Bixby and Hope Center. Looks like she won. I hope Wheaton's watching this from her cell.'

'Not that we're bitter or anything,' Reed said and she poked him.

The picture changed to Hope Center, an excerpt from the exposé Pope had aired months before. Bixby and Thompson had been determined to test therapy methods that had been rejected by every reputable group, so they'd started Hope Center. Further investigation had shown impropriety in handling state funds as well as kickbacks from pharmaceutical reps who wanted their meds to be exclusively administered. Teachers were fired before they could become suspicious. Then the unforeseen happened and Andrew Kates had brought the spotlight on Bixby's life's work.

Pope had tracked Bixby to London where he'd hoped to lie low until excitement from the Kates case had blown over. Then he'd planned to quietly resume his work, but Pope's story had resulted in the closing of the school and the placement of the kids elsewhere.

'I hope those kids get a chance at real rehabilitation,' Reed said as Pope signed off.

Mia blinked up at him, surprised. 'I thought you didn't believe in rehabilitation.'

He shrugged. 'Maybe for some people. It's worked for Kelsey.'

'But she's still in.' Parole had been denied once again.

He hugged her close to him. 'Next time.'

'Maybe.' Mia shook off her dark mood and crawled from the bed. 'But it's not a day for the blues. Get up and get dressed, Solliday. I can't be late.' He didn't move, instead rolling to his side to better watch her get dressed. 'Reed, hurry. You know how long it takes you just to pick out your shoes.'

'Shoes are an important accessory. You *won't* wear boots to the church. Please?'

'No, I bought these.' With a grimace she held up a pair of sexy little sandals with a killer heel. 'I'm going to hurt my feet for a kid who won't even remember it.'

'I'm sure you'll remind her when she's old enough,' Reed said dryly, choosing his suit. 'It's not every day you become a godmother, Mia. Suck it up and wear the shoes.'

Mia picked up the photo from her dresser. The infant was wrinkled, but to Mia she was beautiful. Faith Buchanan, Dana's child. She'd be Aunt Mia to this baby, too. But it was okay, because to Jeremy she'd be Mom. He hadn't called her that yet, but it was coming. She wasn't sure what she'd do the first time she heard it. Probably the same thing she did the first time Reed told her he loved her, which was to cry like a baby herself.

'Mia? Are you going to stand there looking in the mirror all day? I need help with my buttons.'

She blinked, unaware that her gaze had lifted to her own reflection. Setting the picture back on the dresser, she quickly worked Reed's buttons up to his collar, tied his tie, and secured his tie tack. 'How did you manage before me?'

He kissed the tip of her nose. 'It took me a lot longer to get dressed. Plus I ate my hot dogs dry and slept alone.' He grinned down at her. 'My quality of life has drastically improved.'

She had to laugh. 'So has mine.'

Acknowledgements

Marc Conterato, for all his medical know-how.

Cristy Carrington, for showing me the secrets of enjoying poetry and for her gift of the poems 'Us' and 'casper.'

Danny Agan, for answering all my detective questions.

Cindy Chavez, for answering my questions on foster care.

RJay Martin, for introducing me to his firehouse; and Jana Martin, for introducing me to RJay.

My fellow members of the Tampa Area Romance Authors, for support on everything from police funerals to sororities. You all are wonderful.

Julie Bouse, for sharing the story of her own family. Best of success to you, sweetie.

Any mistakes are my own.

About the Author

RITA Award-winning author Karen Rose has always loved books. Jo Marsh from *Little Women* and Nancy Drew were close childhood friends. She was introduced to suspense and horror at the tender age of eight when she accidentally read Poe's 'The Pit and the Pendulum' and was afraid to go to sleep for years, which explains a lot . . .

After earning her degree in chemical engineering from the University of Maryland, Karen married her high school sweetheart. She started writing when characters started popping up in her head and simply wouldn't be quiet. Now she enjoys making other people afraid to go to sleep! She lives in sunny Florida with her husband and their daughters.

Karen was honored and totally thrilled to receive the Romance Writers of America's highest award in 2005 – the RITA for Best Romantic Suspense for *I'm Watching You* (Warner Books, 2004).

Visit Karen's website at www.karenrosebooks.com for more information on Karen, her books, and upcoming events. She loves to hear from readers, so please contact her at karen@karenrosebooks.com.

Lifeguard

James Patterson & Andrew Gross

Everyone out of the water. LIFEGUARD. A killer read.

The perfect job. Working for an easy-going boss at his sprawling luxurious mansion by the sun-kissed beach, watching beautiful women walk by.

The perfect girl. Tess – gorgeous, funny, apparently very rich and crazy for him.

The perfect score. Five million up for grabs. And to get his share, all he needs to do is trigger three house alarms to throw the cops off the scent of the real robbery.

Could things get any better for Ned Kelly?

But things don't go according to plan. And when Tess is brutally murdered and the others involved in the robbery are massacred, Ned is the prime suspect. With danger at every twist and turn, he's running for his life.

The perfect Patterson. Working with Andrew Gross, James Patterson skilfully delivers an addictive cocktail of suspense, surprise and tension that will keep you gripped right up until the last page.

Praise for James Patterson's bestselling novels:

'A master of the suspense genre' *Sunday Telegraph*

'Unputdownable' *The Times*

'Brilliantly terrifying . . . so exciting I had to stay up all night to finish it' *Daily Mail*

0 7553 2569 9

headline

Now you can buy any of these other bestselling
Headline books from your bookshop
or *direct from the publisher*.

FREE P&P AND UK DELIVERY
(Overseas and Ireland £3.50 per book)

Straight into Darkness	Faye Kellerman	£6.99
Smoked	Patrick Quinlan	£6.99
Creepers	David Morrell	£6.99
Immoral	Brian Freeman	£6.99
Thorn	Vena Cork	£6.99
Double Tap	Steve Martini	£6.99
Hen's Teeth	Manda Scott	£7.99
The Patriots' Club	Christopher Reich	£6.99
Double Homicide	Faye & Jonathan Kellerman	£6.99
Never Fear	Scott Frost	£6.99

TO ORDER SIMPLY CALL THIS NUMBER

01235 400 414

or visit our website: www.madaboutbooks.com

Prices and availability subject to change without notice.